A Long Way from Ordinary

Clementine hesitated for a moment, composing her thoughts and feelings about last night's incident and the news Hank had brought her along with the warm biscuits this morning. She tucked in a few loose tendrils and made sure she had no biscuit crumbs on her face before marching over to the curtain. When she flung it open, the men in the bathtubs scrambled to cover their bits with small wash towels.

"What in Sam Hill?!" Jack yelled, splashing around like a dog.

"Close the damned curtain, woman!" Boone scowled, wrapping his arms around himself and making a show of shivering.

Clementine turned and pulled the curtain closed behind her.

A flurry of expletives from both men filled the room.

"I meant with you on the outside," Boone growled when she turned back to them.

She focused on Jack, who was in the tub on her right. His jaw was covered in blond stubble, his hair sticking up like crooked gravestones. "Don't worry," she told them, fighting not to grin. "There appears to be just enough bubbles to cover whatever you boys are hiding." Feeling a bit ornery after a night of worrying about them, she glanced at Jack's tub and raised an eyebrow. "Besides, Jack doesn't seem to need many bubbles anyway."

The unbruised side of his face crinkled in a frown. "Ha ha. For your information, I happen to have—" He stopped abruptly when she took a step closer to him. Mumbling, he began to gather and pile even more bubbles.

"Why do you have the curtain between your two bathtubs tied back?" she asked, glancing away to give Jack a moment of privacy. "Are baths a community event where you're from?" She focused on Boone. The grin she'd been holding back broke free. "Would you both be in the same tub if it were big enough?"

"Well, aren't you the funny one this morning." Boone's eyes crinkled in the corners. He looked at her wool shirt. "Care to join?"

"Thank you, I will." She dragged a chair from the other side of the curtain and placed it between the tubs, settling in near Jack's feet.

"Oh, good," Jack said, rearranging his cloth under the water. "Here I was afraid this was gonna be a quick visit."

Dear Reader,

When I was young I wanted to be a mountain man. The kind with a raccoon hat and the skin of some rugged animal, taken in a rugged way. The kind that could skin a rattler with his foot long Bowie knife, eat it, and then pick the bones from his teeth with the same knife.

In actuality, I was the kind that dons his dad's threadbare ol' wool work coat and holsters up his nickel plated (plastic), ivory handled (also plastic) cap pistols in a handsomely tooled leather (scruffy belt and duct tape) holster. The role of the Bowie knife was convincingly portrayed by a piece of flatware from the kitchen. Or in a pinch, a stick got the job done. Sheath? "Put it down in your sock," the expedition advisor (mom) would say.

Anyway, the mountain man in my mind stands on a snowy ridge, holding his hand up to his brow, the rays of the sun silhouetting a hardy mountain of a man to full advantage. That's the guy. That was me. Eight or ten years old, in the 'wilderness' of uncivilized hills behind my family's small farm.

I climbed and explored endlessly. It was my pastime since television was three channels, if we were lucky. On the surface, it might seem a sad, lonely image, but that couldn't be further from the actuality of it.

Through my teens I haunted those hills. Neither the humid heat of a summer day nor the snowy cold of winter could stay the adventurer from his destiny of tramping old, overgrown logging roads or slip-sliding up and down deer trails. I probably knew that area better than most.

I envy, a little, Clem, Boone, Rabbit and Hank their adventures in the snow-covered Black Hills of the Dakota Territory.

Ann and I hope you enjoy the adventures of our wayward heroes in the Black Hills.

I leave you with words of wisdom passed down from the likes of Hank and Uncle Morton:

"There are two theories to arguing with a woman. One doesn't work very well. The other doesn't either."

Sam Lucky

A Long Way From Ordinary

Book 2

Ann Charles
Sam Lucky

COPYRIGHT 2019 ANN CHARLES & SAM LUCKY

For Uncle Fred
We Miss You

A Long Way from Ordinary

Copyright © 2019 by Ann Charles & Sam Lucky
Prescott AZ, USA

All rights reserved. Except as permitted under the U.S. Copyright Act of 1976, no part of this publication may be reproduced, distributed, or transmitted in any form or by any means now known or hereafter invented, or stored in a database or retrieval system, without the prior written permission of the author, Ann Charles.

This book is a work of fiction. Names, characters, places, and incidents are the product of the author's imagination or are used fictitiously. Any resemblance to actual persons, living or dead, business establishments, events, or locales is coincidental.

Cover Art by C.S. Kunkle
Cover Design by B Biddles
Editing by Eilis Flynn
Formatting by B Biddles

Library of Congress: 2019919304
E-book ISBN-978-1-940364-65-0
Print ISBN-13: 978-1-940364-66-7

Acknowledgments

Whew! We did it! Another book in the Deadwood Undertaker series is finished and in your hot hands. Our first celebratory idea was to run away to Italy and eat cheese until we couldn't move, but we decided instead to thank some folks first, so here goes. Thanks to:

Our kids, Beaker and Chicken Noodle, for asking us over and over "Are you done yet?" You two are wonderful motivators. Ha!

Our First Draft team: Margo Taylor, Mary Ida Kunkle, Kristy McCaffrey, Jacquie Rogers, Marcia Britton, Paul Franklin, Diane Garland, Vicki Huskey, Lucinda Nelson, Bob Dickerson, Marguerite Phipps, Stephanie Kunkle, and Wendy Gildersleeve. You were amazingly fast at reading and giving feedback. We appreciate you putting us at the top of your to-do list.

Our editor, Eilis Flynn, for your help during the busy holiday season.

Diane Garland, WorldKeeper extraordinaire, for making room in your brain and on your worksheets for more characters, places, and plot threads.

Our Beta Team for stepping up during crunch time and not letting Christmas slow you down.

C.S. Kunkle for giving our readers some visual ideas of what's happening on the page.

Our readers—Your cheers and excitement about book one, *Life at the Coffin Joint*, gave us lots of gumption to keep on writing.

Author C.M. Wendelboe for reading the book so quickly and giving us a kick-butt cover quote.

And our newest cat, Clementine, for distracting us with all of your playing and purrs and other adorable antics. You're almost as badass as your namesake in this book.

Also by Ann Charles

Deadwood Undertaker Series
(written with Sam Lucky)
Life at the Coffin Joint (Book 1)
A Long Way from Ordinary (Book 2)
Can't Ride Around It (Book 3) (Mid 2020)

Deadwood Mystery Series (Book #)

Nearly Departed in Deadwood (1)
Optical Delusions in Deadwood (2)
Dead Case in Deadwood (3)
Better Off Dead in Deadwood (4)
An Ex to Grind in Deadwood (5)
Meanwhile, Back in Deadwood (6)
Wild Fright in Deadwood (7)
Rattling the Heat in Deadwood (8)
Gone Haunting in Deadwood (9)
Don't Let It Snow in Deadwood (10)

Deadwood Shorts: Seeing Trouble (Book 1.5)
Deadwood Shorts: Boot Points (Book 4.5)
Deadwood Shorts: Cold Flame (Book 6.5)
Deadwood Shorts: Tequila & Time (Book 8.5)
Deadwood Shorts: Fatal Traditions (Book 10.5)

Jackrabbit Junction Mystery Series
Dance of the Winnebagos (Book 1)
Jackrabbit Junction Jitters (Book 2)
The Great Jackalope Stampede (Book 3)
The Rowdy Coyote Rumble (Book 4)
In Cahoots with the Prickly Pear Posse (Book 5)

Jackrabbit Junction Short: The Wild Turkey Tango (Book 4.5)

Dig Site Mystery Series
Look What the Wind Blew In (Book 1)
Make No Bones About It (Book 2)

AC Silly Circus Mystery Series
Feral-LY Funny Freakshow (Novella 1)
A Bunch of Monkey Malarkey (Novella 2)

Goldwash Mystery Series (a future series)
The Old Man's Back in Town (Short Story)

"A man who carries a cat by the tail learns something he can learn in no other way."
~Mark Twain

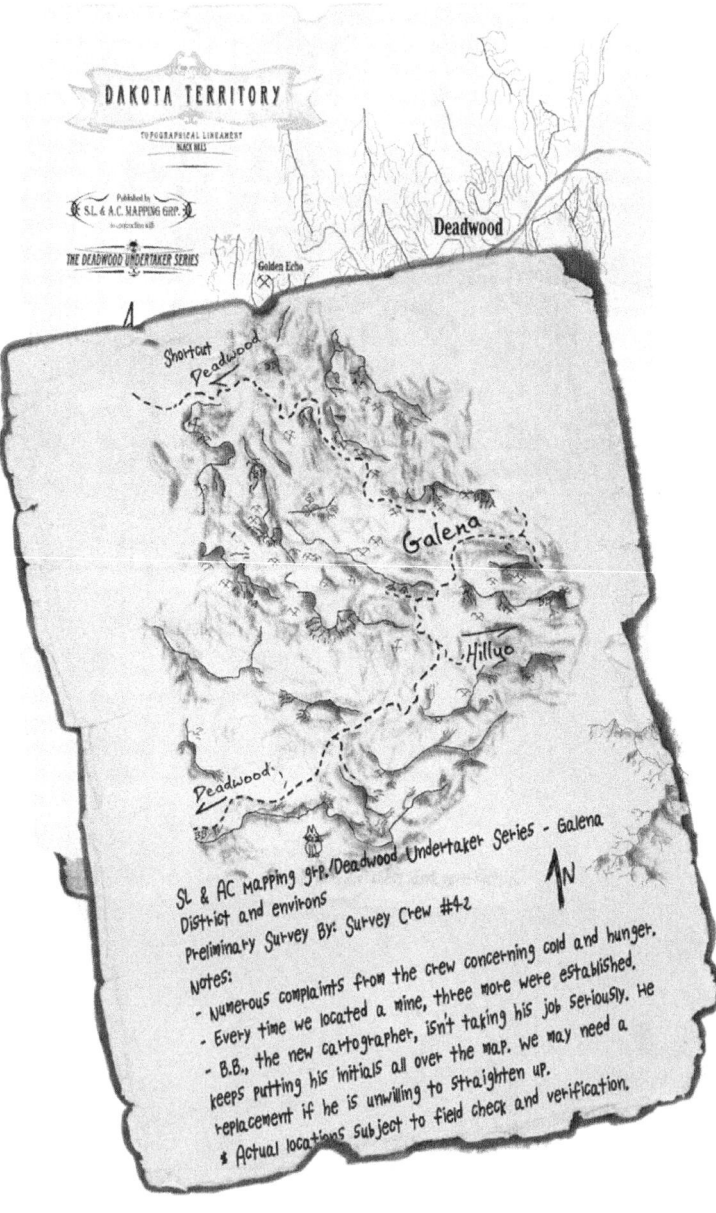

One

Late 1876
Deadwood, Dakota Territory

Waves of death were crashing into The Pyre, drowning Clementine Johanssen in corpses.

Today, for the first time in weeks, her undertaker exam tables were empty. Finally, she had a moment to sort through the signs of devilry she'd been finding on more and more bodies each day. These brandings and other strange markings made on the flesh of the dead—what did they mean to Deadwood's future? To her future?

Not one to sit idle while she pondered, she grabbed a bucket and brush. Who to hunt? Who to slay? Who to let live? Answers eluded her as she worked through the afternoon. There was too much death clouding her vision.

She was brushing the last of the whitewash on the back wall of the parlor when the front door banged open. An icy gust swirled around her legs, peppering her with snow, blowing away the smell of wet wood walls.

Hank Varney stomped across the threshold, as he tended to do, and knocked clumps of snow and mud from his boots. "Miss Clem, you ain't gonna believe what I seen!" He waved a rolled-up news sheet above his head, then frowned at the bucket of whitewash next to her. "What are you doin' that for? We just washed that not more'n two months ago."

"Hank, would you stoke the fire, please?" She winked at her assistant and nodded toward the door. "If we're going to heat all of Deadwood in the middle of winter, we'll need the stove good and hot."

"Huh? Oh." He kicked the door shut. "Street's a-bustlin' this evenin'. Word is population is growin' by a few hunerd a day now in the Hills. Guess they don't know all the good placer claims is gone already."

Clementine could believe those numbers based on the increasing number of "customers" adorning her tables. The lure of gold in the Black Hills drew fortune seekers like locusts. In turn, opportunity filled the coffers of many who preyed on those new arrivals, tempting the gold-seekers with vices and profiting from their weaknesses.

Hank hung his coat and hat on a wall peg and turned his attention to Tinker, the three-legged dog, who was working on a chunk of beef bone near the stove while she kept Clementine company.

"Hiyo, Tinker. I see you're 'bout done wrestlin' with the cow I brung you."

He plopped down beside her, crossed his legs, and dropped the paper next to him on the floor. Tinker wormed into his lap and nuzzled and nipped at his hand as the pup had done nearly every day since her *compadres*, Jack "Rabbit" Fields and Boone McCreery, had left for Santa Fe weeks earlier. Not that Clementine needed to keep track of how long they'd been gone, because Hank was.

The two gunmen had made a friend in Hank. Clementine, too, for that matter, in spite of her reservations about emotional attachments. More than once over the last few weeks she'd found herself looking toward the south, wondering if the travelers would return as they'd promised Tinker. She tempered her hope with reality. There was a lot of trail between Deadwood and Santa Fe filled with all manner of trouble, including the perils of winter weather. They might have changed their minds about returning to this cold, lawless frontier. In Santa Fe, they had a freight business to run, a ranch to work, friends to help pass the time, and probably plenty of sunshine.

If common sense ruled their actions, she doubted they'd come back. The only thing waiting for them here besides Tinker and Hank was death. Clementine could feel a storm brewing over the northern Hills. A tempest not of wind or snow, but of malicious intent and foul deeds. She'd been bred and raised to fight. They hadn't.

Neither had Hank, for that matter, but no number of warnings had convinced him to find employment elsewhere. She couldn't have wished for a better assistant or friend. Watching him play with Tinker fueled a comforting warmth she'd not experienced since leaving her childhood home many, many years ago.

The dog squirmed around to face Hank and thumped the back of his hand with the peg leg Jack had rigged for her.

"Ow! Appears to me yer better at walkin' with that thing than you are sittin' in my lap."

Tinker wiggled her rump and yipped at him.

"She's healed up real good while the boys are away, Miss Clem."

She glanced at the paper on the floor next to him. "Hank."

His attention was focused entirely on Tinker. "You know I brought you somethin', don't ya? Course I did." He drew a piece of jerky from his coat pocket. "Uh oh," he said and stuck it in his mouth, his eyes wide.

The dog scolded him with a series of quick yips.

He pulled the jerky out. "Ho ho! Tinkerdoo. I'm just foolin' with ya." He held the jerky out and she grabbed it with her teeth, carefully avoiding his fingers.

"You're a good little girl, ain't ya? Just a good little girl." He scratched behind her ears and grabbed her front paw. "Next time I'll get ya—"

"Hank." Clementine balanced the brush on the rim of the bucket.

He stopped mid-handshake and looked up, still holding Tinker's paw, waiting for Clementine to continue. His eyes creased in the corners; his brown, wavy hair curled over his collar. For a moment, he looked much younger than his forty-plus years. Just a boy and his dog.

She pointed at the sheet of paper. "What did you read that you came to tell me?"

"Oh!" He picked up the paper. "It's the *Trailblazer*."

"So I see." Deadwood's newspaper office was located several buildings down Main Street from The Pyre.

"You remember we blasted the Bloody Bones pretty good?"

"Of course."

The whole Bloody Bones mine incident was still fresh in Clementine's memory, from what Jack had found in the adit to the battle they'd all fought in the cavern shortly thereafter.

"You remember I said two kegs should do?"

She nodded.

Days after what Hank liked to call the "Battle of Bloody Bones," Clementine and he had hauled two full kegs of blasting powder into the adit and placed them near the entrance to the cavern. Their intent had been to seal off the mine, down deep in the preexisting tunnels past the cavern used by their foes to retreat. Where and to what they had retreated, Clementine didn't know.

But as it happened, the blasts from Jack's sawed-off shotgun during the battle had triggered cave-ins that efficiently collapsed those tunnels. With that task done, she and Hank had decided to use the powder to bring down the side of the hill, closing off the entrance to the mine. They hoped to keep gold seekers from meddling inside of Bloody Bones and once again freeing the troublemakers hidden deep within its rocky guts.

"And you recall the *Trailblazer* had somethin' to say about the blast." Hank frowned at the paper. "*The ground shook,* it said."

It had shaken, knocking the snow off the pine trees all around them as they watched the hillside cover the mine's entrance. Hank's mule, Fred, had plopped his hind end down on the ground and let out a squeaky wail until the rumbling stopped.

"*Big doings apparent in Gayville,*" he continued. "All the way to Deadwood it shook, people talkin' ever'where about it."

Tinker wiggled off his lap and thumped over to her pile of blankets by the stove where she began to gnaw on the hunk of jerky she held between her paws.

"It was quite impressive," Clementine said, grinning at the memory of Hank cursing and tugging on Fred the Mule so they could hightail it out of the area and back to Deadwood before they were spotted by anyone.

"Prob'ly shouldn't have used quite so much powder, I s'pose." He rubbed the back of his neck.

"It should stay sealed. At least for a while."

He shook his head again. "I surely hope so." He held the paper up for her to read. "Look here what it says."

She read the first item aloud:

Winter reaches the Black Hills

> *The Hills are draped with increasingly mountainous drifts of snow and thrashed by icy winds. The resiliency of Deadwood's citizens is tested to breaking, and still unfriendlier times approach as we near the beginning of winter ...*

"Not that one, Miss Clem," Hank interrupted.

"Funny, I could swear winter arrived weeks ago."

This was Clementine's first taste of the snowy season in the Black Hills, but not her first experience with severely cold weather. Her childhood had been spent enduring long, dark,

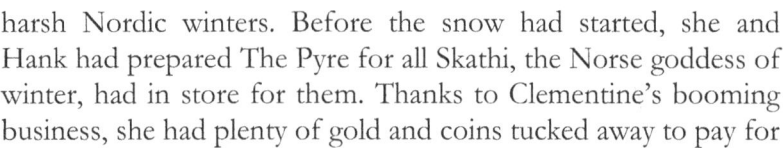

harsh Nordic winters. Before the snow had started, she and Hank had prepared The Pyre for all Skathi, the Norse goddess of winter, had in store for them. Thanks to Clementine's booming business, she had plenty of gold and coins tucked away to pay for food and other supplies.

In short, Clementine was ready for anything Deadwood could throw at her. Anything related to weather, in any case. The *other* problem she might encounter was another story. Time would tell.

Hank stood and brushed Tinker's fur from his trousers. "Down the page a ways."

She read another:

Icy death in the streets of Deadwood
Hundreds of penniless and newly arrived citizens find adequate accommodation and nourishment woefully lacking in Deadwood. Exposure dispatches many and threatens more …

"Not that one neither, Miss Clem. Down the page, toward the bottom. Goes onto the next."

She pointed at the article about icy deaths. "We certainly have seen more than a few dead from exposure come through The Pyre the last couple of weeks, especially with the temperature dropping lower every night."

"Yep." Hank snorted. "Fred the Mule can't hardly keep up."

"I don't know what we'll do if this continues on like it is. Ling and Gart have bodies stacked like cordwood in the shed out back. Near full to the rafters." Her two-man, grave-digging crew had been scratching their heads lately about what to do with the corpses until they could put them in the ground. "Have those boys had any luck thawing the earth enough to dig at Ingleside?"

"Yup. But it's a slow, cold job. Can't keep up with the current business we're doin' here. 'Specially since extra fire fuel's hard to acquire presently, what with ever'body fightin' for wood and coal oil. Reminds me. Earp dumped his logs out front. I'll help the boys saw it up and stack it out back so's nobody gets the temptation to borrow it. Anyway, Ling sounds near to quittin' but Gart likes the pay, and if Gart don't quit, Ling won't neither."

"They're due some bonus. Maybe a few extra coins will keep Ling happy."

Hank grunted in agreement. "I s'pose you still need to thaw the dead out, at least an itty bit, 'nough to see if they been stuck or not. And check teeth."

"More than ever."

Signs of trouble had been showing up more and more often in the last couple of weeks in the form of two different symbols she'd found on several corpses. The *caper-sus* emblem, which looked like a goat melting into a pig, seemed to be spreading. In addition, each victim with this branding or ring had been slain in a similar method—first a slicing of the tendon that Clementine figured was meant to hobble, and then a deep thrust of a blade through the lower jaw up into the brain or between the ribs to pierce the heart.

Quick, efficient deaths.

"The killer is back to work. But I haven't noticed any missing teeth since Big Joe." Awhile back, a few bodies had come through The Pyre missing a canine tooth.

"Don't comprehend takin' teeth from a dead man." Hank wrinkled his upper lip and poked at an exposed canine. He shuddered. "Downright revoltin'. Savage. Ain't enough to lay a man out, gotta violate his body, too."

Savage? Clementine considered that. There was something to this style of murder beyond desecration or defilement. In each instance, the tooth had been taken post mortem, and always the maxillary canine. Something else was at play here. Ritualistic perhaps, or possibly a trophy for a kill.

Hank was right. "It does seem savage, doesn't it?" Unlike the other execution-style killings.

"Yup. Causes me some infirmity to think 'bout it." He leaned down and stroked Tinker's back, probably more to calm himself than Tinker.

In any case, there was an assassin out there responsible for some of the deaths. The slayings were precise, calculated. Clementine wondered if she were being taunted?

Or was the killer like Clementine, an executioner hired to complete a job? If so, who would benefit from these deaths? She had heard the words "rogue executioner" discussed last month behind closed doors. Perhaps this slayer wasn't a rogue at a—

"Miss Clem, it's the next one down there, toward the bottom."

She focused on the sheet, scanning to the next item.

The rush is on! Again.

Recall, if you will, a few weeks previous, the earth rumbled. The blast rattled glass and tin. Its origin, now established and confirmed, the abandoned, or rather previously abandoned, Golden Echo, in the area northwest of Gayville.

"Shouldn't-a used so much blastin' powder," Hank said softly. "I knew better."

"What's done is done. After what we went through in that mine, we wanted it sealed. Both of us did." She squeezed his shoulder. "And I was glad to have you by my side, Hank."

He raised one side of his mouth into a lopsided smile and nodded at the paper for her to continue.

The subsequent search exposed neither the scoundrel responsible nor any victim of same, but the revelation of things more interesting indeed. Gold!

Prospector and city dandy alike commenced scouring the hills behind Gayville in hopes of finding the next Comstock.

The claim was legally located, prospected and staked, but the owners, numbering and including three brothers, have been missing for slightly short of five months.

Reports indicate color varying from dust to nuggets as large in size as to fill a man's open hand is being taken from the mine and it is said that veins run thick and deep into the mountain.

The mine is generally considered abandoned, whether legally or otherwise, and as such, is claimed by an assembly of men of the opportunistic sort.

Consequently, discord and hostility proliferate in the area with four deaths and many fracases reported.

We note that there has been neither demonstrable concern for the three brothers nor discernible intent to verify their well-being.

Increasing numbers of men continue to converge on the area with equipment and a dismaying number of firearms.

It is the opinion of the Trailblazer staff that the town of Gayville, possibly with the help of the miner court of Deadwood, should rectify the growing problem without delay.

"Damn it," Clementine muttered.

"That was my assessment."

"We're sitting on one massive powder keg here in the Black Hills, Hank. They'll open the Golden Echo mine again and follow that gold seam into the earth. To the very end. There's no stopping it. The gate will be opened again … eventually."

And then all hell would break loose.

Hank cocked his head and frowned at her. "We'll go right up that mountainside and seal it up again." He nodded once, apparently agreeing with himself.

"Perhaps, but not yet. I think we have time until they remove all of that rock." The gold would keep luring them back, though. The avarice of men was so heightened by the prospect of striking it rich in these hills that Clementine didn't think sealing off the mine again was the final solution. She'd need to exterminate the vermin at the source. "Besides, that's not our biggest problem at the moment."

One of his eyebrows shot up. "It ain't?"

She didn't know if Hank was prepared to hear the extent of what she suspected was happening in the Black Hills.

Men and women were pouring into the gulches and filling them up with humanity. It was a virtually endless supply of *livestock*, as Clementine had heard them called. Humans arriving in the Hills with not a penny in a pocket, their last few dollars spent on the trip here, only to find that gold did not pave the streets. There were no fist-sized nuggets to pick from the streams as they had been told. Even worse, the prospects of anything regarding financial security did not materialize the moment they stepped from their horses or carriages. In short, they had arrived in the cold, icy realm of Helheim, or whichever version of the Underworld they preferred.

These desperate souls offered a unique opportunity for the worst sort of evil. The increasing number of bodies bearing rings, burn scars, and tattoos of the *caper-sus* emblem supported Clementine's suspicion that someone was recruiting these people to build an army. Or armies.

But who was killing them? The rogue executioner? If so, to what end? Could Clementine's benefactor have summoned more than one slayer to do his bidding?

Aha! Maybe that was the answer. She looked at Hank. He stared back with both eyebrows raised, but she wasn't prepared to share her suspicion just yet.

She changed the subject. "Were you planning to stop by the Cricket this evening?"

He scrunched up one side of his face. "Don't cotton to that place. Swearengen likes them prizefights. Rowdy crowd there. That man sells a ruckus, that's what I say. Swearengen's a swindler, that's what *they* say. Don't cotton."

"Then where? Belle Grande?"

"Prob'ly. Lose my money there, though. Cardsharps. Good beer. Prob'ly go th—"

A series of thumps on the front door interrupted Hank.

"More business, maybe." He opened the door to a tall, lean man wearing a thick sheepskin coat.

"Jack Rabbit!"

"Ho there, Hank!" Jack Fields's grin lit up his face. "Damn, it's good to see you!"

Hank reached out and bear-hugged Jack, lifting the taller man off the ground. He shook him and then dropped him back onto his boots.

Another man stepped into the doorway behind Jack, his shoulders wider, his head a few inches taller, his black hat marred by a single bullet hole.

"Boone!" Hank grabbed Boone McCreery's hand in both of his and shook it vigorously. "It sure is mighty good to see the both of ya! Look, Miss Clem, it's the Santa Fe Sidewinders." He stepped aside and pushed the pair into the room, closing the door behind them. Tink leapt up and yipped and danced around their legs, licking their fingers when they tried to pet her.

"Howdy, Miss Clementine. You're a sight for tired eyes." Jack grabbed the hat from his head, put it to his chest, and bowed toward Clementine.

"Hello, Jack." She crossed the room and hugged the blond traveler. He smelled fresh from the outside. The leather of his coat felt cool under her hands. "It's good to see you two here, safe and sound," she said as she stepped back and turned to Boone, meeting his green eyes. "Welcome back, Boone."

Boone raised his hat to her and then whipped it against his leg, powdery snow swirling to the floor at his feet. "Rabbit's right, Clementine. You surely are a sight for some tired eyes."

She laughed, looking down at her old wool shirt and denim

men's trousers. "I'm a sight, all right." Clementine hugged him. Boone was one of the few men she'd met who stood taller than she, besting her by a couple of inches. His short beard tickled her cheek before she pulled away. When she stepped back, she feasted her gaze on the two men, far too happy to see them again. "You weren't due in for another couple of days, according to Hank."

"That is correct, Miss Clementine," Jack said. "But Booney here kept pushin'. Nickel and Dime ain't none too happy about it neither."

Boone glanced at her, the look on his face edging on sheepish. "A winter trail isn't a place to waste time, especially in Wyoming or the Dakota Territory."

"That's sure enough," Hank said. "You both got real clothes, looks like. Glad to see it. Winter's just gettin' started around here." Hank rubbed the sleeves of their thick sheepskin coats.

"So you know," Jack said to Boone, "I still didn't like the ride up here from Santa Fe any more than I did last time. Hey, Tink!" Jack dropped to his knees and began to ruffle the dog's fur. He smooshed his face against hers. Tinker mirrored his excitement with a swooshing rump and slobbery tongue, yipping and whining her excitement.

Clementine chuckled, glancing up to find Boone watching her with a hint of a smile. "You did a fine job taking care of Tink, Clementine. Thank you."

Her face warmed at his gratitude. "It was my pleasure. She's a sweetheart. Hank helped as well, bringing her bones and treats each morning."

Hank waved off her words, grinning as he watched Jack play with Tinker. "I'll get Keller to squeeze Nickel and Dime in at the livery. You boys got a place to sleep? Doesn't matter, you stay with me, up in Keller's hayloft above the stable. He charges me enough to cover you two along with me."

"With the line forming out front, I'm guessing business must

A LONG WAY FROM ORDINARY 13

be good." Boone pointed his thumb toward the window.

Line forming? "What do you mean?" Clementine asked.

"The body you're storing out front?"

Clementine exchanged frowns with Hank before striding to the door. She marched out onto the porch with Hank on her tail.

Out front were the four coffins Ling and Gart had propped up against The Pyre's façade. "Advertising," Gart had said.

Three of the pine boxes were empty. She stood in front of the fourth, her hands on her hips. A body had been placed neatly in the tipped coffin—a man with his hands folded over his lower abdomen, as if prepared for a parade of mourners to pass by and pay respects.

"Where'd this'n come from?" Hank muttered under his breath, scratching his jaw.

"What the hell is going on, Hank?" Clementine asked in a quiet voice. She glanced up and down the street, wondering who might have left this dead man on her doorstep.

"I surely don't know, Miss Clem. I'll take him in and put him on the table."

Jack stepped out to help Hank carry the body into the exam room. "It's a fine welcome back to Deadwood you arranged for us, Hank. Thank you kindly."

Hank snickered. "Happy to accomodate, Jack Rabbit."

After they'd settled the dead man on her exam table, she donned her leather work apron. "You boys can warm up by the fire if you'd like." She pointed toward the parlor. "There's coffee on the stove and some of those biscuits you like left over from breakfast. Hank has been doing his best to fatten Tinker and me up while you've been gone."

She followed the men into the parlor while tying her apron.

Boone slid out of his coat and carefully picked up Tinker. "You're looking like a young pup again, girl. I see Clementine and Hank have taken extra good care of you." He sat in one of the chairs by the fire with Tinker on his lap. Jack poured a cup of coffee and plopped into the chair beside Boone.

"I'll be just a few minutes." With that she left them to it and crossed into the exam room, where she prepared her instruments and grabbed her notebook.

Hank joined her shortly. "Who would have left him without informing us?" she asked.

He shook his head. "No rigor in him. Ain't frozen stiff. Wasn't there when I came in neither. Purt near fresh."

He fetched the measuring rule and they began the exercise they'd completed too many times to count since Clementine had hired him as an assistant at The Pyre a few short months ago. They measured the dead man's height and guessed his weight. Hank waited by the exam room stove while Clementine circled the table, scrutinizing him from head to toe.

The body was well-dressed, compared to most in Deadwood. Wool coat, hat, and pants. Sturdy leather boots.

She took up her notebook and wrote:

> *Adult male, approximately mid-twenties. Appropriate attire for winter in Deadwood. Apparently well-nourished. No sign of exposure. Beard matted with blood but the injury is obscured.*

She'd explore that wound shortly. Setting down her notebook, she looked over at Hank. "Let's remove his clothes."

Hank grimaced. "Don't like this part."

"That makes two of us."

He started tugging on the dead man's boots while Clementine worked his arms free of the coat. Hank draped a muslin rag over the corpse's waist, muttering something about letting the man keep his "dignity."

Clementine stood over the body, staring at the brand on his chest. *Caper-sus* again.

"The placement of that brand reminds me of the man left at the back door shortly before Boone and Jack left for Santa Fe."

"If you say so, Miss Clem."

Oh, right. Hank hadn't been there to see that one. Boone and Jack had helped relocate the body to her table that day.

"Boone! Jack!" She called toward the parlor. "Will you come in here, please?"

She began checking the pockets of his coat as she waited, looking for anything that might help identify who she had on her table. She found a piece of paper in one pocket, unfolded it and read:

Are you paying attention?

"Are you paying attention?" she repeated aloud.

"What's that, Clementine?" Boone joined her. He did a double take at the corpse on the table. "He's been branded."

"Just like before," Jack said, leaning against the other exam table.

They confirmed her memory.

"Look at this." She handed Boone the note and began examining the man's body. She found no sign of any other injuries save the blood-soaked beard. He even had all his teeth. She felt around under his chin and found a small puncture.

"Jack, will you hand me that metal rod on the tray over there?" She pointed at the tray of instruments near her desk.

He obliged. "What's that for?"

She held the rod up between them. "You might want to look away," she said and then eased the rod into the hole under the dead man's chin. She leaned closer, listening, and slowly pushed it up until it clunked against the inside of his skull.

No familiar clink of steel against lead.

"He wasn't shot." A glance up at her companions found each had turned a pale shade of gray, their faces a mixture of cringes and pained expressions.

She slowly moved the rod around in a small circle, exploring, trying to assess the damage done by … what? A blade? She pulled the rod back out. It came free with a sucking slurp.

All three men groaned.

"Miss Clem," Hank said, his whole face pinched tight. "That's revoltin'."

Boone turned away, saying over his shoulder, "Sounded like you were stirring porridge."

Jack headed for the door to the parlor. "I'm gonna visit Tink."

She wiped the rod clean with a strip of cloth. "I suspect this man was slain by the same individual who left the corpse at my back door before you headed for Santa Fe."

"Same brand too, isn't it?" Boone still had his back to her.

"Yes. But this man is different."

He turned, his gaze narrowed. "How so?"

"He's well-dressed and fed. He's been taken care of or had the wherewithal to take care of himself."

Boone shot a quick look at the dead man. "The body left at the back door was extra lean," he said. "Hadn't been eating too well for a while. Clothes were threadbare. You're right. You make something of that?"

"Maybe." She crossed to her desk and pulled a piece of paper from her drawer, handing it to Boone, who had followed her. "This is the note from before you left. It's the same handwriting."

"Looks like it." He frowned down at the two notes. "Not signed with the letter P, though."

Clementine nodded, focusing on the corpse again. " 'Are you paying attention,' " she repeated the words on the paper. "If I were to guess, this man was higher up in rank. Possibly."

"Have you seen any rings or brandings with the *caper-sus* emblem since we left?"

"Yes, but not during the first week. Business has been up in general—namely due to exposure, accidents, and murders. But none of those who came through The Pyre during the first week after you left wore the sign. Then it started up again, slowly, one a day, sometimes two. But now we're seeing it more and more." She looked to Hank. "Right?"

"Yes, ma'am. Downright busy with 'em anymore."

"There's something else," she told Boone.

"Oh?"

"There seem to be two different forms of the *caper-sus* and no discrimination in death." She opened a wooden box on her desk and pulled out two rings, handing them to Boone.

He studied each and then held one up. "This one has a curved horn. And this one," he held up the other, "is curled, like a ram. Is that the only difference?"

"That I can see."

"Do you think we're dealing with two different ... what was it you called them?"

"Cults." She nodded. "That would be my guess. It's possible that there are two rivals vying for control here in the Black Hills."

He lowered the rings, his gaze searching hers. "What aren't you telling me?"

"It's possible that one of them is led by the benefactor with whom I'm contracted to help."

Boone leaned against the desk. "It's becoming apparent there is a lot you know that Rabbit and I don't."

Clementine grimaced. "This reminds me of a quote from the saga of Hen-Thorir, an old Norse tale my amma used to tell me."

"Amma?" He handed her back the rings.

"My grandmother." She tucked them in her desk drawer.

"So this story is about heroic Vikings battling impossible odds and all that?"

"Not quite. It's a tale about infighting that develops between neighbors and includes some people being burned alive and others beheaded. But it does end with a marriage, if that makes you feel better."

"What's the quote, Miss Clem?" Hank asked.

" 'That which has a bad beginning is likely to have a bad ending.' "

Boone frowned at Hank. "Has she always been this uplifting?"

"That's a question for later." Hank patted Boone on the shoulder. "I got just the place for you and Jack Rabbit. Good steaks and beer and maybe we can shuffle some cards. Then I'll take you boys back to my roost for some shuteye. It might smell some, but it's comfortable and *almost* warm."

Two

Boone followed Hank out the door of The Pyre into the late afternoon shadows with Rabbit trailing behind him. He winced through a cold gust. While they'd been inside, the sun had disappeared below the rim of the gulch and taken the trivial amount of warmth it'd conveyed along with it.

Nickel whinnied at him from the hitching post. Taking his piebald's reins, Boone indicated for Hank to lead the way.

With a nod, Hank cleared a path for them toward Keller's Livery, pushing through the throng of humanity filling the street. Occasionally, he'd pause to wait while Boone led his horse around dense groups of miners, stacks of freight boxes, or piles of lumber. Behind Boone, Rabbit cursed and complained to Dime, his buckskin horse, about the street being so thick with people that he couldn't even cock his pistol.

That was probably a good thing at the moment, considering the abundance of those goat-pig tattoos that Clementine and Hank had been dealing with at The Pyre lately. Something was brewing in Deadwood, and Boone had a feeling they just might wind up in the middle of a stampede if they weren't careful.

They were nearing the stables when a stumbling boozer fell into Hank, grasping at his coat sleeve to keep upright. The drunk burped and let loose with *blawph* accompanied with a blast of vomit that had Boone back stepping in a hurry. Hank managed to pitch sideways, almost enough to avoid the river of yellowish-green vileness. Almost. The gush fanned across Hank's knee in an arc before he could move his leg out of the way, the muck running down his leg and into the cuff of his pants.

Christ! Boone covered his nose with his sheepskin jacket against the sour, awful odor of partially digested whiskey, corn, and chunks of things he didn't even want to try to identify.

Rabbit gagged behind him.

He looked back to see Rabbit resting his forearm on Nickel, alternately breathing deep and then gagging again. "Don't you retch on Nickel, you little nancy!"

Since they were kids, Rabbit had been a sympathy vomiter, and on more than one occasion he'd lost the contents of his stomach from the smell of bile alone.

"Git off!" Hank said disgustedly, pushing aside the drunk who was pawing down the length of Hank's coat before landing on his side in the frozen mud and snow of the street. Hank grabbed a handful of snow and rubbed it down his pant leg.

Boone pointed. "You got a cuff-full there yet." He waited for Hank to finish cleaning up and then pulled on Nickel's reins. "Let's get some distance from this tangle."

"Smell's gonna make me go, too, goldurn it." Rabbit spit. "Gotta get away from it." He pushed past Boone and led Dime around the boozer and his steaming pile of overindulgence, making his way down the street toward Keller's livery stable.

Boone followed. "Seems busier now in Deadwood," he said to Hank, who was walking beside him. "Half again as many folks, maybe, as there were when we left."

"That's prob'ly about right."

"We saw more cabins on the way into town, too, and some farther out than there were before."

"Yep. Poor suckers jus' keep comin'. Thinkin' there's somethin' here for 'em. Like they's all gonna get rich."

Boone paused with Hank, taking in the changes along the street. "More businesses, too."

"Half of 'em is new since you was here." Hank swept his hand up the line of buildings on the left and back down the buildings on the right. "We got banks and dry goods and mercantiles. More saloons. You can have a tooth pulled proper by a barber, even. Some places built right up over where tents was sittin'."

They started again, catching up with Rabbit, who was still making his way to the livery. His head swiveled back and forth as he gawked at the people and buildings that filled practically every space available in the narrow gulch.

"I might have thought the weather would discourage this kind of settlement," Boone said.

"You'd think. But it don't. Ain't many payin' jobs back east. Not good-enough pay, nohow. Ever'body comin' out west to make a go of it. Ask me, they came to the wrong place. Ain't no jobs here, neither."

Boone shook his head. The Civil War had left a lot of folks in a bad way both mentally and financially.

"Here we are," Hank said as they neared Keller's Livery. He hustled past Rabbit and tugged on one of the massive stable doors.

"Right inside, if'n you please, sirs." Hank bowed and ushered in Boone and Rabbit, along with their horses. "Feelin' on top now, Jack Rabbit?"

"Doin' fair, Hank." Rabbit scanned the clean and well-kept livery. "Keller still in charge here?"

"Yep. Wishes he weren't, tho'. Ain't happy. Grumbles a lot. Says it ain't worth the work. Wants to head back east to the missus and his family, he says."

Hank opened the gate to one of the stalls. "There's room enough for yer two fellas in there. Hello, Fred."

The horses trotted into the stall and whinnied, rubbed noses

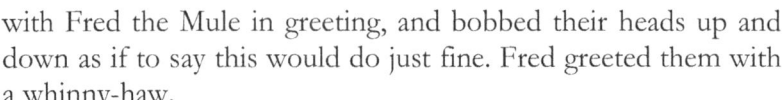

with Fred the Mule in greeting, and bobbed their heads up and down as if to say this would do just fine. Fred greeted them with a whinny-haw.

The sight of the greeting made Boone smile. "Old friends meeting up fresh from the trail."

"Ha! Ain't that right." Hank slapped Boone and Rabbit on the shoulders. "Just like us. Sure is good to see you two fellas. Weren't the same with you two traipsin' across the countryside, leavin' business to me an' Miss Clem."

Rabbit grinned. "You're a right nice sight yourself, Hank."

Boone agreed, thinking back on that day at the Bloody Bones mine. How Hank had probably saved his life, and maybe Rabbit's. Possibly Clementine's, as well. He had shown himself to be a man of quality. Honorable. Good-natured, to boot. Exactly what Boone looked for in a friend.

After he and Rabbit had unsaddled, brushed, and fed Nickel and Dime, they climbed the steep stairs with their bedrolls on their shoulders to the hayloft acting as Hank's current residence.

"Wait here." Hank shuffled off across the loft, skirting shadowy obstacles in the feeble glow from the burning lantern below. He reached the far corner and struck up a lantern sitting in a washtub on a sturdy-looking table. He tapped on the tin tub. "Gotta take care with fire and oil in a place like this. Lucky there ain't much hay up here right now. Too busy in Deadwood these days to keep a loft full."

Boone surveyed the enormous upper story of the livery. In one corner, Hank had pushed aside the hay and stacked sacks of grain into walls to hold it back. A box frame of lumber covered with blankets sat next to the table.

"We'll fix you boys up with a couple-a beds, blankets, all that. Be snug as ticks on a hound."

Boone dropped his bedroll next to the table. "This will be mighty fine, Hank." Especially after being on the trail in the cold and snow for too long. He sat in one of the three chairs surrounding the table. "Three chairs, Hank?"

"There's three of us." Hank plopped onto the seat beside Boone. "Miss Clem don't come up here much. Ain't fittin' for a fine woman like her."

Clementine ... She'd felt soft when she'd hugged Boone hello. Warm under her manly shirt. Her auburn hair had tickled his cheek, teasing him with a hint of lavender when he'd breathed her in. Clementine certainly was *fine*. Especially with those long, long legs.

Boone blinked away his musings about the woman whose impression had troubled him periodically on the trail to and from Santa Fe. It wouldn't do to have Rabbit noticing his preoccupation with Clementine, not with the heartfelt praises his partner had been doling out left and right for her along the trail.

"You even have some niceties," he said to Hank. "Pictures."

"Feels more like a home to me thatta way."

"Window framed with a curtain." Rabbit pulled the curtain aside and looked through the glass. "Stars are handsome tonight."

"Hoo hoo!" Hank slapped his knee. "Like bein' in a real house, ain't it?"

Rabbit moved to a picture strung up with a piece of rope over a hay hook stuck between sacks of grain. "Who is this? Looks like you and President Grant and a couple other people."

Hank smiled wide and nodded his head once, hard. "That there was *before*. Back when—"

A sudden flurry of snorting and blowing from below interrupted Hank.

"Somethin's spookin' the horses," Rabbit said.

Boone froze, listening. "Sounds like Nickel and Dime."

"Fred and yer horses are right below us."

Rabbit grabbed his pistol and hurried down the steps.

"Ain't usual, havin' problems here in the livery. Prob'ly just the reunion goin' on still." Hank stomped his foot, jostling the hay on the floorboards. "You three donkeys settle in!" Snickering, he poked Boone in the shoulder with his thumb. "Fred gets cantankerous when I call him a donkey."

Judging by Hank's reaction to the commotion, Boone relaxed. But to be sure Rabbit was covered if there was trouble waiting below, he stood, stretched, and grabbed his pistol.

"Jehoshaphat!" Rabbit's voice resonated with disgust rather than alarm. "Somethin' died down here! Boone! Hank!"

The livery door creaked open and then slammed shut. Silence followed.

"Rabbit!" Boone descended the steps.

Down below, a sour, rotting stench hovered in the air, pervading the livery. "Oh my—thunderation!" He covered the lower part of his face with the inside of his elbow and rushed for the door.

Outside, Boone found Rabbit talking to a familiar face— Keller, the livery owner and blacksmith. They'd met him inside the stable last month when they were on the hunt for Uncle Morton. Tonight, Keller's square shoulders and massive arms were cloaked in a thick wool coat. Boone could see crystals of frost on his dark handlebar mustache when he reached them.

"Rabbit, what the hell?"

"Mr. Keller here saw me step out the door. Come to see who I was and introduce himself, then recognized me from before when we were lookin' for Uncle Mort."

"Keller. I remember." Boone shook the livery owner's calloused hand and then asked Rabbit, "What happened in there?"

Rabbit scrunched up his face. "Didn't you smell it?"

"It's a stable." Keller was unapologetic.

"Yeah, but that ain't no stable smell. It's like something died a while back and commenced to decline straight away." Rabbit buck-snorted out each nostril. "Can't get that durn smell outta my nose."

Keller nodded knowingly as Hank walked up. "You can blame ol' Hank here for that."

"Keller-man!" Hank patted his shoulder. "Yer off fer the evenin', I thought. Got that bellows for the forge all fixed up."

"I was across the street when I saw Jack come out the door," Keller explained.

"These are the two I told you 'bout. Fresh in from Santa Fe."

Keller's mustache twitched when he smiled. "Remember you both. You find your man Morton?"

Boone nodded with a slight grimace, edging aside the gut-wrenching memory that Keller's question spurred. Rabbit turned away and frowned down the street.

"That's good. That's real good. Sorry about the wagon and the team, though. If I'd known …" Keller shook his head. "Business. Well, anyway, make yourselves to home then, boys. I'm bound for a drink."

"That's a good idea. Due for a libation myself." Hank patted Boone's shoulder. "Whadda ya say?"

Boone glanced to his partner for an answer, but Rabbit was busy staring at a sage hen displaying her assets in the front window of the brothel next door.

Hank pointed at his belly. "Could do with a piece of meat and a tater in here."

"I'll catch up with you boys later." With a finger salute, Keller headed toward the saloon across the street.

"We might wanna talk about this livery of yours later!" Rabbit called after him, receiving a raised hand in acknowledgment.

Boone eyed Rabbit. "What's that again?"

"Think about it, Booney. Entertainment next door." He nodded toward the brothel. "Food and rot gut across the street." He pointed his thumb over his shoulder at the building where Keller was headed.

"Hmm." Boone watched Keller disappear into the saloon. "Probably not cheap, though, what with Deadwood being a

boom town and all." Rabbit had a habit of chasing any opportunity he thought might fit his current situation, but it was freight contracts that were on Boone's mind.

"And think of this—"

"Wait one damn minute!" Boone turned to Hank. "What the hell did Keller mean, 'Blame ol' Hank here' regarding that smell?"

Hank's focus dropped to his feet. He began pushing a hunk of frozen mud around with the toe of his boot. "Well ..."

"What?" Boone pressed.

"It's Fred."

"Fred your mule?" Boone's brow tightened.

"Is ol' Fred sick?" Rabbit joined in.

"The new stable boy Keller hired gave him barley. Doesn't seem to cause no discomfort but gets to workin' on Fred's innards. Gives him the vapors."

"I'd say it causes some amount of discomfort. Works on my innards, too." Rabbit waved his hand in front of his face.

"Oh, that's nothin' compared to the time he chewed open a sack of barley that had got wet. Fermented. The smells that come outta that mule's backside that day. Whooee!"

"Raises quite a stink, I bet, considering the smell in there right now." Boone couldn't imagine it being much worse. He hoped he didn't have to find out firsthand anytime soon.

"Beer's just as bad." Hank scrunched up his face. "Ho ho! Boys down at the Cricket thought they was funny fillin' a bedpan with beer and feedin' it to ol' Fred when I was busy losin' my as—ante to 'Crazy' Charlie Wickam. If I didn't know better, I'd think he was a-cheatin' me that night. Swearengen, he owns the place. He don't care about card cheats, but he runs the place as he sees fit, I reckon. Won't get my stake no more, though. Besides, he runs prizefights there. I don't cotton to men beatin' on one another with their bare knuckles for money. This here town is a life-or-death kinda town. You fellas know that better'n most. Ain't no need for it." The smile left Hank's face. "Anyway, Fred got that bedpan stuck on his nose, started tossin' his head this-a-way and that." He shook his head, the memory apparently coming to the surface, and scowled. "That disturbs my demeanor a little now that I think on it. Poor ol' Fred the Mule ain't fodder for no frolics."

"Scallywags." Rabbit offered.

"So, Fred gets the vapors." Boone brought the conversation back around to the current problem.

Hank shook his head once more and then seemed to snap out of the memory. "Yep. Ever' once in a while."

"And his stall is right under where you shack up?"

"Yep." Hank aimed his finger at Boone. "Now I see the point you're pokin' into my backside, Boonedock. But it ain't as bad as all that. He don't always have the vapors, and when he does, it don't always get up to the loft."

Rabbit laughed. "Fred and his furious fanny. Wind's kickin' up in Deadwood tonight! Maybe we should call him Skunktail."

"Flatulent Fred." Boone chimed in, trying to bring the smile back to Hank's face.

A grin spread wide on Rabbit's face. His eyes glinted.

"Don't say it," Boone said.

"Fartin' Fred!" Rabbit ignored him, hooting and slapping his thigh.

"Come on now, boys," Hank said between snorts and coughs of laughter. "If Fred heard you he'd be upset. He don't mean to stink the place up. He jus' likes to eat." He wheezed out a round of laughs. "Fartin' Fred the Mule. Ho ho!"

Still grinning, Rabbit rubbed his stomach. "Speaking of eatin', I'm hungry enough to chew on a saddle blanket."

"I got the place fer you boys." Hank took off down the street without looking back.

Boone glanced at Rabbit as they followed Hank. "I hope the livery airs out by the time we finish filling our bellies."

Rabbit chuckled. "Nickel and Dime are gonna be good and surly."

"It's going to take a couple of apples to keep them from dumping us on the ground next time we climb into the saddle."

"Not a couple, Booney. More like a bushel."

An hour later, Boone had finished a respectable supper in a little café with pretense enough to pass as a theater. Ten or so tables, each barely accommodating four chairs, were crowded too closely together into the front of the room.

Along the back wall, a short and shallow stage had been built right on top of the existing floor. Boone figured four girls could dance on the stage at once—if they were coordinated. Currently, there wasn't a woman in sight.

A half-height piano, tapped at by a mediocre pianist, sat nestled in the back corner at the end of a bar that ran along most of the length of one wall. Fancy the bar was not, though it was assembled mostly out of smooth-cut lumber, which was a rare commodity in Deadwood.

"Damned fine meal, Hank," Boone said, watching Rabbit finish what was left of the man-sized portion of steak and eggs, along with a hunk of fresh bread. Boone had enjoyed the same meal because it happened to be the extent of the items listed on the menu board hanging beside the kitchen door. "You're surely the man who knows the *what* and the *where.*"

His stomach full for the first time in days, Boone sat back, sipped at his mug of beer, and watched two painted ladies in bright, frilly dresses weave through the crowd and step up onto the stage. As the piano player picked up the pace, they began to shake their enticements.

"Surely was, Hank." Rabbit pushed his empty plate away and began picking at his teeth with his Bowie knife.

Boone frowned. "Manners, buckaroo. We're not alone on the trail anymore."

Rabbit frowned back at him. "Yes, father." Then he

mumbled, "Tryin' to get a piece of meat outta my teeth, wasn't I?" He leaned back and began to nurse his beer.

"You boys made good time there an' back." Hank wiped his plate with the last piece of his bread. "Santa Fe, I mean."

Boone shifted, resting his elbows on the table. "Trails were clear. No trouble on the way south. Not much to speak of, anyway. On the way back ... well, let's just say Rabbit can't help but be Mr. Johnny-on-the-spot." He glanced at Rabbit, who smirked and wobbled his head in jest.

Hank cocked his eyebrow at Rabbit. "There's a story there, I do believe. No trouble gettin' outta Deadwood, huh? That's surprisin'. Paper says road agents are dry gulchin' pert near ever'body leavin' the Hills. Especially stages. Some stages been hit twice right outside of town."

"Just those goin' out?" Rabbit tapped his fingers on the table to the tune the piano player was plunking out.

"Road agents prob'ly figure folks got nothin' comin' in. Stages are loaded with gold goin' out."

Of course, the gold. One stage alone would offer plenty for a man to live for years without want.

"Well, we did get hung up with a couple hard cases, coats closed up high to cover their faces," Boone told Hank, having to raise his voice over the piano's tinny tones.

Rabbit nodded as if he were listening to the table talk, but his gaze was locked on the dancing tails shaking on the stage.

"Bushwhacked us as we rounded a corner in the trail outside Hillyo. Cliff on each side, one going up, one going down. Too steep to skedaddle." Boone aimed a crooked smile at his distracted tablemate. "Rabbit made like he was startled, I don't know, maybe he was. Were you?"

Rabbit scoffed. "Like a kitten facin' a bear."

What was that supposed to mean? "Anyway," Boone continued, "Mr. Kitten here made like he was buffaloed and fell off Dime. I commenced to waving my arms around like I was plumb loco, shouting, 'Don't shoot! Don't shoot!' "

Rabbit laughed, sparing a glance Hank's way. "He sounded like a scared little schoolboy."

"What they didn't see due to my *expert* distraction," Boone said, "was Rabbit had his pistol jerked by the time he landed in the snow. Hid himself behind Dime and took the gun out of one man's hand with the first shot right through Dime's legs. Dime didn't like that, though."

Rabbit shook his head. "I gotta give him a lump of sugar yet or he won't forgive me."

"Second man got a shot off," Boone said. "I heard it go by, but I put a hole through his gun hand before he could light off another. He went all slack jawed staring at the daylight shining through his hand. Took the fight right out of both of them."

"How many times is that I saved your life now, Booney?" Rabbit teased. "Reminds me, I gotta put another notch on my rifle scabbard. I'm gonna need another scabbard if I keep saving your life all the time."

Boone scoffed in return. "You didn't save me, knucklehead. Ever heard of a thing called 'teamwork'?"

"Anyway, they didn't bring enough grit to that fight no how." Rabbit refocused his attention on one of the kicking beauties onstage who was showing handfuls of pink petticoat.

Hank snorted. "Got more'n they showed up for, I reckon. Heartened you two came through it."

"Wasn't much," Rabbit said. "Been through worse." The big flirt smiled and waved his hat at the dancing girl who winked in his direction.

The whoops and shouts grew louder as the girls began kicking high in unison, showing their frilly red bloomers to the patrons.

"Ge ... ings ... d ... down ... outh?" Hank asked.

"What's that?" Boone leaned closer.

Hank scooted nearer to Boone and raised his voice. "I said, did ya get things done down south? With yer freight business?"

"Yep. All taken care of. Our man Carlos is still handling the particulars. Uncle Morton had everything go to us on his death, so we mostly signed a lot of papers."

"We're buying Keller's Livery," Rabbit declared, still watching the frills and lace onstage. His matter-of-fact tone meant he was done thinking about it.

Boone grinned at Hank. "Rabbit thinks he's a big auger sometimes. The idea does warrant some assessment, though. I'm not getting any younger."

Rabbit pointed at him. "You're on the nail head, old man."

"We're practically the same age, hayseed." Boone shrugged. "Sitting in an office would be a preference over a hardwood buckboard seat or on the ground with the snakes and scorpions."

"Talkin' yourself right into it." Rabbit crossed his arms. "Takes you a little longer, I understand. Just let me know when you get there."

Boone chuckled. "Pound sand, Rabbit."

"Carlos runs the place, anyway. And he wants Morton & Son's Drayage. Built-in buyer. Don't make it a hard notion in your noggin."

"I'm thinking about the ranch," Boone shouted over the din of wolf whistles and shouts.

"What? Carlos wants that, too. Said we could visit anytime. Remember?"

Boone sobered. "It's Uncle Morton's." Letting the ranch go felt like hammering the final nail in their uncle's coffin.

"I know, Booney. But he's gone now. We gotta think about us. What are we gonna do? You said yourself that trains are puttin' freighters like you and me outta business."

The piano man ended his keyboard romp and the girls finished their high-leg hoedown, taking bows to the cheers and whoops. The cacophony temporarily halted all conversation in the room.

A gunshot thundered in the café.

"NO GUNS!" The bartender clapped his double barrel shotgun closed and swept the barrels back and forth across the crowd, his thick forearms steady.

The room went silent.

"Apologies, Mr. Bunts," a wheezy voice called out. "Got a little too much ruckus juice in me." The shooter sat and mumbled into his mug of beer.

A tattoo on the bartender's arm caught Boone's eye. "Rabbit. Hank." When both men looked his way, Boone nodded slightly at the bartender. "Right forearm."

Their heads swiveled to stare in unison.

"Keep it subtle," Boone said under his breath in what now seemed a painfully quiet café.

Hank jolted as he locked onto the tattoo. Then he looked up, then back at the bartender, and then up again and quickly to the left. After that, he became engrossed in his boots.

Rabbit shifted in his chair, pretending to focus on one of the dancing girls working her way in his direction, collecting money along with unsolicited pats and squeezes from the rowdy men. Or, knowing Rabbit and his weakness for pretty sage hens, maybe he wasn't pretending.

Christ, this is my posse. Boone scrubbed his hand down his face.

Rabbit turned back to Boone and leaned across the table, his forehead drawn in a deep scowl. "That's a *capsersis* on his forearm, ain't it?"

Hank nodded along with Boone, but the older man continued to deliberately stare down at his boots.

"*Caper-sus*," Boone clarified. "You can look up now, Hank. The bartender's pouring drinks down at the other end of the bar."

The petticoat aiming for Rabbit arrived, twisted him around to face her, and plopped down in his lap.

"Well, howdy, miss!" Rabbit's scowl evaporated in a blink. "Your dancing sure did improve my disposition."

Hank bent Boone's way. "Hoo hoo," he said from behind his hand. "His disposition is on the rise."

"And then some."

"You have something for me, cowboy?" The dancing girl put her arm around Rabbit's neck and pushed her ample breasts close to his chin.

Rabbit grinned wider than his face. "Give me a minute and I will."

"Hey, Loverboy." Boone let his head loll to the side. "She means remuneration for her work on stage."

Rabbit dismissed Boone with a wave and concentrated on the lady in his lap. "Well, Miss …"

"You can call me Bella, sweet thing." She batted her eyelashes and kissed him beside his mouth, leaving a bright red smudge of lipstick.

"Miss Bella, I'd like to thank you for bringing such a pleasin' fragrance in the vicinity of my olfactories. And I'm here to say, you could light up the room in the dark of night with that sweet smile of yours."

Boone rolled his eyes at Rabbit's flannel mouth.

Hank sat back and crossed his arms, his smile almost as wide as Rabbit's.

"Why, thank you, sugar." She ran her fingernails across his chest, real slow like. "Now, about that little present." She rubbed her fingers against her thumb.

Rabbit reached for his boot where he kept his wallet.

"I'll get this." Boone knew from past experience that Rabbit might empty the contents of his wallet, pockets, and anything else under the right circumstances … and one of those circumstances was currently wiggling around on his lap.

A few short seconds after Boone handed Bella a five-dollar coin, the dancer was sitting on the lap of a miner at the next table over. Rabbit stared after her for a moment before turning back to Boone, his big grin still filling out his cheeks. "I like the way she wags her tail."

Boone chuckled. "Pretty tails tend to be your Achilles heel."

"Boys," Hank whispered, motioning them in closer. "That barkeep." They huddled around the table. "That's a *caper-sus* on his arm, all right. Me'n Miss Clem been seein' more and more of 'em lately."

"So she said." Judging by the tension lining Clementine's face when she'd filled Boone in about the growing number of bodies marked with the symbol, they needed to be careful about talking about the *caper-sus* cult out loud in public.

"More'n more all the time." Hank glanced around, adding under his breath, "Prob'ly some in here with us." He was on the same track as Boone.

Rabbit's lips thinned. "Thought we were on top of that after the Bloody Bones. Looks like we got behind headin' south like we did, Booney."

"Not hardly on top of it," Hank said. "But if'n we're on the hunt, I reckon havin' Miss Clem and you two muleskinners at my back, well, I couldn't … I wouldn't want nobody else at my back." He blinked a few times and then bobbed his head.

"We're with ya, Hank." Rabbit punched his arm.

Hank leaned back from the table. "Oh! You said somethin' about no trouble on the way down. So what's this Johnny-on-the-spot about? Trouble on the way back, you said?"

Rabbit glared at Boone.

"Put your stink-eye away. It's Hank. I'm telling him."

Rubbing his hands together, Hank's grin widened. "Let's hear it, Boonedock."

"The night before we headed out of Santa Fe we were saying good-bye to a friend or two and having a drink at El Gato, that's a saloon we tend toward back home. In walks—swaggers, really—a pair of hard cases. Already corned. Real belligerent. Pushing folks aside at the bar. You know the type."

Hank's brow rippled. "Corned?"

"Half seas over. You know, drunk," Rabbit explained.

"El Gato gets that type," Boone added. "It gets pretty rough from time to time."

"Ain't too differ'nt here."

"Right. Well, one of these characters starts singing along with the cantina band at the top of his lungs. Real sour notes, which wasn't anything new, but then he grabs a *señorita* who works there—one Rabbit has a little history with. He starts taking liberties with her. Pawing and grabbing, making her dance with him, intimate like. His *amigo* seemed real amused, but the girl got pretty scared."

Hank tapped on the table. "Some might call that man an animal, but it's my estimation that animals don't do no such things as they get accused of."

"Dumb drunk gump," Rabbit growled. "I tell you what, though, the music improved once I started in singin'."

Boone snickered. "No, not so much. But things did get to hopping. Rabbit insinuated himself between the girl and the *hombre*, subtle like. Took the drunk by the wrist, put his hand on his waist and serenaded him. If I hadn't known better, I'd have thought he was singing him a love ballad. Then he commenced to sashaying the spooney around the cantina, big spinning loops, this way and that."

"He was so whittled all he could muster was a 'Hey now!' " Rabbit told Hank.

"Rabbit dizzied him up real good with all the looping and twirling." Boone looked at Rabbit. "I suspect you were pretty dizzy too, since you were 'half seas over' yourself."

Rabbit guffawed. "Naw. All an act for the little *señorita*."

"He rambled that drunk bastard ..." Boone chuckled at the memory, pausing before continuing, " ... right over to the front door ... " Another chuckle escaped at the memory of Rabbit flouncing and dancing with the drunken horse's ass. "And then right out into the street."

Rabbit sat back with his arms crossed and chin high, grinning like a mule chewing on thistles.

"Then he put a boot to the scamp's ass and sent him face-first in the dirt. Uttering an '*Adios*,' he wiped his hands on his pants, walked back into the cantina, and finished his mescal."

Boone shook with laughter at the memory of all that twirling around. Uncle Morton would have fallen out of his chair with laughter had he been there to see Rabbit's song and dance.

"Hoo hoo!" Hank slapped the table. "Sounds like you, Jack Rabbit!"

"Dumbass couldn't dance any better than he could sing." Rabbit downed the rest of his beer.

"Course, that riled the *hombre's* partner," Boone continued the tale. "He tried to go at Rabbit from behind, but he *accidentally* tripped over my boot."

"Lucky for him," added Rabbit, thunking his glass down.

"Right about then, the *hombre* who got booted comes charging like a bull back into the cantina. He pointed at Rabbit and informed him that he was under arrest for assaulting a Pinkerton agent."

"We couldn't help but laugh at that," Rabbit told Hank while sharing smirks with Boone.

"And that must have really riled the drunk," Boone said. "Because he pointed at me and added, 'That goes for you, too.'"

"I get to laughin' when I'm drinkin' mescal," Rabbit explained to Hank. "Can't help it. Booney neither." He picked up his empty glass and looked toward the bar.

"That's when the Pinkerton on the floor wobbled to his feet. After that, everything went haywire, including—"

"Boone!" Rabbit interrupted, kicking him under the table. "You see who just came in? It's those cocksuckers from Lead. The ones who killed Minny."

Boone sobered, glancing toward the bar without turning his head. Sure enough, Rabbit was right. Anger burned in Boone's chest.

"Rance and Barnes," Rabbit said quietly. "It's them. But who's the man they're with?"

Between Rance and Barnes stood a tall, slender man with a smooth, creamy-white complexion. A long, soot-colored woolen cape-like overcoat hung from wide shoulders. A gray tricorn hat sat neatly atop his slicked hair.

"Rabbit, that big gun. You think it's the man from Lead? He looks young." Boone studied the stranger's profile while he talked with the bartender. The long downward curving nose. The slightly sunken eyes. His demeanor and raised chin exuded self-importance.

"It's that sword-swingin' cocksucker. Gotta be, don't it? What's he think, he's some kinda sailor with that fuckin' hat?"

"What's that?" Hank's brow furrowed.

"The man at the bar—don't stare!" Boone glanced at the stranger again. "Dressed like he's a big show. Looks like he's got that sword on him, Rabbit."

Rabbit nodded as he glared at the trio of men, his contempt obvious to anyone who cared to look.

"He might be the *hombre* we almost got into a scrap with in Lead," Boone continued. "We came a little close to somebody getting killed that day and the odds weren't in our favor."

Hank snuck a peek at the stranger. "Looks like he's got two men with him. I 'member somethin' about that run-in. Killed your uncle's hinny. Roughed up your uncle and sent him outta town without so much as a coat. Into a Black Hills winter. That's a special kinda mean."

Rabbit growled and Boone heard the whiz-click of a spinning cylinder and the click-click of a pistol hammer under the table. *Shit!* When had Rabbit pulled it? Boone shook his head subtly at his partner, but that look in Rabbit's eyes—it was the one that usually preceded the smell of gun smoke.

"The two fuckers with him are the ones who killed Minny,"

Rabbit told Hank. "The red-haired bastard, that's Rance."

"Barnes is the other man," Boone added.

"The big show, huh?" Hank rose all of a sudden and waded through the tables littered with cards and chairs full of butts toward the three men at the bar.

"What the hell is he doin'?" Rabbit grimaced.

Boone wondered that himself. When Rabbit stood to follow after Hank, Boone caught his arm. "They don't know him. You they'll recognize, and then the action starts."

"I'll bring the action with me," Rabbit snarled through gritted teeth. "Sons-a-bitches."

"Hold onto it, Rabbit. You light a fire now and Hank may pay the price. We don't know these men."

"Oh, we know these assholes, Booney."

"You remember what we're dealing with here in Deadwood, right? Remember Gayville? Remember the Bloody Bones? We need to use our heads and back Hank." Boone was ready to jerk his pistol as well. "Just wait it out."

Rabbit sat down again, scowling, his left hand wrapped around his empty beer mug. Boone had no doubt his right hand was gripping his Colt under the table. From this angle, Rabbit didn't have a clear shot, but that didn't matter. He'd make a clear shot if need be. Boone had seen him do it before.

Up at the bar, Hank leaned between Barnes and Mr. Big Show, saying something to the latter. Boone watched the exchange, trying to read their body language because he couldn't make out what was being said. Barnes stepped between the two and pushed Hank away, poking Hank's chest.

Rabbit tensed and half-rose from his chair. Boone reached for Rabbit's arm again, holding his partner steady.

At the bar, Hank raised his hands in front of him and backed away, sliding down the counter a bit.

Rabbit slowly settled in his chair again, his gaze locked onto the trio as they conversed with the bartender, who was all smiles with them. Big smiles, the boot-licking kind. Barnes glanced Hank's way and sneered.

"They look like old friends," Boone said.

"Goat meat. Every fuckin' one of 'em, Booney. They'll pay for Uncle Mort and then some."

"And I'll help you, but now is not the time."

The bartender slid a mug of beer to Hank, who stood a few feet down the bar from Barnes, and then turned back to his conversation with the three high binders from Lead. It wasn't long before Mr. Big Show shook hands with the bartender and sauntered from the café, his palm resting on the hilt of his sword.

Hank weaved back through the tables and rejoined them. "Them hard cases ain't friendly."

"We know." Rabbit's upper lip curled.

Boone watched Hank take a big swallow from his beer. "What were you thinking, going up there?"

"Figured we gotta know what they're doin' here. Overheard somethin' to do with Gayville. 'It's comin' along,' the bartender said. And then the sword man said, 'Lead is ours' and that they was workin' on Galena." Hank squeezed his eyes shut. " 'Galena will come easier than Lead now, since the rout.' That was how he put it."

After another sip of beer, Hank added, "That swordsman looked kinda like he was from the war. That long wool coat. Beard like a lot of them gray coats wore. The sword. Like he was an officer or somethin'. But he sounded like some of the boys I was workin' on the railroad with."

Boone recalled the man's voice from that day in Lead. "Slavic?"

"Maybe. I dunno. Some of the talk with the bartender was French, though. Don't know much French."

"Sittin' on my caboose ain't easy, Booney." Rabbit rapped his knuckles on the table a few times and shook his head slowly.

"I know. It wasn't easy for me, either." Boone wasn't prone

to violence, but the sight of those three had spurred an urge to finish what they started up in Lead, especially now that he knew they'd sent Uncle Morton to his death.

"What do you think it means, *coming along* and *come easier*?"

Boone wasn't sure. "Hank, what do you know about Galena?"

"Little place over the hills thatta way." He pointed toward the wall. "Somebody named it after what's bein' mined out there—silver and lead, too."

"Big as Deadwood?"

"No. A few hunerd, maybe. Lotsa folks movin' in, though. Prob'ly bloom like a flower come spring. Lotsa minin' to do." He tipped his beer, gulping down what was left.

"So these characters are in Galena, too." If it was anything like Lead, they could have it.

Hank frowned. "That ain't all I learned. Those boys with the swordsman had the brand on them, same as the bartender's tattoo."

"Sheeat." Rabbit growled again. "I knew they were more than just regular assholes. Now I *really* wanna kill them."

If Clementine's concerns about the increase in the *caper-sus* cult were on the mark, they'd undoubtedly be running into the three from Lead again. "I think we'll have our chance."

"Say." Hank pushed his beer aside and leaned across the table. "You two run across any of them critters we took care of in the mine on your way back?"

"*Bahkauv?*" Boone shook his head. "Didn't see a one. No white grizzlies or white demons either. Not a sign. I think we scared them back into the hell they came from." At least he hoped so. He'd taken enough of a beating during that battle with them to last a lifetime.

Hank scratched his beard. "I don't know."

"Why not?"

"Well, Miss Clem and I sealed up the Bloody Bones, like we

talked about, 'member?"

Boone nodded. Rabbit pulled in closer.

"We sealed it up good," Hank continued. "At least we thought so. But we made a ruckus and townsfolk, grubbers and the like, came up to peep at the commotion. Now they done found more color up there in that hole and they're openin' it up again. Gonna work it harder than ever."

"Dammit." Rabbit pushed his hat back on his head. "You seen any critters, then? Has Miss Clementine seen any?"

"Nope. Just the *caper-sus* tattoos and brands on bodies at The Pyre."

Boone cursed under his breath. "Looks like we're back just in time for the next round."

Rabbit sprang to his feet, pushed through the crowded chairs and tables, and stormed out the door.

Three

"Wait!" Rabbit heard Boone call as he slammed out the front door of the café.

He'd be damned if he would just sit and let the men who'd beat Uncle Mort and killed Minny walk away. Boone could sit on his ass all night and talk about the best way to handle it, but Rabbit knew exactly how to handle it—with hard punches and hot lead.

"Settle up, that's what we're gonna do, cocksuckers," he said under his breath. "Now, where'd you go?"

From the café's boardwalk, he scanned the street swarming with bodies. There were too many swinging dicks in this town. He climbed up on the café's bench and looked out over the sea of heads. Using a porch post to lean out further, he searched for the gray tricorn hat.

There! A little way up the street. "That piece of shit hat."

The big show was talking to a group of men in front of yet another of the many saloons lining Deadwood's main street.

"Gotcha!" Rabbit hopped down from the bench.

"Rabbit, stop!" Boone snagged the collar of Rabbit's coat, but he tugged free and steamed into the crowd toward the son of a bitch with the stupid hat.

Enough tender footing. Enough fucking around and letting these fuckers have the run of the town. He tightened his fists, his anger flaming in his gut. Minny shot and skinned. Uncle Mort beaten and killed, left for scavengers like his life wasn't worth the price of a shave.

Rabbit's fury burned hotter, racing through him, warming his cheeks in spite of the frigid nighttime air.

Uncle Mort shouldn't have even been in this cursed town. "Too many mangy curs in this place, nipping and barking and biting instead of wagging tails," he muttered as he flexed his right hand, readying for a fight. Uncle Mort had paid a high price, and for what? Asking questions? Being too friendly?

A thicket of scrawny, sullen-faced men in tattered clothes surrounded the big gun in the tricorn hat.

Rabbit pressed into the pack, dividing the men to each side until he could hear the big gun speaking.

"… And your compensation will exceed the inconsequential pittance to which you have become accustomed."

Rabbit paused. It wasn't the bastard from the shabby saloon in Lead, the one who'd run the show from the shadows. He nudged aside a husky lubber in front of him, clearing the path between him and the loudmouth.

Someone shoved Rabbit hard, sending him stumbling into the men in back of him. He rebounded and found himself face to face with Rance, who was standing in front of him, blocking his path.

The asshole shoved his open palm toward Rabbit's face. "Close enough, mush head," he said, glaring.

In a flash, Rabbit plucked his revolver, spun it around, and smashed Rance on the side of the head with the butt. Rance's eyes rolled back and he swayed on floppy legs, lolling this way and that, the crush of men surrounding them keeping him upright for several seconds. Then he began collapsing into the pack, sinking to the ground as the men parted around him.

"That's for Minny," Rabbit told the unconscious prick.

Whoops and angry shouts filled Rabbit's head as the pack

tightened again.

"Sheeat," Rabbit said in a gravelly voice as surly faces pressed closer. "I'll kill every last fuckin' one of you."

The crowd parted suddenly. Barnes stepped in the gap, his pistol pointed at Rabbit.

Rabbit spun his Colt again. C*lick-BOOM!*

Barnes clutched his chest and dropped to his knees, his mouth gaping in a final silent cry.

"And that's for Uncle Mort," he said and used his barrel against Barnes' forehead to shove the dying man backward.

The pack scattered, boots thudding in the snow and mud. Out of the corner of his eye Rabbit saw one man racing toward him. He whirled and cocked the hammer.

Click—.

"Rabbit!" Boone held both hands high in front of him. "Don't shoot."

Rabbit's heart leapt out of his chest. "Jehoshaphat, Booney! You were a second away from leaking when you drink." He nodded at the two men on the ground at his feet. "Barnes is done for. Rance is out cold."

After a glance at the two men, Boone said, "We gotta go." His eyes locked onto something over Rabbit's shoulder. "Duck!"

A searing blast of pain shot through Rabbit's hand. His Colt dropped into the muddy snow. He stared down in disbelief at a sword stuck into the back of his hand, the tip jutted from the middle of his palm. Blood oozed from both sides. When he looked back up, the man with the tricorn hat leered, close enough that his foggy breath washed over Rabbit's face.

"Now now, troubled lad. I bid thee good eve," the man said, his accent soft, like the French trader who'd pay Uncle Mort a visit at the ranch a couple of times a year. "Prithee, why hast thou assaulted my companions?" The bastard turned the sword slightly.

Rabbit cried out in pain, dropping to his knees. He mustered his gumption and grasped the blade with his left hand and pulled. He slid his right hand down and off the sword, his palm smashing into the ground. White-hot pain shot up his arm.

He roared and sprang at the sword-swinging bastard while skinning the Bowie knife from its sheath on his boot—but a spasm of paralyzing pain struck his right hand. The knife, slick with his own blood, dropped to the ground next to his gun.

The swordsman cackled.

Rabbit lunged at the bastard.

A bolt of pain shot down his spine. He crashed to the ground, face-first into the snow and mud. His head spinning, he rolled onto his side and groaned, spitting out dirty snow. There were so many feet all around him. He struggled to focus on his attacker.

"Such animosity, my young friend." Mr. Big Show tapped the tip of the sword on Rabbit's chest. "Mine eyes take interest in thee."

Rabbit squinted up at the man's blurry face and that stupid tricorn. Where was Boone?

The bastard leaned closer, cocking his head. "A familiarity I sense in you ... I've encountered your kind. Full of fire but lacking intelligence." He stepped back and kicked, landing the heel of his boot with a bone-jarring thud above Rabbit's eye.

Rabbit's head lolled. He turned onto his side and tried to push to his knees. Everything turned gray and fuzzy. He closed his eyes and tipped, rolling onto his back again. Daggers of pain speared through his head and spine.

"Prithee, tell. How fares your fiery spirit now?" Rabbit could hear the mock sympathy in the swordsman's tone. "Not well, I presume." He put the tip of his blade to Rabbit's throat. "No matter. Your fate is sealed. I bid thee farewe—"

"Arrgh!" A war cry sounded above the commotion around him.

Rabbit opened his eyes in time to see a blur of motion as something—or rather someone—crashed into the side of Mr.

Big Show. His sword slipped from his grip as he tumbled to the ground, the blur rolling with him. The tricorn hat flew into the crowd.

"Booney," Rabbit rasped, turning his head to watch the brawl.

Boone came out on top of the bastard and began pummeling him. His hands were a blur. When the sword-stabbing bastard reached for his blade, Boone kicked it away.

A gunshot rang out behind Rabbit.

"Ya move, yer dead!"

Hank! Relief flooded through Rabbit, easing his pain.

Rabbit struggled onto his hands and knees, but the world was spinning violently. God, he was going to be sick. He smelled blood. Probably his own. There was no way he could stand, and he didn't really want to anyway. Curling up in a ball and sleeping sounded much better.

Beside him, Boone continued to pummel the bastard with a flurry of blows. "Get him out of here!" he yelled.

Someone grabbed Rabbit by the collar and dragged him to his feet. "I gotcha, Jack Rabbit! I reckon it's time to skedaddle."

"Boone …" Rabbit said, not wanting to leave his partner.

"Don't worry. Said he's got a plan." Hank half-lifted and half-dragged Rabbit through the crowd, leading him away from Boone and the swordsman.

As the sea of bodies closed in behind Hank, Rabbit saw the bastard deliver an upward thrust with the heel of his hand to Boone's chin, making his head snap back hard.

Boone!

Everything went dark.

When Rabbit woke, he lay on his back in a soft bed—his eyes too blurry to make out exactly whose bed.

The comforting rumble of Hank's deep voice nearby kept him from reaching for his pistols. Who was Hank talking to?

Was he in Hank's loft? Rabbit tried to look around, but in the

feeble light everything seemed to have a dark fuzziness to it. His left eye and the side of his head throbbed with his heartbeat.

He remembered seeing Boone roll off the tricorn-wearing bastard and onto his side. "Boone ..." he managed a whisper as his vision began to blacken around the edges.

The darkness pulled him back under.

Rabbit woke again. This time he could only see out of one eye, but it was clear. He was still in the soft bed. How long had he been sleeping?

He tried to rise, but the spinning loft put a stop to his efforts and forced him to return to his back. He lifted his fingers to his eyebrow and then gently touched his eye only to find it covered. A bandage.

Shit. What did that mean?

"Look who's back with us." Hank leaned over Rabbit, his grizzled face softened by the loft's shadows. "You're safe, Jack Rabbit. You're in my bed in Keller's hayloft."

"Wondered," Rabbit croaked more than spoke. He cleared his throat. "What happened? Where's Boone?"

"He's walkin' Miss Clem back to The Pyre."

"He's okay? Miss Clementine was here? How long've I been out?"

"Couple hours, maybe. Boonedock's fine." Hank chuckled softly and shook his head. "He's somethin', Jack Rabbit." He sat on the wooden bed rail next to Rabbit. "I fetched Miss Clem to come and patch up yer, uh, yer head there."

Rabbit laid his palm on the soft linen wrap covering his eye. "She let on?" he asked gravely.

"Well, to come straight at it, and I'm saddened to say it, Miss Clem said she didn't know if'n you'd keep the sight in that eye or not. That bastard put a hard boot to yer head."

An ice-cold lump of dread settled into his stomach despite the layers of blankets piled on top of him. He stared up at Hank, a mixture of shock and disbelief numbing his senses.

"Now I seen that look before, Jack Rabbit, and you can wipe it right off yer face. Miss Clem said chances are good you'll be okay."

He took a breath, reining in his fears. "What happened?"

"You remember anything?"

Rabbit tried to search his memory, but the spasms of pain ricocheting through his head made it hard to concentrate.

My hand ... He grimaced, looking at his gun hand. Clementine had wrapped linen tightly around his palm, leaving his fingers exposed. Blood stained each side of the cloth. He wiggled his fingers and stabbing pang shot up his forearm.

"Fuck!" He frowned at Hank. "What the ..."

Then he remembered. "That cocksucker stuck me like a pig."

Hank nodded. "Ain't normal to see a sword put to use."

"I didn't even see him coming."

"Seemed to me that devil moved almost as fast as Miss Clem."

"I can't remember much from there." Rabbit closed his eye for a moment, thinking back. "Some saphead walloped me from behind."

"Nope. Same devil."

He opened his eye. His attempt at a frown made his forehead ache. "But he was in front of me."

"Like I said, quicker'n a fox. Got beside you and brought the pommel of his sword down on the back of your neck like a hammer." Hank stared at the floor. "Quick, that devil. You didn't even see him from the looks of it. Then *bam* you were down."

That was how it had felt, too. One hard, painful *bam*. "But Boone laid into the asshole pretty good."

"Woo-wee, did he."

"You saved my life, Hank."

" 'Course I would." He softly patted Rabbit on the shoulder.

"I'll get ya some coffee."

After Hank headed down the steps, Rabbit rolled onto his side and sat up. His head throbbed something fierce, but he was up. Almost anyway.

"Hank!" Pain sliced from his ear to his eye, making him wince. "Can you get me the bottle of McCuddle's Original Magical Tonic from my saddlebag?" he asked more quietly, holding his head.

"Surely will, Jack Rabbit," Hank called up from below.

Hank returned a few minutes later with a steaming tin. "Got yourself upright. That's good." He handed the coffee to Rabbit and then pulled the bottle of tonic from his pocket. "Ain't much left. Been curin' what ails?"

"Yep. Boone don't believe it. He's a lunkhead. Don't believe nothing he can't prove." He breathed in the steamy Arbuckles', enjoying the rich coffee smell before taking a sip. Hank had made it good and strong. "So the high binder hit me with his sword. My recollection goes fuzzy from there."

"Yep. You went down like a sack o' oats. After he thumped you, he started spoutin' off a little. Then lit in with his boot. More'n a few in the crowd was ready to bushwhack you. I was almost to you but I had to jerk my pistol and light off a round, threatenin' like…"

"Heard it. You saved my life, Hank."

Hank shook his finger at Rabbit. "Stop it now. You was laid out good, but still movin'." He took a quick drink from his cup. "Anyway, scamps in the crowd lookin' to help rough you up backed off after that. All 'cept a couple hard cases. They kept comin', but for me. I didn't see 'em at first, had my back turned."

Rabbit nodded his head slowly, carefully. He'd been so focused on Mr. Big Show he hadn't paid attention to the rest of the crowd. Uncle Morton had warned him time and again about controlling his temper. He blew on the steaming coffee.

Hank smiled. "That's when good ol' Boonedock took over. He yells out, 'Hank! Behind!' So I got my pistol turned quick as I could. He told me when we was goin' to get you he'd sneak around behind the high binder, but when he saw the two comin' for me he came to help. Anyway, he slipped in behind one and grabbed his chin and twisted his head so fast an' hard like to broke his neck. He was on the second before the first hit the ground. Did some sorta—" Hank weaved his hands around and wiggled his fingers. "Like that. Couldn't see, really, but the second fella dropped like Boonedock done stole the life outta 'im. Woo-wee. Don't want that man's ire directed at me, I'll tell you what."

It'd been a long time since Rabbit had seen Boone fight like that. Damn, without meaning to, he'd dragged both Hank and Boone into his fight.

Rabbit scowled. His neck ached. His face ached. His eye ached. "That Big Show took care of me quick."

"Yessir. Painful to see, but that weren't no normal man, case you didn't figure that part. Miss Clem didn't think so neither. Prob'ly wasn't human at all is her thinkin'."

It dawned on Rabbit he hadn't been figuring on that part at all. "Sheeat, of course." Now it made sense. The sword-stabbing son of a bitch was one of those *other* kinds. "So, how did Boone take him down, then?"

"Surprise, I'm guessin'. After he was done with the two scamps, he saw the boss man with his sword at your throat and charged him. Sounded kinda like he did in Gayville, goin' all pirate again with an 'Arrgh'." Hank snickered. "He's funnin' with you all the time about them pirates, but I think he likes 'em, too."

Rabbit smiled at the thought. Even that hurt now. "Open that bottle for me, will ya?"

Hank twisted the cork from the bottle of the McCuddle's tonic and handed it to him.

Rabbit stared at Hank. "Ain't but a few men in this shitty world take the time or trouble to save my life. You've done it twice now."

Hank studied the coffee in his cup then looked into Rabbit's one good eye. "Yer my friend, Jack Rabbit," he said with a single nod. "You and Boone both. Besides, I think Miss Clem kinda likes havin' you two around."

Rabbit patted Hank on the knee. "Likewise, Hank. You'll probably get the chance to pull my ass outta the fire again, way things are goin' here." He tipped the elixir bottle, chugging the last of it, and then pursed his lips and squinted at the bottle with his one good eye. "Hmm. Gone a little sour." He shook the bottle and peered into its mouth. "I'm out. Hope McCuddle is still in town."

"If'n he is, I'll find him for ya."

"So, Boone had a pl ... a pl-aan?" Rabbit was beginning to feel groggy, his head heavy all of a sudden. The tonic was taking hold quick.

"Yep. He said froggit when bumpin' bist triggit," Hank said.

"Whaaat?" Hank's body stretched up and up, twisting and spinning toward the roof. Rabbit tried to blink the whirling images back to normal, peered at the bottle again, and then frowned. Tonic seemed stronger this time for some reason.

"Binda lacky grack mosin' flow?" Hank shrank back down toward Rabbit, his face huge and swirly.

"Haaank? Wha …? Uncle Mooooor …?" It might have been the tonic, but he could swear he saw Uncle Mort standing beside Hank.

The world faded into darkness again.

Four

The morning brought Clementine sunshine, cold winds, and a black eye. Although the black eye belonged to one Jack "Rabbit" Fields, of course, not her. Not this time, anyway. Odin knew she'd had her share of them over the years.

Last night, moments after she'd finished washing up for bed, Hank had rushed into The Pyre, his eyes wide and cheeks extra rosy, and sputtered out a tale about a fight that had left Jack in dreadful shape. She'd pulled on her trousers, boots, and wool coat. Grabbing her apothecary case and journal, she blew out the lantern and locked the door behind her. Deadwood was full of desperate folks looking for easy money or goods that could be quickly sold for a coin or two, and Clementine had a bit of both.

She hurried after Hank to Keller's loft. He hadn't been exaggerating about the extent of Jack's wounds. While Hank hovered over her shoulder and Jack groaned and squirmed, she'd cleaned the wounds on his hand and the side of his head. Eventually, he'd stilled, his pain rendering him unconscious.

She'd pulled out her journal then and taken notes in case Jack's wounds worsened and they'd need to see Doc Wahl. She also had the notion that it might be useful to keep track of her three companions' injuries throughout the duration of what was to come, if for no other reason than to compare scars later.

In her journal, she'd written:

Probable fracture of the zygomatic and frontal bones near the supraorbital margin.

And after having Hank turn Jack onto his side:

Moderate swelling and evidence of contusion along the cervical vertebrae.

Upon a closer inspection of Jack's hand, she'd added:

Penetrating trauma—Right hand originating from the back of the hand through the palm. No discernible damage to metacarpal bones or flexor tendons.

All of her findings matched Hank's description of the *shindig* in the street, as he put it.

Shortly after she'd applied her poultice and bandaged Jack as best she could, Boone had joined them in the loft, offering to escort her back to The Pyre.

They'd rushed through the chilly night, their boots crunching in the snow.

"Jack was extremely lucky," she told Boone, glancing his way. "A fraction of an inch to either side and the days of using his gun hand might have been over."

He huffed, sending a puff of steam into the night. "Rabbit should have waited for Hank and me to take on that bastard. He almost got his throat sliced tonight."

According to Hank, Boone was the reason Jack was still breathing. "Maybe your lucky hat was at work somehow."

"Maybe," he said, but he didn't sound like he believed it.

When they reached the front door of The Pyre, she eyed him up and down in the feeble light. "You want to come in and let me look you over?" She'd noticed back in the loft that his knuckles were bloody. Had he taken any punches or kicks from the swordsman after Hank hauled Jack away?

Boone held her gaze for several beats in silence.

Her pulse picked up speed, along with her breath.

"What is it, Boone?" she whispered, wondering if he was hurt more than he was letting on.

"Nothing." He turned away. "I'm fine. How about you open the door and let me make sure you don't have any visitors waiting for you inside?"

His chivalry made her smile. She extracted the skeleton key from the hidden pocket she'd sewn into her coat. It had been a long time since anyone had worried about her entering a dark room—anyone besides Hank.

"I appreciate your gesture, but I'm no shrinking violet." Not to mention Tinker was inside playing guard dog from her bed by the fire.

"I noticed." He took the key from her fingers, his touch lingering long enough for her to notice. "But it'd give me some peace of mind after what happened earlier in the street." He unlocked the door and eased inside.

Clementine followed, waiting in the parlor with a sleepy Tinker while Boone moved from room to room. The spicy scent of frankincense lingered in the parlor thanks to the incense sticks Hank had brought her from Soon Lee Curio next to Kee Luk laundry. It almost hid the fact that this was a place of death.

Boone joined her and handed the key back. He smiled down at Tinker and scratched her behind the ears, earning a couple of licks before Tinker returned to her bed next to the stove.

"Find anything worth noting?" she asked, tossing the key in a small bowl on her desk.

"Your weapons cupboard is locked."

Which was how she'd left it. She unbuttoned her coat. "I take great care with my tools of the trade. In the wrong hands, they could wreak havoc."

He tipped up his hat. "In the right hands they can slay a white devil."

"Technically, I slew him with his own blade." She shrugged

off her coat. "What else did you find?"

"Your bedroom smells like something sweet."

That would be jasmine. She paused, eyebrows raised. "Is that bad?"

Had he expected something antiseptic, like the raw alcohol she used when cleaning up after the dead? Jasmine was another scent of incense Hank had brought, along with several others she had yet to try.

His gaze lowered to her neck. "I expected lavender."

Lavender oil was mixed into the soap she'd bought from Hildegard.

"My soap has lavender in it. You have a keen nose, Boone McCreery. Tinker must take after you."

"You tend to leave a mark."

Before she could ask what he meant, he took her coat from her and hung it on a peg near the door. "The fire could use another log."

"I'll probably let it bank for the night, unless you plan to stay and let me take care of your knuckles and whatever else needs attention."

He smirked. "You don't miss much, do you, Clementine?"

"Not on my good days." She stared up at him, liking the warm feel of him here in the parlor with her probably more than was wise. Undertaking was such a bleak business. Cold and lonely. Killing wasn't much different.

"Let me help you, Boone," she said quietly, wanting to keep him a little longer.

He frowned. "Not tonight." He stepped around her toward the door. "I need to check on Rabbit."

"Hank is there. He'll watch over him enough for all of us."

"I could use some rest after the long ride north."

"Of course." She was being foolish about keeping him here. She opened her drawer and pulled out a small sack she'd made from the same heavy canvas material they used to wrap bodies

for transport. "If you're not going to let me help you, take this."

"What is it?"

"Fill it full of snow and place it on your knuckles to bring down the swelling." When he stared at the sack, she shrugged. "Or send it with Hank for biscuits in the morning like I do."

Boone took the canvas sack and tipped his lucky hat at her. "Lock up behind me, Clementine. You may be a hellcat in a fight, but some devils can sneak up on a person."

She smiled. "Come and get me in the night if Jack takes a turn for the worse."

A short time after he'd left, she crawled into bed and closed her eyes. But sleep eluded her until long after Deadwood quieted down for the night, her mind filled with questions … Who was the lightning-fast man with the sword that Hank had described? Was he of the same ilk as the white devil she'd battled in the Bloody Bones mine? How did he play into her reason for coming to Deadwood? Had Jack and Boone's actions stirred up even more potential danger for them and Hank? Should she seek out the swordsman on her own before he and his minions sought retaliation?

Eventually sleep had come, and now that the sun was up and shining brightly, she intended to find some answers to her questions and more. According to Hank, who'd stopped by to drop off biscuits shortly after dawn, she'd find those answers at The Dove, Deadwood's finest brothel and Clementine's favorite place to find a hot bath and hearty meal.

The street was busy this morning, filled with men, horses, wagons, mules, and a couple of stray dogs. Clementine stepped onto the porch of The Dove, tapped the muddy slush from her boots, and entered into a parlor decorated with red curtains and furnishings, lace-covered girls, and perfumed air.

She greeted Jurgen, the doorman, with her customary *Guten Tag.* However, while she normally veered right into the kitchen, this time she took a left.

She hesitated outside the door shingled with the sign "Available Bath." Knowing Hildegard Zuckerman's penchant for cleanliness in her establishment and her not-so-soiled doves *and* the amount of grime covering many of her clientele, Clementine supposed "Mandatory Bath" might more aptly fit the pre-poke requirements for patrons.

Through the door was a large room filled with several baths. She paused inside next to a long dressing mirror. Though not as well decorated, the bathing area was similar to the private room at the other end of the building that Clementine visited from time to time to clean the filth and ugliness of Deadwood's streets from her skin. This room accommodated six narrow bathing areas complete with bath, chair, and a curtain for privacy. A cast iron stove sat near the opposite wall with chairs semi-circled around it. The smell of lemons and lavender filled the humid air.

"Good morning, Clementine," Hildegard said quietly, her smile reaching her dark eyes. Her white-blond hair was pulled away from her slender face with combs but tumbled down her back in long ringlets. Her deep scarlet dress made her creamy skin look almost luminescent. Dressed in her usual wool shirt and trousers, Clementine felt like a toadstool next to the willowy young madam. Maybe she should look into having a dress or two made and have one of Hildegard's girls cut and style her long hair.

Then again, why? The dead men on her table didn't care what she wore and dresses tended to get in the way during fights, not to mention making sneak attacks nearly impossible. Besides, she hated wearing dresses.

But still, it would be nice to feel like a female now and then. It'd been a long time since she'd had a man in her bed.

"Good morning, Hildegard," she said, smiling back. "Hank has informed me that you have two special guests availing themselves of your bathing services."

Though her relationship with Hildegard had started with

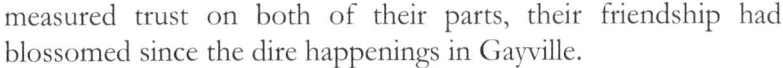

measured trust on both of their parts, their friendship had blossomed since the dire happenings in Gayville.

Hildegard raised one painted eyebrow. "Friends of yours?"

"My colleagues from Santa Fe." She had told Hildegard about Boone and Jack after the Bloody Bones incident.

Hildegard pointed to the closed curtains near the stove. "The other baths are empty this morning. Jurgen will assure your privacy until you leave. I'm sure you have dealings to discuss."

"I appreciate your confidence in this matter."

Hildegard cast a glance toward the curtains. "Will your visit be a surprise?"

"Undoubtedly."

A sly grin passed between them. "It's to their fortune that Alexey made sure there were many bubbles this morning." She patted Clementine's arm. "We must speak soon." She left, closing the door behind her.

Clementine hesitated for a moment, composing her thoughts and feelings about last night's incident and the news Hank had brought her along with the warm biscuits this morning. She tucked in a few loose tendrils and made sure she had no biscuit crumbs on her face before marching over to the curtain.

When she flung it open, both men scrambled to cover their bits with small wash towels.

"What in Sam Hill?!" Jack yelled, splashing around like a dog.

"Close the damned curtain, woman!" Boone scowled, wrapping his arms around himself and making a show of shivering.

Clementine turned and pulled the curtain closed behind her.

A flurry of expletives from both men filled the room.

"I meant with you on the outside," Boone growled when she turned back to them.

She focused on Jack, who was in the tub on her right. He'd removed the bandage she'd wrapped around his head and eye. His elbow rested on the edge of the bathtub, injured hand in the air, bandage intact. His eye was swollen but looking surprisingly good, considering the size of the boot-heel shaped bruise above his eyebrow. His jaw was covered in blond stubble, his hair sticking up like crooked gravestones.

"Don't worry," she told them, fighting not to grin. "There appears to be just enough bubbles to cover whatever you boys are hiding." Feeling a bit ornery after a night of worrying about them, she glanced at Jack's tub and raised an eyebrow. "Besides, Jack doesn't seem to need many bubbles anyway."

The unbruised side of his face crinkled in a frown. "Ha ha. For your information, I happen to have—" He stopped abruptly when she took a step closer to him. Mumbling, he began to gather and pile even more bubbles.

"Why do you have the curtain between your two bathtubs tied back?" she asked, glancing away to give Jack a moment of privacy. "Are baths a community event where you're from?" She focused on Boone. The grin she'd been holding back broke free. "Would you both be in the same tub if it were big enough?"

"Well, aren't you the funny one this morning." Boone's green eyes crinkled in the corners. His hair was wet and slicked back, already washed maybe, but his jaw was dark with stubble yet, like Jack's. A razor, strop, brush, and shaving soap were set out on the chair next to him. He looked at her wool shirt. "Care to join?"

"Thank you, I will." She dragged a chair from the other side of the curtain and placed it between the tubs, settling in near Jack's feet.

"Oh, good," Jack said, rearranging his cloth under the water. "Here I was afraid this was gonna be a quick visit."

No such luck for him after yesterday's tomfooleries. "You're playing poker with a cold deck these days, Jack."

His brow tightened. "What's that supposed to mean?"

"You killed a man last night."

"Barnes," he said with a nod. "He killed Minny. And beat

Uncle Mort."

"I know, but you were not even one day back in town. According to what Hank overheard this morning while waiting for Aunt Lou's biscuits at Grand Central Hotel, you are beginning to build a name for yourself in Deadwood. That's dangerous."

Jack shrugged. "Let 'em come."

"Really?" Boone chimed in. "After getting your caboose handed to you by that swordsman right in the middle of the street? If I hadn't taken him down, at least long enough to get you out of th—"

"You killed *two* men last night, McCreery." Clementine turned her glare on him.

"Hmm. Buzzard food." He scratched his jaw. "Both of them dead?"

Jack grunted, playing with the bubbles floating over his tender bits.

"Didn't think that second one …" Boone trailed off, his brow lowering as he lathered his washcloth with soap.

"Word has it," Clementine continued, "Marshal Stapleton wants to talk to Jack about the shooting." Clementine focused on Mr. Quick Draw to keep from looking at where Boone's washcloth used to be. "Is that the kind of *Let 'em come* you mean?"

"It was self defense. He'd-a shot me, no question."

"Oh, I believe you, but you could have avoided all of this."

"Clementine is right." Boone scrubbed behind each of his ears with the wash towel, then his face. "We're not saying he didn't have it coming. There're just other ways of handling a situation. Usually." He slid under the water, dunking his head.

Clementine glanced at the bubbles slowly dissipating in Boone's bathtub, catching peeks of skin and dark hair underneath. Apparently, Jack was the shy one of the two this morning. Boone returned topside, water running down his face.

His green eyes locked with hers, his gaze intense for several heartbeats before shifting to something more guarded.

The sound of the outer door banging into the wall made her start and look away.

"Boonedock! Jack Rabbit!" Hank's voice practically rattled the rafters.

"In here, Hank." Jack placed his revolver on the chair next to him.

Clementine frowned at the gun. Where in Hades had he been hiding that?

Hank pitched the curtain wide, keeping his gaze averted. His coat and tattered hat were still in place.

"Hank!" Boone and Jack protested in unison, sinking lower into the water.

"Sorry, boys." He closed the curtain and turned toward the tubs. When his sights landed on Clementine, he snapped to attention. "Miss Clem! Why, I never." He looked at Boone and then Jack, pointing his thumb toward Clementine.

"Miss Clem's here."

"Yeah, she sure is," Jack groused.

Hank moved around to the front of Jack's tub. After he hung his coat and hat on the back of the chair sitting there, he picked up the gun and settled in for a spell, placing the pistol in his lap.

Clementine returned to Boone, her focus remaining firmly topside this time. "This swordsman, he was in charge?"

"Definitely." Boone leaned his head back against the bathtub, his mouth barely above the waterline. "Rance and Barnes were his muscle. They were offering jobs to men right on the street. And I didn't get the idea they were mining jobs."

Hank pulled a short knife and hunk of wood from his pocket and began shaving slivers from it.

"The same man who was in the café talking to the bartender?"

"Yep," Jack answered, watching Hank examine the chunk of

wood from different angles.

"Strange accent?"

"A mite," Jack said. "Like before, in Lead, some kind of European. German maybe is my guess, but it sounded smoother. Mixed with a lot of French words. Don't think it was the man from Lead, but sounded something like him," he added, apparently pondering to himself. "Don't think it was."

Hildegard had spoken of another. One who would challenge Masterson. Was this swordsman Masterson's foe?

"He wore the sign of *caper-sus*?" she asked.

"The men with him did. Hank, what was it Mr. Big Show said to the bartender in the café?"

Hank stopped whittling and squeezed his eyes shut. "Gayville is comin' along again after the collapse, and the man with the fancy hat said *Lead is ours* and somethin' about they was workin' on Galena." He commenced whittling again.

The swordsman had to be Masterson's rival, recruiting his *livestock* in the street. Blatant. Flagrant. Flaunting his presence for all to see. The antithesis of Masterson, whose desire was to remain unnoticed in the shadows, concealed.

If the pompous sword slinger were using the sign of *caper-sus*, why were there two different forms of the sign showing up on Clementine's tables? What was Masterson using as his mark? He must have some way to identify his sheep as well. A way for them to identify each other.

There were so many treasure seekers flocking to Deadwood and the surrounding hills now. A practically endless stream of people who were soon to be disappointed by the lack of opportunity. Many were already starving or freezing to death in the streets with no means to improve their condition. A choice between allegiance or ghastly death was really no choice at all. They were easy prey for one promising riches, shelter, and food to fill an empty belly.

The means to grow an army here showed more potential than

any Clementine had experienced. Would she need to eradicate not just *others* banned in the Black Hills, but throngs of humans as well?

Her thoughts drifted back to that dark day when she was forced to decimate an entire village worth of men who had sworn allegiance to a power-hungry demon of old. She shuddered at the memory of all that blood.

"Chilled?" Boone asked, interrupting her thoughts.

She looked over to find him studying her. What would he think if he knew of her brutal past deeds?

"I'm fine." She straightened her back, pushing the screams and other sickening sounds of death from her mind. She needed to talk to Hildegard and see what news she had of this swordsman. "How are your knuckles?" she asked him.

"I'll live. It was a minor scuffle."

She snorted. "Two men dead? With your bare hands?"

"Here you go, Jack Rabbit." Hank plopped a wooden duck into Jack's bathtub and grabbed another piece of wood from his pocket.

Jack picked it up and examined it. "That's a cute little ducky, Hank." He put the duck back in the water and pushed it around in the bubbles. "He needs a lady duck."

Her attention returned to Boone, who stayed submerged up to his chin still holding her stare. He churned the water with both hands, making new piles of bubbles.

"Yep," he finally answered her. Then he sank down into the water, submerging up to his green eyes, still watching her.

"I suppose that means you don't want to talk about it anymore." When Boone stayed put, rising only to take a breath before sinking down again, she turned to Jack. "What about you?"

Jack continued to push his wooden duck around the bathtub, casting passive glances at Clementine.

Hank looked up at her without raising his head from his

whittling. "Guess they don't wanna talk about it."

"Stubborn cusses." She crossed her arms. "Well, since you two didn't stay down in Santa Fe, I can assume that you have come back to the Black Hills to either avenge your uncle Morton or help with our escalating predicament." She included Hank as her partner in this mess since he refused to have it any other way. "In either case, both of you need to re-examine your manner of problem solving before this worsens into a situation bigger than both of you put together." She focused on Jack. "Would you agree, Mr. Fields?"

"I'll take 'em down any way seems necessary."

Clementine nodded slowly. "Therein lies part of our problem." She stood. "I'll leave you two gentlemen to your bubbles and duck. If you could stop by The Pyre this afternoon, we can consider how you can help in this *caper-sus* predicament."

"We'll be there at two," Boone said without consulting his partner.

"Tinker and I will be waiting. Hank, a moment." She waved for him to follow her.

When they were back in The Dove's front parlor, she led Hank over to an empty red velvet chaise in the corner. Pink feathers were strewn here and there on the cushions. "What are we going to do with those two, Hank? I'm not sure they fully comprehend what we're up against here."

He dropped his hat onto the chaise, sending feathers flying. "Maybe not, but those two will fight right alongside of ya, jus' the same."

True, but she didn't need to risk them dying alongside of her if they weren't able to keep their heads in the midst of battle.

"Wonder what one of these fancy soft chairs costs," Hank said, running his hand over the velvet upholstery.

She glanced toward the door that led to the kitchen and the staff's private chambers. "I need to speak with Hildegard. We're caught up at The Pyre, at least for the moment, so you don't need to worry about returning there any time soon."

Hank brushed a stray pink feather off his hat. "I might head out and pick at my claim a little. Waste of time tho', really. Ain't much color and the ground's frozen. Takes the fun out of it. Need to find that man for Jack Rabbit first, though. McDonald, think it was."

"Why?"

"Jack Rabbit's lookin' fer a dose of his magic elixir. Thinks it's curin' him quicker than nature ever could."

Magic elixir? Curing him? She chuckled at the thought of a tonic with actual magical abilities coming from one of the snake oil salesmen loitering around town. "So, Jack's not acknowledging any special influences from *my* magic poultice, I gather."

Clementine's amma had educated her in the different medicinal properties of many plants and animals in the world around her. Prepared in the appropriate way, whether ground, dried, steeped or blended, the effects of many of those concoctions might be interpreted as magical.

"McDougal, was it?" Hank scratched the side of his head. "McDiddle … no. Bustle. McBustle. Hmm. That don't sound quite right, either."

"Hank." She plucked another pink feather from his shoulder, letting it drift onto the seat next to him.

"Yes, Miss Clem?"

"McCuddle."

"That's it! Say, how'd you know?"

"There's been talk. Some believe his elixir actually *is* magical. Apparently Jack is among them."

"Now I ain't sayin' it's true, but Jack Rabbit believes it, and if he believes it …" Hank snorted, brushing another pink feather from his pant leg. "Well, there's power in that."

Clementine didn't disagree. She patted Hank's shoulder. "Good luck in your quest for some magic potion. I'll see you later at The Pyre. We could go to supper, perhaps?"

"I'd be honored, Miss Clem. I'll round up the boys and we'll have us a steak." He headed for the door, pink feathers flying in his wake.

Clementine blew out a breath. Now where was Hildegard?

Five

Clementine's search for The Dove's madam led her through the kitchen. The perfumed air of the parlor faded, replaced by the smell of chicken soup. A pot simmered on the large cook stove; a loaf of bread sat on the wood block next to it, waiting to be sliced. Her stomach growling, she continued through the room to a doorway that opened into the private bathing area.

On the other side of the door, she stopped and listened. Two of The Dove's working girls were singing together while bathing behind closed curtains. The song sounded soft and sad, reminding her of the old French lullaby her amma had sung to her while the winds howled outside her bedroom window in the dark of winter.

"Clementine," a voice called from her right. Hildegard stood at the far end of a narrow hallway in front of her private chambers. She waved for Clementine to join her.

"I assume your associates' baths were acceptable?" Hildegard said as she closed the door behind them, leaning back against it.

"I left them to their troubles and bubbles for now."

"Would you like me to have a couple of my girls see to their needs?"

Clementine had a feeling the *needs* to which Hildegard referred weren't trimming their fingernails and washing between their toes. She shrugged. "That's their business, not mine." Although her gut burned at the idea.

One of Hildegard's painted eyebrows inched upward. "Are you certain about that? They are quite charming, especially the fair-haired one, and both well-versed on manners."

It wasn't the fair-haired one who was giving Clementine pause this morning. Her gaze narrowed. "What's your point?"

"You are female under those trousers."

"I am also an Executioner."

Clementine had learned long ago to keep her liaisons with the opposite sex brief and impersonal. The times she had allowed anything more, as evident by repeated performances in and out of her bed, her companions had been slain by enemies of her profession. Were she to give in to what was currently a mere sexual interest and pursue satisfaction found in the meeting of flesh on flesh, she'd risk losing someone's life along with a growing friendship.

Friends were hard to come by in her line of work.

Sex wasn't.

"You are part human, too, *Scharfrichter*." Hildegard smiled. "I will have Dmitry and Alexey shave your associates today."

Clementine looked away before Hildegard could read the relief on her face. She turned her attention to the madam's quarters. The room was mostly the same as when she'd been there almost a week prior. A fire popped and crackled in the stove near the plush green velvet chair that had become Clementine's favorite during her infrequent visits. The subtle odor of alder smoke from the stove mingled with the floral incense burning on the side table, the combination making Clementine feel the urge to sit a spell and enjoy the quietness.

She pointed at the steaming teapot on the wood stove. "Is that tea?"

"It is. Freshly brewed."

From a large china hutch, Hildegard fetched light blue

porcelain cups that, unlike the chair, were *not* Clementine's favorite. The delicate porcelain cup reminded her of an eggshell. One sneeze and she'd likely crush it into crumb-sized pieces in her large hands.

"Several events have occurred since you were last here that almost led me to pay you a visit at The Pyre." Hildegard poured the hot tea into the dainty cups. "Especially in the last day or so."

While Boone and Jack had been on the way to Santa Fe and back, Clementine had come to The Dove less and less, fearing the risk of exposing Hildegard to Dominic Masterson—or to someone, *or something*, potentially worse.

Clementine relaxed into the soft cushion of *her* chair next to the stove as Hildegard sank into its twin. She held the teacup up near her nose and inhaled. "Floral. Fruity. This must be difficult to obtain here. Everyone wants coffee." She puffed out her chest. "Tea's fer the delicate li'l ladies!" she said in a deep, gravelly imitation of the quintessential bad-tempered miner she was accustomed to putting up with in the streets of Deadwood. "Tea's fer the weak!"

Hildegard chuckled, a warm, breathy sound that reminded Clementine of the wind blowing through the pine trees. "It isn't easy, but I have ways. I have enough to spare you a tin."

"That would be wonderful." The tea tasted slightly sweet. She could get used to such niceties. Next time she signed a contract to kill, she was going to insist on a better ruse to hide behind than the town undertaker. Something less foul. Maybe a gunsmith. Better yet, a blacksmith. Then she could make her own weapons for finishing the task.

"I do, when luck prevails, receive a box or two of Mettwurst. I'd be happy to share that, as well. Dmitry has an excellent recipe."

They fell into a comfortable silence for a sip or two.

Clementine shifted in her chair. "I believe that I am often being watched now. We should be careful. I would not want you to be harmed because you meet with me in private." She lowered her tiny cup. "You or Miss Hundt."

Miss Hundt was an old friend of Hildegard's from Germany. The first time Clementine had met the other woman, she'd warned Hildegard that Clementine was a *Scharfrichter*, not realizing Clementine was eavesdropping. She had yet to learn what Miss Hundt's purpose was in Deadwood, and Hildegard was close lipped when the subject came up, but she assured Clementine that the other woman was an ally.

Hildegard's teacup looked less child-sized in her long, thin fingers. "Of course you are being watched."

"You refer to Ludek," Clementine said to the madam. "I am aware he has been keeping an eye on me."

Ludek was Hildegard's spy, for lack of a better word. The man was a ghost to most, but Clementine had caught sight of him in the corners of her eyes now and then while walking out and about on her own business. He would be there until she looked his way, and then he'd be gone. She'd tried to track him once or twice to no avail. Such was the way of a "ghost."

"I speak of another, lingering in the shadows. Always at the edge of my sight." Clementine leaned forward, resting her elbows on her knees. "I find it strange that I've seen nothing of Masterson. I expected there to be no end to him or his attempted manipulations after the incident at Bloody Bones mine. Yet, nothing." Her benefactor's silence was more troubling than his badgering would have been.

"That is peculiar," Hildegard said with a frown. "I suspect he is re-grouping after his defeat in the Bloody Bones."

"*His* defeat? You mean because I executed that pale bastard guarding the gate?"

"*Ja. Herr* Masterson's *weißer Hund*." She took another sip. "That kill probably thwarted, or at least delayed, any plans your patron may have had regarding that particular threshold."

Well, his *weißer Hund* shouldn't have taunted Clementine when she had him by the throat. "I understand that, but why would his white dog," she used the English version of the German word since her accent wasn't as smooth as Hildegard's, "wear a ring with the sign of *caper-sus*?"

"Ludek believes that it is possible *weißer Hund* was acting on behalf of *Herr* Masterson's adversary."

"A traitor? I recall you telling me …" What was it Hildegard had said? She closed her eyes for a moment, focusing. "Your words about these white dogs were, 'Due to their unbending loyalty and ferocity, they are often given greater responsibility,' I believe."

"Your memory serves you well." Hildegard toasted her with her teacup. "It is unprecedented, true. At least to the extent of my knowledge. However, *Fräulein* Hundt and Ludek agree on this belief." She shook her head slightly. "Unprecedented."

So was Clementine working with the likes of Hildegard, Hank, and the Santa Fe Sidewinders. While killing was rarely repetitive in style and circumstances, there was usually a certain grinding feel to it after a while. Deadwood, however, along with all of its offenses, offered a refreshing change. Although that could quickly become a *deadly* change if Clementine weren't careful.

The stove ticked from the violent swirl of fire in its belly. The flames inside Clementine were swirling as well now. She pushed to her feet and crossed to where the incense burned on the side table, watching the spiral of smoke rise and dissipate.

"Do you recall my description of Masterson's reaction to seeing the ring with the *caper-sus* insignia?" she asked Hildegard, thinking back to the evening after defeating the white devil and his pack of *Bahkauv*. Masterson had charged through The Pyre's front door and confronted Clementine for going against his orders to not travel to Gayville or its vicinity.

"Naturally."

"Betrayal by one of his trusted would explain his agitation

when I showed him the ring." At the time, Masterson had threatened under his breath to rip out someone's throat. Someone other than Clementine, but of whom he spoke she wasn't certain.

"Yes. If his adversary by some manner succeeded in turning his *weißer Hund*, I imagine he would be extremely distraught. He might find it difficult to trust any within his legion."

"Including me. Although I don't consider myself among his ranks." Clementine might be in Deadwood due to a contract with Masterson, but that didn't make her one of his subjects. Executioners were notorious for their lack of prejudice when it came to killing along with their inability to heed orders when it came to living.

"Yes."

"For good reason," Clementine added.

"Undoubtedly. *Herr* Masterson's actions substantiate something else as well. *Fräulein* Hundt and I have discussed this situation at length, and she believes he is losing control of his fiefdom. Or at least he thinks he is."

"Do you agree with Miss Hundt's notion?"

"It is possible his control is slipping. The mining in this area has caused much damage to certain boundaries, and there is little reason to believe it will all stop anytime soon." She tapped her fingernail on her teacup. "No. More men will come. They will dig farther. Deeper. Even now more death is being unearthed."

Death? She must be referring to more metaphorical gates, like the one in the Bloody Bones mine. "You think the Bloody Bones is only the beginning," Clementine stated.

Hildegard nodded. "The Bloody Bones is indicative of what is to come. The mine has been reopened, allowing access to and from what lies beneath it."

"Damn." In spite of the newspaper article Hank had shown her yesterday, she'd hoped they had more time before Hell came to dinner.

"Miners are dying in the depths of that vile place. Again," Hildegard said, her tone heavy. "But the threat does not emanate from the same source, I think."

Clementine tilted her head. "Not the same ... There are more gates in the Bloody Bones?"

"You fought and killed many *Bahkauv*. Can you describe the injuries dealt by those beasts?"

"Lacerations in parallel groups of three or four, generally six inches to a foot in length. Like those made by a thick-clawed predator. Not unlike injuries sustained from a bear attack, but much deeper and longer gashes than a bear might make."

"As I thought." Hildegard sipped her tea while staring Clementine in the eye. "The men dying in there of late are being ripped in pieces."

"A *Bahkauv* might do that, given enough time."

"No, *Scharfrichter*. Ripped *into* two pieces."

Great Odin's spear! This was definitely not more *Bahkauv*.

"Hank and I used too much powder. We roused suspicion and curiosity with the blast and ended up causing exactly what we were trying to prevent."

Hildegard set her empty cup on the table next to her. "It would have been opened again in any case. Either by mining activity or by someone who wanted it open. One way or another, this was inevitable."

"What else is down there?"

Hildegard gave a small shrug. "That is beyond my knowledge at this time."

What did Hildegard mean by 'someone who wanted it open'? "You think the mine was re-opened for a purpose other than seeking gold?"

"It is possible."

"Who would conceive of such a thing? To what end?"

"Perhaps someone with a desire for vengeance against humanity." She gave a small smile, as if they were discussing tea again. "Or merely a challenger for *Herr* Masterson's domain. Tell me, what do you know about this character wielding a sword in the street?"

"Ludek informed you of last night's events?"

"Yes. He believes there is *ein Emporkömmling* in Deadwood intent on acquiring control over this domain, or at the least attempting to weaken *Herr* Masterson's hold."

Clementine cocked her head. "*Emporkömmling*? I've not heard that term before."

Hildegard steepled her fingers together. "One who believes he is to be raised to a position of consequence, deserved or not. A showman, if you will. They are usually pompous and imperious, which rests well with this one's exhibitionism and the hubris he displays."

Clementine nodded knowingly. "He's an upstart!"

"An upstart, yes."

"Hank overheard him say something about the fact that they were working on Galena. The Upstart said Galena would 'come easier than Lead.' What do you make of that?"

"This is not surprising. If we are accurate in our assessment and he means to usurp *Herr* Masterson, then chaos is his ally. Not only does it distract and occupy your patron, but it also lessens *der Emporkömmling's* exposure if the Council begins an inquiry. He can deny any involvement, or he can simply propose that *Herr* Masterson is unfit and advocate for his removal."

"The Council?" Clementine had heard of this entity in passing over the years, including a mention once by her grandfather after the slaughter.

Hildegard waved her off. "We will not discuss that at this time. You would be wise not to speak of it as well."

Her grandfather had said as much about this so-called Council when she'd asked back then. She didn't press him then and she wouldn't press Hildegard now. But one of these days …

"It appears I have a big problem even if Masterson isn't my

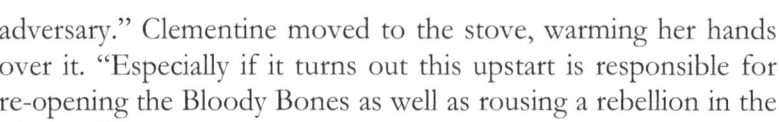

adversary." Clementine moved to the stove, warming her hands over it. "Especially if it turns out this upstart is responsible for re-opening the Bloody Bones as well as rousing a rebellion in the Black Hills."

"Agreed. We need to know more about *der Emporkömmling*. Judging by the confrontation between him and your associates, he demonstrates no misgivings in displaying himself and at least some of his abilities in the presence of humans."

"He's blatant." Clementine wasn't sure if this showed true confidence, making him a dangerous opponent, or if it were merely a show of intimidation without substantial backing. She clenched her hands into fists. There was one way to find out.

"Engagements for control over domains are not uncommon." Hildegard's chair creaked. The sound of tea being poured into a cup followed. "But his overtness strikes me as somewhat unusual. Yet Ludek has had some difficulty learning anything about him. He is elusive even as he pontificates in the streets of Deadwood."

"He must be newly arrived here or we would have come across him before now." Clementine returned to the chairs and the fresh cup of tea Hildegard had poured for her, taking a sip. "Is this a *special* tea? Something to cure my ailments? Give me the eyesight of an eagle?"

"Merely tea." Hildegard grinned. "Although it has been known to sweeten even the most sour disposition, even that of *ein Scharfrichter* who denies her need to bloom when there are perfectly good human males available to water her flower garden."

Clementine laughed.

"You see, it's already working." Hildegard raised the cup to her lips.

"You do realize it is bad luck to make an Executioner laugh, right? The sound of our laughter alone will make your brain seize up, catch on fire, and melt out of your ears."

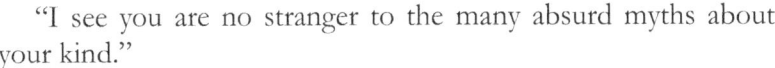

"I see you are no stranger to the many absurd myths about your kind."

"My amma taught me well about the pitfalls of interacting with *others* who are not as blind to my true identity and purpose as humans, nor as tolerant."

Hildegard stared into Clementine's eyes, sobering. "I am confident that you are *ein Scharfrichter* unlike most others who relish in being unrelenting, unforgiving, and deadly. Befriending you is dangerous for me, for many reasons. *Fräulein* Hundt misses no opportunity to remind me that *die Scharfrichter* are a breed alone. She fears for my life and beseeches me to keep my distance from you, as is common among *our* kind."

Clementine finished her warm tea in a big gulp. She set her empty cup on the table between them and smoothed her trousers with her palms. "I appreciate your courage and friendship, Hildegard. Killing makes for a lonely journey through life." Speaking of killing reminded Clementine of the folded scrap of paper in her pocket.

"I have something else to share." She pulled out the note and handed it to the madam.

"Are you paying attention." Hildegard read the note out loud, and then she refolded it, setting it on the table between them. "Tell me."

"I found that in the pocket of a moderately well-dressed and fed, but very dead man. He had a puncture wound on his chin. The injury penetrated all of the way through to the skull." She pointed to the top of her head. "That's a long, slender blade."

"Our mysterious assassin is still in town, I see."

"And still killing. The man also had a burn scar on his chest in the form of a *caper-sus*."

Hildegard sat silently for a moment and then nodded slowly. "If we are to believe that the *caper-sus* insignia is being used by *der Emporkömmling* or *Herr* Masterson, then this assassin must be working against them. A hired killer, perhaps. Or possibly an avenger. Or maybe a rogue *Scharfrichter*."

Hildegard and Miss Hundt had spoken of the rogue *Scharfrichter* before. The situation, timing, method, and precision used in these executions—and that was really what they were, not murders ... "When you say 'hired,' you mean by Masterson or the Upstart?"

"Yes. However, based on the notes you have shown me, I'd place my bet on the latter—a rogue."

Clementine nodded, thinking back to all of the deaths she could attribute to the assassin. Did they all have the sign of *capersus*? She hadn't been keeping track in the beginning, damn it.

"Ludek has been continually frustrated in his attempts to observe her," Hildegard continued. "His reportage on the killings is sparse at best."

Ludek's lack of success was no surprise, really. Executioners were hunters by nature. Few could spy on them without being caught ... and then killed. "You realize Ludek's life may be in danger if this *Scharfrichter* feels threatened by him in any way."

Clementine would hazard a guess that the rogue had already assessed that Ludek was not a threat, or he would be dead by now.

"I suppose it could be *der Emporkömmling*." Hildegard crossed her arms. "He is good with a sword, as your associate found out last night."

Yes, Jack did. "I am with you—it's another *Scharfrichter*. We need to find out her purpose here." Other than to harass Clementine for not doing her job well enough. She stood to leave. "It appears I have much work to do in addition to attending to the dead in town."

"And your associates?" Hildegard rose as well, walking toward the door. "What of their future in Deadwood?"

She had a feeling Hildegard was asking for more than just formalities. She would need to inform Ludek of their purpose in all of this. "I'll need to prepare all three of them for what is to come." She thought of Hank in the Bloody Bones and his fight with Masterson's white dog. "Although Hank may well have things to teach me."

Hildegard nodded. "I'll tell Ludek to redouble his efforts with *der Emporkömmling*." She smiled up at Clementine, but her eyes were lined with concern. "We'll see what he can learn about this pretentious swordsman while you prepare for battle."

Six

Boone rubbed his smooth chin. Those crazy Russian twins at The Dove sure knew how to give a close shave. They'd worked those blades like they'd been handed to them straight out of the womb. Hell, they'd spent more time arguing about whose minced meat and potato *pirog* tasted the best than they had scraping whiskers.

There was nothing like a pair of vociferous Russians with cutthroat razors to make a naked man in a tub of water sit real still. By the end, he and Rabbit were raring to get dried and dressed, not to mention hungry as grizzlies in spring. After agreeing to return another day to judge the twins' *pirogi* dishes for themselves, they'd tipped their hats at the ladies lounging in the main parlor and scampered out the door and back to the livery.

Now, a few hours later, Boone sort of wished they'd stayed at The Dove and taken the twins up on their offer of chicken soup and fresh baked bread in the kitchen. He had no doubt that the soup would have tasted far better than the gray slurry this little café called gravy, and the bread would've been soft compared to the rock-hard, two-day-old biscuits. It was a surprise that the bitter coffee here hadn't sprouted all new whiskers on his chin.

"Hank ain't coming?" Rabbit asked, bringing him back to the present. "I thought he was joinin' us for a cup of coffee."

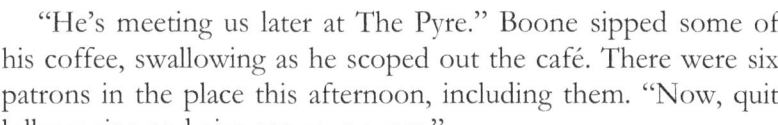

"He's meeting us later at The Pyre." Boone sipped some of his coffee, swallowing as he scoped out the café. There were six patrons in the place this afternoon, including them. "Now, quit lollygagging and give me your guess."

Over their meal, they'd resumed the freight wagon guessing game they'd started on the way into Deadwood days ago.

"Fine. You sure the three bags of beans, six bolts of cloth, two crates of Remingtons, a barrel of whiskey, and a piano ain't all of it?"

"I'm sure."

"Pretty much all of it, then. Most of it." Rabbit sounded sure, nodding. "Considerin' that piano and the size of the wagon."

Boone chuckled. "Nope. Remember it's a Kilkenny Overlander."

Rabbit scowled and then winced, gingerly touching his swollen eye, which was looking better already.

"There's plenty more," Boone added. He pointed at Rabbit's face. "Can you see out of that purple puff of an eye?"

The swelling had diminished considerably, but Boone wasn't sure whether Rabbit's quick mending was due to Clementine's care and poultices or to McCuddle's "magical" tonic. He'd hear no end of it if Rabbit clung to the notion that it was the latter.

It was also possible that Rabbit was just healing fast. He always had since they were kids. "A strong constitution, that boy's got," Uncle Morton would say. Thanks to Rabbit's many wild hairs, their uncle had abundant opportunities to comment on Rabbit's seemingly better than average ability to bounce back from physical adversity.

Rabbit closed his uninjured eye and forced his puffy eye halfway open. "Your punkin' belly is filling my view."

Boone turned away. "Cut that out. It's all clouded with blood and squishy looking." He shuddered, glancing at Rabbit through a squint, glad to find he was back to using his good eye. "Reminds me of that humdinger of a shiner you got when you were ten or eleven. What was his name who gave it to you?" Boone snickered. "Deadbeat, wasn't it?"

"His name was Granger. You only called him 'Deadbeat' because all he ever did was eat and sleep. Says you. He had a big personality and did lotsa things. You hurt his feelin's calling him 'Deadbeat' all the time. And, by the way, he was my *compadre*. A better *amigo* than you."

Boone leaned back in his chair, grinning wide. "How's that?"

"For one, he didn't try to boss me around all the time."

"No. He just threw you to the dirt every time you tried to crawl on his back. I don't know why Uncle Morton didn't make sausage out of him."

"Not *every* time, only when he wasn't in the mood for a ride. Besides, Uncle Mort liked Granger more than he liked you. Told me hisself."

"Himself," Boone corrected. "And he did not like that pig better than me. He got a chuckle out of you riding that pink skin. Listen to you. A pig with feelings. Pigs don't have feelings. Or moods either." When Rabbit jutted his chin, Boone held up his hand. "Okay, okay. Maybe he was moody at times. But horses are meant to be jockeyed, not pigs."

Rabbit scoffed. "Granger was big enough to ride and not so high off the ground as a horse. Perfect for a kid."

"I bet Hank would get a kick out of that story."

Boone took another drink of coffee, watching two of the patrons rise and don their long coats and felt hats, leave some coins on the table, and head for the door. Businessmen, by the looks of them. No rings visible, but they could wear a *caper-sus* brand or tattoo under their fancy clothes.

"Don't you tell nobody about that. People don't never understand about a buckaroo and his pig."

Boone grinned. "That much is true."

"Speakin' of Hank, you give him his LeMat yet?"

"Nope." Boone had picked up the pistol down in Santa Fe.

It'd been well taken care of and shot as true as his Colt. "It's still in Nickel's saddlebags. Thinking about giving it to him for Christmas."

"That's a good idea, Booney. He's gonna get a kick outta that fire breather. Ain't nobody got a pistol with a shotgun barrel under. Not no one I've seen anyway."

"Hope so. He seems partial to his bow but he's good with a pistol, too. I think he'll like that leather you tooled for a holster—real nice."

"Thanks, Booney. Worked on it every night the whole trip up here. I might as well save it for Christmas, too." Rabbit gulped the last of his coffee from the tin cup, sat back, and studied Boone.

Boone held his gaze. "Why are we here, Jack?"

Rabbit scratched his jaw. "Argh. That's still tender a little."

"I didn't realize you caught one there." Boone leaned across the table, studying Rabbit's face.

"Ain't nothin'." He waved off Boone's concern and sat back.

Returning to his question, he added, "It's revenge for Uncle Morton, I know, but—"

"I ain't here for revenge, Booney. I'm here to *avenge* Uncle Mort. Pure and simple. It's a reckoning."

"I gotcha. But is that it?"

"Ain't that enough for ya? After what they did?"

Boone thought on that for a moment. Of course he wanted to punish all of those heartless bastards who were up in Lead that day Uncle Morton was treated so callously and sent out into the cold and snow with only what he could carry.

"How about add Minny in?" Rabbit said. "And Tink, too?"

"Reason enough, sure." Boone nodded slowly. "What about Clementine, and Hank?"

"Well, sure, they figure in. Shit, Booney, we don't even know what they're up against." He opened his mouth, apparently intending to add something more, but closed it again.

Boone studied Rabbit's expression, seeing the lines of tension around his mouth and good eye. "You had a taste, I think, in the Bloody Bones. And in the street the other night."

"I got shanghaied is all." Rabbit looked down at his bandaged hand. "I just needed to get to my guns."

"Maybe." But Boone knew better. Rabbit *did* get to his gun. He'd had it in hand and ready to fire. He'd been outmatched by the French-speaking swordsman, plain and simple. It was only with luck, and Hank's help, that Boone was able to get Rabbit clear before the son of a bitch slit his throat. He'd high-tailed it out of the brawl before the swordsman got the upper hand on him, too.

"I know that look. What's on your mind, Booney?" Rabbit shifted in his chair. "What are you diggin' for?"

"I don't know. Just assessing. There are big problems here in the Black Hills."

"We've had our share of trouble before."

Boone nodded. "And we've become more than a little friendly with a couple of people here."

"Miss Clementine and Hank."

Boone finished off his coffee. The tin cup clattered on the table, sounding louder than usual in the nearly empty café. "Seems those two are in for it and here we are chasing our own tails."

"Sort of, but if our obligation to Uncle Mort happens to have us ride alongside them, then where's your quandary?"

"It's not about that." Rabbit wasn't grasping that Boone was wrestling with the idea Clementine and Hank might be reason enough to abandon their lives and friends in Santa Fe.

"What, then?"

"Tell me something. Why are you so jo-fired ready to buy Keller's Livery? What in this big world has you thinking you even know how to run a livery?"

"You know and I know that either one of us can run that

livery. And I'll tell you what else, Booney. You remember where Tink came from?"

"Good ol' Saint Nick dropped her off on Christmas," he shot back with a grin.

"Ho ho. You sure are funny." Rabbit smirked. "I saved that sweet girl from that pack of coyotes when she was just a li'l pup and you know it."

Boone nodded.

"And you remember those kittens? Their momma killed by a rattler?"

"Yep."

Rabbit had a touch of callousness in him since he was a youngster, maybe because of the grisly wagon train affair that had ended with their parents buried along the trail, but especially since the shoot-up in Denver. Walking into that blood-splattered saloon changed him. Not so much in a self-destructive, fuck-the-world sort of way, but more in how he handled the inequities one sees in everyday life. He had no patience or tolerance for tormenters or antagonists—even more so when it came to cruelty to an animal.

"Found homes for every one of 'em." Rabbit tapped the table with his fingertip to end the sentence.

"You did, and I had to do your chores that day while you wandered around town playing with those kittens." Boone hadn't minded the chores since Rabbit was saving the kittens, but he still liked to give him grief about the extra load. "What's your point with all this? I thought you were going to tell me why you're all fired up about that livery. Wasn't too long ago you were gung-ho to expand the drayage business into Deadwood."

"Old news, Booney. We got the money. We can draw against the ranch in Santa Fe. We got the opportunity, and Keller wants to sell. It's a good, well-built building."

"Why Deadwood?"

"I don't know." Rabbit stuck his hand in the air to get the

attention of a girl wandering from table to table filling coffee cups. "Feels right. Don't it?"

Boone pushed his cup toward her as she filled Rabbit's.

Come to think of it, there was something about Deadwood. The Black Hills. Hank. Clementine. Something that had hooked onto him and wouldn't let go. Something he didn't want to let go. Was this what Rabbit was feeling? An obligation to stay. No, that wasn't right. It was more of a …

"Booney!" Rabbit swayed his head back and forth in front of Boone. "Where'd you go? The girl just filled your cup for ya."

"Thanks much, miss." He smiled at her.

Her cheeks turned pink. She curtsied awkwardly, almost spilling the coffee, and then hustled off to another table.

"That one likes you. Must be the shave, 'cause you normally ain't much to look at."

Boone chuckled. "She's a kid." He had his sights on someone older. Taller. Ass-kicking.

"As I said before your admirer showed up, this feels right, don't it? Deadwood? Keller's?"

Boone started to nod, but then shook his head slowly. "I don't know."

"What don't you know?"

"What about Uncle Morton's ranch? How do we run it from up here?"

"Carlos wants it if we don't."

"And if we do want to keep it?"

Rabbit shrugged off Boone's question. "Carlos is lookin' after it fine, like he always did. Maybe one or both of us head on down there from time to time. Check up on things."

Boone glanced at the regulator on the wall. "Shit! We were supposed to be at The Pyre fifteen minutes ago." He gulped half his coffee and then stood. "Pay the girl. I'll get the saddlebags."

* * *

Let another's wounds be your warning.

Clementine poured some raw alcohol on her cloth, soaking half of it. She splashed a little more on the examination table, her mind returning to that last body the rogue executioner had left on her doorstep.

Why the notes? Killing she understood. She'd been trained long ago on the quickest ways to take a life, as well as the not-so-quick ways for those pests who needed to suffer a little before returning to the earth. But these notes left behind …

"What do you think, Tinker?" she asked the dog, who was watching her from where she lay sprawled on the floor in the opening between the examination room and parlor.

Tinker lifted her head long enough to let out a short bark, then returned to snoozing.

"I quite agree. This rogue is either enjoying a gloating game or seeking a cohort in battle."

Let another's wounds … be her warning. The quote her amma had said periodically to Clementine while teaching her about their family's calling in this world kept repeating in her thoughts. The line came from one of the many Norse tales of passion and struggles passed down verbally from generation to generation.

If she were to heed the quote, that meant the slicing of the Achilles tendon followed by the precise piercing of the brain or heart, as had occurred to a previous victim, was to be a warning. But in what way? In the manner of execution? Was the method used necessary for some reason? Or should she be focusing more on what it says about the Rogue?

Let anoth …

The front door of The Pyre creaked open, followed by the sound of footfalls on her parlor floor. Tinker looked around. She whined, and then scuttled into the parlor.

"That a girl," Boone's deep voice came from the parlor.

Clementine dropped the rag on the cleaned examination table and peeked into the parlor as Jack closed the door behind them. Her questions about the Rogue pushed aside for now, she watched in silence as the two men greeted their old friend.

Boone squatted and scratched Tinker behind the ears. "You're looking spry. Have Clementine and Hank been feeding you proper? Looks so." He patted her rib cage.

And then some, Clementine thought. Tinker ate as much as she did some mornings.

Tinker nipped playfully at Boone's knuckles and wagged her tail so hard it wiggled her entire back half.

"Howdy, ya furry mutt." Jack kneeled next to Boone, patting Tinker's back. "Where's the leg I made ya?"

The dog bounded up and over Jack's knees, across the room, and down the hall, her claws *scritch-scritch-scritching* on the rough plank floor all the way down to the end of the hall. There was a *whump* as she crashed into the back door and then *scritch-scritch-scritch* up the hallway again.

"You see that, Rabbit? She hops on that one back leg better than if she had two."

Jack stood and scratched his head under his hat. "Boy howdy! I guess she don't need that wooden leg no more."

Tinker had been practicing her three-legged racing daily while playing fetch with one of Clementine's old socks filled with dried beans. The wooden leg he'd made almost slowed her down now.

The dog raced back into the parlor and veered toward Boone and Jack in an arc that skimmed the stove. She crashed into Boone hard enough to knock him onto his ass, sending his hat flying. She pinned him to the floor and licked his face as if he were covered in honey.

"Come on now, Tinker." Boone blocked his face from her tongue while Jack laughed down at him.

Clementine decided to join in on the fun. "Well, Tinker, look

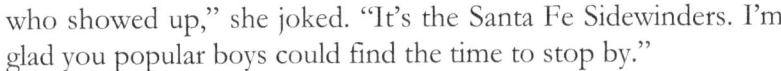

who showed up," she joked. "It's the Santa Fe Sidewinders. I'm glad you popular boys could find the time to stop by."

"Clementine." Boone sat up and then stood, brushing off his backside. "Apologies for our tardiness."

"Afternoon, Miss Clementine." Jack took off his hat. "My eye is healin' up quick."

She stared at the results of his street fight. The swelling was down some from this morning when she'd visited him during his bath. "Your magical elixir?"

"Well, I reckon so." He held up his palm toward her. "Not to discount the nursin' you did. Fixed me up proper, and for that I'm grateful."

"You're welcome." Clementine crossed her arms and leaned against the wall, shooting a wink in Boone's direction. "I noticed this miraculous elixir has something of an intoxicating and debilitating effect on the imbiber."

Jack's smile was borderline sheepish. "It was too old, I think. Mighta been damaging my sensibilities a bit."

Boone guffawed. "It gets you drunk, you dunderhead." He walked over and scooped up his hat. "What I can't come round to is why."

"Why what?" Rabbit frowned at Boone. "It don't get me drunk, it just gets me a li'l loopy while it fixes things inside me. Along with Miss Clementine's medicines, of course." He shot her another mollifying grin.

"After all of the things that have happened to you from imbibing that charlatan's concoctions, not to mention all of the other snake oil you've gulped down in the past, *why* haven't you learned your lesson?" Boone brushed the dust off his hat, telling Clementine, "Hell, they've made him so sick I'd swear he's turned green. Fevers. Chills." Boone marked off each entry by extending another finger. "Hallucinations. Remember that?"

Jack flapped his thumb and fingers together, imitating what she assumed was supposed to represent Boone's flapping jaw.

"Feel that, Miss Clementine? Wind's blowin' again."

Clementine chuckled at their teasing. They reminded her of another old Norse proverb about being young and journeying alone until becoming lost. *Rich I thought myself, when I met another. Man is the joy of man.* Did these two understand how rich they were? A stab of envy made her breath catch. She certainly did.

"Ain't no call to be a curmudgeon about it, Booney. Ain't hurting you none when I drink the stuff."

Boone pointed at Jack. "You tried to stop that stagecoach coming into Santa Rosa because you were all-fired sure there were pirates inside doing whatever swashbuckling things pirates do. Me trying to stop you the whole time. That coach gunner pert near filled us both with buckshot!"

"Now hold on one ding-dang minute. Them boys were pirates, and they was—"

"Sure they were," Boone interrupted, his eyes twinkling. "That was right after you had a good dose of … what was the name of that one? Can't remember, but that stuff had you seeing the chickens dancing at the ranch shindig too."

"They *was* dancing!" Jack looked at Clementine. "Potts is a damn fine fiddler. A feller and a chicken can't help but dance when he rosins up his bow."

Clementine laughed at the little jig Jack demonstrated for her.

"Where did the chickens learn to dance?" As soon as Boone asked it, he scowled, seeming to realize the futility of the question.

Jack looked at the dog. "I bet Tink knows. She was always hanging out in their coop, lettin' them hop on her back."

Tink seemed to grin up at Jack. When he made a twirling gesture with his hand, she did a little spin on cue.

"*Tink* taught them?" Boone shook his head. "Rabbit, I swear, engaging with you in your tangents loosens my grasp on anything resembling a logical argument." He knelt beside the stove and picked up the iron poker.

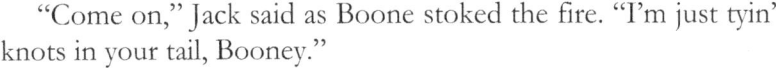

"Come on," Jack said as Boone stoked the fire. "I'm just tyin' knots in your tail, Booney."

"And I'm just going to stab you in the ass with a hot poker." He aimed a mock stab in Jack's direction.

Jack dodged, laughing. Tinker joined the fun, barking and hopping around the two. "I keep an open mind about such things. You consider everything. Want a reason for everything. I don't. I'm willin' to accept a few things now and then that don't make no sense if you look at them too close, that's all."

"Okay, *mi hermano*." Boone set the poker in the ash pail next to the stove. "You go on not making sense, and I'll go on—"

"Needin' a reason for everything," Jack finished for him.

Clementine had witnessed them finishing each other's sentences before. She had a feeling that due to a connection forged by shared trials and trauma over the years, they often knew what the other was thinking. A kinship that would not easily be torn apart by greed nor time.

Boone's face split into a crooked smile. "Dancing chickens."

Jack grinned from ear to ear, spreading his arms wide. "Come here, scallywag."

Laughing, Boone backed away. "I'm not going to hug you, ya nancy."

Jack settled for playfully punching Boone in the shoulder. "Boone loves me," he said to Clementine.

"With that ugly eye, he might be the only one," she teased.

"I'm liking Clementine more and more every day," Boone told Jack, his gaze warm when it moved to her.

"Too bad she likes you even less than me," Jack joked back, stepping between them. "Do you know if Hank found McCuddle?" he asked her.

"He did, and he procured three more bottles of that elixir."

"Three?" Boone asked.

"One for me." Clementine lifted her chin in the face of any reproach he might aim her way. "I'd like to know what's in this wonder liquid that could heal Jack so quickly."

"It's a magic potion, ain't it, Tink," Jack said, patting the dog on the head.

Tinker looked up from the dried pig's ear she was chewing on and let out a bark.

At Boone's raised brow, Clementine shrugged. "I'm always on the lookout for new creations." She rubbed her hands together. "Now, injured eye and hand notwithstanding, we have some training to do." Waving for them to follow, she headed for the hallway to her room at the back of the building.

"Training?" she heard Jack repeat.

"The lady awaits," Boone replied. The thud of footfalls followed.

Seven

Long ago, in a country far away that was even colder than the Black Hills, lived a young girl who spent hour upon hour, day after day, year after year learning how to kill all sorts of nightmare-inducing beasts. Now that girl had become a woman who was a pinch wiser and a lot more scarred on the outside thanks to numerous hand-to-hand clashes with a sharp-toothed *bacraut* ... or ten. But how did this woman go about preparing two hard-headed men for beasts and battles that required far more training than time allowed?

Since leaving The Dove, Clementine had been trying to come up with the answer to that question. It was time to see if Boone and Jack truly intended to follow through on helping her quell this *caper-sus* uprising.

"What sort of training?" Jack asked as he followed Boone into Clementine's quarters where she kept her weapons locked away in the large, sturdy cupboard Hank had crafted for her months ago.

She pulled out the key she kept strung on a strip of leather around her neck and opened the steel lock with a twist, swinging the doors wide. "This sort."

Weeks prior, she'd shown Boone and Jack her array of weapons. Finely cleaned, oiled, and sharpened, the tools in her arsenal were balanced on wooden pegs and hung from hooks on the back of the cabinet and the insides of the doors. Dozens of razor-sharp blades glinted in the afternoon light coming through the single window above her narrow bed. There were as many shapes and types of metal as there were long, short, curved, and straight weapons. Flails and maces waited for their turns in battle, their wooden handles stout, their weight finely balanced. All were meticulously maintained and ready to deliver damage in the proper hands—namely hers.

Clementine smiled at the sight of the armory she had amassed over many years. Some pieces had been passed down from her ancestors, while others were collected as victory trophies from uncommon or fierce adversaries. Each weapon told a story of blood, sweat, and death. Her story.

"Now we're in the biscuits!" Jack clapped his hands together, which spurred a howl of pain.

Boone chuckled. "Did you forget about that sword hole in your hand? Maybe pour a little tonic on it to make it feel better, clodhopper."

"Maybe put my fist on your nose to make me feel better." Jack's grin took the sting out of his words as he cradled his bandaged hand.

Blood darkened a spot on the bandage covering his palm, spreading as Clementine watched. "I can put some poultice on that and re-wrap it if you're inclined, Jack."

"Thank you, Miss Clementine. Maybe later."

"Aren't you going to threaten to box her nose, too?"

"Naw, Booney." Jack let his bandaged hand sag to his side, studying the weapons. "I'll stick with practicin' my fisticuffs on your ten miles of rough trail."

Boone laughed as he joined Jack in front of her cupboard. He sobered as he took in the view, whistling under his breath. "I'd sure like to see you in action with a few of these beauties, Clementine."

"That'd be a sight." With his uninjured hand, Jack reached for the longest, broadest, shimmering double-edged sword. Displayed in a red velvet-lined case in the center of the cabinet with the letters *VLFBERHT* etched into the blade, it was a stately monarch upon its throne, steeled and ready to command. The other impressive, yet less grand, weapons of the cabinet lay in wait.

Of course, Jack went for *that* sword. Clementine would have too, given the choice.

His finger grazed the pommel. "I think this one will—"

"No." She caught his wrist.

"But—"

She held Jack's stare for a moment before looking at Boone.

"That sword, gentlemen, is an *Ulfberht*. It has been handed down through my family line for centuries. It's made of the finest steel, and its craftsmanship is still revered even now centuries after its creation."

Boone's eyes widened as he leaned in closer. "Where was it made?"

"In what is now known as *Deutsches Reich*. Germany. There is no better sword and only I wield this one."

She deftly lifted it and spun it in a precise, sweeping arc down, around, and up over her head. The sword felt like an extension of her—balanced for speed, weighted for strength, honed to kill.

She turned toward Jack. He took two steps back as she swung the blade, stopping it inches from his chest, holding steady.

"Damn." He blew out a breath, his blue eyes crinkled at the edges. "I'm gettin' some heart-bustin' feelings about this girl, Booney."

"Be careful, *hombre*. That 'girl' can pluck out your heart and dance the flamenco on it without breaking a sweat."

Clementine laughed, letting the sword fall to her side. "I don't know that dance, but Hank has taught me an Irish jig that makes me sweat plenty."

"Maybe Rabbit can teach you the flamenco. He's pretty good with the twirling and foot-stomping, especially after half a bottle of tequila."

"Miss Clementine, could you slice Booney into four quarters for me with that fancy blade of yours?"

She looked at Boone and lifted the blade, pretending to consider Jack's words. "Maybe later. I'm very fond of this blade, but I use it only out of necessity, and right now we need Boone in one piece."

Jack stared at the sword, shaking his head. "You could have sliced me like a fish with this beauty and not left a scratch on it."

"Impressive indeed." Boone held her gaze. "You swing it like it was made just for you."

For some reason, she blushed at his words. Or maybe it was the admiration in his green eyes. Turning away, she waved her hand in front of her other weapons. "In most instances any one of these would be more than adequate. I save this piece for special occasions." She nestled the *Ulfberht* into the folds of the velvet-lined case.

"Now you sound like Booney and his old Winchester."

She crossed her arms, eyeing them both in turn. "You two will need to become more proficient in bladed weapons than you are with firearms."

Jack's face lined from forehead to chin.

Boone's gaze narrowed.

Before they started arguing otherwise, she added, "I think you learned in the Bloody Bones, at least to a limited extent, what we will be facing as we move forward. That is, if you both are still *fired up* to join the fight."

"Nice wordplay," Boone said. "But I'm not *fired up*."

"I'd say not." Jack moved toward the cabinet again, glancing repeatedly at Clementine and then the *Ulfberht*. "My guns seemed to work just fine before, long as we shot 'em in the head." He ran his palm over the hilt of the Flammard, a long, slender, wavy-bladed sword that hung near the *Ulfberht*. Did his fascination with swords have anything to do with being impaled by one? Or had he always been drawn by sharp blades, like she was?

She stepped back, letting him heft the Flammard. "There are many foes that won't fall to your guns as easily as the *Bahkauv*."

Boone snorted as he inspected the weapons along the other side of the cabinet. "*Easily*, she says." He ran his fingers over the bone handle of the black scimitar she had won from the pale devil in the Bloody Bones mine—Masterson's white dog. A worthy trophy to add to her collection. He touched the flat of the blade carefully, his expression cloaked.

What was he thinking? Was he remembering fighting with the pale devil last month in that cabin in Gayville? Or the attack in the mine when she shoved that very blade up through the white dog's chin after he'd angered her with his threats.

"It really happened," he said almost too quietly to hear, answering her questions.

Jack patted him on the shoulder. "Oh boy, did it ever." He touched the area above his injured eye and winced. "And then some."

Clementine stepped over to her bed, giving them space to soak up the situation. "The Bloody Bones. The *Bahkauv*. The pale devil." Or *weißer Hund*, as Hildegard called it. "That all happened, and as I've said before, that was only the beginning." She dropped onto the thin mattress, staring down at her hands where they dangled between her knees. "There are things of this world that are easily heard. Seen. Felt. Things you deal with every day and think of as normal. This is the world in which you have lived all of your years." She frowned at them. "Now you will need to learn how to survive in mine."

Both men turned to face her, Boone with folded arms and Jack with his head slightly tilted to the side. She had a feeling the Santa Fe Sidewinders were going to be a tough audience. If she were going to train them as efficiently as possible in the short time they had to prepare, she was going to need to grease the wheels a little. She needed to deliver her lessons in a manner that matched their personalities and strengths. Make it clear the level of danger they would face, yet convey this with a note of humor. Make it feel as natural as their own exchanges. Maybe include …

An idea struck her. She schooled her expression. "In your many travels, have you ever seen things that made you question your sanity?" Her focus moved from Jack to Boone. She lowered her voice and added, "Hellish things?"

Boone rolled his shoulder, appearing to shrug off her question, but his gaze remained wary.

Jack smirked, aiming his thumb toward Boone. "I question his sanity every day. Sometimes more than once."

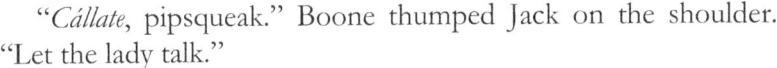

"*Cállate*, pipsqueak." Boone thumped Jack on the shoulder. "Let the lady talk."

"Don't call me pipsqu—"

Clementine interrupted him. "Have you ever been scared stiff? So afraid that you couldn't even will your legs to move?"

"Well, there was a rattler in my bedroll once," Jack started.

"You're raising my dander!" Boone threatened to wallop Jack again.

"And that saloon girl in Wichita with the extra-long toes," the jester re-started.

Biting back a grin, Clementine leaned forward. She dropped her voice to a whisper. "Have you ever been in so much pain that you longed for death's sweet relief with every single breath?"

Jack opened his mouth, but then closed it, looking like he'd swallowed a bug.

Now she had his attention. She held his wide-eyed stare, fighting to remain solemn. Adding a scratchy growl to her voice, she tried to emulate the haggard old woman in her childhood village who often joined her amma in throwing the rune stones during the solstices. "That dark moment when your life is nothing more than a meaningless bauble in a sadistic game played by a wicked, bloodthirsty demon that feeds off of your fear and suffering while your life force spills from your veins and your guts pool around your feet?"

"Holy hell," Jack whispered.

"Only death will not be the end of it," she croaked.

Boone's brow tightened. "Why not?"

"In my world, you could suffer cruelties beyond your most horrifying nightmares. Agonizing, gruesome torture with no end, not even in death. Forever and ever." She breathed the words, finishing with, "And ever."

Jack gaped at her, his typical cocky grin absent. One blond eyebrow shot up while the other hesitated, as if uncertain which way to go.

Boone's face seemed a shade or two paler. His Adam's apple bobbed. "But you ... I thought ..." He sent a worried frown at Jack and then back at Clementine. "When Rabbit and I ..."

A squeak of laughter escaped from Clementine's throat.

Boone's gaze narrowed, his chin lowering.

Another laugh leaked out. And then several more. "Great Odin's beard!" She fell back onto her bed, letting out a belly full of laughs. "You should have seen your faces."

"Miss Clementine," Jack scoffed. "Were you just pullin' our legs? Tryin' to scare the piss out of us?"

"More like the piss and vinegar," she said between her giggles, sitting up and wiping the corners of her eyes with her blanket. "Did it work?"

Jack sputtered, ending his verbal stumble with a fat grin.

Boone chuckled. "When it comes to Rabbit, you'd have better luck eating soup with a knife." He returned to the weapons cabinet.

"Ignore Booney. He don't know gunpowder from pepper."

"My world isn't as bad as all that," she said, sobering. "Well, not usually."

"What do you mean, *usually*?" Jack asked.

She walked over and peeked out the window at the shed where she had frozen bodies stacking up. Bodies with the *capersus* brand or tattoo on them. "Although I do need to address a serious insurgence situation growing here in the Hills."

"You mean *we* need to address it," Boone said while holding the bone handle of the pale devil's black blade in his hand.

"You boys say you're ready to throw in, but I'm not sure you realize what you're in for." She shifted, looking at them in turn. "We've talked about this before, but now I'm asking for your word. If I commit to training you, I need you to pledge to see it through."

Boone looked at her, his poker face in place.

"This is about more than simply bringing to justice those

responsible for the death of your uncle," she said.

"It's a reckonin'!" Jack piped in.

Shaking his head, Boone returned the blade to the cupboard. "Rabbit learned a new word, and he likes to use it now." He smacked Jack's shoulder with the back of his hand. "You were saying, Clementine?"

"I understand that a big part of why you're doing this has to do with your uncle. However, ultimately, if the numbers of *others* swarming the Black Hills are allowed to grow unconstrained, then the pestilence will spread across the land and envelope every town and city around. Eventually, it will even spread beyond the Hills."

"And *that* is why you're here in Deadwood, isn't it?" Boone asked. "To contain this plague?"

Before she could answer, Jack cut in. "How many of these *others* are there, do you reckon?"

"Possibly legions by now."

"Okay. A legion is a lot, right? Kill a lotta bad guys. I can do that." Jack jerked his pistol with his left hand and aimed it at the wall. "Bang! And if they happen to be the rotten sons-a-bitches that killed Uncle Mort, even better."

Clementine sighed. She said to Boone, "Didn't follow that through to the end, did he?"

Boone scoffed in reply. "He's always in too big of a hurry to wait for the end."

"What?" Jack was now pretending to shoot at the knots in the ceiling boards. "*Pow! Patwing*—that was a ricochet 'cause of my off hand."

"Jack, focus."

"I am. You have my word, Miss Clementine. I pledge to stand by you no matter the beastie comin' our way." He holstered his pistol and sauntered back to the open cabinet door. "Do we get to choose our weapons now?" Without waiting for her answer, he leaned closer to her grouping of blades. "Since I can't have the fancy sword—what was it called? A Herbert? I think I like this one with the wavy blade."

"A Flammard." Clementine joined them at the cabinet. "I removed it from a particularly belligerent yet vain foe who smelled like roses."

"You mean this desperado of yours stunk?" Jack clenched the grip, his eyes on the blade.

"No, I mean it was encaged in the branches of a century-year-old rose bush because the fragrant flower and its brambles are a trap for its *kind*."

"It looks deadly," Jack said, letting his fingers explore the blade and hilt.

"Some might think that. On the contrary, it's not. While I've had some success with it, the sword actually does little to aid the wielder due to the poor balance of the pommel and the tendency for the blade to quickly lose its edge. One who bears it exhibits ignorance and inexperience in the art of battle. Its sole usefulness here is decoration—and to remind me not to turn my back on a *bannik*."

Jack let his hand fall from the Flammard. "What's a *bannik*?"

"An evil fairy that likes to look in mirrors too much for its own good."

"Well, which should I use, then?" He scanned the other weapons in the cabinet, apparently eager to choose something, anything. He didn't understand yet that as much as he chose the weapon, the weapon chose him. Or that no matter if he was armed to the teeth, his adversary might foul his perception of reality. That certain of the *others* he might face could fight him not just physically, but psychologically as well.

She closed one of the cabinet doors. "I believe it would be best for both of you to begin with a trial."

Boone backed away and crossed his arms. "Let me guess, things aren't necessarily as they seem."

"Ahh, you are reading my mind, Boone." She nudged Jack

aside and closed the other cabinet door.

"Guess that means Rabbit doesn't get a sword." Jack scowled, crossing his arms, too.

"Not yet. Your first training task is to spend two days in Deadwood without arousing any suspicions. Both of you." She slid the lock in place. "Without engaging in any fights. Without causing any trouble at all."

They protested in unison, Jack including several curse words in the process.

"And," she interrupted their grousing, "you must go about your normal daily business. Hiding out in Keller's Livery drinking and playing cards for two days doesn't count."

"Don't be ridiculous," Boone said.

"We don't cause problems," Jack added. "We *solve* problems."

"Mr. Fields," she said, tapping him on the chest. "What I've learned about you in the short time we've known each other is that you are always on the prod."

"She's seen your poker hand, *bandito*," Boone said.

"While that facet of your temperament can be useful," Clementine continued, "it is of no help in our current situation. So, if I hear of any dustups, frolics, mills, rows, scraps, sloggings, or brushes, the two-day trial starts again."

"Frolics?" Boone grinned at Jack. "Did she say frolics?"

"I don't cause no kerfuffles," Jack told her.

"Yes, you do, Jack. And none of that, either."

"Stealth," Boone said simply. "We can do stealth, Rabbit."

"Are you going to watch us for two days straight?" Jack asked, apparently searching for an angle already.

Clementine measured him from head to toe. Jack raised wrinkles and Boone smoothed them out. She'd seen their song and dance in action. "I have my ways. Trust me, I'll know."

Jack growled, aiming a grimace at Boone. "She's starting to sound like Uncle Mort."

"Maybe he's haunting her now," Boone replied.

"Don't you start hounding me about Uncle Mort's ghost again, Booney. I know what I saw."

Before they'd headed back to Santa Fe, Jack had claimed to see their uncle's ghost in this very room. He hadn't mentioned anything about this specter since returning to Deadwood, but then again he'd been busy landing in hot water his first night back.

"I have a feeling it'll take more than two days for you gunslingers to finish this trial." Clementine locked the cabinet and tucked the key back in her shirt. "You'll start the two days over every time I hear of the raucous doings of a pair of Santa Fe Sidewinders."

"Start *over*?" Jack said, his voice higher.

"Besides, you could use a day—or five—of recuperation."

"Sheeat." Jack tucked his thumbs in his gun belt, scowling. "Are we gonna let this stand, Booney?"

Boone regarded Clementine, his jaw clenching and unclenching. "I reckon we don't have much choice, partner."

Eight

The next day ...

Boone glanced at his untouched beer, wondering why he ordered it in the first place. He'd rather have whiskey, but Yellow Strike served raw alcohol mixed with burnt sugar and passed it off as whiskey. The saloon seemed to be plenty busy this afternoon, filled with all sorts of Deadwood's rowdiest clientele ... and some of its smelliest. Several of the miners were an outstanding testament to the lack of enough bathing houses in Deadwood. Next to these shovel slingers, a well-used spittoon smelled like roses.

Rabbit and he had survived twenty-two hours—wait! Boone glanced at the regulator on the wall. Make that twenty-two hours and thirty-two minutes of Clementine's challenge without a single *frolic*. At least he was pretty sure they hadn't had a frolic.

Convincing Rabbit to steer clear of two bar fights and a belligerent panhandler had taken some doing, but through the years Boone had become adept at pulling Rabbit's biscuits from the fire. In any case, they hadn't heard from Clementine since their probation had started, so Boone was perfectly happy to believe that all was well.

Of course, there was the possibility that Rabbit was up to no good this very minute. Hell, it was entirely likely that Rabbit

would, at any minute, land himself in jail or in the town news sheet.

Boone scanned the room, looking for his partner. Porter, the barkeep, held sway over the bar lined with fortune seekers of various shapes and sizes. Drink girls and wag-tails roamed the room filling drinks and dance cards.

It seemed such a short time ago that he and Rabbit first arrived in Deadwood and walked into Yellow Strike saloon, looking for Uncle Morton. The only discernible difference in the place now was the number of clients. There were more. A lot more, and vices were peddled freely to flannel mouths, big guns, and dusty miners alike. Boone imagined it was an easy task in Deadwood to satisfy any libidinous ideation the morally depraved could conjure.

The chair next to him scraped across the floor, pulling him away from his thoughts.

His new companion, a spindly little old man with short, rough cut whiskers, rapped on the table quickly with his bony knuckles. His head swiveled this way and that as he regarded the saloon, like a lizard watching beetles.

He looked familiar. "Howdy, old-timer." Boone held his hand out for a shake, but the geezer was more interested in scrutinizing the raucous lot of saloon patrons.

"Dan'l Boone, Dan'l Boone, dead too soon that Dan'l Boone," the man sang absently, still knocking his knuckles on the table in an uneven rhythm.

"Do I know …" Then it hit Boone. "Ah!" He recognized the old fart from the first time he and Rabbit had come to Yellow Strike. He couldn't remember his name, though.

"Keeping above the snakes, looks like, Mr. …" He came up blank. "I don't recollect your name. I'm Boone, but it seems you remember that from when we met last time."

"Boone Boone Boone. Dead too soon." The old guy spoke in a quick staccato and still didn't spare him a glance. "Where's that boy? All a'fir. Got the spit and vinegar in him. Where's he, where's he, where's he? Need him, too."

The old-timer locked onto a dandy at the bar and froze. The well-dressed dude had one foot on the bar rail and one thumb hooked on his suspenders. He seemed to be pontificating at a fellow who was filthy with the sweat, mud, and weariness that came with placer mining. The sort of man Boone was becoming accustomed to seeing in Deadwood.

The old man pointed a gnarled finger at the dude but quickly pulled his finger back as if it had been bitten. "That'd be one." He continued to stare at the man, unmoving. "'Nother, 'nother. 'Nother one. Ever'where now, they's ever'where." He licked his lips. His focus shifted from eyeing the dude to measuring up Boone's beer.

"Boone knows. Boone knows. Shared his whiskey with ol' Buck. Buck knows what shares with him."

Boone pushed his beer toward the old man, who nabbed it and gulped it all down, losing a good portion of it down his chin and shabby wool coat. He clunked the mug on the table and began surveying the room again, his knuckles taking up the irregular beat he had momentarily suspended.

"So, Buck, you cut your beard short. I didn't recognize you at first."

"Hey, boys!" Rabbit dropped into the chair next to Boone and set two mugs of beer on the table hard enough for the foam to spill over the rims and down the sides. "Who's your fr— I know you! Tried to steal my whiskey last time. Kept talkin' in riddles."

"This here is Buck, near as I can tell," Boone said. "He has a preoccupation with, well, anything in this saloon but me, apparently."

"Good to lay my peepers on you again, Buck. Didn't catch your name last time. 'Buck' seems fittin'." Rabbit waited for a reply but Buck continued to survey the saloon, spending extra time on the fancy-dressed dude at the bar.

"Well then, Mr. Conversationalist, mind if I talk to my partner?" Rabbit turned to Boone. "Keller says he owns the lot next to the livery. He's sellin' it along with the livery. Wagons and such, too. Everything on the lot."

Boone nodded. Rabbit was like a bloodhound on the scent with this buying the livery idea.

"Keller Keller, he's an upright feller," Buck chanted.

Rabbit glanced at Buck and then continued. "He says if anybody shows up with real money, he's takin' it."

Buck's hand froze mid-knock as he watched the dude make his way toward the door. Boone kept an eye on Buck, who followed the dude's progress as he pushed the swinging doors open and disappeared into the darkness outside.

The geezer resumed knocking after the man left. Although, each time Buck's gaze swept across Rabbit's beer he'd pause.

Boone chuckled under his breath. What was this old-timer's story? "Rabbit." He dipped his head toward the old man and then Rabbit's beer.

Rabbit shook his head, scowling. "Ol' geezer tried to suck my whiskey last time we were here. Didn't get it then and he ain't gettin' my beer neither." He pulled the mug close.

"Scaly boy don't share," Buck grumbled.

Boone chuckled again. "He just wants a little sip."

"What is it with this ol' coot? Said a word to you?"

"Not so *to* me ..."

"Wouldn't even know we was at the same table as him exceptin' he keeps makin' comments. Like he's here but not here, know what I mean?"

Boone nodded.

"There's Hank." Rabbit waved high and wide.

Hank pushed his way through the thicket of occupied chairs, grabbing an empty one on the way, and pulled in next to Buck.

"Howdy, fellas. Looks like you been adopted by ol' One Horn

Buck."

Rabbit looked at Boone and grinned. " 'Course he knows him."

Boone wasn't surprised Hank knew Buck either. Hank seemed to know most everyone in Deadwood. "Did you say 'One Horn Buck'?" he asked Hank. "What's that about?"

"Two horns, they's two horns on 'im," offered Buck.

"Good ol' One Horn." Hank patted the older guy on the shoulder. "Did some huntin' and prospectin' out in Nevada with Buck and Tennessee Pete. Called him 'Tennessee' on account of he left Philadelphia for Tennessee. Carpetbagger, I guess you'd call him. Met him in California."

Rabbit smirked at Boone. "Makes sense," he said, but then shook his head.

Boone didn't follow either, but waited. He could see Hank wasn't quite done with his tale.

" 'Course, it wasn't Nevada at the time. Utah Territory, was it?" Hank furrowed his brow and studied the table. "Maybe still Mexico … no … what'd they call it?" He stuck his finger in the air and with a deep and official-sounding voice said, "And this great territory of Nevada will become a state before the decade is done." Then in his normal voice he added, "Yep. That was it."

"So, One Horn Buck?" Boone attempted to steer Hank back to the original subject.

"Oh. 'Course. Best placer miner in the whole of the Hills. 'Til his brain cracked. Went an' saw too much, I'm thinkin'." He winked at Buck.

Boone watched Buck for a response. The old guy's cheek and eye ticked in a quick squint. Did he just wink back?

He looked to see if Rabbit had seen that, but he was entirely occupied with a tight-fitting, lacy red dress on a curvy damsel sashaying toward the piano through the thicket of drinking and gambling. Feathers from her black boa floated to the floor in her wake.

The piano player jumped into a lively melody, and the damsel jumped right in after him, singing loud enough to fill the saloon over the whoops and catcalls. She swished her dress right and left while she sang.

> *Minin' these hills might kill you boys,*
> *Shovel and pick be your only toys.*
> *Back breakin' work always fills the day,*
> *And in the end you never know,*
> *If you'll even get to collect your pay.*
>
> *Up early come mornin' and plenty work 'til it's dark,*
> *Feelin' is generally that your outlook is stark.*
> *The Hills are a-shakin' and rollin' all day,*
> *It's back breakin' work for you men, no it ain't play.*
> *With industrious souls of all color and principle,*
> *It's a minin' man's world for those that's invincible.*

The piano player continued playing as the woman bowed and took kisses and pats from the gentlemen at tables near the piano.

"Aw, that's a shitty ditty," Rabbit said, turning to Boone.

Hank laughed hard. "Hoo hoo! Which one of 'em is off key, the piano or the lass? Might be both!" He hooted again.

"What we need is Abigail." Rabbit grinned. "Sweetest voice in New Mexico, I swear. We should convince her to come up here, Booney."

"Her voice can lead a man from the darkness."

"So can her …" Rabbit cupped two large imaginary breasts in front of his chest.

Boone laughed. "She can ease the troubled libido, sure enough."

"Oh hey! Jack Rabbit!" Hank pulled two bottles from the inner pocket of his coat and clunked them onto the table. "Found McDoodle. He's headin' to Cheyenne in a day or so, he says."

"McCuddle," Boone corrected.

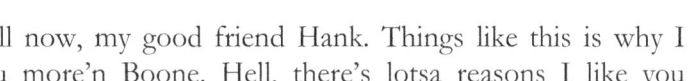

"Well now, my good friend Hank. Things like this is why I like you more'n Boone. Hell, there's lotsa reasons I like you more'n Boone."

Boone laughed again. "That's fine. I'm starting to prefer Buck over you, anyway. He makes more sense than you do when he opens his mouth."

Rabbit grabbed a bottle of snake oil and twisted the cork free. He held the bottle toward Boone. "This is the liquid that heals a man's infirmities." He took a sip and wiped his lips with the sleeve of his coat. "Ahhh. I feel it workin' already. Best I've found yet, I think." He leveled a self-satisfied look at Boone and pushed the cork back into the bottle.

"You may be healing, but your mouth is impaired. Nothing but poppy cock coming out of it."

"Hoo hoo, you two." Hank elbowed Buck. "Like they're married, huh?"

"Shut up, Hank. And thanks for this." Rabbit tapped one of the bottles.

"McCuddle's got the magic," Buck chimed in while continuing to survey the room.

Boone, Rabbit, and Hank all looked at Buck for a second.

When the geezer didn't say anything more, Boone reached for one of the bottles. "Dammit. Send it over. It's spirits, that's all."

Rabbit held a bottle out toward Boone, but then pulled it back. He raised an eyebrow. "Now, don't go drinkin' it all, Booney. Just a sip."

"Bah!" Boone grabbed the bottle, popped the cork, and smelled it. He jerked back. "Smells like that shit Uncle Morton put on the horses' legs when they got an abscess." He peered in the bottle. "Why is it black?"

Rabbit snickered. "It's okay if you're scared."

Dammit. If Rabbit drank it, so could he. Boone took a healthy swig. The assault on his mouth made his pucker pinch tight. The fiery bite of spices and herbs coated his tongue and oozed down

his throat. It felt as if it were melting skin along the way. He coughed and wheezed, breaking into a series of sneezes as the vapors seeped into his nose, burning deep.

He sputtered. "How can …" *cough*. "How can you drink that …" *sneeze, cough*. "That shit. It's like hot tar."

Rabbit roared with laughter.

Drool ran down the side of Boone's mouth. He wiped it away with his sleeve. "Sweet Irene! That juice packs a punch." Fire burned his tongue and seeped down his throat. He coughed again.

"You gonna live, *hombre*?" Rabbit asked between snorts and chortles. "I shoulda warned you. It ain't for the delicate. I did tell ya, though. Only a sip."

"It was a sip!" Boone glared at Rabbit and Hank through watery eyes. They were laughing and slapping the table.

"Hooo! Take the starch outta ya?" Hank said between guffaws. "Can't hardly breathe, ya got my squinny up."

"You too, Hank?" Boone's nose was running now. Peppers. He tasted peppers. And corn alcohol. And who knew what else since his tongue was probably melted by now.

"Now I know why you like this swill. It's got alcohol in it."

"McCuddle's cures the sickness," Buck interrupted, and then he pushed to his feet and hobbled toward the bar.

Rabbit pointed his thumb at Buck. "He knows."

"What is it with Buck?" Boone asked as they sobered up. "You know anything more about him, Hank?"

"Only some. He worked a claim just up the gulch a piece, not too far from Gayville, matter of fact. Worked it hard and pulled a fair amount of color. Was doin' right well for himself then all sudden like started actin' off his nut. Kept sayin' he'd seen it. It was here."

"It?"

"The 'ruin,' he called it. 'The ruin is here,' he'd say. Ever'body asked, 'What's a ruin?' He'd just answer, 'I see it. Corruption.'

We all thought he worked himself too hard. Cracked his nut."

"Near Gayville, huh?" Rabbit asked.

"Yep. Knowin' what we know now, more apt to give pause, you reckon?"

Boone nodded. "I'd say."

"You want some more, tenderfoot?" Rabbit held out the bottle of elixir.

Still wiping tears from his eyes from the last drink, Boone waved him off. "Hank, you reckon we can get some sense out of Buck?"

"Hard to say. Worth throwin' a bone. See if the dog'll fetch."

Boone scanned the bar for Buck. The geezer had made his way down to the far end and was wedging between wiry, tired-looking hairy men in filthy clothes. From the looks of it, Buck was trying to snag an unguarded beer or tin of whiskey and pissing off a few drinkers in the process.

"Feelin' any effects of your venture into the world of magic there, *amigo*?"

"Shut up, Rabbit. Why don't you go fetch Buck?"

"All right, all right. Where is … oh, I see him. Let me finish my beer first."

"So." Hank leaned back, grinning at each of them in turn. "Miss Clementine has you two sidewinders behavin' like choir boys, eh?"

Rabbit growled. "*You whippersnappers can start working with the swords after the two-day trial.*" He spoke in an approximation of Clementine's voice. "*Jack, fetch a pail of water. Boone, chop some wood for the fire.*"

"She didn't say that," Boone told Hank. "We're about one day in, one day to go. Then we start working with the cutting steel."

"Cutting ste … ? Oh, the blades." Hank chopped at the air.

Rabbit lifted his beer. "Maybe I don't want nothin' to do with her toys."

"We're almost there, Rabbit. Besides, like Clementine said,

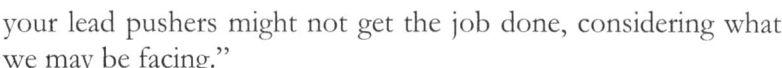

your lead pushers might not get the job done, considering what we may be facing."

Rabbit flapped his thumb and fingers together. "Waa waa waa. That's what I hear coming from your lips, Booney."

"Stop doing that."

"I would like to get me some payback on that high-falutin', hat-wearin', sword-swingin' bastard, though. Maybe this time get the jump on him."

"I get the feeling that won't be easy." Boone rubbed his sore knuckles. The ones he'd used to batter the French swordsman before escaping the fracas.

"I suppose. Probably backed strong. But we have Hank!" Rabbit punched Hank in the arm. "And Miss Clementine." Then he turned to Boone. "Then there's you."

Boone smirked. Apparently Rabbit was forgetting that he'd quite probably saved his life. "Finish your beer and go get Buck."

Rabbit gulped the last of his beer and surveyed the bar. "Where is the ol' …"

Boone searched the bar, too, and caught sight of Buck curled up on the floor not far from where Boone had sighted him moments before. How many drinks had he pilfered or wheedled from the other drinkers around him?

"He's on the floor, Rabbit. Probably tangle-legged from overindulging in poached libations."

Hank furrowed his brow. "Don't think that's so." He rose and made a beeline for Buck.

"Rabbit, go get him up and help him over here."

"*Rabbit, go get him up.*" Rabbit mimicked Boone's deep voice. He rose and waded after Hank toward Buck. Over his shoulder he hollered, "Can't just say he's corned. Can't just say that."

Boone returned his attention to Hank. As he bent to grab Buck, a particularly well-ginned digger with a fur hat put a boot to Hank's rear and shoved. Hard. Hank tumbled forward over Buck and landed on his side, shoulder first.

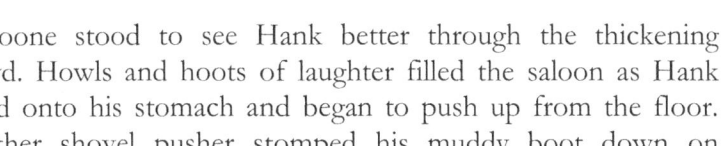

Boone stood to see Hank better through the thickening crowd. Howls and hoots of laughter filled the saloon as Hank rolled onto his stomach and began to push up from the floor. Another shovel pusher stomped his muddy boot down on Hank's back, slamming him down to the floor, renewing the laughter and hoots throughout the saloon.

No good pickled assholes! Boone made for the bar, pushing through the crowd of unbathed, foul-mouthed miners. He elbowed and rammed his way through, no longer able to see Hank or Buck, catching only glimpses of Rabbit.

Suddenly, the crowed parted. A thick miner clad in a wool coat fell like a tree, landing with a *whump* on the floor about ten feet in front of Boone.

The crowd let out a collective "*Whoa!*" Then the laughter resumed and the crowd closed in again.

Shit! That looked like Rabbit's handiwork. The fool was in no condition to be fighting.

The crowd grew louder, bumping up against each other and him more, like a herd of cattle itching to stampede.

Where was Rabbit? This motley mix of drunks and gold diggers might kill him. Or Hank.

Boone pushed against the mass of bodies, arriving in time to see Rabbit swing his uninjured hand in a wide, backhanded upward arc. He connected with the nose of a scrawny but belligerent-looking cur coming at him from the side. Blood squirted from the attacker's nose as he toppled backward.

Boone pushed with everything he had as the mass tried to close again in front of him.

BOOM! Crash!

The throng of drinkers "Whoa'd" again. They dissipated away from the bar this time, leaving Rabbit standing alone, his pistol pointed at the ceiling. Boone could see the rage glittering in his eyes. His good eye, anyway. The other was still too puffy and purple to tell.

Overhead, a beautifully painted glass chandelier studded with burning candles swayed to and fro, its dangling decorative pieces clinking together. Dust and shards of broken glass rained down around Hank, who was trying to pull himself and Buck up from the floor.

Boone hustled over to Hank and Buck. The chandelier shook and jingled above. As a screech filled the saloon, Boone helped Hank drag Buck aside. They'd barely cleared the area when the chandelier plummeted to the plank floor with an ear-splitting crash. Glass shards shot out like bullets, peppering everyone nearby, including Rabbit, Boone, Hank, and Buck. A fine glass dust rose in a colorful billowing cloud.

"You okay, Rabbit?" Boone asked in the silence that followed.

Rabbit leaned back against the bar, his jaw slack, gaping at the heap of broken glass.

Taking that as an affirmative, Boone looked at the man standing next to him. "What about you, Hank?"

Hank rubbed his shoulder. "Feelin' better than I ought, I expect. Here. Up off the floor with ya, Buck."

Boone joined Rabbit at the bar.

"Never shot a fancy light before." Rabbit scratched his head. "Ow!" He pulled a shard of glass from his hair and dropped it. He scooped his hat from the floor and banged it against the bar. Glass shards tinkled as they hit the floor. "You look peppered, Booney."

"What in the hell happened here!" shouted a stout, black-frocked man at the top of the stairs. He rapped his brass-handled cane on the railing and then clomped down the stairs, leaning so far forward Boone thought he might topple over. He stopped at the pile of chandelier and then growled through pinched lips. His whole body shuddered as he turned his hard, squinty-eyed gaze to the glass-speckled men in front of him. He looked Boone and Rabbit up and down, one at a time.

Hank sidled up next to Boone and whispered, "Uh oh. That's

Angus Monty. Owns the place. Mean sonofabitch."

Boone grimaced. "Nice shootin', Tex," he said to Rabbit through stiff lips.

Angus snorted like a mad bull. "I'll be havin' a word with you boys!"

Nine

The next day after that ...

"One day?" Clementine sat on the edge of her desk in the parlor, holding the *Trailblazer* news sheet in one hand. She stared at Jack, and then Boone, waiting for an excuse or explanation.

Both men avoided looking at her. Instead, Jack lounged on the floor playing with Tinker, and Boone was taking an inordinate amount of time braiding three thin leather straps from his seat next to her stove. She would have laughed if they weren't both in front of her, and if this didn't put them both at greater risk of ending up on her examination tables.

"Nothing to say? Well, let's see what the *Trailblazer* has to say about the goings-on last evening." She deliberately held the news sheet high out in front of her and stretched it tight between her hands.

"It says here:

The Curtain Dropped at Yellow Strike (and too, the chandelier)

The entertainment oriented establishments along the main thoroughfare in Deadwood have gained reputation throughout the surrounding hills of sundry and perhaps occasionally coarse operation.

Such standing may be warranted, judging from the unremitting turmoil with which this harried town was burdened yesterevening. The commotions appear to be worsening in both length and scale with insufficient law to curb the wanton and lascivious appetites of weary miners.

"This town does have some surly sorts roaming the streets," Jack said, glancing up at Clementine from his tug-of-war with Tinker.

"Stocked plumb full with degenerates," Boone added. He continued to focus on braiding the straps.

"Degenerates, right." Clementine shook her head. While she hadn't fully expected Jack and Boone to last two days without some sort of scuffle, she didn't think they'd make enough commotion to end up in the damned paper.

Jack frowned at Boone. "What are you gonna do with that watch fob yer making, Booney? You ain't got no watch."

When Boone just shrugged, Clementine continued reading ...

Witness, evidence to the veracity of said statements provided by Marshal Stapleton:

- Eight drunken malfeasants of varying degree

- Two knife fights ending in serious injury

- Various and multiple discharge of firearms within trade establishments

- Various and multiple discharge of firearms in the streets of Deadwood

- Numerous lascivious public displays

- Destruction of property at Yellow Strike Saloon—to wit destruction of one French Renaissance chandelier by an individual known as Mr. Sidewinder. Value: seven

hundred fifty-five U.S. dollars

- Two larceny ...

Clementine lowered the news sheet in time to see Boone aim a deeply furrowed brow at Jack and mouth, *What the fuck?*

She tossed the paper on her desk and crossed her arms, waiting to hear what Mr. Sidewinder and his sidekick had to say about their newfound popularity.

"Don't look at me like that, Booney. I had to give the marshal a name." Jack turned to her. "Didn't give him Jack Fields. Or Rabbit. Or Hank. Or," he bobbled his head, "or the famous Boone 'Big Britches' McCreery. Just Santa Fe Sidewinder."

"That's the same name you called me in front of McCuddle," Boone said. "And the name you've spread around town some."

"That's all I could think of while I was busy picking glass outta my hair."

Boone grunted. "Great."

"They was kickin' poor ol' Buck. I had to help him. And Hank, too."

"What about Hank?" Clementine frowned. "Did you two get Hank into some kind of trouble?"

"No, ma'am." Jack scratched Tinker's back. "Hank was helping Buck up off the floor when some bastard kicked him down."

Clementine rubbed the back of her neck, trying to picture the scene. "Who's Buck? And why was he on the floor?" She held up her hand. "You know what? Never mind that. Is Hank injured?"

"He's fine." Boone glanced up from his handiwork. "Strong constitution, that man has."

He was right. Hank could weather a stiff breeze without having to bend into it. "Did the marshal talk to you? Wasn't he looking for you after the fight in the street?" The marshal had been pretty lenient so far. Hell, with all of the killing going on, he was undoubtedly preoccupied.

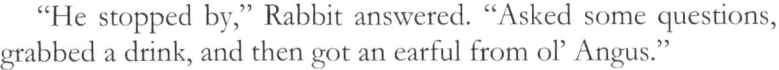

"He stopped by," Rabbit answered. "Asked some questions, grabbed a drink, and then got an earful from ol' Angus."

"And?"

Rabbit snorted. "Hank and Booney can charm the *pantalones* off a *vaquero* sittin' in his saddle."

Boone shook his head at Clementine. "I don't charm cowboys." He scowled at the news sheet. "How did they get that in the *Trailblazer* so quickly? Less than a day. Bad timing for us."

"Booney, you wore Diego's pants home from *La Fiesta del Otoño* that time and don't try to deny it."

"He lost those to me fair and square, no charming needed."

Clementine crossed her arms, waiting for them to return to the problem at hand. Odin's beard! These two bantered and bickered almost as much as Alexey and Dmitry. "Are you two almost done?"

"Those pants were something, weren't they?" Boone continued, his braiding progress slowing for a moment. "Studded with silver *and* turquoise."

She fought back a grin. "I guess you're not done."

Boone stood and held out his hand, palm up. "May I have your key?"

She looked at his hand, her gaze narrowing on it. "What?"

"The key. The one that unlocks the cabinet in your room."

Her squint lifted to his face. Why? They hadn't made it through the two days yet.

"Trust me, Clementine."

"Trust you?" She picked up the paper and held it up in front of him. "After you two managed to stir up this much dust?"

"It wasn't as bad as that." Boone took the sheet and tossed it aside. The paper landed on the floor near Jack and Tinker. "Trying to make their little newspaper interesting is all."

"Besides, we didn't cause no trouble," Jack said, turning his head sideways so he could read the print. "Just ended it. Like I said we do." He spoke as if it were a matter of fact.

She guffawed at their laughable explanation, but slipped the tattered leather strap that held the key from around her neck and handed it to Boone. He pulled his Bowie knife from its sheath, cut the frayed leather lanyard, and slid the key free. Then he returned the knife, sat in the chair, and began weaving the key onto the leather strips along with a small silver sun, the rays made of turquoise.

Oh, that's what he was making. She watched his fingers weave. Long, skillful fingers. His knuckles were mostly healed, the skin still slightly pink over the …

"Boone and me are thinkin' ol' Buck might be an interestin' man to converse with," Jack said, snapping her back to reality.

She looked toward the exam room, focusing on the empty tables, hoping neither Jack nor Boone had caught her staring too long. "Why's that?"

"Seems he was a normal sort, but according to Hank he might've seen somethin' that knocked his kettle sideways. Says some stuff that gets you to wonderin'."

"Okay, let's try this on you." Boone stood and raised the lanyard. He stepped closer to her. "Hmm. Let's see here. Permit me?"

Before she could find her tongue to tell him she could do it herself, he moved aside a few tendrils of her hair that had escaped her long plait and slid the lanyard over her head, pulling her hair through as well. He studied where the key rested next to the sun against her upper sternum and then straightened the leather, brushing her collarbone with his knuckles.

Clementine swallowed a tickling flutter rising from her chest.

"That should keep your key safe," he said, his voice even deeper than normal.

"And what's this?" She held up the silver sun.

"I got it from a Hopi medicine man when I was younger. He told me it would encourage the sun to return at the end of winter."

She smiled. "Thank you. I have a feeling we'll need all the help we can get to make it through to spring."

He took a step back and cleared his throat. "The thing is, Rabbit, it's not easy to get anything out of Buck. He just rambles." Boone returned to the chair next to the stove, sitting heavily. "Seems to know about you, though," he said to Clementine.

Jack frowned up at her. "Unless I disremember the first time we met him, he said something then about you taking care of them, uh … them whangdoodles, I think it was. Knew your name, too."

What in tarnation were whangdoodles? Clementine touched the sun Boone had given her, rubbing the metal between her thumb and fingers. Who was this Buck character? Why would he know her name? More important, what did he really know about her?

"Buck spotted a dandy in the bar last night," Boone said. "A real barber's clerk. He said, 'There's one.' " Boone pointed, reenacting the scene for them. "Said it like that gentleman was something special, and not a good kind of special."

"We need to get Hank here," Jack chimed in. "He said ol' Buck talked about seein' somethin' called 'the corruption.' "

"And that's when Buck went loco," Boone finished.

Clementine grabbed the other leather chair and pulled it closer, joining them with her elbows on her knees. "I've not heard that term applied to anything of significance here in Deadwood, except possibly to describe Angus Monty and his kind. They're corrupt as hell."

"You mean the guy who owns Yellow Strike Saloon?" Jack scoffed. "Fucker holds remarkable contempt for anyone who shoots his lights out. Accidentally."

Boone chuckled. "Knucklehead."

A realization dawned on Clementine. "Jack, did you shoot that chandelier on purpose?"

Jack shrugged. "Accidents happen."

Of course he did! Jack didn't miss with a firearm. His aim was always spot-on, no matter which hand was doing the shooting. Perhaps it was possible, after all, that he might be more dangerous to the *others* with his firearm than she'd first thought. Well, maybe not with his firearm, but with something else equally as deadly in skilled hands.

"Angus Monty is a no-good sheepherder," Jack added.

They all nodded.

"Corruption," she said, searching her memory.

Both men watched her in silence.

"Corruption," she repeated, closing her eyes.

There was something in her past about corruption. *Korrupsjon. Verval.* She let her mind wander through her past, through the languages she knew. *Die Verderbnis.* Memories of a battle fought long ago returned in violent starts. A pestilence had left the

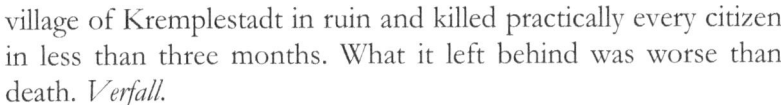

village of Kremplestadt in ruin and killed practically every citizen in less than three months. What it left behind was worse than death. *Verfall.*

"*Der Verfall,*" she whispered, opening her eyes. "Could it be?"

"Could what be?" Boone asked.

Jack furrowed his brow. "Was that German?"

"I believe so," Boone answered, his brow mirroring Jack's.

Clementine's thoughts returned to that horrific battle …

"Many years ago," she told them, "at the start of my fifteenth winter, my afi—my grandfather—and I journeyed to a village two days' travel from our home. He'd told me that we were going to visit *liebe Freunde*, good friends of his, but his mood was solemn that day, his face lined with tension, which was not normal for him or my amma."

"What was normal?" Boone asked.

"Uncle Mort usually laughed through half of his lectures." Jack added, petting Tinker's back.

"He was often stern, and deadly serious about my training and responsibilities in this world. But there was another side to him, a gentle and kind side." Clementine's throat tightened from a wave of homesickness. She smiled in spite of the lonely ache. "He also had a wonderfully devious sense of humor. Well, maybe a little too devious, if you ask my amma, who suffered from some of his most devilish pranks."

"Your amma?" Jack asked.

"That's her grandmother," Boone told him. He turned to Clementine. "Your grandf—afi, I mean, trained you? For combat?"

She nodded. "And for many other things. He was my mentor, along with my amma. While he trained me physically, she taught me to speak the many tongues I would need to know and the medicinal properties of plants. Other things, too." Just as they had her mother before her. "Because of my grandparents, I am able to fulfill my purpose."

Jack leaned back on his hands. "Which particular purpose?"

"To kill."

"Your parents?" Boone's tone was somber, as if he could guess the answer to his question.

Most of what she knew of her mother was not memories, but rather stories told by her amma. Her father was never known to any other than her mother, and she'd taken that secret to the grave with her. "I'll save that tale for another time."

Boone shifted, stretching his long legs out in front of him. "You said your grandfather's mood was solemn. Why would he be solemn when he was taking you to visit his Frud ... Frueden ..."

"*Freunde.*" She clasped her hands. "It turned out that we weren't going for a visit after all." She stared down at her hands and told them the story.

"As we neared the village, my afi began to act more peculiar. Instead of using the main road into the village, he detoured into the forest, using the cover of trees as we continued. He remained watchful as we trekked through the forest, pausing every so often to listen and sniff the air. While he'd used such methods during my training, there was something different this time. The tension felt stronger, more tangible. I had the feeling he feared that we were being followed or that we might be seen.

I began to wonder if he was really uneasy, or if this might be another prank. Or maybe he was using the trip to the village as an opportunity to sharpen my skills. He often told me *die Schläue*, above all else. That meant if skill and luck fell short, stealth might win the day. 'Be ever vigilant,' he would warn me time and again.

When we arrived on the outskirts of the village, he

stopped and took me by the shoulders. 'My little *Liebling*,' he said—that was what he called me when I was younger. 'We have a task to accomplish. This village is diseased.' He removed his pack and began pulling weapons with which I had trained daily under his supervision. 'It is a disease that has overtaken the village,' he continued. 'The few elders who have managed to keep their sanity and courage have called for a Summoner, to lure those responsible from hiding.' "

Clementine reached for her cup of tea on her desk, wetting her throat with the cool liquid. "This disease my afi was talking about," she explained, setting her cup on the desk. "It was *Draug*—the dead who walk."

Jack's eyes widened. "Sheaat."

Boone grimaced. "Like how dead? You mean fresh? Or rotting, like with maggots and skin falling off?"

"Fresh. Mostly, anyway." She returned to her story ...

"It is said, and I believe it is possible after my experience that day long ago, that weak-willed or intellectually inferior humans can be raised from their graves and enslaved by certain *others*. That was what had happened in that village weeks prior to our arrival, and the Summoner had been called upon to expose the *other* responsible before everyone in the village was killed and re-born as *Draug*.

The good news was that the Summoner had arrived and succeeded partly, luring several *Draug* to him. The bad news was that the local villagers believed he was a witch and was responsible for the disease. They burned him to death before he could draw forth the *other* who'd brought this terror to the village.

This Summoner had been my grandfather's ally for

many, many years. The news of his death both saddened my grandfather terribly and inspired him to loose me on the village and do as I'd been trained. To fulfill my role as a slayer, even though I was still young.

As we stood hidden amongst the trees, he told me I would see things in the village that would shock me. He warned that I might feel fear and confusion, but amma and he had trained me well. 'You must remember,' he said, handing me some of the weapons I'd favored during training, including my Eagle Claws. 'Strength of mind grants strength to body. Strength of body follows strength of mind. You must control your repulsion. You must control your fear.' He kissed my forehead and told me he would be beside me always. Then he made me promise not to look for him during the battle, that I was to remain focused on the task until he said it was finished.

We entered the village, concealing ourselves in the afternoon shadows as best we could."

Clementine paused and stared at the embroidered Helm of Awe cloth hung over the front door. She definitely could have used the Viking symbol of protection and victory that gruesome day. The reek of death in the village streets had made her retch more than once. The low, guttural moans of the *Draug* had haunted her dreams for many weeks after it was over. Their flesh had been bloated and blackened with decay, much of it hanging from their bodies like torn garments.

Dragging her gaze back to her audience, she continued ...

"The horrors that I experienced that day still weigh heavy in my heart. There were rotting remains scattered everywhere. People, livestock, dogs. All had been chewed upon to the extent that it was difficult at first glance to accept what I was seeing. Time and again, I had to look away from the sight of such ghastly deaths, covering my nose to block out the stench of decayed flesh. But afi would force me to turn back and look at what remained. 'You must witness this, Slayer. All of this.'

As we moved through the village, we dodged several *Draug* that roamed the paths and trails between the cottages. Others were so busy gnawing on the putrid flesh of the dead that they didn't see us slip past them.

I remember hiding in a barn. The cattle had been gutted, their eyes gouged out and their tongues had been chewed off. Afi whispered a prayer to Odin and then told me that we must slay the villagers. All of them. The disease had spread too far. It was too late to save the people of the village and none could be left alive. You see, we couldn't risk the disease spreading to other villages. To our village.

When that was done, we would need to find and slay he who'd stirred the *Draug* to rise.

My afi's final words before the fight were, 'Guide your weapons well. Take the heads.' "

Clementine looked down at her hands again, remembering the bloodshed. Stabbing and slashing and slaying. Mewls of hunger for flesh. Shrieks of fear. Screams of pain. And then she held a head, empty eyes staring up at her. With more *Draug* attacking, there was no time for remorse. She'd tossed her trophy aside and moved to the next, slaying again and again. Finally, blood and silence was all that was left in the village.

So many lives wasted all because of one *other*. She squeezed her hands into fists and plowed forth with her story …

"We slew an entire village of *Draug* that day. At the end, putrid flesh and blood covered us from head to toe.

When it was over, I asked my grandfather why we had needed to sneak into the village since we'd just made more commotion than a harvest festival.

He said, 'Surprise, my little *Liebling*. If the one responsible had been alerted to our presence too soon, we would have had to face him as well as the *Draug*. A difficulty to be avoided, if possible. Remember, when confronted with multiple enemies, you must try to divide them, especially when your foe is strong. Now, we have abolished his horde so he must face us, alone.' "

"Sheeat." Jack pushed to his feet, moving over to sit on the edge of the desk. "You weren't done yet?"

She scoffed, knowing what was to come for her and her grandfather. "Not quite."

"Were these *Draug* difficult to kill?" Boone asked.

"I'm sure you two remember the creatures we fought in the Bloody Bones."

"*Bahkauv*," they said at the same time.

"You may also recall that I was not apprehensive to go against them, regardless of the fact that there were many."

"You kicked some *Bahkauv* ass," Jack said, nodding his approval. "And that white devil. Kicked his ass, too."

"Then you should understand when I tell you that I never want to see another *Draug* as long as I live."

Jack shook his head. "Damn."

"What about the *other*?" Boone pressed. "How did that go?"

She leaned back in the chair, crossing her arms ...

"We waited in the village square. When I asked my afi why we sat in the open, rather than attempt to ambush the *other* or go hunt it down, he said that we had exposed ourselves by slaying the *Draug*. There was no hiding or hunting to be done now."

She blew out a breath. "I tell you, until that day, I'd never known afi to show fear, yet the haunted look in his eyes when he said those words chilled me inside and out."

"I remember the feeling at that moment well. Terror and dread equally making my pulse pound. A sense of utter helplessness weighing down my limbs. The suffocating sensation with each breath born from being exposed with no defense except the weapons we held in our hands. Oh, I remember it very well."

"How old were you again?" Boone asked.

"Fifteen winters."

"A kitten still," Jack said.

"Maybe," Boone agreed. "But that kitten had sharp claws."

True, but sharp claws were of no use against some demons …

> "The sun was setting when a lone figure appeared in the distance, strolling toward us as if on a leisurely walk along a forest path. As the bastard drew closer, I could hear him whistling.
>
> Afi shielded his eyes from the evening sun over the stranger's shoulder. 'It can't be,' he whispered, taking a step back.
>
> 'What is it?' I asked him.
>
> 'No. It cannot be,' he said, his eyes filling with tears. 'No, no no,' he kept whispering."

Two matching frowns were aimed in Clementine's direction.

"You see," she told Boone and Jack, "while many *others* will attempt to attack you physically, there are some that will attack your thoughts as well. These attacks on the mind can be powerful, devastatingly so. I'm less susceptible to them simply because of my lineage and the innate defenses that come with my blood line, but the two of you have no natural resistance."

She focused on Jack, who was more at risk until he accepted that his guns weren't the answer to all things. "These *others* will make you see things that aren't there. They can crawl inside your mind, find those fears you normally keep deeply and safely hidden, and use them against you." She turned to Boone. "Worse, they'll use those you love to break your spirit. Even capable men such as yourselves may fall to their will."

Boone nodded slowly. "And this happened to your grandfather?"

"Yes. He believed he saw his friend, the Summoner, alive and in good health coming toward him. Now, I believe my grandfather had an idea he was being deceived, but the wickedness at play in his brain was so potent, so overpowering, that he ran to the *other*, his arms outstretched. He did not see what I saw coming. Not its thick hunched shoulders, nor the blades it carried, nor its misshapen head with sunken black eyes, flat slitted nose, and long sharp teeth."

The front door slammed open.

A fresh gust of icy air blew in, followed by Hank clomping inside. "Gotcha 'nuther frozen one, Miss Clem." He patted the body wrapped in waxed canvas that was propped on his shoulder like a log.

"Damn it, Hank!" Boone covered his heart as he leaned back in the chair. "Knocked a year out of me, I think."

"You scared the shit outta me, you ol' mule." Jack cursed a few times, scrubbing his hand down his face.

Hank took the body into the other room, set it down on her exam table, and then returned, unbuttoning his coat. "That one's gonna need to thaw," he told her. "What's goin' on in here? You tellin' these boys ghost stories?"

"I'm telling them about Krempleschtad."

"Whoo wee! That's a good'n. Did ya git to the ..." He ran his finger across his throat.

"Hank!" The guys bellowed in unison.

Grinning, Hank moved closer to the stove and warmed his hands.

Jack turned to Clementine. "Your afi? What happened?"

She returned to her lesson for the Santa Fe Sidewinders …

"Afi ran to the creature, thinking it was his friend. It wasn't, of course. The bastard flicked my grandfather aside as if he were nothing more than a child's doll. Afi flew across the courtyard and slammed into a wall of rock. I thought he was dead.

The *other* focused on me then. I could feel it trying to reach inside of my head, like a tickling sensation in your throat that you can't quite scratch.

I glanced over at where my afi lay and a rage like I'd not felt before burned in my stomach. I wanted to rip it to pieces. I took a step toward the creature, Eagle Claws raised. All of afi's training about planning an attack, approaching a battle with controlled moves, preparing for what I can't see, keeping a calm head—that all was gone. My focus was on killing. I wanted revenge for afi, for the villagers I'd had to slay, and for all those who'd had the unfortunate fate of meeting this bastard before me. I took another step, my body trembling with fury.

But then I remembered my amma's words: *Strength in serenity.*

'What has happened here, child,' the *other* asked. Anger rippled from it through the air, making my hair blow back.

Strength in serenity.

I focused on tempering the burning rage in my stomach, the fury making my muscles quiver, the wrath causing my heart to pound. As my head cleared, I did as I'd been taught and channeled all of that energy through my muscles. It filled me with confidence, determination, strength. At that moment, I felt like I had no equal in battle, no rival that could not be vanquished. I had the eyes of an eagle, the strength of a bear, the quickness of a fox.

I'd found my strength in serenity.

The *other* came at me fast, in a blur, swinging. But I was ready. Its first mistake was that it took me for a simple village child thanks to all of the blood and decaying flesh disguising my true scent. Its second was that it didn't duck fast enough when I swung back with my blades. When it was over, the *other* had been divided, head from body, and conquered. Its reign was over."

"What happened to your grandfather?" Boone asked.

"Afi lived. He had many injuries, but he was an exceedingly stout man and my amma was an amazing healer. We eventually came to call that day *Tag des Verfalls*, which means the 'Day of Decay.'"

Both Boone and Rabbit sat in silence. They stared at her as though they were trying to see into her head. They reminded her of the *other* that day so long ago, trying to read what she had hidden behind her eyes.

Clementine stood, rubbing her hands together. "And that, Sidewinders, is your lesson for today."

Boone's brow wrinkled. "Strength in serenity?"

"No, I think she's making a point that we can't shoot everything that comes at us."

"You're both correct. If I had apples, I'd give one to each of you star pupils."

"I knew these boys would catch on quick as chain lightnin'." Hank clapped and headed for the door. "Well, I'll be back momentarily. Got another'n down the street near the mercantile. Slipped on the ice and clunked his noggin on the pickle barrel. Done jus' like that." He snapped his fingers. "That's what they's sayin' anyhow."

Clem closed the door behind Hank, leaning back against it.

Boone's brow was still wrinkled. "It was a rite of passage, wasn't it?"

Clementine nodded. "And a final test of my years of training. There are some things that can be learned only on the battlefield, such as maintaining focus when facing death."

"I get it," Jack said. "It's like an initiation. You became a real slayer that day."

Boone smiled. "An official Executioner."

Clementine nodded again. *Ein Scharfrichter*, according to Hildegard and Miss Hundt.

"And your gr—your afi had no lasting effects from that collision with the wall?" Boone asked.

"He had a limp after that. His leg had taken the worst of the impact with the rock wall. But he recovered otherwise."

"You're saying Rabbit and I are vulnerable to these *others*." Boone frowned at the floor, slowly shaking his head. He wasn't asking, more like letting those words sink in. "That they can get into our heads."

Clementine could see the alarm in his eyes. "Yes. Many of them can and will."

"And you're thinkin' this mind stuff has something to do with what ol' Buck mentioned." Jack wasn't asking either. "That corruption business being in Deadwood."

"I think it's possible the two are related. We need to talk more with Buck."

Boone tapped his fists on his knees. "Is there anything that can protect us from those bastards getting into our heads?"

She pondered that for a moment. Being who she was by blood, she hadn't concerned herself with protection of this sort for some time. "There are shields. But it's never a sure thing. You'll need to be prepared."

"Dammit, Clementine. How do Rabbit and I," he held up his hands and wiggled them around, "*prepare*, for something like that?"

She smiled. "With my help, of course."

He settled back into the chair, his dark gaze steady on her. "Okay. I trust you."

"Don't worry, Booney, I gotcha, too," Jack said. "So, we talk to Buck. Probably best we all corral the geezer. He's a slippery critter. Git him by the neck." Rabbit clenched his fist in the air.

Clementine nodded, but her thoughts returned to that dark day. So much blood. Too much death. Most of it on her hands.

"I get what you're sayin', Miss Clementine." Jack's voice pulled her back to the present. " 'Don't go off half-cocked, Jack,' is what you're sayin'."

A short laugh escaped her lips. "I'm glad you understand, Mr. Quick Draw."

Vertical lines creased his forehead. "Ain't gonna come easy, though. Warnin' you is all. Ain't gonna come too easy for me. My gun hand tends to do the thinkin' sometimes. Then my head finally shows up at the shindig wondering what's goin' on."

She joined him at her desk, squeezing his shoulder. "Believe me, I understand. But maybe this is a good opportunity to work on that, since your gun hand is on the mend."

He smirked down at his bandaged palm. "I reckon you're on the gold with that idea."

Clementine moved over to the doorway of her examination room, wondering exactly what she'd find wrapped up in the waxed tarp Hank had left her—besides another dead body.

She looked back at them. "I have some thawing to do with

this one." She thumbed toward the frozen body. "With the other body Hank is bringing, I'll be busy for the afternoon. You two will need to find something to occupy your time unless you want to get your hands dirty with me." She started to turn toward the exam room, but then stopped. "Oh. One more thing. Your two days start over again."

"Sheeat!" Jack frowned at Boone. "So it starts now? Not tomorrow morning. Right?"

Boone slapped his thigh and stood. "Two days. That's not bad. I think Rabbit can keep his hands to himself for that long."

Jack flapped his thumb and fingers together. "That's what your lips are doin', Booney, in case you didn't know."

Smiling, Clementine left them poking at each other in the parlor. If old Buck was right about the corruption, training Boone and Rabbit was going to take more than just weaponry practice.

A lot more.

Or they might end up dead way too soon.

Ten

And the next day after that ...

It was difficult to discern exactly where the town of Galena started, Rabbit decided as he followed Hank and Fred the Mule into the gulch. Tents and cabins were strung sparsely along a creek that appeared occasionally from beneath a thick but dusty blanket of snow.

"That, Hank my friend, was one hell of a trail. And with Fred dragging a wagon loaded with picks 'n hammers 'n kegs of powder, too." He whistled his admiration, patting Dime's neck.

Hank shot a grin back his way. "Fred surely is a hearty beast."

"And plowin' snow most of the way." Fortunately, it was the light and powdery kind, cold enough to freeze the horns off a billy goat. Rabbit's whiskers were inadequate cover for a day like this. "Must've been better than two miles worth of hill gettin' here. Seems we came around the corner a little."

"Too bumpy to come straight 'cross them hills." Hank jutted his thumb over his shoulder at a nearby ridgeline. "No trails cut through the snow thataway, no how."

The trail they'd taken hadn't seemed to diminish the difficulty to a great extent. It had been forged through undulating terrain, following the path of least resistance—or not. But it had leveled somewhat as they entered into a gulch obviously scoured and flattened with sediment. It was a gulch much like that in which Deadwood rested, high ridges to each side that would prove impassable in winter, excepting through smaller side gulches wiggling off into the distance occasionally.

When they came to a stop in front of a small cabin, Rabbit climbed down off Dime and helped Hank untie the ropes securing the crates and barrels to the wagon. They hefted one of the heavier crates onto the porch.

"Good to have your help, Jack Rabbit." Hank smiled through gray whiskers coated with a good layer of frost. "You're savin' an ol' man's back. But you deserve some pay, helpin' with the load and all."

"Happy to help a pard, and I don't want no money." Rabbit adjusted his wool scarf, tucking it further down into the front of his coat. "*And* you ain't old. Not too, anyway."

Hank sniggered and then coughed. "Damned cold air. Disturbs the bugs in my lungs."

"Let's grab the rest." Rabbit led the way back to the wagon.

Unloading the equipment was heavy work and the frigid, dry air burned Rabbit's throat and lungs, but it felt good to get blood into his muscles after the long ride from Deadwood. Jolts of pain from his injured hand, head, and neck slowed him some, but not much. He pushed through that pain into the fatigue of honest hard work.

He noticed Hank puffing big clouds of steam, too. The older man knew how to grind, that much was sure.

They finished unloading the equipment and sat on the back of the wagon, catching their breath.

"Where's your man with your pay?" Rabbit glanced at the dark cabin. No smoke billowed from the stone chimney.

"Ever'body around here is up in the hills workin' adits. It's mostly silver and lead minin' around these parts."

"Paid first then?"

Hank grunted.

"Smart." Rabbit's gaze roamed the hillsides. He pointed at the tall stand of pines across the creek. "I'd wager Deadwood probably looked like this not too long ago."

Hank shielded his eyes from the sun that sat low in the afternoon sky. "Reminds me of whiskers on a man's chin, only the whiskers on these hills ain't been shaved yet like in Deadwood."

They sat for a few minutes, chewing on some tough pieces of peppery beef jerky. They finished their meal with some sweet dried apricots that Hank had picked up from who knew where. Occasionally, Hank would rise and dump a tin of oats into Fred the Mule's grain bag, sharing with Dime, too.

"Damn mule never is satisfied. Eat my supper, too, if'n I let him. Ever'time I do that, though, it gives him the vapors." Hank didn't seem to be in any particular hurry and Rabbit wasn't inclined to get in a "flustration" at this very minute either, especially since time spent away from Deadwood was time that trouble couldn't find him. And the clock on Clementine's damned challenge kept ticking.

He bobbled his head. " 'Two days,' she says."

"What's that, Jack Rabbit?" Hank looked over from where he stood in front of Fred the Mule. He held the mule's jaws in his hands and bonked his forehead against Fred's, then came around the wagon and sat beside Rabbit. "Two days fer what?"

Rabbit didn't feel like talking about that particular bother, so he changed the subject. "How'd you come to be in Deadwood, Hank?"

Hank scratched his chin, closed an eye and looked at the sky. "What say we bag us a rabbit? Make some stew. Maybe, we get lucky and find us a deer or a goat."

Apparently, Hank wasn't keen on that subject either. That was fine. Hunting something sounded good right about then anyway.

Rabbit scanned the ridges, along one side and then the other. "You know these hills?"

"Good 'nough to hunt."

"Don't got my Sharps."

"Don't need no cannon for rabbits, Rabbit." Hank snickered at his play on words. "You handy with that six shooter on yer hip with yer good hand?"

Rabbit jerked, spun, and slotted his Colt with his left hand, more from reflex than for show.

"Woo hoo! That is a fast pistol. Shortened the barrel, did yuh?"

"Quicker on the pull," Rabbit said, a little surprised that Hank noticed the custom barrel, since most didn't. "Ain't so good at a distance, though."

" 'Tween us we'll get one or two, jus' the same. And I got my bow, you probably noticed."

Rabbit had noticed. He wouldn't have put much stock in someone's ability to bring down a rabbit or especially a deer with that bow. But Hank wasn't just *someone*. Rabbit had seen him go to work with it. If they came across a deer, it was more than likely going down with a wooden arrow in it rather than a lead bullet.

"Let's get us some stew fixin's." Rabbit checked his revolver and slung his full bandoleer over his shoulder.

Hank loaded up his pack, spun the cylinder on his revolver, and slung his bow over his shoulder. "See you in an hour or two, Fred. You stay outta trouble now, ya hear?" After a pat on Fred's head, he started up the hillside behind the cabin.

Rabbit shook his finger in front of Dime's big brown eyes. "You help keep Fred outta trouble now."

Dime whinnied and tossed his head. He shifted his weight and bumped Rabbit with his rump, knocking him hard enough that his hat tumbled into the snow. Fred snorted at Rabbit as he picked up his hat and smacked it against his leg.

Cursing under his breath about the lack of respect from the two ornery critters, he took off after Hank, lining up behind him.

"Let's go get us a *Bahkauv*!"

Hank stopped and turned. "Now don't you be startin' with that kinda talk when we's headed into the woods, Jack Rabbit. You'll get my sensibilities hackled up."

Rabbit chuckled. "Yeah. I don't suppose we wanna wrangle any of them vermin without Miss Clementine swingin' her fancy finger blades around. What do you figure a bunch of those boys is called? A herd?"

"How 'bout a flock?"

"Too civilized," Rabbit sniffed, the cold air making his nose drip. "Cute little birdies is a flock."

"A pack. Like a pack of wild dogs."

They certainly had attacked like wild dogs, even though they looked more like big ugly cats. "That seems fittin'."

"It's bad luck is what I'd call it."

Rabbit chuckled. "Yeah. Bad luck for them if they run across us again."

"And Miss Clem."

"Sure as a bear has hair."

"We should spread out a little." Hank started moving again, lumbering up the hill.

Rabbit swiped his nose with his handkerchief. "I'd rather jaw with you than bag a rabbit."

They huffed up the hill, cutting a trail through the snow that was knee-deep in the openings between the pines. They paused every few steps to listen and watch, resting longer occasionally when Rabbit's lungs burned. Hank, on the other hand, didn't seem to tire so rapidly. He was probably accustomed to the hills and plowing through drifts.

Rabbit preferred a little more heat in his winter and a lot less snow. Although if he and Boone were going to buy Keller's Livery, he'd need to get used to this sort of weather.

"Ain't so cold as it's been, that's one for the goo—shhh." Hank stopped in his tracks and pulled the bow from his back.

Stringing an arrow, he crouched down into the snow.

Rabbit crouched too, and spied the quarry: a white rabbit not thirty yards up the hillside. It stood on its back legs near a dense thicket, its ears and eyes intent on something farther up the hill.

"Let me shoot it," Rabbit said and pulled his pistol.

The other rabbit turned its head and looked directly at the men.

"Quiet now," Hank whispered. "He heard you."

Both men remained still until the rabbit focused up the hillside again.

"You ain't gonna hit that from here, are you?" Rabbit was sure the distance was too great for bow and arrow.

"Shh." Hank looked back at Rabbit, his eyes wide.

"Well, sheeat."

The rabbit looked at them again.

Hank continued to stare at Rabbit.

"Okay, okay," Rabbit whispered and grinned at Hank. "Get 'im."

As soon as the rabbit looked away, Hank stood tall and drew the arrow back, taking aim. *Thwwwp!* The arrow flew. In a blink it struck home.

"Bull's-eye!" Rabbit cheered.

"Took him quick. Didn't feel a thing. I don't like animals sufferin' unduly." Hank trudged up the slope and bagged the rabbit. "Probably another'n around here someplace. Didn't even need to hunt that one, really. Appeared pretty as you please."

"We get another one and that's enough for you and me and Boone and Miss Clementine." Rabbit glanced around, peering through the pine trees. "Maybe still get a deer. Wish I had my Sharps."

They continued their hunt, trudging through the snow, veering along the hillside below the crest of the ridge. They searched for tracks, listened for the sound of a scurrying critter beneath the whispering pine needles overhead, and paused now and then to rest.

At one point, they stopped and sat on an old log under a pine with branches bushy enough the snow hadn't built up around the trunk.

"You recall I told you I was out in Nevada Territory huntin' with One Horn Buck and Tennessee Pete?" Hank asked.

"Yep. Hunting and prospecting, you said."

"After I finished with helpin' building the railroad, there was something that drew me to Nevada Territory. That's the way it goes for me. I get this feelin' I need to be in a place, so I go. Tried to resist it a time or two, but it gets to bein' like an itch. Keeps itchin' 'til it gets scratched, meanin' I go. Never been able to explain it so I kinda give in and go. Well, I got this itch to go to Nevada Territory. Met up with Tennessee Pete in a town in California. Can't remember the name."

"Nevada is where you met One Horn Buck?" After Hank nodded, Rabbit sniffed and asked, "How'd he come by the name One Horn?"

"That's what I called him back then. It stuck." Hank leaned over and buck-snorted into the snow, and then he wiped his nose with a raggedy cloth. "I was helpin' him track the biggest-of-the-big bighorn up the side of the Sierras for a week, maybe more. Climbin' rocks. Up one side of a hill, down t'other. Run clean outta hardtack and jerky, we did. Had to hunt for ever'thing."

He rubbed his gloved hands together. "He was a wily sonofabitch, that sheep. He'd catch a whiff of us and up he'd go. Up and up. Clear up the mountainside into the snow to near the tippy tops of the range. We was half froze and starvin' when we finally got him cornered on a flat 'tween a cliff on one side and the dropoff on t'other. Poor beast couldn't climb the cliff, too steep, and didn't want to jump over t'other side. Ol' Buck sighted him up in his rifle. Just before he shot, the bighorn took a flyin' leap over the side. Musta been outta its mind with fear." The corners of Hank's mouth drooped. "Don't like bein' the cause of a fine animal feelin' thatta way."

"After all that time and work Buck didn't get his bighorn?"

"Well, believe it or not, Buck went after him. Over the side."

"You shittin' me?"

"No siree, Jack Rabbit. Over the side ol' Buck went after that bighorn. Made it a ways down on snags and rocks. Weren't a bad mountain climber, turns out. Lost his footing, though, and fell the rest of the way like the sheep did. I watched him tumble prob'ly a hunerd feet or so down the mountain. He stopped up not too far from the sheep, turned out."

"I'll be a son of a gun." What kind of man went over a cliff like that? Ol' Buck was crazier than Rabbit, hands down.

"I climbed back down the mountain the way we come. Took me two days, stuck eatin' squirrels an' such. Found the sheep and Buck in a pile of rocks. The sheep was all broken up from fallin' down the mountainside. Buck was in sore shape, too, so I set up camp and cooked up what I could find of that bighorn. Fixed up Buck best I could. Found one horn from that sheep but couldn't find t'other."

"One horn." Rabbit nodded. He wondered how much of that fall had rattled Buck's brain bucket. Hell, maybe he'd been a little *loco* before whatever he ran into in Gayville stirred his pot.

"Yep. Few days later, I worked up a travois. I figured the best thing I could do was extricate Buck outta them mountains and head for town. Damned if I didn't end up pullin' Buck and that horn all the way down the mountain."

Rabbit stared at Hank with more than a little awe. "You dragged him the whole way?"

"Sure. He couldn't walk. Had two broke legs and I don't know what all else." Hank chuckled, crossing his arms. "Buck carried that damn horn for a year after that." He hooted, scaring off a pair of jays from a nearby tree. "He'd hand it to the barkeep and say, 'Fill 'er up,' and then try to pour the whole of it down

his throat. Couldn't, of course. Too big. Soaked his shirt and the front of his trousers tryin'."

Grinning, Rabbit said, "Sounds like some of the characters I know from El Gato saloon in Santa Fe."

Hank shook his head. "He'd hold the horn in front of his pants and chase the girls around the saloon. You think he's loco now, naw, *that* was loco. Sometime after that, it was stolen when he got too corned in a brothel in Virginia City. Some say it's hangin' on the wall there now, but I ain't been back to see fer myself."

"How big was the horn?"

"Damned big." Hank put his hands in front of him to indicate the width. "Wide as your shoulders maybe."

"Damn is right." Rabbit would have liked to have seen that big ol' sheep standin' on a ridge. He watched snow sprinkle down from one of the pine tree limbs across the way, thinking back on his trip north with Boone. "You know what *loco* thing I seen lately."

"Fred the Mule drink hooch?"

Rabbit laughed loud, probably scaring off all the critters in the area. "I'd like to see that." He sobered. "I seen a man out in a stream, dead of winter, dudded head to toe in black. Black pants, black frock coat, and black top hat, runnin' a sluice. Like he just arrived from Sunday prayers at the church."

Hank grunted, looking up the hillside. "Gold drives a man to do things that ain't necessarily his characteristics otherwise. It's a funny thing."

"Never seen that before." Rabbit stared at Hank's profile. His nose was crooked partway down. Must have had it knocked sideways somewhere along the trail. "Don't seem to have that influence on you."

"Naw. Don't got that urge. Like I said, I get to itchin' a little and find myself needin' to mosey to a place. No tellin' where it might land me."

"Landed you in Nevada Territory."

"Yep." Hank shot him a grin. "Ol' Buck and me and Tennessee took up huntin' there—well, Tennessee and me mostly, anyway. Buck turned a fair pan after runnin' down that bighorn sheep, so he could make his livin' prospectin'. He hunted with Tennessee and me just for the company, I suppose. Anyway, Tennessee and me hunted and sold the meat to minin' interests, big and small. Kept whole camps in meat sometimes. Huntin' was good then."

"Probably ain't what it used to be around here." Rabbit scanned the hillside in front of them. "Ain't seen one deer yet."

"Might. Might not. Yer right 'bout big game. Ain't so many no more, and they's smarter. Know to keep a man at a distance, like they do a big cat."

Rabbit pulled some jerky from his coat pocket and tore it in half, handing a piece to Hank. "You reckon we'll see the other side of all this *other* stuff?"

Taking the bit of jerky, Hank shrugged. "I believe we have a good fightin' chance. Miss Clem will git you boys trained in the blades and subterfuge. I'll do my best to do my part, and with Miss Clem, well, I think it's those beasties that need to be concerned."

Hank's mellow tone was reassuring. Rabbit stood and stretched. "You like Nevada?"

"Had a few experiences I'd just soon forget. These things goin' on here? Ain't the only place. Just as soon disremember losin' Tennessee." Hank's face went slack, his gaze lowering to his hands.

"Sorry to bring it up, Hank." Rabbit scanned the hillside again before pulling back and checking out the area around them. The lengthening afternoon shadows made it easier to see the complexion of the snow. "Hey, I see some tracks over yonder." He leapt up. "Rabbit tracks," he told Hank.

Hank followed. "Looky here. That's one big rabbit."

He turned to find Hank pointing at Rabbit's boot prints in the snow.

They both chuckled and followed the other tracks along the side of the hill with Rabbit leading the way.

"Whup," Rabbit whispered, stopping Hank. "There he is. Other side of that log. See the ears?"

"I see him. Can't get a shot."

They snuck up alongside an outcropping of rock, attempting to flank their furry prey. All at once it dashed up and over a hummock a few yards farther on.

A short hike and they were standing on top of the hummock while the rabbit rested at the edge of a small clearing a little way back down the hill. In spite of the snow, Rabbit could make out the telltale shape of flattened-out mine tailings toward the downslope edge of the clearing. Stumps of trees peppered the area. He'd bet Boone's lucky hat there was a mine nearby in the hillside. They must have taken the timber for shoring.

"Looks to be an adit down there." Hank pointed at the tailings, apparently reading Rabbit's mind.

"Thought so. Can you get a shot at the critter?" He pointed at the rabbit, which had scampered farther away while he wasn't paying attention.

"Too far away," Hank said. "Let's circle 'round down to the left and move up on him."

They worked their way closer, keeping trees and bushes between them and the rabbit until they were below the lip of the tailings. The rabbit hopped through the snow on the other side.

Hank grabbed his bow and strung an arrow. He stood, aimed, and let fly. *Thwwwp.* The arrow veered left and disappeared into the snow beside the rabbit, startling it straight into the air and then down over the rim of the tailings on the opposite side of the clearing.

"Dangnabbit!" Hank lowered his bow. "Wind caught it."

"That's what I saw," Rabbit said sarcastically as he climbed onto the flattened tailings. "He's gone, I think." The tracks led down the tailings and disappeared into a heavy thicket. "Little buggers are fast."

"Jack Rabbit, looky here." Hank's voice sounded higher than normal.

Rabbit turned around. "What is it?"

Not twenty feet off was a heavy iron gate covering an adit dug into the side of the hill.

Rabbit frowned at the adit. Blackness oozed from its hollowed depths, shrouding everything on the other side of the iron gate with darkness. He took a step toward the mine, hesitating. "Just an ol' mine," he said under his breath, but dread weighed heavy on his shoulders and squeezed the cheerfulness out of him.

Memories of finding Uncle Mort flooded his head. His uncle's battered, limp body and broken bones left in a loose pile in that cold, damp mine. Since that day, he'd had many dreams ending with his uncle's dead, pale eyes staring into nothingness. Sometimes Uncle Mort would be struggling to speak to him, his mouth moving awkwardly as he reached for him with a bloody—

Rabbit stumbled backward, away from the memories, away from the mine. He bumped into something solid.

"Easy there, Jack Rabbit." Hank turned him around and held him by his shoulders, peering into his eyes. "What's got you spooked?"

"Uncle Mort …" was all he could get out before his throat closed up tight.

"Ah. Your uncle." Hank nodded. "You were the one who found him in the Bloody Bones. I can understand you feelin' a bad way about that, but this ain't the Bloody Bones. Your uncle ain't in there." He patted Rabbit's shoulders. "You stay right here. I'm gonna have a look-see through that gate."

"Thanks, Hank." Rabbit breathed deep and watched Hank move toward the gated opening, his steps slow, cautious.

"That's a heavy gate," Hank said without looking back. "Those bars are as fat as my thumb."

"You see anything inside yet?"

"Nope. Big lock on a chain. Takes a key."

Rabbit inched closer, his nerves steady once again.

"Not much snow here." Hank indicated with both hands the area of leveled-off tailings that formed a gravel platform under their feet. "Hard to read any prints."

"Probably workin' this mine." Rabbit caught up with Hank. "Maybe locked away a thick vein behind that gate."

Hank nodded.

Closer to the gate, Rabbit's eyes began to adjust to the darkness within the adit. The sun's descent below the ridgeline helped as well, making the snow around them not nearly as bright.

Hank put his face up to the thick bars. "Looks a mess inside, but don't see no minin' equipment."

Joining Hank at the bars, Rabbit studied the thick iron up close. Not much rust on it yet. He could almost slip his head through into the mine.

"What's all over the ground in there? Rocks?" Hank asked.

There was something hanging on the wall just inside the gate. A couple of things, actually. Rabbit squinted into the darkness. What were …

"Sheeat!" Rabbit stepped back quickly. "Shackles!" He pointed at the iron restraints hanging from chains bolted into the wall. His gaze darted. He felt vulnerable all of a sudden without his favorite sawed-off. "I should've brought Boss, too," he said as much to himself as Hank.

Hank stood his ground, peering through the bars. "Blood on the ground under 'em, and a bloody scratch ma— Thunderation!" He backed up, too. "Saw fingernails caught in those rocks. Looks like they was torn out trying to get free of them shackles." He shuddered and then returned to the bars again.

Rabbit frowned at his hunting partner. Hank was one tough *hombre*. Blowing out a breath, Rabbit returned to the bars, too.

"Lots of blood," he told Hank. "Mostly frozen. That must be why it don't stink." He sniffed, smelling damp dirt. He concentrated on the shackles. "Size for a regular man, looks like."

"That ain't piles of rocks you seen, Jack Rabbit." Hank turned to him, his cheeks paler than usual. "They's parts."

"Parts?" Rabbit began searching the floor. Parts of what? The piece on the floor had short stems sticking out of it that looked like … "Oh fucker! That's a hand." Several more lay nearby it.

"Boot over there, I think." Hank stood up tall but didn't back up. "Still has a leg sticking partway out."

Rabbit began to see what Hank was describing. Partially eaten hands, feet, and other torn or chewed parts that were unidentifiable littered the ground. He looked at Hank, who was looking right back. Hank's wide-eyed stare and open mouth probably mirrored Rabbit's.

A shadowy something rushed at them from out of the darkness and crashed against the gate.

They both stumbled backward, falling on their asses.

A long, hulking arm with smooth scales shot out between the bars. Claws as big as Bowie knives arced upward before sweeping down fast and hard, snagging the very tip of Hank's boot. The arm tugged, hauling Hank closer.

"Arr!" Rabbit sprang up and grabbed onto Hank's thick coat. He lunged backward, wrestling Hank free from the beast's grasp, but not his boot.

A deep, shrieking roar echoed out from the adit. For a moment, Rabbit thought he could feel the ground shake.

The creature swiped at Hank again, one yellow eye looking out through the bars, the thick arm and long claws outstretched. Rabbit dragged Hank farther from the gate, moving him safely out of reach. The thing pulled its arm back and faded into the shadows, taking Hank's boot with it.

Rabbit glanced down. "You still in one piece, pard?"

"I dunno." Hank's eyes were squeezed shut.

Rabbit checked Hank's calf and foot. A wool sock still covered both. "I don't think he got you."

Hank sat up and opened one eye. "It didn't get me? It didn't get me." He opened his other eye and squinted toward the adit. "Got my boot, though."

Whatever lurked in the adit let out another shrieking roar, sending a shiver down Rabbit's spine. It crashed against the gate again, the thick iron shuddering under the thing's weight. Two scale-covered, muscled arms shot through the bars this time, along with a rounded scaly snout with deep slits on top and long fangs jutting out. Two yellow eyes stared out through the bars as it swiped at the men.

"Sonofabitch!" Rabbit jerked his pistol and took aim.

Boom! Whap! The bullet tore into the flesh of one paw, spraying dark liquid into a crimson bloom. The creature squealed and both arms disappeared back through the bars in the blink of an eye. The squealing and panting grew fainter.

"I think it's backing away," he said to Hank.

Hank stood, frowning down at his bootless foot. "That didn't look like no *Bahkauv*."

"Nope." It didn't sound like one either, and this fucker's arms were scaly, not covered in black fur.

Inside the dark adit they heard the *scritch-scritch-scritch* of claws on rock.

"Oh, shit," Hank said right before the beast crashed into the gate again with enough force to bend the iron bars outward. Metal shrieked against metal. The chain snapped taut against the lock.

The huffing sounds from inside faded into the darkness again, but didn't go away entirely.

Rabbit tilted his head, hearing heavy, raspy panting. "Fucker's still there," he whispered. "Trying to break through is what he's doin'. He almost broke that lock. See?"

The lock still held, but had been stretched and twisted out of shape by the chain.

Rabbit's heart galloped in his chest. "I don't think that thing will take another hit."

"Ain't no good runnin', then. Missin' my boot, anyhow." Hank raised his pistol and waited. "Ready?"

Rabbit was one step ahead of him, his pistol cocked and aimed. "Sure wish I had my Sharps or Boss. Come on, you bastard."

On cue, the creature rushed out of the darkness and crashed into the gate again, both arms reaching, claws swinging, yellow eyes bulging as it pushed against the bars.

Boom! Boom! Boom! Boom! Boom! Boom! Boom! Boom! Boom!

Clickclickclickclickclickclickclickclickclickclick ...

"Jack Rabbit! Yer out!"

"So are you!"

The creature squealed long and high, reminding Rabbit of hog killing time at the ranch. It retreated into the darkness again, still squealing.

The gate creaked open a few inches as the chain clanged and clanked, link by link, to the ground.

Rabbit shared a wide-eyed look with Hank, and then they both began to reload as quick as their fingers could work.

"He don't know he broke through, does he?" Hank finished loading and spun the cylinder.

Rabbit's gun was pointing and waiting. "Stand and fight?" His gaze darted between Hank and the open gate.

A shriek echoed out from the darkness.

"RUUUUUN!!!" they yelled at the same time and raced through the snow over the edge of the tailings toward Fred and Dime.

Eleven

Meanwhile …

Afternoons were short in the gulch, but the sunshine on Boone's hat and coat helped take the bite out of the icy breezes sweeping the street. He meandered up one side of Deadwood's main street and down the other. The town smelled better today for some reason, fresher, less like a dirty mining settlement. Could be due to the dusting of snow last night that coated all of the soiled spots around the young town. Or maybe he was just getting used to the place.

He bought a small bag of hard candy from the mercantile and contemplated buying a new hat. But he didn't. The good luck charm with a bullet hole in it was comfortable. A small part of him wondered if maybe it actually did bring good fortune. After all, his luck seemed to improve when he donned the black gambler-style hat. The irony of it being a gambler made him chuckle from time to time. Boone was about as ready to part with his money playing games of chance as Rabbit was ready to put down his Colt.

He stopped across the street from Keller's Livery.

A livery. Uncle Morton was probably turning in his grave that his boys were even thinking about a livery. But above all, Uncle Morton was a businessman. He'd raised Rabbit and Boone to be the same.

Another gust of wind swept down the street, taking a bowler hat with it. Boone watched the hat roll and bounce past him like a tumbleweed back on the ranch.

The problem he was having now was he couldn't get a gut feeling about Deadwood, possibly because he still wasn't sure that giving up his uncle's drayage business was the best idea. He had yet to follow up on his uncle's contact here in Deadwood, the one he and Rabbit had learned about before heading back to Santa Fe. It might be worth the trouble to see that through. Maybe establish a route from Laramie. Or Yankton.

What should we do, Uncle Morton?

Asking that was pointless, really. Uncle Morton was the one originally trying to expand the freight business to the Black Hills. To Deadwood, especially.

Boone hadn't ever voiced his opinion to his uncle, but his gut said that the railroad would be the end of Morton & Sons Drayage. Long haul freight would end up on trains, leaving the scraps of business-to-business short-distance haulage to freighters like them. *Around town.* After the things he'd seen and places he'd been, Boone wasn't about to settle in and run milk to little old ladies in their house dresses *around town*.

Of course, what was running a livery? Raking and shoveling straw and horseshit.

"Aw, damn." He popped a hunk of hard candy in his mouth and continued up the street. Before long, he found himself in front of The Pyre, contemplating going inside …
She's working.

Sure, but she's working alone.
Might appreciate the company.
Might appreciate working alone, too.
Who wants to be alone with a corpse?
She has at least two tables' worth of buzzard food to work on, though.
Nice. Probably not too proper to think of the dead that way.

You gonna stand here and talk to yourself or go in?
"Going to," not "gonna." You're starting to sound like Rabbit.

Done thinking it over, Boone opened the door.

"Clementine?" he called as he stepped inside and closed the door. "Oh!" He blinked when he saw her sitting at her parlor desk. "I didn't realize you'd be in here."

Clementine looked up from the small journal he'd seen her writing in several times before. Her braided hair looked soft and shiny, her skin smooth as silk. "Good afternoon, Boone. I work *here*, not sure if you realized that." Her slight smile showed that she was playing with him.

Boone chuckled. "I mean here in the parlor. I thought you had work to do." He pointed toward her exam room. "In there. With a couple of … ah … icicles."

"Boone McCreery, did you make a joke?" Her smile widened. "It turns out both icicles are solid enough to thwart my advances, so I'm waiting while I warm their dispositions."

"Care to join me for a hot cup of coffee? I thought maybe I—well, we if you're so inclined—could grab a biscuit at Grand Central Hotel."

She looked back down at her journal for a couple of seconds and then nodded. "That sounds good. Let me finish up these notes and then we can go."

While Clementine wrote in her book, Boone settled into the chair by the fire. He picked up Tinker's tattered play shirt and dangled it on the dog's snoring nose. She woke instantly and shook her head, then took the bait and chomped onto the shirt, tugging at it.

After several minutes of playing, he glanced at Clementine. "She's healed up all the way except for the leg. Maybe ready to go outside, you think?"

"She's ready," Clementine said, closing her journal. "She's loaded with energy and needs to use it in some way besides running up and down the hall."

"Ha! That sounds like Tink."

Clementine stood and stretched her back. The thick, gray knitted shawl she wore over her pale blue shirt made her eyes look the same color as dark snow clouds. "I'm done here. Let me get my coat."

A few minutes later, they had settled in at Grand Central Hotel's last empty table with cups of coffee for each of them. Boone set his hat on his lap. Apparently, escaping the cold afternoon breezes was a popular idea around these parts.

"Is that typical?" He was still simmering after witnessing no fewer than four rude gestures directed at his companion along with three offensive comments about her manly appearance. "Can't make up their mind if they want to bed you or fight you, apparently."

Clementine shrugged. "It happens often enough. I appreciate that you were able to let it pass." She smoothed the stained linen tablecloth next to her cup. "Your two-day challenge is still intact."

For now, anyway. She didn't know how close a couple of those bastards had come to being face-down in the muddy slush of the street wishing they were dead after what he wanted to do to them.

"Just so you know, Clementine." He fiddled with the brim of his hat, glancing her way. "It is my opinion that there is not a single masculine trait observable anywhere on your person."

She squinted at him. "Thank you, I think."

That hadn't come out quite like he'd wanted. He looked her in the eyes this time. "What I mean to say is, your appearance is pleasing to any normal man."

Her gaze didn't waver. "What about the abnormal ones?"

He chuckled, liking the shape of her lips even more when she pursed them like that. He looked away and scanned the room. "Where are those blasted biscuits? A man could starve waiting for something to eat around here."

A nasal-heavy voice from the table next to theirs cut in, "Why don't you have *him* kill your supper for ya? Got man-hands big enough to strangle a bear." Hoots and laughter followed.

When Boone turned to see which of the four assholes had said it, none of the men were looking at him or, more importantly, Clementine.

He donned a false smile and looked back at Clementine to read her reaction.

She raised an eyebrow in his direction, a half-smile tipping one side of her mouth.

Boone leaned in closer to her, his forearms on the table. "You think Buck knows anything about our little problem?"

She leaned in, too. "I think it's at least worth talking to him. I'd be interested to find out what he meant by ... " She glanced around and scooted in closer, mouthing the word *corruption*.

Clementine was close enough now that Boone could smell the soap she used. It reminded him of when he'd stand in the desert lavender that covered patches of empty range near the ranch. He and Rabbit used to play in those lavender-covered fields when they were younger. Rabbit would pick a sprig of it, stick it behind his ear, and tell Boone to ask him to *la fiesta del danza* with a big dumb grin on his face.

"Lavender," he said, warmth spreading through him at the sunshine-filled memories.

Her eyes widened slightly. "What about it?"

Shit. He didn't mean to say that out loud. "I can smell it on you. It reminds me of home. Of Santa Fe."

"Least one o' them cowhands smells purty," the nasally voice threw out. The other table exploded into laughter again.

Boone turned in his chair. "You boys working up a problem over there?"

They ignored him.

Clementine laid her hand on his forearm. "Don't," she said.

At her touch, his head of steam dissipated. What were they

talking about before the lavender soap? Oh yeah, ol' Buck.

The assholes at the next table over hooted and whistled. Boone frowned their way, watching as the frazzled wait girl dropped off a plate of biscuits and topped up their cups of coffee. As she left, one of the louts laid a firm palm to her rump. *Smack!* Louder hoots and hollers erupted. The girl's cheeks turned beet red. She scurried away, squeezing between the tightly crowded tables in the dining room.

"Your piece is prob'ly as sweet as your momma's," the same nasally voice taunted her. She aimed a quick frown at the table of degenerates, her eyes red and watery.

Boone shook his head. "What kind of men ..."

Clementine squeezed his forearm. "You'll be in a punch-up every day in this town if you can't let things like that go."

"Well, you can't treat a girl that way," Boone grumbled through gritted teeth.

Clementine let go of his arm, sitting back in her chair. "Tell me, Mr. McCreery. A man your age, is there no Mrs. McCreery?"

"What do you mean, my age?" He wasn't that much older than her, was he? Boone took a breath. *Simmer down, cowboy.* "When it comes to women, Rabbit has a lot more ..." He paused, searching for the right words. "Rabbit is ... let's just say he's more successful with women than I am." A little less picky about sage hens, too.

"Looks like you're purty good at holdin' hands with the men, though," the jackass from the other table cut in. More laughter and snickering followed.

Boone shot out of his chair.

Clementine stood with him. She looked him straight in the eye. *No*, she mouthed, grabbing his arm again.

He let her pull him back down into his chair.

The wait girl appeared with a plate of biscuits, almost dropping them from her trembling hands. Clementine caught the plate and set it down, smiling and thanking the poor girl.

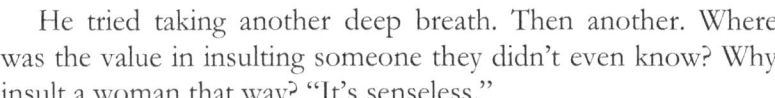

He tried taking another deep breath. Then another. Where was the value in insulting someone they didn't even know? Why insult a woman that way? "It's senseless."

"Agreed." Clementine smiled. "Have a biscuit."

Boone grabbed one. He tore into the warm, slightly salty bread like a hungry dog with a piece of meat.

Clementine took a smaller, less energetic bite of her biscuit. "Mmm. Still warm." She took a sip of coffee. "So how do you think Jack and Hank are faring in Galena?"

"Li'l doggy likes his bone," their neighbor goaded.

Doing his best to ignore the asshole, Boone picked up his cup of coffee and swallowed the contents in one gulp. The hot, bitter liquid burned all the way to his stomach. Fuckers. Gotta interrupt a pair just trying to have a cup.

"Tell me about your ranch in Santa Fe," Clementine urged.

He appreciated her trying to distract him from the problem next door. He reached for another biscuit.

The wait girl returned with the coffee pot, trying to skirt around the troublesome table next to Boone and Clementine but to no avail. One of the ill-mannered scoundrels halfway stood and grabbed the girl by the arm.

"I need some lovin', darlin'. Sit with me a spell." He pulled her hard and she lost her grip on the tin coffee pot. It crashed to the floor, black coffee pouring out and seeping down through the cracks between the planks.

"Aw. She spilt the coffee, Slats," another bastard at the table said to the grabby jerk. "You better give her a spankin'."

"No, no, no, no, no!" The girl sobbed and beat frantically against Slat's arm, her hits feeble compared to his iron grip.

Boone turned to Clementine, his squint so narrow he could hardly see her.

She scowled back and nodded.

He was up and standing between the sobbing girl and the man in a heartbeat, breaking Slat's hold on the girl. He glanced around the table. Four men. Probably good for all of them if they didn't pull knives or guns. "Gentlemen. I believe I'll give the little lady a hand with that coffee. My cup's dry."

Boone turned to the girl, who was rubbing her red arm. "Afternoon, little miss." He picked up the coffee pot and set it next to Clementine. "What's your name?"

"J ... Joa ... nie," she blubbered through tears.

"Joanie. I like that name." He looked at the floor. Most of the coffee had run through or soaked into the floorboards. "Well, Joanie, I think it's not so bad. Nothing to clean up, and there's probably more coffee in back, right?"

"Hold on there, pard," Slats said. "We're gonna sit and talk a little."

Boone pointed to his chest and then Slats. "We are?"

"No, asshole, me an' her." He tried to grab Joanie again, but she dodged sideways out of his reach.

"First," Boone said, nudging Joanie behind him. "I'm not your 'pard.' And second, it's not 'me an' her.' That's just sloppy English." He grabbed the empty coffee pot off the table.

Clementine chuckled softly.

"Fuck you, pard. Now send the girl over here."

"You just had a good idea about sitting and talking. I think you ... Slats, is it?"

The asshole nodded.

"You and all your 'pards' here should have a little talk. Put your formidably fat lunky heads together and work out a nice combination of words for a sincere apology to little Joanie here. And while you're at it, maybe a nice group of words for Miss Johanssen over there, since you seem hell-bent on insulting her, too. For no reason, I might add. How long is that likely to take you mushheads? Because I'll order another cup of coffee if it'll be a while."

The four halfwits exchanged glances as if they didn't understand what was happening.

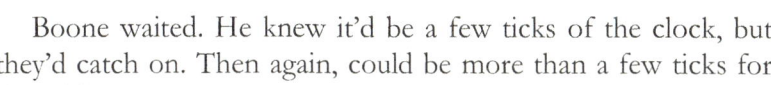

Boone waited. He knew it'd be a few ticks of the clock, but they'd catch on. Then again, could be more than a few ticks for these idiots.

Slats was the first to come around. He stood, his forehead pinched tight. "You think you—"

Boone didn't let him finish his sentence. He pulled up hard with his right knee and caught Slats square in the nuts. Slats bent forward, letting out an *oof!* Boone swung the coffee pot around and smashed it hard into the side of Slats's face. *Clang!* He crumpled to the floor. That was the end of Slats.

"That's one!" shouted Boone.

Cheers and applause filled the dining room.

The other three stood, their chairs flying backward into the surrounding crowded tables. The man nearest took a step toward Boone.

"I should at least know your name," Boone said and then raised the coffee pot to eye level. The man lunged and Boone jabbed the pot quick as lightning right at the man's unprotected nose. *Clank!*

The attacker stopped on the spot and grabbed his nose. Blood gushed between his fingers and down the front of his shirt.

Boone stepped back and kicked out hard, catching the bloodied mess in the stomach, sending him flying backward into the crowd.

"Two down."

Another wave of cheers swept through the dining room.

Wham! Something hard hit Boone on the back of the head. He tumbled forward. He'd barely hit the floorboards when Clementine pulled him up so forcefully that his feet almost came off the floor.

It took a split second to get his bearings, and during that time someone grabbed his arms and pulled them behind him, exposing his torso. One of the two remaining louts appeared from the side and landed a powerful blow to his rib cage, knocking the air from his lungs. Boone gasped for breath. The son of a bitch pulled his arm back for another shot, his fist aimed at Boone's face.

In a flash, a familiar boot swept in from Boone's left and connected with the man's neck. He heard a *crack*. The guy slumped to the floor at his feet and lay there, moaning.

Still trying to draw a good breath, Boone raised his fist high in the air and thrust his elbow back. It landed in his captor's ribs. A huff fanned the hair on the back of Boone's head. The arms holding him went limp. Boone raised his other elbow and spun around, catching the man square in the jaw. Something crunched under the weight of his elbow. His captor stumbled forward, ramming head-first into a chair before hitting the floor.

The dining room was a hell storm now, with several more rough-looking patrons fighting each other. Over what, Boone couldn't tell.

He glanced down at Clementine, who was kneeling next to the man she'd kicked in the neck. Boone grabbed his lucky hat from the floor. "Clementine, we gotta get!" He pulled her upright and nudged her toward the door, pausing on his way out to toss several coins on the counter to cover the cost of their food and some of the damages. Joanie stood behind the counter. She was nodding at the pile of Slats on the floor, a satisfied smile on her face.

Outside the hotel, Boone and Clementine rushed along the boardwalk toward The Pyre.

"Are you hurt?" he asked.

"I wanted to kill him." Her voice was monotone, making him wonder if that was a good or bad thing in her mind.

"But you didn't."

"No."

He tipped his hat as they neared a pair of ladies coming out of the mercantile, slowing and stepping aside to make way for them on the boardwalk. They stared after Clementine with pinched lips.

"She's something, isn't she," he said to the ladies and then caught up with the long-legged hellcat. "Clementine, remind me not to ask you to join me for coffee in the future."

She laughed.

He liked the sound of it. She should laugh more often. "And weren't we talking about stealth?"

"Yes." She stopped in front of The Pyre and pulled out her key. "By the way," she added, her eyes sparkling with amusement. "Your challenge starts over again."

"Dammit!"

Twelve

The next afternoon ...

"Wake up!" Boone squatted next to Rabbit in the livery loft and pinched his nose shut. When Rabbit inhaled a long rattling snore through his mouth, Boone squeezed that shut, too.

The knothead had been sleeping long enough. Boone had been working on reviving Rabbit for half an hour, but so far the mind-numbing qualities of McCuddle's Original Magical Tonic had outmatched him. The damned snake oil had kept a firm grip on Rabbit's sensibilities throughout the morning and then some.

After a few seconds, Rabbit shuddered, swiping at his nose.

Boone dodged the slap and kept his hold. "No, you don't, buckaroo. Wake up!"

Rabbit shook free of Boone's hold and sat bolt upright. He drew his pistol and pointed it at nothing, except his pistol was on the table. "I'll put one right in your—" He stopped, his gaze darting around the loft, and then he tried to focus on Boone's face. "Wha ...?"

"Time to get up, Mr. Minstrel." Boone stood. "It's afternoon. You've been sleeping for three days now."

"Wha ... ?" he repeated, squinting at Boone.

"That all you got, lover boy? 'Wha?' You lose your tongue to that swilly hooch?"

Rabbit shook his head and then winced. "Ooh! That spins a little."

"You're still drunk. Surprised you didn't lose your stomach. Not yet anyway, I suppose. Get up."

"I didn't get drunk. Where are we?"

"Are you joking with me now? We're at The Hacienda Hotel in Santa Fe. You don't remember?"

Rabbit's eyes opened wide. He stared up at Boone. "We're in Santa …"

"You've been having some strange dreams, *amigo*. Talked in your sleep. Mumbled something about monsters. Deadwood. Amazon women. That last one doesn't surprise me since you romanced every woman at the hotel dance."

Rabbit's jaw went slack. He scanned the room around him and then turned back to Boone. "Fucker. Ain't no hay in The Hacienda Hotel."

Boone leaned back and laughed. "Had you for a minute. Hank has some rabbit stew all cooked up on the forge downstairs. Threw in some carrots and spuds. Smells good." Lucky for them, Fred had his vapors under control at present. Much more from the back end of that mule and Boone would be off his supper for a week.

"Stew? You jokin' with me, Booney? I feel like the burnt bottom of a stew pot right now." Rabbit held his head in both his hands.

"They'll be up momentarily to eat with us, so you better put some trousers on." Boone grabbed one of the chairs they'd brought to Hank's loft earlier in the day and dragged it to the table. Then he grabbed another one. "Got enough chairs for everybody now."

Rabbit patted around him on the bed. "I lost my trousers. Who's *they*?"

"You could just stay in your flannels. You apparently don't mind going out in public that way anyway."

"Booney, I surely do wish you'd stop fuckin' with me."

"I'm sure Clementine won't mind. She's seen worse, I'd wager." Boone pointed toward the end of the bed. "Your pants."

"Miss Clementine?" Rabbit squeezed his eyes shut and opened them wide.

"She's downstairs with Hank. Like I said, they'll be up directly with that stew."

Rabbit threw the blankets toward his feet. He popped out of bed and immediately began to tilt to the right. He hunched over, spreading his hands out and down toward the ground as if he could steady the world around him. "Hold still."

"Easy, Mr. Minstrel. Maybe you should crawl."

Rabbit grabbed his trousers and jammed one leg in and then the other, almost tipping over each time. "Why do you keep calling me 'Mr. Minstrel'?"

"On account of your vocal prowess. And your dancing isn't bad either."

"Booney, if I didn't have a church bell clangin' in my head, I'd wallop you upside yours."

"You'd try. Why don't you sit and recollect your run to Galena. Clementine will want to hear it, and Hank has been close lipped, waiting for you to wake up, Mr. Winkle."

Rabbit dropped into a chair and nestled his head into his folded arms on the table. "Okay, tell me. Who's Mr. Winkle?"

"Rip Van Winkle. Read a little now and then."

"Fuck you."

Boone sank into the chair next to him. It was becoming obvious that Rabbit wasn't in the mood to be tormented. Unfortunately for Rabbit, Boone was in the mood to do just that.

"Do you recollect anything that happened this morning? Or last night, for that matter?"

Rabbit looked at him with his good but bloodshot eye, and then he slowly shook his head.

"This should be good, then."

"Goddammit, Booney."

Boone chuckled. "Do you remember anything about Galena?"

"Yes, I remember *anything* about Galena, snapperhead." Boone recognized the tone in Rabbit's voice. It was the same huffy tone he used when Uncle Morton chided him for wasting time catching frogs in the pond instead of slopping the hogs or graining the chickens.

It made Boone smile. "Uncle Morton would tan your hide, you talk to him like that."

Rabbit's mouth curved up in a cockeyed smile. " 'Member when I tried stuffin' hay down the back of my pants so the lickin' wouldn't tarnish my goods so bad? Made Uncle Mort laugh so hard he couldn't catch his breath. Said, 'You wanna look like a scarecrow, git out in that bean field and start pluckin' weeds. Scare them birds off.' " Rabbit snorted. "Can't even remember what the lickin' was for."

Boone nodded. "Those were good times. Didn't know it at the time."

"Didn't get the lickin', though." Rabbit's smile held a dose of sadness.

"Never was that bad anyway. Uncle Morton talked like he was mean, but he wasn't. Did a lot of talking, though."

"More talkin' than beatin'."

Not anymore, a voice said in Boone's head. He shook it away.

"Boonedock!" Hank called from the bottom of the stairs. "Come rope this stewpot up."

* * *

"This rabbit stew smells so good, Hank." Clementine leaned over the tin pot sitting on the rough-cut table and took another whiff of the stew. "All I need is a hunk of bread for dipping."

"Wish it had more rabbit in it, but that second little bugger got lucky, eh Jack Rabbit?"

Clementine had been pacing the floor of her parlor since the two men had returned from Galena last evening. Jack had eaten and gone straight to bed with a headache. After stowing the wagon and bedding down Fred the Mule in the livery, Hank had filled Clementine in on the trip but included remarkably few details. They'd delivered their freight. Fine. They'd gone hunting. Fine. They'd found a gated mine with something interesting inside. Not fine. Then he'd mumbled something about needing a drink and disappeared into the throng of humanity filling the streets.

"I wish you'd tell me more about your trip to Galena, Hank," she said as she blew on a spoonful of stew. "I don't understand why we needed to wait for Jack to wake up."

"No intent to be shifty, but best that we waited, Miss Clem. I'd surely be disinclined to misinform you or leave somethin' out in the tellin'. It was best to wait."

Huh. Hank could be as stubborn as her amma during an Old German lesson. It was pointless to badger him. She dumped her spoon in her mouth, savoring the salty broth, soft potatoes and carrots, and chewy meat. Hank sure knew his way around a good stew.

"All right, but Jack is awake for the most part. Tell me now."

"I'd rather Booney tell me why he keeps calling me 'Mr. Minstrel,' " Jack grumbled from the chair next to her where he leaned his head on one hand while stirring his steaming bowl of stew with the other.

"He doesn't remember anything?" Clementine questioned Boone and Hank. They both shook their heads.

"What's the last thing you remember, Jack Rabbit?" Hank tore a hunk of bread from the crusty loaf and handed it to Boone.

Jack squinted one eye. "Let's see. Last night, I came up here with Booney after dinner. Couldn't sleep." He poked gingerly at

his head. "Headache. Prescribed myself a dose of McCuddle's and got into bed." He scratched his jaw. "That's it, I think."

Boone smirked. "You don't remember anything from this morning?"

Jack resumed stirring. "No ... wait. Maybe ..." He stared intently at his stew. "Seems I mighta gotten up this morning early, still had a knockin' noggin, so I took another sip."

"A sip? Or a swig? You told me to sip it. Remember?"

"Don't reckon I recall. Thought the sip last night might need some reinforcement this mornin'."

"You don't remember getting out of bed in nothing but your flannels?" Clementine asked.

They all snickered except Jack, who glared at Boone.

"Booney, you fucker. Wasn't sleepin' no three days. Always gotta be messin' with me."

Boone continued to chuckle. "Maybe think twice on that magical tonic next time."

Hank dipped a hunk of bread into the steaming bowl of gravy, meat, and vegetables. "Nice flannels, Jack Rabbit. 'Course, red sticks out a little. And you're missin' a button on yer trap door. Part of one cheek keeps peekin' out."

A wave of laughter welled up again for all but poor Jack.

"Okay, you pie eaters," the odd man out growled. "Spill the bucket."

"You want to tell him, Hank?" Clementine was more interested in watching Jack's reaction to the story as it unfolded.

"Surely." Hank stuffed the stew-soaked hunk of bread into his mouth. "You were a sight, Jack Rabbit," he slurred around the mouthful of bread. "Miss Clem and me saw the whole thing. I was sweepin' the porch in front of The Pyre. Way down yonder in the Badlands, I heard a commotion fit to wake the bears in the hills. Thought it might be a dust-up or some such, but then the music got rollin'."

"Music?" Jack stuffed a hunk of potato into his mouth.

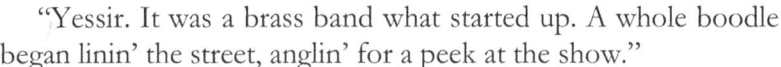

"Yessir. It was a brass band what started up. A whole boodle began linin' the street, anglin' for a peek at the show."

"It was a parade." Boone sipped his coffee, his eyes full of mirth.

"Yes, indeed," Hank said, slurping a spoonful of stew. "It was one of them fancy-type processions they have back east. Come up the street. Band playin'. Mayor Farnum in a swanky buggy, standin' and wavin' at ever'one."

"What's this got to do with me and my tonic?"

"Gettin' there, Jack Rabbit." Hank wiped his mouth with his sleeve, grabbed his coffee tin, and sat back. "I rushed inside The Pyre, told Miss Clem to put a coat on an' come watch the procession—well, *parade* is what Boonedock calls it—workin' its way up the street." Hank started to snigger, his whole body shaking. "Hoo hoo. I can't tell no more. Miss Clem, you tell it."

"Happy to, Hank." She pushed aside her empty bowl, rubbing her hands together. "We were watching the parade when all of a sudden a nearly naked man leapt up into the mayor's buggy. He stood up tall right next to the mayor and saluted him, then stuck out his hand for a shake."

Jack scowled. "I still don't see—"

"Keep listening and I'll tell you," she cut him off. A bubble of laughter escaped before Clementine could stop it. "The mayor looked like he was seeing a ghost, but he stuck out his hand anyway. The bushwhacker took it and pumped it like he'd grabbed a hold of a snake and was trying to shake it to death."

Boone laugh-snorted, spilling a bit of his coffee.

"Then the crazy rooster started dancing to the brass band. He kept hold of the mayor's hand and began to dance with him."

"Texas two-step," Boone said, wiping off his trouser leg with a handkerchief.

"Hoo hoo!" Hank slapped the table, making the bowls and cups rattle. "Bushwhacked the mayor in his buggy. That was a sight!"

Jack squinted at Boone. "'Texas two-step,' you say?"

Boone grinned. "That's not the all of it. The bushwhacker noticed a few calico queens singing and dancing to the band up on the balcony at the Diamond Belle."

Jack rubbed his head, his whole face lined in one big cringe. "Four girls, was it?"

"Yep. Mind if I continue the tale?" Boone asked Clementine, who ushered him onward. "Bushwhacker hopped down from the mayor's buggy, slipped and fell on his bare ass, jumped back up, and climbed onto a horse. Then the son of a gun stood on the saddle and climbed the porch post like a coon after an apple. He was on the balcony with the girls in no time."

Jack scratched his jaw. "Pretty spry, sounds like."

Boone's shoulders shook as he grinned at Jack. "This Romeo proceeded to bend each girl over backward, one by one, and kiss them. When he was done romancing those sage hens, he started dancing the two-step again, all the while singing 'My Old Kentucky Home' as loud as he could."

Rabbit looked at his lap. "That's a good song."

"Sure is, *amigo*, but it wasn't the song the band was playing."

"Ho ho! Comin' to you now, Jack Rabbit?"

"Yeah," he said sheepishly. "Might have a recollection or two." His cheeks were blushed in dark pink. "Ginger and Toula. Don't remember the other two."

"I sent Hank to fetch you," Clementine told him between giggles. "By the time he got up to the balcony, you were on the floorboards."

"Out cold," Hank added, holding his belly as he laughed. "Girls tried to wake you up but they couldn't. Them doves kept callin' you Sidewinder. Said they'd be happy to nurse you back to your right mind."

"Sidewinder." Grimacing, Jack straightened his back and stretched his arms high. "Mighta mentioned that, I suppose."

"They sure was sweet on you after all of that kissin'." Hank made a smooching face and kissed the air a few times, inspiring a fresh burst of laughter from Clementine and Boone. "I carried you back here to sleep it off. Boonedock helped git you up the stairs there."

"Think that will make the next news sheet?" Clementine asked, wiping the tears from the corners of her eyes. She should be chastising the Sidewinder, but it was all so funny that it didn't seem worth getting excited about right yet.

Jack sniffed. "Boone screwed up your challenge when he got in that fight at the café." He pointed at her. "Seems I remember hearing you were more than willin' to partake in that scuffle, too."

"Clementine didn't step in until I was in the thick of it and you're changing the subject." Boone leaned forward, sobering as he stared at Jack. "Lay off the tonic, *amigo*."

"It's helpin' me heal up," Jack said.

"Might be it was Clementine's help, not that snake oil."

"Right. That too."

"Don't be a knucklehead. That tonic is not magical."

Jack's chin jutted. "You don't know."

"I know what it looks like when you make an ass of yourself."

Thor's thunder! Clementine needed to rein in this squawking hen party before feathers started flying. She returned to the question that had been burning in her mind since last evening. "What happened during your trip to Galena?"

Jack turned to her, his brow wrinkled. "Hank didn't tell you?"

"Thought the story would be better if'n we was both tellin' it," Hank answered.

"Why don't you start," Jack told him, picking up his coffee cup. "I don't feel like waggin' my chin much yet."

Hank spilled the story of what sounded like two men on an uneventful trip to deliver supplies. Jack had nothing to say about it until Hank began describing a massive iron gate protecting a mine they'd come across near Galena, and then he paused and looked at Jack.

"We came across another beastie," Jack told her. "It was locked away in that mine, but there's more." His story about shackles and body parts had her lowering her cup to the table.

"Those poor souls," she whispered.

His description of the attempted attack through the iron bars by a creature that had no business being in this realm made her mind whirl with questions. Was the gate keeping the creature in? Or was it keeping other things out? Was the beast protecting something? Was there another gate deeper inside the earth? Was this mine similar to the Bloody Bones, providing an opportunity for *others* to travel where they were not allowed?

Boone tapped his fingers against his cup. "Was the creature similar to what we faced the first time we rode into Deadwood?"

Jack shook his head. "This one had smooth scales, like snake skin sorta."

"Tell 'em about the teeth, Jack Rabbit."

"Long and sharp. Four inches or so, don't ya think?"

Hank nodded. "Them claws stuck in my boot was prob'ly that long, plus a little more."

"You shot at it?" Boone leaned his elbows on the table.

"Yep. Hit it, too, at least once," Jack said. "In the hand, or paw, or whatever that devil has. Emptied my pistol into it. So did Hank. No way we didn't hit it at least a couple more times."

"So, it retreated into the mine when you two fired at it." Clementine was a little surprised that bullets were able to make the creature back off. Maybe it was the sound of the gunfire as much as the bullets, which would be especially loud echoing through a cave. "The two of you are very lucky."

Jack nodded. "I think we sank a lot of lead into it, but we didn't kill it."

"Nope." Hank tapped his spoon on the table. "When we was heading out, I was busy drivin' Ol' Fred through some precarious terrain with one cold foot, but Jack Rabbit thinks he saw it a few times. Following us, it was. Had Ol' Fred keepin' the pace up pretty good."

"Wish I'd had my Sharps."

"I'm not sure that would have helped," Clementine told him.

"Suppose you're right. But it woulda made me feel better."

Clementine looked across at Boone and found him watching her as he sipped his coffee. She had a feeling he was waiting to see what her reaction to this news would be. Or hear her decision on what to do about it. Or both.

"What do ya think, Miss Clem?" Hank stared at her, too, now.

Galena. She hadn't been there yet, only heard about it. Guess it was time to take a cold ride on Fenrir over that way and investigate the mine Jack and Hank described.

But what of Masterson? He hadn't expressly forbidden her from Galena, but it was certainly possible that the goings-on in Galena were somehow part of Masterson's overall plan. How would he feel about her conducting business there? Then again, what did his opinion matter if there were a threat that needed to be removed?

Maybe this creature had something to do with the *Emporkömmling*, as Hildegard called him. What had Hank overheard the Upstart say the first night Boone and Jack were back in town? Something about having Galena under their control?

"I don't know, Hank." She looked from Boone to Jack, holding her cards close to her vest. "I'll have to ponder on it for a bit."

How soon could she set out for Galena? More importantly, should she take the three of them on the hunt with her and risk their lives, or go it alone like she always had before?

Thirteen

A few days after that ...

Rabbit watched as Boone slowly turned the pages of a small booklet he held flat on the table.

"What's that, Booney?" Lounging back in his chair, Rabbit kicked up his boots on the bale of hay he'd dragged closer to the table.

" 'The Celebrated Jumping Frog of Calaveras County.' "

Rabbit pulled his pistol and slowly turned the cylinder. *Click, click, click.*

Boone continued reading.

"Done with all that highbrow literture then?" *Click, click.*

Boone shifted in his chair and glanced at Rabbit. Anyone else would have missed the subtle squinty-eyed look Boone gave him, but Rabbit didn't.

Click, click, click, click.

"Literature," Boone corrected without looking up from the pages of the book. He propped his elbow on the table and cradled his chin in his hand, an obvious attempt to concentrate on what he was reading.

"Thought you said it was somethin' about a frog."

Click, click.

" 'The Celebrated Jumping Frog of Calaveras County.' Mark

Twain."

"Sounds kinda light-minded for you. Frogs jumpin' around and all." *Click, click, click.*

Boone's eye twitched.

"Now take pirates." *Click, click, click, click.* "Pirates is somethin' you—"

"Rabbit! I'll string you up for the coyotes if you keep rolling that cylinder."

Rabbit grinned. "I think I need a drink. Wanna head on down to Yellow Strike and grab one with me? Maybe we can talk some more with Ol' One Horn."

"No. We'll wait and talk to him when Clementine is ready."

Rabbit spun the pistol this way and that on his index finger. "Ain't seen no coyotes around these parts. Reckon there must be. Coyotes are clever. Live anywhere, seems to me."

Boone closed the book, sat back, and stared at Rabbit.

Holstering his pistol, Rabbit folded his arms behind his head. "I like it here."

"What? In the loft?" Boone stuck his hands inside his sheepskin coat. "Too cold."

Rabbit ignored the gravel in Boone's voice. "With the forge down there and all that horse meat on the hoof, seems pretty warm to me."

With the additions and changes to the loft made by the three of them—him, Boone, and Hank—Rabbit figured Keller's Livery was becoming a passable comfort. Blankets of any sort were practically impossible to come by in this overcrowded, underprovisioned little burg, but Hank had somehow appropriated a cart full. From where, only Hank and Jehoshaphat knew.

They'd built rough straw-and-blanket beds framed with scrap lumber Hank had been storing out back of The Pyre.

He and Boone both had readily taken to cooking beans and hunks of meat in Hank's huge iron skillet nestled in the coals of the livery forge. Rabbit was continually impressed with Hank's ability to procure vittles—a slab of beef, a bag of potatoes or carrots. He managed a tin of salt or pepper or sage for the savories and even sugar every now and then for the gritty coffee Boone cooked up. According to Hank, taters weren't worth eatin' without a little sage-n-salt and pork fat. "Put some flavor to it," he'd say.

With Boone's cooking and Hank's steady supply of vittles, they ate surprisingly well, and so did Keller. Miss Clementine had even joined them for a few meals. *Eatin' good, sleepin' good.* Hell, he was downright comfortable.

"Say, you think Miss Clementine is thinkin' on makin' a visit to Galena?"

"I believe she is."

"Hasn't mentioned it. Thought she woulda mentioned it." Rabbit couldn't help but feel at least a little betrayed at the notion of her not including them. "Thought we were a posse."

"Not yet, I think." Boone crossed his arms. "We haven't even completed her first challenge."

"To hell with that challenge. Don't it seem this two-days shit is a thing you tell a small fry? 'Wash the dishes, you'll get a chunk of sugar.' Before you know it, she'll have us playin' Bo-Peep or some such nonsense."

Boone raised his eyebrows.

"Aw hell, Booney. Don't start huffin'. I'm just jawin' is all."

"I'm not *huffin'*," Boone said flatly. "But you and me, we might have different ideas on why we're here."

"Maybe, but I'm not sure I'm ridin' along with that confounded challenge no how." Rabbit bobbled his head at the idea.

It'd been over a week since Clementine had issued her challenge to him and Boone, and they'd twice almost completed the two-day test. Almost. But between the two of them, they couldn't seem to keep from becoming a scene, one way or another, sooner or later. It'd be spring before they went two days without causing a ruckus—according to Clementine, anyway.

According to Rabbit, though, his days were like a smooth rolling freight wagon on a sunny day. He almost had Boone convinced that buying a livery was the smart play. At least he was pretty sure he almost had him convinced. They were eating good. He'd made a few acquaintances, mostly female, in the saloons and theaters along Main Street. Better yet, he'd found a good friend in Hank, and probably Clementine, too.

Yep, Deadwood was one big, never-ending *fandango* for Rabbit. Santa Fe was home, but it didn't compare to the excitement of Deadwood.

"You ever give a thought maybe there's something more to that test of hers?" Boone's question brought Rabbit's attention back from its wander.

Rabbit studied Boone for a moment. The fact that Miss Clementine was forcing them to prove they could abstain from ruckus chafed at his patience, and now Boone was offering the idea that there might be something more to it. Wasn't it enough that she wanted them to cower like newborn pups in the corner?

"Like what? Like maybe we put on skirts and work at the café. Maybe we collect laundry and wash it clean for all the fine gentlemen in this here burg."

"Huh?" Boone looked at him like Rabbit had been tipping the magical tonic again. "Skirts? Where do you come up with this shit? Never mind. I'm only thinking out loud. Might be there's something else she's trying to find out about us. Like maybe testing to see if we're ready up here." He pointed at his head. "See if we maybe decide to call it quits and head back south."

"Well, I don't need no testin'!"

"Take the simmer out of it for a spell, Mr. Chile Pepper. The stakes are different now. All we've done. All we've seen. Road agents. Scofflaws."

Rabbit shook his finger at Boone. "Fuckin' Pinkertons."

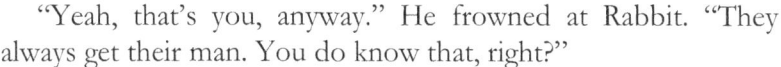

"Yeah, that's you, anyway." He frowned at Rabbit. "They always get their man. You do know that, right?"

"I know, I know. I'll probably be dealin' with that foot stomper sooner or later. Chase me up here, though? Maybe not."

"Nevertheless, we've come up against some real outlaws and always come out ahead. If we stay this course there's no doubt we'll be coming up against things that aren't normal in this world. Nasty things that would just as soon see us dead."

"Like Uncle Mort." The image of his uncle's torn body and dead eyes flashed in Rabbit's mind. He quickly shooed it away. Boone always did have a way of bringing reckoning to the table.

"You strong on the thought we should head home then?" Rabbit asked. "Back to Santa Fe? Back to drayage and ranchin'? Mind our business and let them that's equipped handle things here?"

Boone slowly shook his head. "I don't see how we could. Do you?"

"Nope. Miss Clementine and Hank. Don't need no other reasons."

"That's right. But we have other reasons, too. The way Clementine tells it, if we let these beasts roam, and more get out and spread, then we got bigger trouble."

Rabbit stood, breathing in deep. "I'm with ya, Booney." He punched Boone on the shoulder, hard, but not too hard. "I'll be there to pull your ass from the fire, don't go frettin' it."

Boone laughed. "Jackass. You might remember, somebody in this loft not named Boone got worked over like a stolen mule not too many days ago."

Rabbit touched his almost healed purple and yellow temple. It still ached a little. "Don't recollect any such."

"Yeah, I don't imagine you would."

Rabbit looked up and around the rafters of the livery. "Built strong, not like that smoke shed you built out by Uncle Mort's butcher shack."

Boone dropped his chin and shook his head. "Here we go."

"Dust devil took it right down, didn't it? Two pigs' worth of pork in it." Rabbit laughed so hard at the memory that he snorted.

Boone grinned. "You sound like that pet hog of yours. You're forgetting he was on the rough from eating those fermented apricots. Damned pig helped some in taking down that shed. You remember that?"

The main door to the livery creaked open and slammed against the wall.

"Boonedock! Jack Rabbit!" Hank hollered from downstairs.

"Up here, Hank!" Rabbit hustled over to the narrow stairs and looked down. The urgency in Hank's voice put a giddy-up in Rabbit's step.

Hank shot up the steps and into the loft, almost ramming into Rabbit, who dodged at the last moment. Hank blasted over to the table, panting as he faced Boone.

Rabbit shrugged at Boone's questioning look.

"You boys ..." Hank bent over and put his hands on his knees, still panting, "... got to get ... your gear!"

"Hank, what's wrong?" Rabbit asked.

"Miss Clem," he wheezed.

Boone shot to his feet. "What about her? Is she hurt? Does she need help?"

"She's gone!"

"What? Gone?" A rock sank in Rabbit's stomach. It can't be. Surely he didn't mean ... *dead?* Rabbit led Hank to a chair.

Boone turned his own chair so he sat directly in front of Hank. "Tell us what happened. What do you mean, 'gone'?"

Hank reached into his pocket and withdrew a crinkled piece of paper. He held it out to Boone.

Rabbit studied Hank's face. Wide eyes and red blotchy cheeks. Another rock dropped in Rabbit's stomach.

Boone began to read from the crinkled paper:

Hank,

I've decided an investigation of Galena is in order.

Don't follow.

Please take care of Tinker until I return tomorrow.

Also, it would be best if you failed to mention this to the Sidewinders.

Clementine

The three of them were silent for some moments. Hank's panting was the only sound other than the occasional nicker or shuffle of hooves from below in the livery.

Finally, Rabbit broke the silence. "Didn't waste no words cuttin' down her posse, did she?"

"When did she leave?" Boone asked Hank.

"Don't know for sure. Prob'ly two, maybe three hours ago."

"Sheeat." Rabbit kicked an empty chair, sending it tumbling.

Frowning, Hank wrung his hands. "I was down to my claim. Came back to see Miss Clem at The Pyre. Thought she might use some help, but she was gone. Left the note on her desk."

The angst in Hank's voice tugged at Rabbit's heartstrings. He patted the older man's shoulder. "Ain't your fault, Hank. That woman has too much stubborn in her. We could spread it around to a herd of burros."

"That's so," Boone chimed in.

"You boys ain't lyin'. But I gotta get after her. She may need me. Wanted to stop by and give you the chance to come along, if'n yer inclined."

Boone looked at Rabbit and nodded once.

Rabbit nodded back. "She's got three hours on us, you say?"

"Pert near. Prob'ly. I got all my needs down below. Bow, pistol and ammo, some grub an' such. I'll get Nickel and Dime saddled if you boys wanna collect yourselves. Might be out fer a couple nights. Might be we have us a run-in."

"Galena." Rabbit frowned at Boone. He holstered his sawed-off and started plugging his customized bandoleer with shells and shotgun cartridges from his saddlebags.

Hank disappeared down the stairs as Rabbit grabbed his sheepskin coat and mittens. "Get movin', Booney!"

Boone was standing but not moving. "I was just thinking."

"Stop thinkin' and move." Why did Boone always have to think a thing into the ground?

"Have you considered Clementine may have some reason she doesn't want Hank or us there? We might turn into liabilities. Get in her way. We don't know."

Rabbit stopped stuffing jerky into his saddlebags to stare at Boone. "You mean to tell me you're willin' to stand there and think about whether you're ridin' out?" He snorted. "Well, if that don't beat all. Miss Clementine could be in the dire right now, and there you stand, thinkin'." He returned to packing the rest of the jerky and then started in on the boxes of shells he'd been storing next to his bed.

Boone held up his hands. "All right. But we got to be smart about things now. We can't—"

"Comin'?" Rabbit grabbed his bags and headed for the stairs.

"Never mind." Boone trailed off into a mumbling rant as Rabbit hit the first step, saying something about "half-cocked *compadres*."

Hank had both horses and Fred the Mule out of their stalls and saddled by the time Rabbit reached the ground. Nickel appeared to have picked up on Hank's urgency and was snorting and nickering and pawing at the ground. Dime joined in as soon as he saw Rabbit. Fred chewed on a mouthful of grain and watched Hank finish up cinching Nickel's saddle. Tinker stood next to Hank, her tail wagging as she looked up at the horses.

"How do, Karl," Rabbit said to the livery owner who watched Hank from a nearby stall rail, a familiar makeshift leash in his hand.

"Afternoon, Jack." Karl Keller wiped his hands on a rag before taking Rabbit's outstretched hand.

Tinker came run-hopping over. Rabbit knelt to scrub her back. The pup licked his hand and then walk-hopped into Dime and Nickel's open stall, snuffling through the straw-littered floor.

"I see Hank has saddled you with Tink already."

Keller looked at Tinker, who was digging away in the straw now. "Not a problem. I'm partial to dogs, and she's a good one, seems like. A real hoot, hoppin' around on that one back leg." He smiled. "Maybe she can catch those damn rats that've been chewin' my bridles."

"Howdy, Karl." Boone descended the stairs and joined Rabbit beside Keller.

"Boone." He took Boone's hand and shook it hard. "Jack here got you convinced? Money invested well is well-spent money, my daddy always said. Lot next door included, wagons and all. I'll put the cost of your uncle's wagon and team toward the price."

Rabbit watched Boone's expression as Keller's words sank in. *Almost convinced, more like.*

"Working on the details, Karl," Boone answered. "It's a heavy price. Not that I fault you for that. Deadwood booming the way it is, only fair a building such as this should fetch a worthy price."

"I'll get him there, Keller." Rabbit moved over to Dime while buttoning his coat. "Just don't sell to no one else in the meantime."

Boone grinned. "Mr. Negotiator over there."

"Shut up, Boone." Rabbit plopped his saddlebags on Dime's rump.

"So, you're good with Tinker for a day or two?" Boone followed Rabbit's lead and threw his pack onto Nickel.

"No problem." Keller followed Tinker into the stall, talking softly to the dog while holding the leash out to lasso her.

Boone moved closer to Rabbit, speaking low, "Doesn't make

much sense, does it, running off without us like that?"

"Nope." Rabbit cinched his gear tight behind the saddle on Dime's back.

"She'll get herself killed is what she'll do." Boone finished securing his pack to Nickel.

"Don't talk thatta way, Boonedock." Hank joined them, hefting his substantial pack onto Fred, who grunted under its weight. "We'll be there directly. I know a shortcut."

Rabbit had a feeling Hank knew shortcuts all over the West.

"You fellas know what you're doin'?" Keller had returned with Tinker, who was trying to tie knots around his legs with the leash. "Looks like a storm's a-comin' and the sun's on its way down. Dark probably by the time you get to Galena."

"Thanks for your concern, Keller," Boone said. "We'll manage along." The grimace on his face showed less confidence than his words, though.

"We'll take Hank's shortcut," Rabbit added.

Hank grunted. "My thinkin' too." He opened the door to the livery and led Fred out with Rabbit and Boone following behind.

"All righty, Hank," Keller said from the doorway. "Take care of these boys. I'd hate to see the new owners of the livery dead before they even signed the papers." He laughed, waved, and closed the doors behind them.

Rabbit scowled at Boone, thinking about that beast behind bars in the mine near Galena. "That wasn't funny."

"Yeah. It is funny," Boone said, climbing onto Nickel.

Rabbit hopped onto Dime. "How's that?"

"He thinks we're buying that livery." He turned to Hank. "Let's hit the trail."

Fourteen

Fenrir's long, muscular legs made easy work of the trail to Galena, leaving Clementine free to enjoy the view from high up on the Morgan's strong back. The horse whinnied now and then in response to Clementine's rhetorical questions, and snorted when she wanted a break to rest and stick her muzzle in the feedbag.

Clementine hadn't been to the tiny mining town, but after hearing plenty of Hank's stories over the last few months, she felt as if she knew the place. Except for the presence of the *capersus* cult, it didn't sound any different than the multitude of other mining camps that had popped up in the Black Hills.

The terrain was certainly the same. Long, wiggly ridges joined and then split randomly across the countryside. Large pine trees jutted from the deep snow like a thick set of quills from a porcupine's back. Shallow valleys divided the ridgelines here and there, while streams cut deep through others. Periodically, she could hear the sound of water gurgling under the snow.

As she cleared a group of pines, she scanned the hillsides and craggy ridges. In the late afternoon sunshine, the snow sparkled like millions of stars on a moonless night. The sight took her breath away ... or maybe that was the freezing wind that had hit her as soon as Fenrir had stepped out into the clearing.

Enchanting beauty aside, she was under no illusions here. Monstrosities had been set loose and her duty was to rid the Hills of their foulness. She was, fundamentally, a merchant of death.

Listen to yourself, a voice in her head chided. *Merchant of death? Have we slipped back into the Dark Ages? What next?* She laughed. "Maybe we'll battle a dragon, right, Fenrir?"

The horse bobbed her head with each step and neighed.

Clementine drew her dagger from its sheath at her calf and held it high. "I will slay yon dragon with icy cold steel, oh brave Fenrir. I will slice flesh from bone with a blade of reckoning. I will lay bare the length of its spine and rend head from body with naught but these two hands." She laughed again, louder this time. It echoed off the sides of the gulch.

Fenrir craned her neck and with one eye held her gaze on Clementine for a moment before turning her attention forward again.

"Ahhh, I see. You fear I'll alert to our presence the very beasts of which I speak. You may be right, my friend." She leaned down and patted Fenrir on the side of the neck. "But allow me the occasional random soliloquy, won't you? I promise not to turn into Don Quixote and begin tilting at windmills, although I might prefer to battle Quixote's imaginary ferocious giants rather than tricksters the likes of Masterson and his foes."

As they continued along, Clementine's thoughts returned to the conversation she'd had with Hildegard earlier about Galena. The madam had sneaked to The Pyre before dawn, shrouded in a long cloak that hid her white hair and everything south of it.

Clementine had been awake when Hildegard knocked, working on a corpse that had thawed enough for her to make proper preparations for the old man's journey to the afterlife. This one had no tattoos or brands, only the usual signs of malnourishment and tuberculosis.

Hildegard's visit had been short and sweet. She'd spoken of

several troubling realities, but one in particular had spurred Clementine to pack enough food and gear for a couple of days and head for Galena without even waiting for Hank to show up for their usual breakfast of biscuits, coffee, and gab.

Children.

Clementine shook her head in disgust.

Days ago, Clementine had told Hildegard about Hank and Jack's discovery in Galena. The madam had sent Ludek to investigate Galena more thoroughly. He'd located the mine, but found it secured with thick iron bars and what looked to be a new, heavy iron lock.

But that wasn't what had Clementine rushing into battle.

According to Hildegard, Ludek had returned from Galena during the night with disturbing news. Deducing from his description of the ample signs of struggles and activity at the entrance of the mine, and taking into account Hank's and Jack's descriptions of the beast that tried to attack them, Clementine reckoned that she would be facing a *Höhlendrache* before the night was through.

Furthermore, she and Hildegard now suspected the mine was a gateway, same as the Bloody Bones.

Clementine shifted in her saddle, easing a small ache in her lower back. It'd been awhile since she'd ridden this far over rough terrain. She scouted the hillsides as they rounded a bend, searching for signs of civilization, but found nothing. The wind made it hard to hear anything other than Fenrir and her own breathing.

In Ludek's estimation, Hildegard had told her, someone had been feeding or sacrificing humans to whatever was inside the gate. However, the remains of the victims that Ludek found were not those of adults. The features were too small.

Too small.

Hildegard hadn't asked Ludek for further details on that part of his report. She couldn't bear to hear it. Her eyes had filled with tears when she'd told Clementine about it.

Children!

"What kind of sick bastard could do such a thing?" she asked Fenrir. Was the French swordsman in the tricorn hat behind this? According to Ludek, his name was Augustine and he'd only recently arrived in the Hills, which made Clementine wonder if someone had brought him here or if he were here of his own accord.

The horse bobbed her head again, and then pushed onward through a deeper patch of snow.

The thought of what was happening in this new town had Clementine bristling to take up her weapons. Ludek's news solidified her resolve to cleanse Galena of the pestilence that besieged the mining camp. Unfortunately, the same flare of temper that had spurred her to head out for Galena immediately had also distracted her from proper planning for the trip. In her haste, she'd left a couple of things behind, including a spare pair of gloves.

She scanned the shadows under the canopy of evergreen branches that were drooping low with loads of snow. She would welcome open conflict to subterfuge while traveling out in the open like she was, this or any day.

Shortly, they came across a trail well traveled by wheels and hooves. Galena was near. Fenrir's hooves thumped dully in the compacted snow and frozen mud. Another cold blast pushed them to the side.

Fenrir snorted and huffed.

"I know, and I'm not happy about it either, but someone has to take care of this problem before any other children are sacrificed." Clementine cringed in the wake of another stiff wind. "If it's any consolation, you're not the only one upset with me. I'm sure Hank has discovered my absence by now and is angry, worried, or disappointed in me. Or all three." She leaned into another gust, thinking about Hank and how she'd come to enjoy the steadiness of his friendship day after day. "He's a remarkable man, isn't he?"

Fenrir nickered as if she understood the question and agreed.

"A true Renaissance man. He has the uncanny ability to know what I need and when I need it. Even before I need it." She pondered that for a few hoofbeats. "Peculiar, don't you think? Yet trustworthy to a fault."

Fenrir's ears pricked forward. She let out a short, bold neigh.

"I agree. He's a diamond in the rough here in the Hills."

Clementine pulled an apple from her haversack and bit a chunk from it. "I probably should have brought him along."

She'd been second-guessing her decision to leave him behind since she'd left Deadwood. "But if something happened to him, I'd never forgive myself." From what she'd learned from her afi about a *Höhlendrache,* it was a formidable opponent for most slayers.

Her decision not to invite Boone and Jack was still sound. The Sidewinders weren't ready. Or at least she didn't think they were. There was no way she was going to spend the rest of her days having their deaths on her conscience.

"Why do I even care, Fenrir?" Was she becoming soft and frail with age? She thought about that for a moment and then dismissed the idea. No, frailty was not one of her weaknesses. Kindness, however, seemed to keep uprooting her sensibilities. There was a time not so long ago that she wouldn't have allowed anyone to come too close. She'd learned the hard way early on in her travels the strength of one and the weakness of many in her line of work. Death was a way of life for a slayer. Affairs of the heart, no matter the duration or intensity, were a way of death.

"But those two boys do make me laugh." The lightness they brought along with them was addictive. Although they were impulsive at times, periodically to the danger of their own health. Yet they were kind. Hotheaded, certainly, but so was she at times. Compassionate too, especially when it came to their uncle and their animals. A distraction, for sure, each in their own way. Rabbit with his guns and Boone with his ...

"Enough," she growled under her breath and tried to push thoughts of the two from her mind.

The sparkly snow around her turned gray. She looked up at the sky. Dark clouds churned, blotting out the sun.

"Well, Fenrir, those clouds intend to keep us in Galena tonight, I'd wager. Let's hope the citizens there are more friendly than those in Gayville, but if Jack and Hank are correct, it's unlikely."

A tiny snowflake struck her cheek.

That felt more like ice than snow. She looked up again to see the beginning of the fall—millions of tiny white dots swirled downward gracefully, as if dancing on the wind. An icy gust buffeted the two of them.

Fenrir lowered her head against it and whinnied.

Clementine squeezed her arms to her torso against the cold fingers of air creeping through the seams of her coat. "Great," she told the horse. "Apparently it wasn't cold enough already."

Fenrir plodded on through the gathering blustery snowstorm, past cabins and tents spread along the creek to a cluster of log shacks and more tents with no discernible roads between. This camp was larger than Gayville, but not by much.

As she neared the small town buildings ... a livery, an assay office, and a mercantile, to name a few ramshackle structures ... it became obvious which building served as the local gathering place for the residents of Galena. A somewhat larger log building sat apart from the others at the base of a rock escarpment at the far end of town.

As she drew closer, she reined in Fenrir under a group of low pines next to the livery. Out of the wind and snow, Clementine took stock of the saloon, including the able-bodied souls being swallowed into its warm innards as well as the drunken retches being disgorged into the blowing snow. Two rough-cut windows framed the door, but were too dirty to see through, especially at a distance. The steady rumble of conversation could be heard each time the door opened, silence falling along with the snow when it closed.

"Best to determine the lay of the land first, Fenrir. Besides, I think I'll have more success at the mine at dusk, when the light is failing." Thanks to this storm, nightfall would come a little sooner. From her estimation, she had about three hours until she needed to be at the mine.

After watching the saloon for a few more minutes, she tucked her braid underneath her wool coat. Then she loosened the flaps on her beaver cap, pulling them down over her ears. She'd need to hide her identity in this place, and not just the fact that she was female, which would garner unwanted attention. Stealth was required while on the hunt to ensure success. She took off her scarf and slipped it inside of her coat, wrapping it around her breasts and cinching it tight over the two wool shirts she wore. She double-checked that the tiny muslin sachet she'd made containing various dried herbs and spices still hung from her neck and then straightened her coat buttons. The thick wool fabric helped hide what remained of her curves, but she hunched forward slightly to make sure.

Disguise in place, she led her horse in a slow arc toward the saloon, glancing this way and that out of habit as much as caution. There were *always* dangers, both large and small, her afi would remind her time and again, and his maxims were usually correct. At times like this, she needed to rely on senses beyond mere sight to detect signs of trouble.

As she neared the building, the shingle hanging above the door became legible.

She reined in her horse abruptly. "You know what that is, Fenrir?" she murmured, peering up at the sign through the blowing snow. "That's the sign of *caper-sus*, is what that is."

She scanned the saloon and surrounding buildings. She

couldn't feel any eyes upon her at the moment, but her quarry obviously held sway here. "There are things to learn here," she told the horse. "But we must be careful."

She had little fear that Fenrir would be in peril while she went inside the saloon. The formidable size of the horse alone was enough to dissuade most with malicious intentions, and her brusque and ill-tempered demeanor toward men persuaded the rest that this horse was no easy prey.

She dismounted and draped Fenrir's reins over the hitching rail. Two other horses tied to the rail farther down looked their way and neighed, their manes blanketed with a dusting of snow. Fenrir tossed her head and looked the other way.

Chuckling at her horse's aloof response, Clementine loosened her pack enough to extract her haversack, which she'd filled with several smaller weapons and a couple days' worth of provisions. She hefted the bag over her shoulder and then ran her hand up Fenrir's cheek. "*Noen gang klar*," she whispered, warning the headstrong mare to stay aware.

Fenrir flapped her lips, pawing at the ground with one hoof.

"Don't worry. I'll be back. I'm just going to check things out. No fighting, I promise." With a final pat on the mare's neck, Clementine headed for the door.

Inside, thick clouds of smoke roiled in the gust of wind that entered with her. The din of conversation quieted. She scanned the room, noting six faces turned toward her, openly staring. The same number of men returned to their beers, cards, and chatter without a second glance.

It was busier than she'd expected at this time of day. Must be the snow keeping these miners from their claims. No soiled doves lounged amidst the men. No piano was to be found. This establishment was intended for two things, drinking and cards.

She dipped one shoulder slightly and shuffled to the bar, adding a limp for good measure. She dropped her haversack on the dirty floor at her feet and faced the barkeep, chin tipped low.

"Whiskey," she said in a tone as raspy and deep as she could muster. As soon as he slid the glass in front of her, she threw it back, ordered another, and tossed a coin on the rough-hewn bar.

Grabbing the second glass, she picked up her bag and shuffled to an empty table next to the wood stove where the lighting was dimmer. Sinking into a rickety chair closest to the warm stove, she leaned her forearms on the table, keeping her chin to her chest.

A glance from under her lowered lashes found four faces still turned toward her. Their body language and expressions showed a mixture of curiosity and animosity. She'd need to keep an eye on them and her blade close at hand.

Twelve souls total occupied chairs or stood at the bar, although three or four more lanterns were needed to chase the shadows from the far corner. There could be one or two more in that darkness, and with the two barkeeps, that made possibly sixteen altogether. In addition to the four who continued to watch her brazenly, three more kept an eye on her as well, but their observations were subtler. As for the rest, it was difficult to tell. She had already spotted five *caper-sus* rings being flashed about while holding cards and drinks, and one carving of the telltale insignia into the clapboard wall at one end of the bar.

Another symbol she didn't recognize was carved at the other end. It was in roughly the shape of a human skull but with a grossly protruding jawline and sloped forehead. The cheeks ...

"Interesting to find you here drinking whiskey," a smooth voice said low and quiet next to her ear.

"Jævla!" Clementine muttered in her native tongue and jerked back, spilling a few drops of her drink.

"The use of profanities is unwarranted," her visitor added in Norwegian, surprising Clementine again. This time she didn't flinch—she frowned instead. "I would expect your kind to favor mead from the horn of a bovid." The timbre of the stranger's voice was that of a very young man, yet even and confident with an accent that Clementine couldn't place.

What did the stranger mean by "your kind"? Clementine turned her head slowly.

Occupying the chair next to her was a slender figure dressed in a five-button Union soldier sack coat and a wide-brimmed black felt hat tipped low to cover the eyes. A gray wool scarf wrapped up the stranger's neck, stopping just below a set of lips. No mustache lined the smooth upper lip, reinforcing Clementine's estimation of youth based on voice timbre.

Young or not, Clementine knew better than to underestimate a stranger. Besides, something about this one had the back of her neck tingling. She lowered her hand to her thigh, her fingers inching toward the handle of the dagger in her boot sheath.

"The object you reach for is unnecessary," the stranger said in a silky voice, still speaking in Norwegian. "At least for the moment."

Clementine scoffed, but slid the dagger from the sheath anyway and held it at the ready under the table. She kept her chin low as she studied her new companion as best she could out of the corner of her eye.

Who the hell was this soldier? When she'd counted heads in the place, this shady tenant had eluded her somehow. Who would have the skill and stealth to sneak up on her so easily?

"Very well," the stranger said. "Brandish a weapon if you must, but I am not here for you. On the contrary, *you* may very well be in a position to assist me."

Wait! Could this be Ludek? Had Hildegard told him to follow Clementine? The skin above the scarf was creamy, but not unusually so. The nose was petite, but not unnatural in any way. Clementine experienced no sense of danger, which she would expect if this was an *other*. Besides, why would Ludek approach her so blatantly? And hadn't he just returned to The Dove this morning?

She turned and looked the stranger in the eye, noticing prominent cheekbones above the scarf. "I like whiskey," she replied in a deep raspy voice, staying in disguise.

The lips above the gray scarf wrinkled in a sneer. "Of course. It is a crude and grotesque libation. It is only fitting that your kind would make the choice to engage in such brutish behavior."

There was that "your kind" remark again. Clementine bristled under her thick coat at the underlying insult. If this stranger were Hildegard's spy, surely he knew better than to anger a *Scharfrichter*.

"You have me at a disadvantage," Clementine said in German, switching to Hildegard's favored language.

"Of that I am certain," the stranger returned in matching tongue. "German. I have always found it to have an uncivilized, annoying resonance. Too much phlegm is involved." The stranger leaned closer and sniffed at Clementine's neck, whispering, "Enough pretense. You must realize you aren't fooling anyone in this establishment, excepting the *humans*." The soldier's voice dripped with contempt on the last word.

The Stranger sat back. Was this one of Masterson's crew? Was her benefactor having her followed now after the incident in Gayville?

"Although," the stranger continued, "I do find it remarkably clever that you've chosen to hide not only your identity, but your scent as well."

Clementine stilled. The sachet of herbs and spices that she wore had always worked before when around *others*. Why wasn't it working now? Or was it? What was this stranger?

Two more men stepped inside the saloon, greeting the bartender like an old friend. They joined the four who were still watching her and now her tablemate. Finger pointing and whispering followed, and then there were six pairs of eyes on them.

Hel's bones! Clementine didn't have time for this. "Enough games," she whispered in German. "State your purpose."

The stranger *tsked*, saying in English, "You need to learn to control your temper, *Scharfrichter*."

Clementine growled in her throat. "I said enough. State your business or move along."

"Business at hand, I presume." The stranger smirked above the scarf. "Fine. I'll elaborate for you since you seem incapable of reaching conclusions relying solely on your acumen."

Wait a second. Clementine took a closer look at the stranger, shifting her focus. Not Ludek, he wouldn't dare treat her with such disrespect. Not one of Masterson's crew either.

Your kind.

Ah, of course! Bold, unusual stealth, condescending at every turn, dressed in bulky clothing, a higher than normal voice for a male soldier. This must be …

"I am here to cleanse this establishment, as I believe are you." The stranger gestured toward the *caper-sus* carved into the wall.

"The Rogue Slayer," Clementine said under her breath.

"At long last, you've arrived. Congratulations, but I do have to say there was generous assistance. Although I would prefer you not call me 'Rogue.' "

Wait until she told Hildegard who she'd crossed paths with in Galena. Finally, they might have some definite answers to several burning questions on who and why.

Clementine sheathed her knife and then lifted her whiskey glass. "The word seems fitting, given your proclivity to meddle in the affairs of *others*." She took a drink, wishing she had some of her amma's sweet mead instead of whiskey to wash down this encounter.

"I find the moniker vulgar," the Rogue said. "Nevertheless, I am encouraged. At long last you have begun to perform your task. It had occurred to me that you might not understand what needs to be done. My presence remedies your shortcomings."

"I am not in need of your help with my task."

Clementine scanned the room. No one seemed concerned about her or her companion, save two of the original six who had watched her enter the saloon. Those two continued to cast glances in her direction.

"Ah, but you've proven quite the opposite. We will start here." The Rogue swept her hand in an arc, indicating the entire room.

"Start what? The patrons in this saloon are not why I came to Galena."

The Rogue sighed, muttering something under her breath in what sounded like French. "I do not understand your hesitation to accept what you were born—and most likely contracted—to do. This saloon must be cleansed. The chattel must be freed, and that requires purification by the blade."

Clementine scowled. This rogue was a fanatic. Clementine had witnessed on her exam tables the blade work to which she was referring. "No. These are not someone's property or slaves,

they are just men looking to survive."

"Yet they have chosen a path that will result in their deaths."

"Some of them, yes. But others are here because they are desperate to survive." When faced with starvation and the harsh winter elements, the *caper-sus* brand and the protection and pay it offered was their only salvation.

"They will kill indiscriminately if ordered," the Rogue stated.

Some might, but not all. "I will not take their lives. They need only to see the error in their judgment."

"Irresolution has befallen you. Or perhaps placidity." The Rogue scoffed. "No matter. I shall purify this place unassisted by you, it seems."

"You will not." Clementine wasn't sure what edicts the Rogue obeyed, but she was fairly certain the term *rogue* was fitting—although it was entirely unorthodox. Never had she met nor heard of a rogue slayer. Of course, it was possible her tablemate had been summoned. But two slayers? In the same region? It would be an extreme rarity.

The Rogue stared at Clementine, her nostrils flaring slightly. "You consider me subordinate? To be commanded?"

"This is my warrant. My territory. I will handle it as I see fit. You must stop interfering."

"You appear to be disinclined to perform the commission. I am here to remedy that. Must I remind you that I have saved your life more than once."

Clementine's gaze narrowed. "I'm more inclined than you know, and my life needed no saving by you or anyone else." She paused, taking a calming breath. Now was not the time to let her anger rule. She downed the last of her whiskey, setting the glass upside down on the table. "You must end your intrusion and let me do my work. The mine is the source of the infestation here, not this saloon."

The Rogue's chin lifted. "This building is infested with chattel. I intend to cleanse it."

"Who summoned you?"

"Together we shall be done with this task presently."

"Who summoned you?" Clementine repeated, this time in French.

The Rogue stilled. "That is not your concern."

"I can only conclude that you have *not* been summoned. You have no edict. No proclamation. You don't belong here. Furthermore, your presence endangers the balance. You must cease your interference."

The Rogue stiffened, lines forming around her lips. "I wouldn't need to be here if you would only manage your charge."

Clementine crossed her arms. "You are a rogue with bloodlust, and that is dangerous."

"You presume to imply that you do not share the same quality?" The Rogue scoffed. "*We* are dangerous."

Clementine bristled. She had spent many long hours during the years since leaving her grandparents struggling with the idea that her life was dedicated to death. Her only redemption came with the idea that it was a necessary, grisly task that few others could perform. But while killing was what she was born to do, she was no murderer.

"Abide by the rules of our vocation," Clementine said.

The Rogue huffed. "So be it. The *lieutenants* are your concern. You are unaided in this task." She stood and bent close to Clementine's face. "Know this," she whispered. "When you die, I will be here to restore order from the chaos you left behind."

In a blink and a flash of blue, the Rogue was gone. The door swung shut behind her. The two watchmen at the other table noticed her exit but quickly refocused on Clementine with renewed interest.

Clementine lowered her chin again, cursing under her breath. She might have to kill that uppity rogue before this was done.

She flipped her glass right side up again and pretended to

glance toward the bar while searching the room with her eyes. Was the Rogue right? Was she going soft? These men were clearly in league with the *caper-sus* cult. Were they aware of the creature in the mine that was being fed children? Were they the keepers who were "collecting" the creature's meals?

The door slammed open and Hank stormed inside. He craned his neck this way and that, looking for her, no doubt. Jack was right behind him.

Clementine lowered her chin again, sinking back into the shadows as best she could.

"Don't see her," Hank said, too loudly.

Damn! She hated being right sometimes.

"Keep it down," Jack said as they headed for the bar. He was thumbing the hammer on his pistol.

The table of watch owls turned in their direction, their focus off of Clementine for the moment.

Movement near the door caught her attention. Boone closed the door behind him. His gaze drifted around the saloon, moving past her without pause.

"*Faen*," she cursed softly. They must have seen Fenrir at the hitching post. She'd have to sneak out while they were bellied up to the bar. She reached down for her haversack, which was caught on the chair leg. A few tugs and she had it freed. She pushed her chair back.

"Leaving already?" Boone sank into the chair that had been occupied by the Rogue only moments earlier.

"Odin's beard!" First the Rogue had figured out who she was, now Boone. Maybe the Rogue was right. Maybe she was losing her edge.

He leaned closer. "I understand why you left." He spoke in a low voice meant only for her. "But we're here now."

"You shouldn't be. The three of you are in danger."

She could hear Rabbit's and Hank's voices at the bar loud and clear. They were bantering loudly about past storms and their

perils in the snow while tossing back whiskey.

"So are you." Boone brushed the snow from his hat. "We're here to help."

"I'm getting a lot of that lately."

He glanced her way. "What do you mean?"

"The Rogue was just here."

Boone looked left, then right. "Here? Now? Where?"

"I said the Rogue *was* here, under the impression I needed help. Apparently, I'm not capable of handling myself these days."

He smirked. "It's not that at all. We were worried."

"Worried? You remember what I am, right?"

He shrugged. "Doesn't make you immune to death. I worry. Hank and Rabbit, too. Get used to it." He glanced toward the bar. "You been up to the mine yet?"

Warmth filled her. She wasn't accustomed to anyone worrying about her. Not since she'd left her grandparents. Not to this extent, anyway. Damn it, nothing good would come of her caring too much for this man, or Rabbit and Hank.

"Not yet." She pretended to search for something in her haversack. "This saloon is a haven for *caper-sus*."

"I noticed."

She stood, hooking the haversack over her shoulders. "We should go unless you feel like slaughtering everyone in here. I'll go first. Meet me behind the livery."

He looked toward Hank and Jack. Clementine followed his gaze, watching the two who were comparing hats with great animation. Too much animation, maybe, judging by the suspicion lining the four watchmen's faces

"Lunkheads," Boone muttered with a small grin.

"They're doing a fine job at distracting, though," she said.

"I'll get them and meet you outside."

She started to walk past his chair, but he caught her coat sleeve. "I noticed a few gunhands loitering near the mercantile when we rode in. Seemed to be looking for trouble."

"Good. I know where they can find it." She left, all eyes on Jack as he pretended to dance a jig around Hank's hat that now lay on the floor.

Outside, the snow kept falling. She looked up at the darkening sky. It was time to go hunting.

Fifteen

Clementine didn't have to wait long for Hank and the Sidewinders to join her. She'd just finished securing her haversack to her pack on Fenrir when they walked around the side of the livery towing Fred the Mule, Dime, and Nickel behind them.

"Miss Clem, I declare," Hank said when he neared. "You gotta be more careful. Leave a note and expect a body to sit on a rock and wait." He somehow managed to sound both exasperated and relieved.

"I'm sorry, Hank, but I—"

"He's right, Miss Clementine." Jack hopped on Hank's bandwagon while he adjusted the large scabbard tied to Dime's saddle. Clementine did a double take at the size of the rifle stuffed in the scabbard. "Worry us sick, runnin' off like that."

Clementine felt guilty, like when she'd broken one of her amma's favorite crystal music boxes. She looked at Boone, expecting admonishments from him as well. He just gave her a lopsided smile and shrugged while adjusting the cinch strap on his saddle.

"I'm not accustomed," she started and then paused, frowning toward the saloon. "I'm not accustomed to working with others."

"It's okay, Miss Clem. You worried us is all. I brought you this." Hank handed her a leather bundle, bound up tightly with straps. "Thought you might need this, since we showed up."

She unwrapped it and peeked inside. He'd brought her spare gloves, along with her throwing knives and the sheathed scimitar she'd planned to give the Sidewinders in the future. "Thank you, Hank." Apparently she did need him this trip.

"Ain't been up to the mine?" Jack hopped lightly and slid a leg over Dime's back.

"Not yet, I wanted to explore Galena first. I thought I'd find out a thing or two in the saloon."

"Them in there ain't friendly, Miss Clem. I shoulda warned ya before."

"I came to the same conclusion straight away, Hank. But they're not our problem, at least not right now. And they're all humans in there, from what I can tell. No *others* to be seen." The Rogue had said as much herself. Clementine pointed toward the saloon. "If we deal with that, it's likely we'll miss our opportunity to handle the hostile situation at the mine."

Boone nodded.

"Humans you say?" Rabbit turned Dime toward the hill. "Not really up to killin' like that. It's something killin' one or two men, then it's something else killin' a whole passel."

"You think like me, Jack Rabbit." Hank climbed on Fred and reined him around to stand next to Dime.

Clementine settled into Fenrir's saddle. "How did you three get here so quickly?"

"Shortcut," Hank said as if their trek from Deadwood were a simple afternoon buggy ride. He spurred Fred toward the center of the camp, adding over his shoulder, "Thisaway, Miss Clem."

She fell in behind him and Jack, but then reined in Fenrir and looked back. "Boone? You standing guard all day, or are you coming with us?"

He stared at her, his head tipped to the side. "Why was the

Rogue really in there?"

"To kill, of course." *The lieutenants are your concern* ... What had the Rogue meant by that? What lieutenants? Clementine frowned about her cryptic parting remark.

"Kill?" Boone's voice brought her back to the present.

"Yes. Fortunately for everyone in there, we had a disagreement before blood was shed. Otherwise, they'd all be dead."

"You stopped him?"

"Who says it's a *him*?"

"The Rogue is a female?"

Clementine smiled at his wide eyes. "Of course, Sidewinder. Executioners are only and always female."

They followed Hank single file up the hill, using the trail blazed by the steam engine otherwise known as Fred the Mule.

"I'm not overly pleased with our timing, Miss Clem," Hank called back to her. "Sun's almost done for the day."

Which was the perfect time to hunt her sort of prey. "It won't make any difference when we're in the mine, Hank."

Jack turned in his saddle to face her. "In the mine, you say?"

"That's right." His grimace made her smile. "If you're worried about going inside, Jack, you can stand watch at the entrance."

"By myself?" He looked beyond her to Boone, who was bringing up the rear of their train.

"Can't very well let a lady go into that mine by herself now, can we?" Boone asked.

Jack grinned. "She'll have Hank. And you, it appears."

"Why, Jack Fields," Boone said. "Does the idea of going into that mine vex you?" Clementine could hear the mirth in his voice.

She joined in the fun. "It's okay, Jack. We'll probably be fine on our own. You can tend the horses."

"I ain't tendin' no horses. But I ain't afraid to say, I am presently disinclined to wander through any mines. The last mine we went in didn't have a whole lot of niceties to offer, if you recall."

"I'll be there to hold your hand, Jack Rabbit!" Hank said from the front of the line.

"Thanks, Hank. That'll do it."

Clementine shifted in her saddle. A heavy knot had begun to tighten in her stomach. Her senses were on high alert, her eyesight and hearing amplified. Her gaze darted here and there as clumps of snow fell from the trees around her, a rabbit bounded through the snow to her left, a bird fluttered in a bush on her right. Sounds of the forest surrounded her—the scratching of a porcupine on a tree trunk, pine needles rubbing together in the wind, the sound of more snow falling through branches. She sniffed, catching the scent of something besides horseflesh, mule, and men. "How much farther, Hank?"

"Fifteen minutes or so, Miss Clem. Wouldn't you say, Jack Rabbit?"

"Feels like," Jack answered.

"You gettin' fidgety, Miss Clem?"

"We're being watched," she said to all of them. "Keep your eyes open."

She heard Boone slide his rifle from its scabbard and rack a shell into the chamber. Jack laid his pistol across his lap and scanned the ridgeline ahead. It was heartening to see them gearing up for trouble, regardless of Jack's protests. Years of traveling dangerous trails had apparently prepared them, if not for what they faced now, at least for a fight, and that was something.

After a few minutes of blazing a trail through deep powdery snow, Hank exclaimed, "Right up here. See the tailin's?"

She could. It looked to be a modest-sized mine judging by the pile of tailings ahead of them. The leveled-off top reached no more than twenty or thirty feet in any direction from the entrance to the adit.

As they crested the edge of the tailings, it became clear to Clementine that the mine had been used for more than extracting precious metals from the earth. The mix of mud and snow reminded her of the streets in Deadwood with boot prints coming and going in many directions. The difference being the generous amount of thick, dark blood mixed with the snow.

"It weren't this bad last time, eh Jack Rabbit?" Hank surveyed the flat-topped tailings. Blood and pieces of mangled flesh were ground into the snow and mud.

Jack shook his head. "Looks like the devil made a stew."

"That's disgusting, Rabbit." Boone walked Nickel up alongside Fenrir. "How many met a bad end here, I wonder?"

"And who?" Clementine shuddered at the memory of what Hildegard had told her. *Children.*

"Jack Rabbit, you reckon that beastie that took my boot coulda done this?"

"I reckon it did."

"Hildegard's man mentioned that the gate was secure when he was here." Ludek had mentioned more than that, but these men needed to keep their heads right now. She'd witnessed their compassion and how it could drive them to take risks beyond reason. They didn't need to know yet that children were being preyed upon.

Hank pointed at the iron bars covering the adit. "That ain't secure."

Boone frowned. "Nope."

"Huh uh. Less than it was when we first came upon it last time," Jack said.

Clementine moved closer to the gate.

Fenrir snorted and tossed her head this way and that, pawing at the ground.

"Don't worry, girl." She stroked Fenrir's neck. "You don't need to go inside. I just want to take a better look."

The gate was hung at an awkward angle from one hinge,

blasted outward by something that really wanted to taste freedom. Judging by the look of the blood-spotted ground surrounding the adit, she figured the creature had caused considerable damage to those who had been nearby when it broke free.

She slid from Fenrir's back and took a slow walk around. Blood and hunks of flesh were everywhere. The sun had sunk below the ridgeline and light was failing, but she could still see the carnage well enough. She scraped at the snow with her boot.

"Hank, what do you see here?" She pointed at the prints on the ground and then indicated toward the wavering line trailing off into the trees.

He swung his leg over Fred's rump and joined Clementine. Bending down, he studied the markings in the snow and then grinned up at her. "Yep. You a tracker too, Miss Clem? Looks to be it headed off thatta way." He squinted at the tree line. "You was right, we're goin' huntin'. Don't know about you, but I'm better in the daylight."

She sighed, searching the trees around them. "I don't need the daylight, but with you three along it might be better to wait."

Boone swung down off Nickel. "We're not thinking it's still in there, right?"

Clementine shook her head. "That feeling I got earlier, I'm confident it's out there." She waved her hand out toward the trees.

"Probably not a bad idea to seal it back up, in any case. If it is a gateway, maybe we can keep more of those things from getting out while we hunt."

"Good thinkin', Booney." Jack was off Dime and headed toward the adit. "I'll help. Watch yourself. If that brute is in there, it comes quick."

"I have you to keep me safe." Boone bent to lift the gate back onto the barrel hinges. "Help me with this."

"Hank, can you see which direction it headed once it left the tailings?" she asked.

He followed the tracks to the side of the tailings and then trailed them with his eyes down the slope and into the trees. "Double sure now that ain't no *Bahkauv*. Don't make the same track."

"I didn't think so either, Hank. Your description sounds like some kind of *Höhlendrache*."

"Hoolindrawers like to eat humans, do they?" Hank turned to her, his face solemn.

"*Höhlendrache*. A cave dragon. They eat all manner of flesh." But prefer young prey.

"Oh. Almost forgot." Hank trotted back to Fred and rummaged in his pack. "Where's ... " he pulled out a rolled-up blanket and set it on the saddle. "Think I put it ... here it is." He pulled a heavy iron lock from the pack. "Here, Boonedock." He handed it to Boone.

"Always got the remedy." Jack laughed. "Hey Hank, you got a *senorita* for me in that bag?"

"Ha! Jack Rabbit. You don't need no help with that, seems to me."

"Come on, Rabbit," Boone said. "Lift this, up onto ..." He grunted. "Yeah. Over. Up. Good."

Boone hefted the gate up onto the hinges with Jack cursing along beside him.

CLANG!

Both men froze.

"Dammit!" Jack said in a harsh whisper. "Best we get this secured in a timely fashion. I don't cotton to meetin' up with that cave dragon again."

"Have you ever come up against a *Höhlendrache*, Clementine?" Boone put all his weight on the latch to bend it straight again.

"No. But I've read about them. Nasty, filthy creatures. You don't want to know what Hildegard's man found farther back in that adit."

Boone and Jack both looked into the darkness of the mine, then at each other.

"Hurry up, Booney." Jack peered over Boone's shoulder as he tried to fit the lock to the gate.

Boone stopped abruptly. "You hear that?" He turned his ear toward the mine and looked at Jack, his eyes wide.

Jack drew his pistol and looked into the dark with even wider eyes than Boone's. "What'd you hear?" he whispered.

"Sounded like a Rabbit's teeth chattering," Boone answered with a straight face.

"Aw, fuck you, Booney." Jack slapped Boone's shoulder. "I'm gonna shave your *huevos* some night when you're sleepin'." He turned to Clementine. "How many different kinds of damned monsters are we talkin' about, anyway? Them *Bahkauv* were bad enough."

Clementine shrugged. "More than a few. Could be hundreds of different species spread around here and there." She'd sure seen her share over the years. "I don't think anybody really knows. But I can tell you, I encounter new … *things* everywhere I go."

"Like this one?" Boone aimed his thumb toward Jack.

Jack squinted at Boone. "That hole in your hat? Two of a kind pretty soon."

Clementine smiled. "They all do have one thing in common."

"What's that?" Boone asked.

"They're all vile menaces that need to be put down. Like the one Jack and Hank saw here." She motioned toward the mine. On second thought, now was a good time to let these three know what they were up against. "Someone was feeding it children."

"Fuck." Jack peered over Boone's shoulder again. "Quit flappin' your jaws, Booney, and hurry up."

"I am. Need to bend this piece over that way a little more." Boone grunted again.

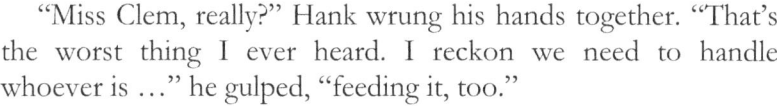

"Miss Clem, really?" Hank wrung his hands together. "That's the worst thing I ever heard. I reckon we need to handle whoever is ..." he gulped, "feeding it, too."

Clementine nodded. "Soon enough."

She couldn't be sure yet who was responsible, but the French swordsman, Augustine, and Masterson were both in a position to control a gateway. What she knew of Masterson didn't lead her to the idea that he was the guilty party. But when it came to it, how well did she really know her benefactor? Hildegard and Miss Hundt both believed Masterson capable of nefarious deeds.

Boone shook his head. "Some kind of world you live in, Clementine." He closed the lock, the clank reverberating into the darkness of the mine.

"Booney, look at that. Down at your feet." Jack squatted and picked something from the ground. He wiped the mud and blood from it on his pant leg and held it up to the bit of light left in the day.

"One of them *caper-sus* rings." Jack handed it to Boone as they joined Hank and Clementine at the edge of the tailing. "The horn is curled."

Boone handed it to Clementine, who studied it for a moment in the twilight before pocketing it.

"That's the same *caper-sus* insignia we saw in the Galena saloon," Boone said, gazing toward the skyline. "You may be able to hunt and track in the dark, Clementine, but like you said, us," he pointed at Jack, Hank, and himself, "not so much."

"I know." She frowned. "That's one of the reasons I came by myself."

"Well." Boone shrugged. "That plan is shot to shit, so ..."

Hank looked back down the way they'd come. "Too far back to Deadwood, 'specially since storm's comin'. Shouldn't drop too much of the white fluffy, might be we could hold up at Hobble's, down in Galena. Known him for a spell now. He'd put us up."

"I'd like a roof over my head right now, but we can't trust

anybody in Galena," she said. Out here under the pines they had less of a chance of being stabbed in the back while sleeping.

Boone glanced at her and then stared out into the forest. "We need to follow that trail, long as we can, before the snow covers it. Then we use Clementine's instincts. You say you can feel when that bastard is close, right?"

She nodded. There was no mistaking the sensations she'd had on the trail up to the mine.

From a young age, she'd been taught that experience in dealing with *others* would raise *bevissthet,* her awareness, but she didn't understand fully what her grandparents meant by this until she started killing. While sparring with her afi, she'd not felt the tightening of her skin when an *other* tried to sneak up on her from behind. Until she'd hunted on her own, she'd not realized she could hear the pounding heart of an adversary hidden in the shadows. Or that she could smell the sharp, metallic odors she came to know as hatred and rage. It took years of actual encounters with enemies to learn how to use *bevissthet* to her advantage.

Her awareness was strong these days when trouble was upon her, but it wasn't what she'd consider enlightening. It didn't tell her what type of creature she was facing, how many there might be, if it had big claws or big teeth, or both. Nor did it tell her if she were the stronger of the two, if she'd easily defeat the creature, or if she was about to get her ass handed to her. That was all up to her to figure out based on what she could actually see and hear.

"My plan was to track this thing in the mine," she told them. "But now we need Hank's skills to interpret those tracks." She pointed at huge paw-like prints that disappeared into the forest. "In spite of this damned snowstorm."

"Been workin' on that, Miss Clem." Hank frowned at the jumble of prints he'd been studying. "I'd say there was a scuffle, here, here, around thisaway." He gestured generously with his arms, indicating the scuffle had covered almost the entire flat top of the tailings. "You say Hildegard's man said the gate was secured?"

"Yes."

"Well, the brute that got my boot, looks like he crashed through that secured gate, knocked a body ass-end over to here." He pointed near his feet. "Ate some on the spot."

"Jeez, Hank." Jack scrunched up his nose. "That's revoltin' "

"Yer tellin' me. Anyhow, musta been two of them *caper-sus* fellas, since the body parts left over indicate such. The brute— what'd you call it, Miss Clem?"

"I think it might be a *Höhlendrache*."

"Hoolindragon. Right." He pointed toward some other tracks. "Deep bootprints there. Looks like maybe somebody carried somethin' off that way." He grunted. "There musta been others—I mean other man men, not *other* men, or *other* monsters. *Others*?" He looked at Clementine for help and continued after her nod. "Or whatnot. Anyways, it musta either ate them two fellas up or they had friends that carted them away. Maybe that. Hauled what was left of them off later. Hate to think that brute, the Hoolindragon, ate two grown men." He shuddered. "Turns my insides to think it. Bones crunchin'. Slurpin' up the—"

"Okay, Hank." Boone held up his hand. "I think we get it." His imagination must have been working along with Hank's.

"That coulda been us." Jack's voice was solemn, as if he could picture it happening.

"Yessir, Jack Rabbit. It coulda. Miss Clem, your Hoolindragon is carrying a long tail. This big around." Hank made a circle with his thumbs and index fingers barely touching. "Took off in a straight line thisaway, swirlin' its tail behind it." He followed the paw and slither tracks to the edge of the tailings with Jack on his heels. "Down over the side right here. Weren't even concerned about coverin' tracks. Course, if'n it's like an animal, it wouldn't have no such concerns."

Jack peered over the edge of the tailings. "Blood in the tracks. Injured?"

"Don't look to be. That blood yer seein' is smashed into the track. Likely to be somebody else's blood. If the ol' Hooly were leakin', I'd expect spots of blood around the tracks. Nope. Don't expect those *caper-sus* boys did any damage at all. None I can tell, anyway. Same as us, Jack Rabbit. All that lead we pushed didn't hurt it one bit."

They all stood for a minute, ruminating on Hank's words.

"We should move." Boone hopped up on Nickel.

Clementine leaped onto Fenrir. "Before we do, you need to know what we're hunting."

"Maybe we killed it. Maybe this is another one," Jack said hopefully.

Clementine shook her head. She hadn't seen an actual *Höhlendrache*, but she had seen drawings of one and read passages about them. Hildegard had concurred it was likely some species of *Höhlendrache* after hearing the description from Clementine and the report of findings from Ludek. In the madam's experience, if there were *Bahkauv*, there were *Höhlendrache*. She'd also warned Clementine that there were other foul beasts that tended to show up in the same regions as *Bahkauv*. All were carnivorous hunters.

"The *Höhlendrache*, if that's what it is, isn't like a *Bahkauv*, although they are often seen in the same territories. They are much larger, often twice as big. And as Jack and Hank found out, they are much more resilient." She looked from Jack to Boone. "We'll need to sever the head completely. It will be deadly until we are successful in that endeavor."

"Okay. Teeth. Claws. Big as a buffalo," Boone summed up.

"Bigger than a buffalo and scaly like a snake," Jack corrected.

Boone nodded. "Fine. Bigger than a scaly buffalo. Take the head. Anything else?" Apparently, he was restless to hunt.

She watched Hank situate himself on Fred. "Yes, there are a

few more things to be aware of before we face off with it."

" 'Course there are." Jack scratched his nose with the back of his glove.

"Don't let it spit on you. It has poisonous saliva. Also, some think its breath is poisonous as well."

"Oh, is that all?" Jack's sarcasm was thick.

"No." She met his gaze head-on. "You might need to cover your ears when it shrieks. It's believed that the screech of the *Höhlendrache* can drive a man insane."

"Sheeat. We didn't get close enough to get breathed or spit on. Heard it wail like a cat in heat when we plugged it, though. Didn't seem so bad, right, Hank?"

"Naw. Curdled your blood, but I ain't crazy so I think that one is wrong." Hank grinned. "Could be it knocked Jack Rabbit a little loose in the noggin maybe."

"Not you too, Hank." Jack shook his head and grinned at Clementine.

The Hank that Clementine knew didn't normally take part in that kind of teasing. It must be something about Jack that brought it out in a person.

"Funnin' you is all, Jack Rabbit. I'm glad to have ya by my side."

Boone chuckled and leaned on Nickel's saddle horn. "Rabbit is what you call a natural target for a daily derisional."

Jack bobbled his head. "Daily *derisional*. Ain't no such word."

"I'll blaze, Miss Clem." Hank unhooked a miner's lantern from the assortment of equipment he had hanging from his pack. "You three stick close, though. Not holdin' much interest in gettin' dressed out like a side of beef same as those boys back there."

"We'll put Rabbit between us, Hank," Boone said. "That way, Mr. Courageous can protect both of us." Boone waited for Clementine to follow Jack, who was tailing Hank, before bringing up the rear.

Clementine steered Fenrir toward the steep gravel bank of the tailings and let her pick the route to the bottom, which happened to be right in the tracks of Fred and Dime.

"Quiet down, jug head," Jack said over his shoulder as Dime slid-walked down the slope. "You wait, Booney. When that Hooly bastard sticks a claw or two in that pumpkin belly of yours, don't come cryin' to me."

Clementine frowned at the sky, which was mostly dark now thanks to the clouds that had returned. They sure could have used some moonlight tonight.

There was one other thing she hadn't told them about the *Höhlendrache*, partly because she wasn't sure if it was a myth or not, but mostly because she didn't want to make them edgier than they were. There was a reason that whoever was jailing the creature had it locked up in the dark. According to legend, the *Höhlendrache* preferred to hunt on moonless nights when its ability to see in the dark gave it an advantage over its prey.

Sixteen

"This ain't workin'," Hank said. "Dark night, too much white fluffy, like somebody laid a blanket across the tracks." He stopped Fred the Mule for what felt like the hundredth time.

Shivering, Rabbit watched Hank dismount to check for prints again. "Fuck, it's cold," he said and tried to sink his head into his collar. It was a good night to be a tortoise.

They had followed the slither and paw tracks as best as Hank could for a little over an hour. The snowfall had stopped but not before doing a respectable job of obscuring the tracks. Thick clouds shrouded the crescent moon, leaving fleeting moments of moonlight by which to see. The feeble glow from Hank's lantern did little to help.

"We should hold up." Rabbit rubbed his hands together. "This thing has led us deep. You know where we are, Hank?" He was tired and it felt like pieces of him were so cold they were about to fall off—or already had and he just couldn't feel it.

"Sure I know, mostly. Holdin' up suits me. Pick it up come daybreak." Hank grunted, switching the lantern to his other hand. He flexed his gloved fingers several times. He must be frosted to the bone, too. Hell, they all had to be, including their rides.

"I'd go along with that." Boone gingerly stepped down from

Nickel. "If I move my toes, I think they'll break off." He brushed away the ice and packed snow stuck to the horse's tail and legs. "Sorry about this, *compadre*. I'm sure you'd rather be safe and warm in Santa Fe nuzzling up to the fillies at the ranch."

Nickel nickered and nuzzled Boone's neck with his ice-crusted nostrils. "Ahhh! That's cold, boy!"

Rabbit jumped down. Jolts of pain shot through his feet and up his legs. Dammit! He should have followed Boone's lead and taken his time dismounting. "Think we risk a fire?"

Clementine squinted into the darkness. "I'm not picking up any scents or sounds out of the ordinary. What do you think, Hank?"

"Oh, I think we're a long way from ordinary, Miss Clem." Hank peered into the darkness around them. "And I think ol' Hooly is miles away and a fire don't matter. Or maybe ol' Hooly has been watchin' us all along, so a fire don't matter. Prob'ly that."

Boone nodded. "Expect you're right, Hank. If we don't warm up, we'll be in sorry shape come morning."

"You get a fire goin', Boonedock. I'll get some grain in the horses and put blankets on 'em."

The cloud cover shifted, allowing the crescent moon to shine through.

"I'll set up the lean-tos." Clementine eased off Fenrir and untied one of the packs behind her saddle. "Will you help me, Jack?"

"I surely will, Miss Clementine." Rabbit looked around in the semi-darkness, trying to memorize their surroundings before the clouds shrouded the moon and everything below in shadow again. "Appears to be lots of boughs and branches downed around here we can use."

As they gathered wood for shelters, he glanced at her several times. He'd been besotted with her from their first meeting and he continued to be still, but something had changed. Everything about her still intrigued him, from her Amazonian size and build to her total domination in combat. She was like no woman he'd ever met. With practice, he was getting better at concealing his fascination with her. The last thing he wanted to be was a flustered gump in her eyes.

What had changed, though, since returning from Santa Fe was that what he felt about her wasn't a physical obsession. He wasn't interested so much in getting her clothes off as he was in seeing her slash, swing, and stab with them still on. In the past, when he set his sights on a woman, it had always been a raw, physical attraction. With Clementine the attraction wasn't really physical, and that was new.

Rabbit dropped an armload of branches next to where she had begun tamping down the snow for the floor of the lean-to. He watched her work for a couple of seconds before heading back into the shadows for more wood.

He thought back to that day in the Bloody Bones. Clementine had rushed into battle, so sure of herself. He relished the idea of fighting by her side again, of watching her spin and lunge and contort her body in battle. She reminded him of the ballet dancers he'd seen in San Francisco, only she wielded deadly sharp blades in her dance of death.

This new feeling Clementine inspired within him might have been borne from the need to avenge Uncle Mort's killers, but now it felt more like a purpose.

He gathered a few more branches and returned to help her finish up the lean-tos. Boone had a good, blazing fire built by the time they were done. They commenced to eating as soon as Hank had the bacon and beans cooked up. The fire heated up pretty much all of Rabbit's parts except the outside edges, and the food and hot coffee warmed up his insides.

"More?" Boone held out a tin plate toward Rabbit with a few hunks of bacon.

"Naw, I'm full. Hand me the coffee, though, and don't give

me any shit about this being my third cup."

Boone had been teasing him about every damn thing throughout the day, but had backed off as the evening wore on. Sometimes when Boone got edgy about a thing, he'd start to take his worry out on Rabbit. He knew Boone didn't mean anything by it and had grown accustomed to it over the years. Most days Rabbit gave the same right back. And Boone knew better than anyone, Rabbit could be a donkey at the dance sometimes.

"It's too cold to lock horns with you tonight."

"You gonna sleep all right out here, Miss Clem?" Hank had laid blankets on the horses and over the top of the branches she and Rabbit had spread out under the lean-tos.

"I was born in the far north, Hank. This is a gentle summer night where I'm from." Clementine spread her arms wide as if to take in the warm evening air.

They all laughed.

She put on a good show, but Rabbit had seen her rub her gloved hands together and stamp her feet every so often as they set up camp.

"If a body don't have reason in it, it don't choose this, do it?" Hank cocked his head. "That make sense to any of you?"

Rabbit chuckled. "Well, you said it, Hank. If it don't make sense to you, there's probably somethin' wrong with it."

"You been drinking over there, Hank?" Boone stuck his palms out toward the fire. "If you have hooch, you need to share."

"Yeah. Spread the heat, Hank." Clementine held out her empty tin cup.

"I ain't drunk, you buzzards." He pulled out a metal flask. "But I do have somethin' you may like."

"Now we're talkin'." Rabbit grinned at the older man.

He'd taken to Hank quickly and the reverse seemed to be true, too. There was something about him that Rabbit couldn't quite puzzle out. It felt like a familiarity that came from years of friendship, yet he'd known him for only a short time. They shared a kinship that Rabbit had only experienced with one other person.

"Boonedock, take a good sip of this." Hank handed Boone a metal flask.

Boone took the flask and gulped down a mouthful. "Holy Moses! That's good. What is it?" He took another drink before passing it to Clementine.

"That, Mr. Sidewinder, is rum."

"You got rum?" Rabbit perked up. Hell, he'd been trying to procure a dose of rum since leaving Santa Fe. It turned out Hank had it all along.

"I do, Jack Rabbit." Hank grinned extra wide, obviously pleased with himself.

Clementine tipped the flask into her mouth. She closed her eyes and swallowed. "Ah, Hank, that is the best hooch I've had since I arrived in Deadwood." She tipped the flask again.

"Come on now. Leave a little for the pirates," Rabbit pleaded.

"Hoo hoo. Thar be pirates in the hills! Shave me timbers."

Rabbit chuckled. "Shiver, Hank."

"I been shiverin' all day, Jack Rabbit."

Rabbit shot Clementine a one-eyed squint. "Arh, lassy, I'll be feedin' ye to the fishes if'n ye drink down all me rum!"

"I don't think there'll be any left for pirates," Clementine teased and took another sip before handing it back to Hank, who took a mouthful as well.

"Mutiny says I! Me aggression is accumulatin'." Rabbit, still squinting one eye, made a fist and shook it at Hank.

"Poor Jack Rabbit." Hank handed the flask to Rabbit. "Drink up! I got a whole bottle in my pack."

Clementine stood. "That reminds me. I think I have some of those dried apricots you gave me in my haversack, Hank. They would go well with your rum."

While she walked over to the lean-to, Rabbit took a big gulp

of rum, wiped his mouth, sighed, and smiled wide. The sweet rum warmed his throat and belly, making him want to curl up with the flask and go to sleep. "Hank, I think I love you."

Hank batted his eyelids. "Aw, shucks. That's the nicest thing nobody never said to me, Jack Rabbit."

Clementine returned with her bag.

"Now I know you're drunk, Hank," Boone said. "Rabbit, give me that back." He took the flask and swallowed more rum. "*Amigo*, all this time I thought you liked rum because pirates drink it."

"Yeah?" Rabbit held out his hand for the flask.

Boone used the flask as a pointer. "You should have told me it's got whiskey beat."

"Quit shaking it, you're gonna spill it. Hand it over." Rabbit grabbed the flask and wiped the mouth of the container on the sleeve of his coat.

"Nice." Boone smirked. "I didn't slobber on it."

"I've seen some of the girls you've kissed with that mouth," Rabbit joked.

Boone shot a glance at Clementine and then glared at Rabbit.

Clementine was busy rummaging through her pack and didn't notice Boone's scowl, but Rabbit did.

" 'Course, that was years ago," he continued in spite of Boone's dirty look. "How long since you had a woman, Booney. Months, ain't it?"

Clementine stopped searching in her pack and stared across at Boone, who was still too busy giving Rabbit a withering glare to notice he had her attention. But Rabbit noticed. He also observed the way she hurriedly returned to her haversack and began shuffling things around inside of it with more vigor than before.

Returning to Boone's scowl, Rabbit mouthed, *What?*

Boone lowered his chin, nudging his head toward Clementine. "There's a lady present, remember?"

Rabbit waved him off. "She ain't even payin' attention, are you, Miss Clementine?" At least she was acting that way now, burrowing in her haversack again like a groundhog homesteading.

"What?" She didn't look up. "No, what do I care?"

Well now, that wasn't what he'd asked at all. Rabbit looked from her to Boone, who was tipping back more rum and frowning into the fire. Apparently, he'd stuck his foot right in the middle of something squishy there. Rabbit turned to Hank, exchanging raised brows with his new *pard*.

"Hoo, Boonedock!" Hank scooted closer to the fire. "I bet you keep back the women with a stick, handsome man such as you. You too, Jackrabbit. Tall, fetchin', strong chins. Like two statues carved by Michelangelo, dontcha think, Miss Clem?"

Rabbit sat up straight and lifted his chin. "I thought that, too." He grinned at Hank.

Boone burst into laughter. "Yeah, you have a real block of stone sitting square on those shoulders, Rabbit."

"Don't be jealous now, Booney."

"These two certainly smell better than most of the men around these parts," Clementine told Hank, smiling as she pulled a small cloth wrapped in string from her haversack. "But that isn't saying much."

She doled out dried apricots as they all continued to chuckle and poke fun at Rabbit, who gave back as good as he got.

For just a moment, the scene took Rabbit back to nights around the campfire with Uncle Mort down at the ranch. They'd had some good times over the years. Too bad his uncle wasn't around to meet Clementine and Hank. He'd have enjoyed their company for certain. Funny, if it weren't for his uncle he wouldn't be here now with these new friends.

Dammit, Uncle Mort.

Rabbit blinked away the sad thoughts threatening to surface, remembering that he needed to find the pendant Uncle Mort had worn around his neck. The silver and turquoise bear that an old Navajo had given his uncle long ago to protect him from evil and give him strength. Rabbit had lost track of it somewhere between Deadwood and Santa Fe, and he could sure as hell use some strength and protection on nights like this.

Boone stood and squinted into the dark forest surrounding them. "Is anybody else worried about the ruckus we're tossing into these woods?"

"Relax, Booney." Rabbit indicated toward the horses. "They'll tell us if anything is around."

Clementine took a sip from the bottle of rum Hank had fetched to refill his flask. "I don't sense that danger is close. The creature might be miles from here by now since we don't know when it escaped." She glanced up at Boone. "It's been almost three days since Ludek investigated the mine and found evidence of a recent feeding." She ended that with a grimace.

"Who is Ludek?" Boone began gathering his gear.

Rabbit tried to remember where he'd heard that name before.

"I don't really know him. He's Hildegard's man. Well, not her 'man' per se, at least I don't think so. More of an employee. Servant. Maybe a friend." She shook her head, offering the bottle of rum to Boone. "You know, I'm not really even sure what their relationship is, only that he watches out for her—and now me, in a way."

Boone took the bottle from her. "You should formally introduce us to the both of them sometime."

He took a swig and then offered it to Rabbit, who waved it off. He'd had enough drink for tonight. Rabbit wasn't keen on sleeping too hard with that Hooly critter lurking out in the trees somewhere.

Boone handed the bottle back to Hank. "I think I'm full of enough rum for now."

"You got the right idea, Boonedock." Hank took one more drink and then corked the bottle. "Rum is puttin' me to bed before I get there. We'll be at it at first light, right Miss Clem?"

"Yep." She helped Hank pack up what was left of their meal.

"Should one of us stay awake and keep an eye out for trouble?" Boone asked. "Take shifts?"

She shook her head. "Everything I've read or heard about the *Höhlendrache* is that it likes the hunt. Sleeping prey is of no interest to it."

Boone snorted. "And I thought grizzlies were worrisome."

She grinned, her eyes teasing. "But if it makes you feel better, you three boys can sleep together like a litter of pups in one of the lean-tos and I'll take the other."

Rabbit laughed at Boone's curse. Yep, Uncle Mort sure would have gotten a kick out of Clementine. Damned *Bahkauv*.

Seventeen

Boone woke to a wet cold horse nose tucked into his neck. "Nickel! Get off me." He pushed on the horse's nose and rolled away.

Laughter filled the air around him. He squinted into the morning sun that was peeking over the ridgeline and through the trees. Clementine, Hank, and Rabbit stood in a semicircle around him.

"Sleepin' with Nickel again." Rabbit crossed his arms. "You two done, or do you need some more time alone?"

Boone growled. It was too early for this shit. "Close your flapping meat, Rabbit."

"Hoo hoo! Never seen a man sleep with his horse before." Hank scratched his whiskered chin. "Then again, there was that one time in Montana Territory …" His attention faded into his recollections.

Boone stood and stretched his back. He sniffed. Someone had made coffee. "Officially, I wasn't sleeping with Nickel, he was sleeping with me."

Nickel struggled to his feet from where he had been snuggled up against Boone's back and pushed at Hank to strap on his grain bag.

Boone stared down at his makeshift bed. Since Nickel was a

foal, he'd made a habit of sneaking into Boone's bedroll in the middle of the night, especially when they were on the trail. "You got hair all over my blanket, you big gollumpus." He shook out the blanket and folded it into a neat, tight square.

Nickel whinnied back without interrupting his breakfast.

"It stopped snowing last night sometime." Hank cinched one of the packs onto Fred the Mule's rump. "Didn't leave too much behind, I should be able to pick up them tracks."

The sun hadn't had much of a chance to cook the chill out of the air. The few rays that penetrated the thick forest struck the swirling steam in the air from the people and snuffling, snorting horses, creating rippling rainbows all around them.

"Here, Hank brought breakfast along." Rabbit handed him a tin of steaming coffee and a hard biscuit, and then started kicking snow into the fire. "We need to take him on the trail with us. His cookin' is a hell of a lot better than yours, Booney."

Boone ignored Rabbit's goading. "That rum of yours took me down to a nice solid sleep, Hank, even as cold as it was." He sipped at the coffee.

"Nickel helped with that last part," Rabbit ribbed him.

"I have something for each of you and this is as good a time as any." Clementine loosened the rope securing the flap on one of her packs. It clanged and clinked as she rummaged through the contents. After a moment she withdrew a curved leather sheath. She held it up by a mottled gray-brown bone handle and slid the blade from the leather. "Do you recognize this?"

Boone knew exactly what she held in her hand.

"Yes, ma'am," Rabbit answered. "That's just what I need." He reached for it.

She pulled back, shaking her head.

"That," Boone said, "is the blade you took from the white devil in the Bloody Bones."

"Stuck it right up through the fucker's chin and stirred his brains with it." Rabbit smiled and nodded.

Clementine handed it to Boone. "This is your weapon. I believe you possess the speed and acumen to wield it."

Boone took it by the carved bone handle and held it up in the sunlight. Its blade curved in a gentle arc and widened toward the tip. It was obvious from the glossy black appearance that it was not steel or iron but some unfamiliar material. He gently touched the blade with his thumb and instantly felt a sting as the blade cut into his flesh. Blood oozed up into a small drop on his finger.

Clementine smiled. "It's remarkably sharp. I was going to suggest that you avoid touching the blade. At least try not to cut any of us. Or the horses."

Boone nodded, feeling like a knucklehead, and pressed against the cut to stem the blood flow. "It's an odd shape."

"It's called a scimitar. It's made to slice through flesh and chop through bone, not hack through armor as a broadsword is. You will need to study your foe's weakness and exploit it."

"I'll tie up that sheath on Nickel's saddle for ya, Boonedock." Hank took the sheath from Boone and headed for Nickel.

"So, I'm in the expectin' frame of mind now," Rabbit said, rubbing his hands together. "Don't suppose you changed your mind and brought me that Olbert, did ya?"

"*Ulfberht*," she corrected. "No. As I said, I wield *Ulfberht*. But I did bring you something I think you'll find interesting. Or rather, Hank did." She pulled a small leather pouch wrapped in straps from her pack and handed it to Rabbit.

He took it but looked somewhat dismayed. He untied the straps and unrolled the bundle. His jaw slackened, his forehead wrinkled. He looked back and forth between Clementine, Boone, and the bundle.

"I think those will fit you perfectly, Jack."

He plucked a small knife from the leather bundle and held it up. "What the hell is this?"

"Some call it a knife," she said with a smile.

Hank nodded. "It's a throwin' knife. Them things are

dangerous. Chinese workin' on the railroad carried them things around. Killed rodents n' such for eatin'. Miss Clem is an ace when it comes to huntin' with 'em."

"What am I supposed to do with these? Join a circus? Booney, you put on a dress and hold a playin' card up. I'll throw one at ya."

Boone could almost read his partner's mind. Rabbit had talked untiringly for years that someday he would carry a sword, like the pirates whose adventures he read. Calico Jack and William Kidd and Benjamin Hornigold intrigued Rabbit to no end. Boone didn't understand the fascination, but he did understand his friend. There was probably mutiny on his mind.

"You throw it. It's made to pierce, not cut." Clementine plucked another knife from the bundle and balanced it on her index finger. "These particular knives are weighted to be thrown by the handle. Put your pointer finger along the top of the knife and wrap your thumb and fingers around the sides. Like this." She held the knife straight out in front of her as she'd described.

Rabbit mirrored her stance.

"When you throw, your body should be straight but leaning back. Raise your arm like this, as if you were preparing to shoot an arrow. Your other hand should be pointing at your target." Rabbit continued to imitate her movements. "Bring your arm back and throw. Your arm should follow through and your hand should cross your body and wind up near the opposite hip at the end of the throw."

Clementine cocked her arm back. "Watch me."

"Why can't I throw it the way that works for me?"

"You can try, but it's more accurate this way." She snapped her arm forward and in the blink of an eye, a small branch fell from a tree twenty feet distant, and then the knife hit the tree. *Thwap!*

Rabbit frowned at the tree. He raised his right arm and let his knife fly. It hit the tree trunk. *Clang!* It bounced off and dropped into the snow.

"Dammit." Rabbit shook his head and rubbed the hand that had been stuck by the Frenchman. "I don't see why I can't be strapped with a sword like Booney."

"Trust me." Clementine patted his shoulder. "You hit the tree. That's better than most their first time. Will you please fetch mine when you go get yours?"

Rabbit grumbled all the way to the tree, digging through the snow while Boone, Clementine, and Hank cinched packs and saddles on the horses.

"Did you pick up the trail, Hank?" Clementine leapt onto Fenrir.

"Surely did, Miss Clem. Lucky for us it stopped snowin' last night." Hank steered Fred down the side of the hill, further away from the mine. And Galena, too.

The bitterly cold morning gave way to a short, sun-drenched lunch on an outcropping of rock before the hunt continued. Boone figured it was almost warm enough to thaw his frozen toes and fingers. They plodded through snow into the afternoon, following the tracks as they meandered up and down thickly treed hills, along rocky ridgelines, and through shallow, treeless valleys. Occasionally, they came upon areas spoiled with chunks of flesh, bone, and blood-soaked snow where an unfortunate deer or elk had crossed paths with the *Höhlendrache*. It was evident by the remains that it wasn't killing to eat, but for sport.

"Where the fuck is this thing going?" Rabbit had vocalized his frustration more than once, voicing Boone's sentiment.

"We're a fair distance from Galena now," Hank said. "Don't know of any settlements out this way. Roubaix is off thatta way a half day or so." He paused to take in the surroundings, as he'd done countless times already. "I think that's so, anyway."

"I can't figure out if it's headed somewhere or just out looking for trouble," Clementine said.

They continued on through the forest. Rabbit voiced his

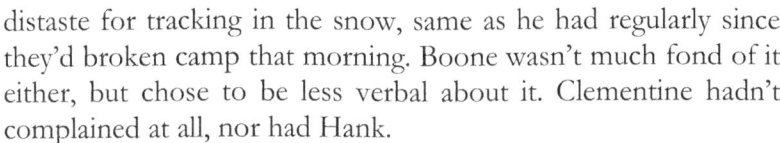

distaste for tracking in the snow, same as he had regularly since they'd broken camp that morning. Boone wasn't much fond of it either, but chose to be less verbal about it. Clementine hadn't complained at all, nor had Hank.

"It seems to me we're circlin' a little, Miss Clem. It may be it has a territory." Hank reined up Fred and scanned the thickly treed valley in front of them. "I believe there's a cabin down in there, if I'm rememberin' right."

They all craned their necks to see a sign of humanity.

"But we got us a problem. The beastie headed up along the ridge, thatta way." Hank pointed up to the right along a narrow ridgeline. "Do we follow him? Or do we head down to that cabin? See what they seen?"

"We need to head to that cabin." Clementine apparently didn't need to think twice about it.

Boone frowned her way. "It'll put us farther behind." He didn't like the idea of another night out in these woods.

"It'll only take a few minutes."

"They might have some coffee brewed, Booney. Let's take a look and then head on." Rabbit had pulled Dime up alongside Nickel and bumped Boone's stirrup with his own.

"Your thoughts, Hank?" Clementine asked.

Hank squinted toward the cabin. "There's something funny down there. Don't seem right, somehow."

Clementine shielded her eyes, following his lead. Boone watched her raise her hand to her chest and take several deep breaths. "There is something ... " She stopped mid-sentence and grimaced. "Wrong."

"You got the feelin', Miss Clem?"

She nodded. "Unfortunately so, Hank."

"Then we'll head on down." Hank started Fred down the hill, weaving between the trees.

Boone fell in behind Clementine with Rabbit bringing up the rear. Winter forests were quiet. Boone knew this, but this forest seemed exceptionally quiet. As they rode toward the cabin, Boone felt as if a heavy rock was sitting on his belly button, squishing his guts. His instincts were speaking loud and clear.

He looked back at Rabbit, one eyebrow raised.

Rabbit nodded, shucked his gloves, and stuck them in his coat pocket. As Boone watched, he tested the hammers on his pistol and sawed-off to make sure they weren't jammed with ice and snow. Boone did the same with his Winchester and Colt.

The cabin looked rickety from a distance, like most they'd seen in the Black Hills. Hastily assembled as protection against a fierce winter.

"Door's open," Hank said as they eased closer.

"Damn, you got good eyes, Hank."

Clementine nodded. "There's something scattered in the snow in front of the door."

Hank suddenly stopped, his jaw going slack. Boone and Rabbit halted next to Hank and Fred, while Clementine kept Fenrir plodding closer. Boone stared at the blood-soaked patches of snow peppering the yard in front of the cabin, his heart thudding hard in his chest.

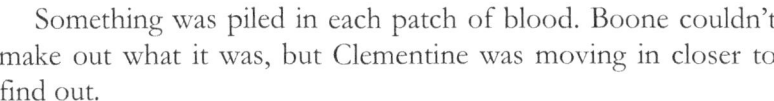

Something was piled in each patch of blood. Boone couldn't make out what it was, but Clementine was moving in closer to find out.

"Rabbit, Hank." Boone pointed at the forest around them.

Nodding, Rabbit began his watch.

Boone reined Nickel toward the cabin, joining Clementine. "What is that?" he whispered.

"I think it's skin."

"What?" Boone tried to make sense of the piles of wet, red flesh.

Her sword drawn, Clementine eased from Fenrir's back and crept toward one pile.

Boone followed, not quite so silently, his pistol ready. They squatted next to the pile of flesh. It glistened in the sunlight.

"It's human."

"Sonofabitch." He stared at the pile, his thoughts reeling. Who? Why? How? "That's gotta be a whole person worth of skin."

Clementine frowned at each pile and then at the cabin. "Three piles. Three people."

Boone gaped at her.

She stood. "We need to check the cabin."

"I knew you'd say that." He motioned Rabbit and Hank forward.

They both jumped down and stared at the mounds of skin.

"That's fuckin' skin, Booney," Rabbit whispered. "People skin."

"Yeah."

"What the fuck happened here?"

Boone shook his head.

"Boone and I will take a look in the cabin," Clementine told the other two. "You both watch for trouble out here." She started toward the cabin then stopped. "Put your guns away. You have proper weapons now."

Oh shit, right. Boone holstered his gun. "I'll get the sword."

When he returned, Clementine started toward the cabin again, moving cautiously. "If we run across anything inside, try to stay out of my way and help where you can. Remember, draw your blade in long downward strokes. Slice through the flesh. Don't hack until you reach bone."

He nodded, his pounding pulse reaching a crescendo as they neared the partially open door. Something had smashed the door in.

Clementine pointed at her chest, then Boone, and then the door.

He nodded again.

With Rabbit, it had always been Boone doing the planning and pointing and door kicking. But here? Now? He was perfectly fine with Clementine telling him how it would go.

She rushed the door, kicked it all the way open, and disappeared inside.

"Damn, she's quick!" he said under his breath. He charged inside, holding his sword in front of him and straight up for fear of poking the pointy end into Clementine. When his eyes had adjusted to the darkness inside, he found her squatting next to something on the floor. What was that? He moved closer. What was left of a body was laid out on the floor next to a table. Blood pooled on the floor around it. He leaned closer and gasped. The shock of realization sent him stumbling backward into the wall. He put his hands on his knees to keep from keeling over.

"Whatever did this is gone now," she said, rising. "We must have just missed it."

Boone stared at the body. "So that skin outside ..." He gulped a wave of nausea. "Not one bit left on the body."

"Completely skinned." Clementine pointed. "There are two others over there and one in the corner."

"Is it me, or are we one skin short?"

She rubbed the back of her neck. "Why would it take human

skin?"

"Hank was right. This is pretty fuckin' far from ordinary." He surveyed the cabin. Nothing seemed out of order. These men, if that was what they were, had been ambushed. They didn't even have a chance to put up a fight. "Whatever did this is gone, you say?"

"Yes, but it happened recently. You see how the bodies aren't frozen." She sighed. "And there is something else."

Boone wasn't sure he wanted to know what the "something else" was. "What?"

"I believe these men were alive when they were flayed. At least for part of it."

"How can you tell?"

"Do you see how the blood oozed here, but not here. The heart was still pumping."

"Jesus, Clementine." He grabbed her coat sleeve. "We should probably get gone." Boone pulled her toward the door, holding it wide for her.

Rabbit waited outside a fair distance from the piles of skin. "What happened in there? No smoke and bullets." Rabbit checked Boone over for injuries. Hank joined them and looked Clementine up and down.

"The owners of those are in there," Boone said, pointing at the three heaps of skin and blood. "Plus one more with the skin missing."

"You mean it *took* the skin?" Rabbit grimaced.

"It looks that way," Clementine said. "Whatever did it is gone."

"Sheeat." Rabbit took a step toward the cabin, but Boone caught his arm and shook his head.

"You don't want to see that." Boone couldn't have been more serious. He'd not seen a skinned human body before and would forever wish he still hadn't.

Rabbit looked him in the eyes for a moment and then slowly

nodded.

"You thinkin' our Hoolindragon did this, Miss Clem? Or somethin' else?" Hank grabbed Fenrir and walked the horse over to Clementine, handing off the reins.

"This wasn't a *Höhlendrache*. They mutilate and eat their victims, but they're not known to flay them alive."

Boone pointed at the ridgeline. "Besides, the tracks we've been following head up that ridge, not down here to this cabin."

Rabbit's gaze darted this way and that, his hands touching the handles of his guns. "Now we're huntin' two varmints?"

Boone shared Rabbit's agitation—his legs wanted to get moving.

"It appears so, Jack." Clementine searched the surrounding hills, her face lined. "I think we should stick to the original trail. This is a problem best left for a future hunt. I think whatever did this is going to be a bigger headache."

Boone climbed onto Nickel, watching the way Clementine continued to scan their surroundings even more so once she sat up on Fenrir. Her back was straight as a board, her head cocked a bit as if she were listening to something.

She doesn't think we're ready for this.

Somehow he knew that without asking her. That may well be true. Who or what skinned four grown men, for chrissake?

Boone fell in behind the other three as they climbed the hill to rejoin the tracks of the *Höhlendrache*.

Midday wore on and the shadows lengthened into a blustery late afternoon. They all hunched forward against the bite of the frigid wind. Fatigue showed on their faces.

Boone was pretty sure that they all would just as soon head back to Galena and warm their feet and hands by a good hot stove as continue this hunt. Even Clementine looked worn, her eyes dull when they met his.

Rabbit dropped back next to Boone.

"What the fuck would do something like that back at the

cabin, Booney?"

Apparently the grisly scene had been working on Rabbit's imagination.

"I mean, what *could* do something like that? We've seen men shot, stabbed, and beat to a pulp. We done a fair bit of lacin' ourselves. But that?" He shook his head. "If that don't beat all."

"I don't know, Rabbit. It's like we've stepped into something and there isn't any easy way to step back out again."

"Yeah."

Hank stopped and slid off Fred's back. He bent and studied the ground, then he looked up at the trees, his face pinched.

"Something wrong, Hank?" Clementine stopped beside him.

"Strange. Tracks just disappear. Right at this here tree." He squinted at the trees behind them. "Damned snow muddles my huntin'."

Rabbit scoffed. "You reckon it up and flew away?"

Hank rubbed his whiskers. "Well, I—"

"No, it took to the trees," Clementine interrupted, her expression lined with deep furrows as she stared toward a thick grouping of pines. "I think *we're* the ones being hunted now."

Eighteen

Clementine searched the growing shadows under the trees for signs of movement. Light was becoming scarce, with the sun about to bid them farewell behind the tall pines and the high ridgeline to the west. Night would be upon them soon, and the hunt had already shifted. The hunters were now the prey.

Four of them against one predator. In this case, a larger number didn't necessarily tip the scales in their favor. It only made for a bigger target.

She'd rather have come alone. She'd only ever hunted with one other—her afi, who was more experienced at hand-to-hand combat than her current companions. Throughout the day, the responsibility that came with keeping everyone alive in the face of death had weighed on her. Now, with Nótt, the beautiful giantess in Old Norse mythology, preparing her chariot to ride across the dark heavens yet again, Clementine hoped she wouldn't let them down.

"Hank." Clementine pulled out her sword and pointed it toward the small clearing near the edge of a rocky outcrop. "We need to get out from under these trees. Now."

He and the Sidewinders followed her as Fenrir led the way. Once in the clearing, Hank hopped off Fred and stepped gingerly toward the rocky outcrop. "Don't nobody go this way. Better

than thirty foot fall down there."

Clementine slid off Fenrir. She eased toward the dropoff, peering over the edge along with Hank. Boone and Jack joined them.

Thick shadows filled the treed terrain below them. Clementine focused inward, centering herself, reaching outward with her other senses. Something was near. Something not normally of this plane. She could feel its growing presence, like cold fingers scraping up her spine, making her muscles tighten and the hair bristle at the base of her neck.

"Anybody see anything?" Jack skinned his sawed-off and cocked both barrels.

"Put that away, Jack. You need to practice with your throwing knives."

He pulled the leather bundle from inside his coat and opened it. "Got it." He slid two knives from it and stowed the leather bundle back in his coat.

"Careful. Those are almost as sharp as Boone's scimitar."

Rabbit stuck one into his belt and grasped the other by the handle.

"I do believe you could do some damage with those, Jack Rabbit," Hank said.

"Prob'ly do more with my sawed—"

"Shhh!" Hank turned his ear toward the hillside above them.

Clementine listened, too. She bent her knees slightly and raised her sword, preparing for battle.

Swish thump, swish thump, swish thump.

Boone and Jack were crouched and waiting for trouble as well, sharing wary looks. Hank had his bow out with an arrow ready to fly. Boone slowly unsheathed his sword.

Swish thump. Swish thump.

Hank suddenly let out a bark of laughter. "Ain't nothin' but a deer lopin' through the snow."

Clementine caught a brief glimpse of the deer as it bounded

and weaved through a thick stand of trees. Hank was right, yet her body tingled with energy, a telltale sign that a threat loomed.

Hank lowered his bow. "Make a man feel beef-headed gettin' spooked like that."

Jack and Boone relaxed their positions, too, but their laughter was edged with tension.

Clementine remained crouched and ready, scanning the trees and shadows, listening to the sounds of the forest.

"Look." Hank pointed. "There's another'n running through over there. We should collect us some dinner, I'm thinkin'."

"I could use a good hunk of venison about now." Jack rubbed his belly.

"Almost looks like they're running from someth..." Boone stopped talking and frowned at Rabbit.

The horses whinnied and tossed their heads. Fenrir pawed at the ground, letting out a shrill neigh. Fred whimpered quietly, moving closer to Dime.

Blood surged through Clementine's limbs, raising the hairs on her skin. "It's close," she whispered.

Hank lifted his bow and strung an arrow again, his stance rigid and his hands steady.

Clementine didn't move a muscle as she watched the deer crash through a bramble of saplings. She tightened her grip on her sword, holding the hilt in front of her with the blade extended, unwavering, above her right shoulder. Her knees were still bent, ready to spring. Her body pulsed with energy and exhilaration, the bloodlust taking over.

She tilted her head, listening. There, under the sound of the pine needles whispering in the breeze, she could hear it.

... *Thump thump. Swoosh thump thump. Swoosh thump* ...

Before she could warn the others, a flash of black rushed past her and knocked Jack backward, landing him in the snow.

Jack!

The creature turned and crouched, preparing to pounce. In

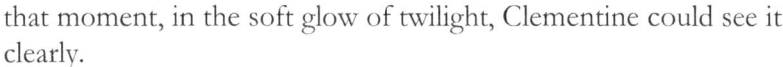

that moment, in the soft glow of twilight, Clementine could see it clearly.

So this was a *Höhlendrache*. The drawings had not done it justice.

The head and shoulders were that of a wolf mixed with a mountain lion with a wide snout and unnaturally long, thick fangs. In place of fur were scales, its skin similar to a snake or a lizard. The front half of the beast rested on two well-muscled legs with massive paws ending in long claws. The back half looked more reptilian, with a long thick tail that bristled with spikes reaching over a foot in length near the tip.

It shrieked and lunged toward her, moving at lightning speed.

Just as the beast reached out to swipe at Clementine with its scaly arm, thick curved claws extended, Fenrir rushed forward and plowed her shoulder into its chest. The blow knocked the *Höhlendrache* sideways, but it managed to catch one of the horse's back legs with a paw. Fenrir went down with a shriek, sliding though the snow, and tumbled over the edge of the dropoff and out of sight.

Fenrir!

With a scream of rage, Clementine charged the beast and swung her sword down, swift and hard, but her blade clanged off the thick scales covering the back of its neck.

The *Höhlendrache* turned and swiped at her. She pitched sideways, dodging its claws, and rolled away through the snow.

Jack pushed to his feet and drew back his arm, preparing to throw one of his new weapons.

The massive creature twisted toward Jack and swung its arm. The back of its paw smashed into Jack's chest. He flew backward again and landed in the snow at the base of a tree near the edge of the dropoff where he lay, gasping for breath.

An arrow *thunked* against the scales on the side of the beast. The wooden shaft splintered on impact and dropped to the ground.

Jack got to his feet again, somehow still holding the knife. He drew back and flung it. The blade hissed through the air and clanged against the beast's side and fell away.

"Damned scales!" he shouted.

In a blink, the *Höhlendrache* whirled toward Jack and lunged. Before he could escape, the beast knocked him onto his back again and stood over him, its long claws spread wide and raised to strike.

Clementine raced toward him, but Dime cut her off and crashed into the creature's back, sending it plummeting over the edge of the dropoff where Fenrir had fallen.

"Dime!" Jack struggled to sit upright, wincing in pain.

Boone stomped through the snow toward Jack. He glanced at Clementine as he passed her. "You okay?"

She had her sword raised and prepared for the creature's return from below. In her experience, these snarly types didn't die that easily.

"I'm fine," she told Boone. She wasn't sure about Fenrir, though. That was a steep drop. If that devil killed her horse, she was going to rip … No. Stop. Strength in serenity. She took a deep breath.

"Remember." She glanced around at the others. "Don't let it breathe or spit on you!"

"Damn beastie broke one of my arrows." Hank strung another one and stood behind Clementine.

"Is that what you two saw in the mine?" Boone checked Jack from head to toe. "You were right. It does have scales. Not nearly as big as a buffalo."

Jack waved him off. "Never mind that. Help me with Dime, he's cast in the snow."

Boone pulled him to his feet. They waded through the shin-deep snow toward Dime, but stopped short at the sound of a screech behind them.

Clementine turned as the *Höhlendrache* crested the edge of the

dropoff to her right. It crouched and leapt. She took a swing at its belly and missed as it soared over her head.

The creature bore down on Dime in great bounds.

Jack skinned his sawed-off and lit a round as the *Höhlendrache* leapt toward his horse.

BOOM!

The beast shrieked and twisted in the air, landing in a nearby pine tree.

An arrow whizzed passed Clementine. *Thwap!* This time the point found purchase in the pit of the creature's arm. It batted at the arrow, breaking it off, leaving the tip buried in its skin.

"Gotcha a weak spot, don't ya, bastard!" Hank rushed closer, strung another arrow, and pulled back on the bowstring.

The *Höhlendrache* hissed at him with a long forked tongue and spat. A glob of goo hit Hank in the chest. He reeled, as if he'd had too much liquor, then fell backward into the snow.

"Hank!" Jack cried and lit off another round at the beast's head.

BOOM!

The creature turned toward Jack and shrieked. It crashed to the ground and charged at Dime, who was still kicking his legs in the air, trying to right himself, Jack's pack weighing him down. Boone stood near Dime's head, trying to grab hold of the bridle as the horse thrashed in the snow.

Clementine ran toward Dime, gripping her sword tightly, but the creature was moving too fast.

Something crashed past Clementine and knocked her sideways. She careened shoulder first into a tree and stumbled, falling to the ground where she landed on all fours, her sword still in hand. She looked up in time to see Fred rush toward Dime with his ears flat, bellowing a drawn-out whinny haw. The mule reared up and kicked the *Höhlendrache* in the neck with one front hoof as the beast swung at Dime.

The creature hissed and clawed wildly as it fell onto its side next to Dime. One set of claws raked down Fred's shoulder, ripping large gashes into his flesh. The mule squealed and stumbled sideways before crumpling into the snow.

The *Höhlendrache* pushed upright and reached out, taking a swipe at Dime's flailing back legs, ripping gashes up one leg and along his haunch. Dime shrieked and kicked frantically at the beast's claws. Blood ran from his wounds, soaking the snow beneath him.

Clementine pushed to her feet just as Nickel swung alongside the beast and let loose with a double back kick. Both hooves smashed into the creature's head with a loud *crack!* It swooned and crashed to the ground.

She knew better than to believe that was the end of it.

Sure enough, the *Höhlendrache* rolled back upright, shaking off the kick. It turned on Boone, who was trying to free his frantic horse's reins that had snagged on a downed tree before Nickel broke his neck.

Clementine wasn't going to make it to Boone in time. "Jack! Use the knife!"

He pulled the knife from his belt, hauled back, and flung it at the creature.

Thwap!

The blade sunk deep into its eye and stuck. The *Höhlendrache* howled and pawed at the knife, knocking it free and into the snow. The beast thrashed and struggled to regain its footing, stumbling into Fred and raking its claws along the mule's shoulder.

That gave Clementine enough time to close the distance between them. She leapt in the air, feet first, and snapped her legs straight, kicking it in the shoulder. The beast rolled onto its back, exposing a long stretch of torso unshielded by scales. It flailed, trying to right itself while lashing out, but she moved in quickly with her sword high. She thrust it down with a roar and sank it into the side of its chest. It shrieked and squealed as her blade rent flesh and sinew.

"*Djevel!*" she cursed and twisted the blade deeper into its chest.

The *Höhlendrache* hissed up at her with its forked tongue, spraying her face with its poisonous spittle. A wave of nausea slammed into her and she reeled back, falling to her knees. She wiped her face with snow and fought the urge to vomit.

Clementine's blade still buried in its side, the beast turned toward her. Dragging itself partway up, it raised a thick arm above her head.

"Arrgh!" Boone charged, his scimitar in both hands, bobbing clumsily out in front of him. He leapt, spun in the air, and arced the blade toward the *Höhlendrache*. Using the momentum of his leap, Boone slammed the scimitar against the side of its neck and pulled it across the flesh, slicing through its soft throat.

Dark liquid gushed from the wound. The creature gurgled. Bubbles of slime and black blood poured from its mouth and the wound. It clawed at its neck as it fell onto the snow.

Boone covered his mouth and nose with the sleeve of one arm and raised the sword with his other. He swung again, smashing through the vertebrae. The head fell away. He dropped to the ground, coughing and gagging.

Clementine rushed to his side. "Can you breathe?" She dragged him away from the *Höhlendrache* while holding her arm over her nose.

Boone took a deep breath and gagged. "Killing that oversized skunk …" he coughed, "will raise somebody's ire, I'd wager." He coughed again. "Go check on Hank."

By the time she reached Hank, Jack had him on his feet. He was wobbly, but standing. Both men had their kerchiefs out and over their noses and mouths.

"I gotcha, Hank," Jack said. "Where'd it get you? I can't see no blood."

Hank shook his head. "Didn't get its hooks in me. Just spit

foulness at me." They frowned at the glob of goo still stuck to his coat. "Got me ta feelin' spooney." He shucked his coat and dropped it in the snow. "That coat is a goner. That beastie keeps killin' all of my clothes."

"It won't be killin' anymore. I'll get you a blanket." Jack headed for the blankets tied to Nickel's pack.

"I'll be back shortly. Tend to Fred and Dime," Clementine told Hank and headed for the dropoff.

She was afraid of what she would find at the bottom. She skidded down the steep hill, using trees to stop her as she slid through loose stones and snow. At the bottom, she rounded a few trees and some high brush surrounding an outcropping of rocks to find Fenrir lying on her side next to a small pile of downed timber. She was not moving.

Her heart pounding, she stopped. "Oh, Fenrir," she cried.

The horse's head lifted at the sound of her voice.

Clementine rushed over to Fenrir, who snorted and whinnied as she approached. The horse's eyes were wide, nostrils flaring as she bent over her.

"Easy, girl. I'm going to help you." Clementine's guts wrenched as Fenrir struggled to stand. She stroked the horse's neck. "Shhhh. Calm down. What did that *djevel* do to you, poor girl?"

A quick check found nothing more than scratches most likely from the trip down the steep drop. So why was Fenrir ...

The horse struggled to get up, but her head appeared stuck to something in the downed timber.

Clementine followed the trail of Fenrir's reins, up and around to a thick branch that had somehow worked its way through part of the bridle near her neck.

"You're tangled!" She laughed with relief. "Oh, blissful Valhalla, you're just caught on the branch!" Clementine blew out a breath of relief. "Let me help you."

She worked the reins free, all the while talking to Fenrir. "You

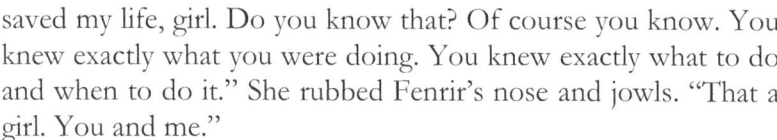

saved my life, girl. Do you know that? Of course you know. You knew exactly what you were doing. You knew exactly what to do and when to do it." She rubbed Fenrir's nose and jowls. "That a girl. You and me."

Fenrir nickered and nuzzled Clementine's hands.

After checking her legs to make sure the horse had no broken bones, Clementine pushed on Fenrir's rump to spur her up. "You should have seen your friends, Fenrir."

The image of Fred's hindquarter ripped open by the creature's long claws flashed in her mind. *I can mend him. I can mend him and Dime, too.* She'd brought along the makings for several poultices in case her battle with the beast had ended with her own bloodshed.

"Hurry, Fenrir, we've got to tend to Fred and Dime!"

"Clementine!" Boone's deep voice echoed through the valley. "Are you okay?

"Yes," she called back, leading her horse around the outcropping of rocks. "And so is Fenrir. We'll need to go around. This hill is too steep to climb. It might be a few minutes. How is everyone up there?"

"Okay. We're trying to tend to Fred and Dime. Nickel is fine. A little disconcerted, but fine." After a pause, he added, "I guess that describes Hank and Rabbit, too."

Clementine smiled, just a little. She hurried up the hill with Fenrir trailing.

It took almost a half an hour to reach the top of the hill. When she arrived at the scene of the battle, Fred was still on his side with Hank and Boone hovering over him. Dime was up but struggling to put weight on his back leg. Jack was cleaning his wounds with a rag, talking to Dime as he dabbed liniment into the gashes.

Nickel stood close by, nuzzling Dime's nose and nickering softly.

"Bleedin's almost stopped," Jack said when she touched his

shoulder. His eyes were watery. "Can't put no weight on that leg, though."

Clementine knew what that meant. Ordinarily.

"See to Fred. Hank is beside himself." Jack wiped his sleeve across his eyes and went back to tending Dime.

As she drew near, Boone looked at her, his face haggard.

"I think," Hank started, his voice cracking. He swallowed. "I think he's a goner, Miss Clem. Oh, poor Fred. Poor 'ol Fred the Mule."

She gently pulled Hank away and leaned closer to study Fred's wounds. The *Höhlendrache* had ripped a set of gouges in one direction and then another, making a crosshatch of oozing wounds on his flank and thigh.

She stood upright, hands on hips, and frowned at Hank and Boone. "It occurs to me, gentlemen, that you apparently have a low opinion of my healing skills." She whistled to Fenrir. When the horse joined her, Clementine loosened the pack that had somehow managed to stay tied to Fenrir's rump in the fall and pulled out her apothecary travel pouch.

"Boone, get me some water and a piece of cloth. Hank, I'm going to need your lantern." Without further ado, she commenced to tending a horse that was in bad shape and a mule that was in slightly worse shape.

Meanwhile, Boone and Jack scratched their heads about what to do with one decapitated *Höhlendrache*.

Nineteen

Hours later ...

Boone had a pretty good idea where Galena was, but he wasn't looking forward to lingering in that town. They hadn't had any trouble the first time, but why push their luck? Clementine, that was why. Confound if she wasn't hell-bent on paying another visit to that saloon. When pressed for what was so damned important about returning to the shithole, she'd muttered something about really needing a drink.

Boone had a pretty good idea about Dime and Fred, too. Clementine had made dandy work of patching them up, but they needed rest and time to heal and warm up some. Deadwood was too far. Goddammit.

He watched Clementine move in harmony with Fenrir as the horse pushed through the powdery snow. Hank and Rabbit had decided not to ride Fred and Dime, given the extent of their injuries. Both mounts were limping badly as it was. Clementine had suggested many times that she take a turn walking while letting Rabbit or Hank ride Fenrir, but neither would hear of it. Boone, on the other hand, had done his share of plodding through snow with cold toes while either Hank or Rabbit rode Nickel.

"Galena is through that gulch and a little ways on." Hank

stopped and checked Fred's wounds. He pointed at Dime and Fred. "Don't think we should push these two past that."

"Daylight is used up today anyway," Boone said more to himself than anyone else.

"What say, Boonedock?" Hank had started up again through the snow. The man was a beast on the trail.

"I say … " Boone ducked a low limb. "We'll need to find a stall or three for these boys, and girl, in Galena."

The sun was gone and a thick blanket of gray and even grayer clouds floated silently above. No stars to look at, but the clouds helped to keep the temperature up a little. Enough to keep his balls from getting brittle at least.

The small collection of shacks, tents, and cabins looked as deserted as they had when they'd previously passed through. The saloon, however, was alive with light and the low rumble of voices. They led their horses and Fred the Mule to the side of the building, away from the comings and goings of the front door.

"Looks busier than before." Rabbit squeezed one nostril shut and blew. "Bastards."

"Hank, will you take the horses on up to the livery?" Clementine asked.

"I ain't lettin' you go in there alone, Miss Clem."

"I won't be alone. I'll have the Santa Fe Sidewinders with me."

Boone squinted at her. "This Sidewinder business has gotten out of hand. People might get the wrong idea." He grinned as he said it, though. He actually liked the moniker … a little.

"What would you prefer instead?" she asked. " 'Mr. Leery McCreery'?"

"Too formal."

" 'Tin horn' suits you," Rabbit offered. "Maybe 'Mr. Molasses'?"

"Those hunks of meat on your face are flapping again, Rabbit."

"Did I offend? I apologize, Miss Nancy." Rabbit curtsied. "So are we goin' in or not? Let's get this behind us. Whatever it is." Rabbit handed Dime's reins to Hank. "You behave yourself, Dime. You're in good hands." The two men exchanged nods and Rabbit pulled the bundle of knives from his pack.

"Gimme Nickel, Boone." Hank held out his hand for Nickel's reins. "I'll be at the livery, anybody cares."

"Jack, if you don't mind my suggestion," Clementine said, pointing at the bundle of leather. "You should put that away and arm yourself with iron. You're dealing with humans now. Mostly."

She slid off Fenrir and handed her reins to Hank, who began a slow trudge toward the livery at the top of a long, steady slope, whistling a tune Boone didn't recognize.

Rabbit smiled wide. "You know how to make a man happy, Miss Clementine." He trotted over to Dime, stowed the bundle of knives in his saddlebags, grabbed his bandolier, and strung it over his shoulder.

On his way back, he drew and holstered his sawed-off a few times, quick as most anyone else could draw a pistol. "Perfect balance."

"Showing off, Mr. Quick Draw?" Boone drew his pistol and began checking the cartridges.

Rabbit held his pistol up to his ear and spun the cylinder. "Makes music, don't it?" He polished the barrel on his coat and holstered the pistol.

"No blades, then?" Boone pointed at the scimitar headed toward the livery with Nickel and Hank.

"No. But I'll need you and Jack to create a distraction while I tend to some business."

Boone studied her for a moment. She wasn't telling him everything. Hiding things from him had better not become a habit. "If we're in for a fight, I think you need to play straight with us. I don't take delight in the idea we're walking into a viper pit."

One of her eyebrows inched upward. "I thought a couple of mean old sidewinders could handle a bar full of trouble. Or maybe I should call Hank back. You and Jack can tend the horses."

Boone scowled at Clementine. "We're good to go."

"Okay, then."

"You line 'em up, Miss Clem." Rabbit skinned his pistol and pretended to shoot three imaginary bad men in front of him. "We'll stack 'em."

Boone fluttered a hand at Rabbit and said in his best Southern belle drawl, "I declare, you handle that six-shooter like a Texan, cowboy."

"Why, thank ya, li'l petticoat." Rabbit used the barrel of his Colt to push his hat up high on his forehead. He holstered his gun, put his hands on his hips, and grinned.

"Who can resist a handsome fella with a big gun?" Clementine joined their fun, pretending to fan herself for a moment. "Now, you two go on in. I'll be right behind you. Make sure you're noticed but don't start a fight. Not yet, anyway." Clementine busied her hands in the pockets of her overcoat.

Boone hesitated, still unsure of what Clementine had in mind. There must be some reason she wasn't spilling the beans on her plan. He could stand here all night and wonder or head in. It came down to trusting her, which he did. Well, that and the fact that Rabbit had already gone inside and was probably almost to the bar by now, flagging down the barkeep.

Boone stepped through the open door. He weaved his way through rough-sawn tables surrounded by scruffy men to the wall-length plank bar.

"Dammit, Brunhilda!" Boone said loudly and slammed his fist on the bar top next to Rabbit. "Where's the nugget?"

Rabbit turned and looked at him, his jaw gaping. But then he caught on. "You know damn well that nugget is mine!" He

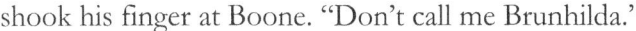

shook his finger at Boone. "Don't call me Brunhilda."

The man behind the bar glanced at them and then returned to pouring drinks.

"Barkeep. Whiskey." Boone shoved Rabbit. "Nugget, I said. I dug it. My claim. My nugget."

"Ain't neither your claim, you sow's ear. Lost it on that last hand, didn't ya? Didn't ya?" Rabbit shoved him back.

"You no-account, carpetbaggin' sheepherder! We wasn't playin' for claims, you idjit." Boone took his hat off and smacked Rabbit on the head with it, then placed it carefully back on his head. He glanced around. Yep. Got some attention already. Mention a nugget in a place like this and it was a surefire thing.

"You call me a sheepherder?" Rabbit adjusted his cockeyed hat. "You sidewindin', fat-headed, banjo-strummin' buzzard. You'd steal the coins off'n a dead man's eyes, wouldn't ya?" Rabbit downed his glass of whiskey and then grabbed Boone's and downed it, too. He leaned in closer and whispered, "I count fourteen. Just enough bullets. Fuckin' lucky."

"Ain't got no interest in stealin' nothin'," Boone continued their farce. "Just want my nugget. And now you owe me a whiskey, you mangy, flea-bitten bovine."

"I'd take ya out back of the barn and shoot ya, but ya ain't worth the bullet." Rabbit was getting that gleam in his eye.

Whoop. Careful. That gleam meant a good, sound belly laugh wasn't far behind.

Maybe it didn't matter, though. The distraction Clementine ordered up was in full swing. Almost everyone in the bar was watching the show now.

"Greetings, my hapless friends."

Boone and Rabbit turned and faced a man dressed in a long gray cape and tricorn hat.

Recognition flashed on Rabbit's face. "Sonofabitch."

"How fortunate I am to find in my purview the very two rascals to which my attention has been centered of late. Well, not

truly centered, I assure you. I would deem you more of a distraction. No, rather, an annoyance."

Rabbit's pistol was suddenly pointing at the Frenchman. With a flick of a long slender sword, the gun fell to the floor.

Boone snatched his revolver from its holster while lurching backward. He aimed it at the Frenchman, but the bastard was one step ahead of Boone. He had the point of his blade pressed against the side of Rabbit's neck.

As Rabbit stood frozen, a drop of blood oozed and dripped from his neck onto his coat sleeve.

Silence filled the bar. The crowd seemed to be waiting with held breath.

"Augustine!" Clementine called out loud and clear.

Boone glanced to his left. Clementine stood tall, seeming to have appeared from nowhere. She must have followed them inside and been watching the entire time.

"Ah! You are accompanied, and by a woman no less." The Frenchman addressed Clementine without taking his focus away from Boone. "You know my name, mademoiselle, but I am somewhat troubled to say I do not know yours."

Boone's trigger finger trembled slightly. The urge to blast a hole in the bastard's head burned in his gut. But if Augustine fell toward Rabbit … If he pushed that blade only a little, Rabbit was dead. Moreover, what if Boone's bullet didn't kill him?

Augustine tipped his head slightly. "Ah. Of course. Your compatriot fared poorly in our last encounter, and you would have as well. But you chose to strengthen your ranks with a *woman*?"

"I count three dead that didn't make it out of Deadwood," Rabbit said.

Shut up, Rabbit! Boone slowly shook his head at Rabbit.

"Face me, Augustine." Clementine shrugged off her coat, tossing it on a table, and raised her fists.

Boone did a double take. What did she have on her hands?

Were those gloves? They looked to be made of some sort of metal ... oh, knuckle dusters!

Boone had first seen the metal knuckles used in a fight at a bar filled wall-to-wall with sailors down near the docks in San Francisco. It wouldn't have been his choice to patronize that particular establishment, but on occasion Rabbit required assistance in removing himself from certain entanglements. When the fight was over, the faces of the men who'd been beaten by the devilish weapons had looked like chopped meat. He cringed at the memory.

Boone had seen knuckle dusters from time to time since then, but Clementine's were unique. Metal smithied into a thick band conforming to the shape of her knuckles. A bouquet of inch-long spikes protruded along the edges of her palms. Boone couldn't see how the knuckle dusters were held in place, possibly with a strap of leather or loop of metal grasped in her palms.

"Face *you*?" Augustine guffawed. "Oh, what new amusement is this?"

The *caper-sus* dog pack in the saloon erupted in laughter.

Rabbit used the opportunity to drop and kick, landing a boot heel on the Frenchman's shin. Augustine faltered for only a moment, but it was enough for Clementine to lunge forward and up, extending her arm in a mighty uppercut. Her knuckles smashed into the underside of his chin. He soared backward propelled by Clementine's momentum and the force of her blow.

Holy shit! Boone gaped. She'd nearly lifted him off the floor.

"Keep his dogs leashed!" Clementine told Boone, and then she took up her fighting stance again, fists up, protecting her body and face.

Boone understood immediately. The pack in the saloon had remained motionless until Rabbit made his escape. Now there was movement everywhere.

Boom! Rabbit's pistol sang out, the quick sonofabitch. Apparently he understood Clementine's order as well and had snatched his gun from the floor while he was down there. "Don't anybody else move a fuckin' finger!"

Boone heard the rumpled thud of a body hitting the floor. They were surrounded still, but none of the bastards wanted a piece of what number fourteen had received.

"Guess that leaves thirteen," Boone said, swinging his pistol back and forth at the crowd of *caper-sus* wearing bastards. "Don't interfere and you can leave with the same number of holes you came in with! We have enough bullets to put one in each of you."

"Jehoshaphat, Booney. Don't talk 'em to death."

Augustine had shaken off Clementine's blow and was holding his sword up, advancing slowly toward her. "A lucky tap, assuredly," he said to her. "Do you propose a duel? My sword against your ... *fists*?" The last word dripped with disdain.

Clementine smiled and motioned him forward.

The Frenchman growled and began slashing the air with his blade in a tornado of movement so quick Boone couldn't follow it. But apparently Clementine could. She blocked a slicing swing at her neck with her steel dusters. *Clang!* Then a thrust at her midsection. *Clank!* Two more sweeping chops. *Ting! Clang!* It looked to Boone like a fast-moving, choreographed dance as Clementine dodged and swung and twisted.

She kicked at Augustine's midsection, landing a blow to his abdomen, the strike knocking him back. He gasped for air. Clementine rolled forward into a somersault and came up hard and fast and using her momentum shot straight up with her arm extended. She smashed her fist into the underside of his jaw. The Frenchman's head snapped back, nearly connecting with his shoulder blades.

Boom! Boone heard Rabbit's gun explode.

Rabbit called out, "Twelve!"

Boom! "Eleven! More's comin', you fuckin' dogs!"

Boone watched Rabbit take aim at number ten.

Rabbit glanced his way. "Booney! Behind yo—"

A crash of searing pain spread over Boone's head, followed by a flash of lightning. Things got fuzzy for Boone after that. He kicked back and his boot connected with something soft. Moving on instinct, he swung around and fired. *Boom!*

"Ten!" Rabbit hollered. "Lay 'em out, Booney!"

Boom! Boom!

"Eight!"

Double barrels of a shotgun appeared over the top of the bar. Damned barkeep! Boone lunged over the bar, landing on his feet on the other side.

Boom! "Seven!"

The barkeep leveled the barrels at Rabbit.

Shit! Boone grabbed a bottle from the bar and flung it at the barkeep. It smashed into the side of his head and shattered, drenching him in shards of glass and whiskey. Blood mixed with the whiskey and ran down the barkeep's face. He squinted through the mess and swung the shotgun toward Boone.

Boone raised his gun in a flash. *Boom!*

The bullet glanced off the shotgun barrel, sending a shower of sparks over the barkeep's face and chest. His clothes and face burst into flames.

Damn. Boone frowned. Must have been the good stuff.

The barkeep screamed, flailing his arms in an attempt to douse the flames but managed to fan them instead. His entire upper body was soon engulfed in blue and orange flames. He ran, smashing through the front door, screaming all of the way, and disappeared into the darkness beyond.

"Six with style!" Rabbit called from across the room.

Boone's head was still throbbing. He spared a glance at Clementine, confident that she had things well in hand, but concerned nonetheless. As he watched, she lifted Augustine high with one hand and drew back her other arm, her fist high and tight, aimed at his face. He hung limp in her grasp.

Boone waited for the knockout blow to hit.

"Booney!" Rabbit's voice was higher than usual.

Boone turned to see three Galena saloon dogs holding Rabbit while a fourth leveled a pistol at his chest.

Without taking the time to think, Boone fired his pistol. *Boom!* The man with the pistol slumped to the ground.

"Five just in time!" Rabbit yelled, struggling to free himself from the three still holding him.

"Shut up, dead man," the man behind Rabbit snarled.

Clementine appeared in Boone's periphery, streaking toward Rabbit. She jabbed straight out, landing a steel duster directly to the forehead of the mangy cur holding Rabbit's left arm. He stood up straight and timbered backward.

Boone let loose on the two left holding Rabbit. *Boom! Boom!*

Rabbit shook himself free as the men slumped to the floor.

"Four, three, two. Thanks, Miss Cle—" Rabbit looked around for Clementine, but she had already dashed out the door. He turned to Boone with a mile-wide smile. "You're developin' some kinda style, Booney!"

"Two more somewhere." Boone scanned the saloon. Everyone was either dead or gone. "Where'd Clementine go?"

Rabbit shrugged.

Shit! Boone headed for the door. Before he'd taken more than a few steps, Clementine returned with Hank trailing.

"Didn't see any, Miss Clem," Hank said. "Came quick as I could when the shootin' commenced, but too late. Not a body came past me. Saw a flamin' man, but that's it." He scanned the room, letting out a low whistle. "Looks like you three were shootin' frogs in a barrel."

"Are you two okay?" Clementine asked.

Boone and Rabbit collapsed into chairs, breathing hard. "No new holes. You, Rabbit?" Boone asked, but he knew the answer already.

"Good to go. You ain't even breathin' hard, Miss

Clementine."

"Augustine escaped."

"How? Appeared to me that you had him wrapped up." Boone couldn't believe he'd escaped after what he saw.

"I had to let him go. It looked like Jack could use a hand." Clementine's brow furrowed as she glanced around the saloon.

"I had him covered." Boone had taken the last two holding Rabbit and was pretty sure he could have laid out the third as well.

"Not quite." Clementine bent and pushed at the body of the dirty dog she'd clobbered in the forehead, coming back up with a small, throwing knife. She held it up. "Bastard had this at Jack's ribs."

The blade was black, like Boone's scimitar. The silver handle was inlaid with engraved ivory.

Rabbit stuck his finger in the new hole in his sheepskin coat. He held up his thumb and forefinger about an inch apart. "I was this close to havin' that thing between my ribs."

Boone raised his eyebrows. "Didn't see that."

"My new coat, too. You bastard." Rabbit kicked the boots of the man who had almost split his ribs.

"Damn. So we lost the Frenchman."

Clementine nodded. "And two others ran when the dustup started, before any of us could take care of them. It's just as well, I guess. Not all of those wearing the *caper-sus* brand necessarily need killing."

"Well, I for one appreciate the timely dispatch of that knife-swingin' bastard, Miss Clementine." Rabbit bowed.

"Happy to help, Jack."

Rabbit pointed at the knife in Clementine's hand. "Can I have that? It is for throwin', right?"

Twenty

Later the next afternoon ...

Clementine eased slowly into the steaming bath water. The small of her back tingled from the heat as she sank inch by inch. "Ahh. That hits the spot." She groaned as the warmth seeped into her bones, enjoying a moment of privacy after days on the trail with Hank and the Santa Fe Sidewinders.

The Dove's private bathing area had been empty when she'd followed Dmitry into the large room, who'd been carrying pots of hot water. He'd filled the tub for her quickly, adding a dash of powder that he said was Hildegard's favorite treat, and whisked the water until bubbles covered the surface. Then he left Clementine with a bar of lavender soap and a promise of fresh warm bread and apple butter after she finished bathing. She'd wasted no time closing the curtains around the tub and stripping down to skin.

After a thorough scrubbing from head to toe, she lowered her eyelids and relaxed in the sweet floral-scented steam. Dmitry somehow knew how to make the water just a tiny bit hotter than perfect. As her muscles loosened, her thoughts returned to Galena ...

She, Hank, Rabbit, and Boone had spent a frigid night in the stables with their mounts before journeying back to Deadwood early this morning. It had been a mostly sleepless night for Clementine in the unheated livery.

Besides the cold keeping her shivering off and on, she had death on her mind, as in the men that they'd left lying in the saloon after Augustine had fled. With the snow and frozen ground outside, she couldn't come up with a discreet way to dispose of all the bodies. In the past after a fight, she had been able to bury the evidence or take flight from the area. And when she slew *others*, their remains usually returned to the earth by turning to dust or smoke.

The frozen ground was damning her to exposure. In more ways than one when she considered the *Höhlendrache* that had died by Boone's blade. They'd tucked its carcass partway under a stone overhang. With any luck, forest scavengers would take care of it over time.

By morning, she'd discovered that her nightlong fretting session had been a waste of time. When they returned to the saloon in the daylight, they found that someone, or something, had carried the bodies away during the night. The tracks in the area were such a jumble that Hank couldn't find any of significance to follow.

At that point, Clementine didn't really want to follow anyone anyway. They all needed to rest, herself included. Their battles along with the brutal cold had taken a toll on them.

As for the missing dead, she was fairly certain none would find their way to her examination table. But if any did, it would be a trail for her to follow. No, the "lieutenants" that the Rogue Executioner had spoken of wouldn't chance leaving her breadcrumbs.

After finally arriving in Deadwood in the late afternoon, the first thing Clementine had wanted to do was to wash the filth of battle from her body. The fetid breath of the *Höhlendrache* seemed to cling to both her clothes and skin. The caressing warmth of a bathing tub to soak her aching muscles and bones wouldn't hurt either. Days of riding a cold rough trail were not for the weak. She had more appreciation for the Sidewinders' journey to Santa Fe and back now.

Upon returning to town, the men had professed a strong desire to avoid the agony of starvation. After securing the horses and mule in the barn, they had gone in search of a thick steak and side of cornbread.

"Bathin' can wait." Jack had put it succinctly when she'd parted from them.

The sound of the door to the private baths creaking open and quietly clicking shut interrupted her thoughts.

"Clementine?" a familiar voice said from the other side of the curtain.

"Yes, Hildegard?"

"May I come in?"

"Of course."

Hildegard pulled back the curtain surrounding the bath, closing it again behind her. "Your cheeks are rosy. Dmitry has the water temperature satisfactory, I hope?"

"Perfect, as usual." Clementine smiled up at Hildegard.

The madam wore a dark green dress this afternoon, her hair coiffured with a few loose tendrils. Her cheeks were dusted with rouge and her lips stained red. Clementine envied Hildegard and her finery. What would it be like to dress in such beautiful clothes day after day instead of old wool shirts and trousers? To wear satin and lace instead of leather aprons stained with blood? To smell like flowers instead of disinfectant alcohol … and death?

"Is Deadwood treating you well today?" Clementine asked.

"The winters are unpleasantly cold, I'm beginning to find."

"Unlike those in the Black Forest?"

Hildegard laughed. "No. Very much like the Black Forest."

"But not quite so severe as Nordic winters." Clementine always shivered when she thought of waking up on winter mornings to start the fire in her grandparents' house. She had experienced enough of both Black Forest and Nordic winters to distinguish them, though neither was pleasant.

"I imagine your night in Galena supports my observation?" Hildegard pulled a chair closer to the tub and sat. "Where did you spend the night?"

Clementine groaned at the memory of her cold, restless night. "We slept in the livery with the horses. Well, the men slept, I found it difficult to relax after the evening's ... festivities." She lowered her voice on the last word in case they had company.

"Don't worry, we are alone." Hildegard crossed her arms. "For the moment."

Clementine leaned the back of her head against the tub. "I met the Rogue in the *caper-sus* saloon in Galena."

One painted eyebrow lifted. "*Caper-sus* saloon?"

"The *caper-sus* was displayed on the shingle outside and on the walls inside. Many, if not all of the patrons, wore it in some fashion."

"Which one? The curved horned or curled?"

"Curled." Clementine shifted, sloshing the water. "The Rogue is as we thought—*ein Scharfrichter*."

"Ludek was certain of that."

"She called the Upstart a 'lieutenant,' I believe." At least Clementine assumed the Rogue was referring to Augustine. She went on to tell Hildegard about the fight in the saloon and how the Upstart had gotten away.

"Did the Upstart know you are *ein Scharfrichter*?"

"Maybe. I indiscriminately displayed my fighting skills for everyone in the saloon to see."

"Surely he could smell death on you anyway."

Clementine shrugged. "I disguised my scent."

"I was unaware you could do that."

"A *Scharfrichter* does not live long without knowing a few tricks." She changed the subject. "Ludek was correct about the

beast in the mine. It was a *Höhlendrache*. But when we arrived, it had escaped. We tracked it for a day and then it attacked us. We slew it in the forest."

Hildegard nodded. "Did *der Höhlendrache* present a challenge to your compatriots?"

Clementine dipped the washcloth in the water and ran it down each of her arms. "The *Bahkauv* presented a challenge due to the sheer number of beasts we confronted. The *Höhlendrache* offered a different type of trial."

"They performed well? No one panicked? No one fled?"

"Correct." Clementine thought back to the Battle of the Bloody Bones, frowning slightly. "Quite the opposite both times, actually."

"Courage to a fault?" the madam asked with a smirk.

"Are you reading my mind, Hildegard?"

"You and I think alike more often than not, *Scharfrichter*. So, *der Höhlendrache* was their first encounter with a *Jäger*." She used the German word for "hunter."

"Yes. We tracked it for some time but it eventually turned the game and started pursuing us."

"That surprised you."

It shouldn't have, but she'd been distracted. "Do I even need to speak, or can you just look into my mind?"

Hildegard chuckled. "Yet you slew it."

"I helped to slow it down a little, but Boone took its head."

"I'm impressed. And the other two men?"

"They helped as well." Clementine took the rag and draped it over the edge of the tub. "Believe it or not, our mounts did, too. Fenrir saved me from potential injury when the *Höhlendrache* came for me."

"Then your *musterage* is nearly complete."

Musterage? What did she mean by that?

"Have you spoken to *Herr* Masterson?" Hildegard asked.

Clementine hadn't given much thought to her patron since

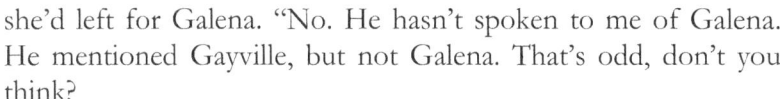

she'd left for Galena. "No. He hasn't spoken to me of Galena. He mentioned Gayville, but not Galena. That's odd, don't you think?"

"Indeed. The Black Hills is not a fractured territory."

"So his charge should include Galena, and yet he has relayed no instructions to avoid that area." Clementine took the whisk Dmitry had left behind on the small side table, swishing the water. "There is something else out there. Out beyond Galena."

"Yes?"

"Has Ludek come across anything that I should know about? Anything you haven't mentioned?"

"Only inconsequential occurrences that he and I and Miss Hundt can handle ourselves."

What sort of inconsequential occurrences? Hildegard did not explain further under Clementine's stare. Apparently, the madam had some reason to keep additional explanation from her.

"On the trail of the *Höhlendrache*, we came across a cabin. Outside, we found three skins—human skins. The door had been forced. Inside we found four skinless bodies."

"Good heavens. A skin was missing?"

"Yes. And it was recent to our arrival. The blood had not yet frozen."

Hildegard's powdered forehead wrinkled. Her hand covering her throat, she whispered, "Could it have followed us, all the way from the Black Forest?" She stood abruptly. "I must talk to Miss Hundt about this." She reached for the curtain and left.

Clementine frowned after her, several questions left unanswered. What was a *musterage*? Was that German? And what were the inconsequential occurrences of which she'd spoken? For slayers, truth and trust were rare commodities when it came to dealing with *others*. What was Hildegard withholding? Clementine wasn't in the habit of considering anything inconsequential.

The curtain parted and Hildegard slipped back through. She

held the same tin Dmitry had carried earlier containing the soap powder used to create bubbles. She also had a large towel draped over her arm. "You may need these." She dumped more powdered soap into the tub. "Stir that up. I'll put this within reach." She laid the large towel on the chair.

As ordered, Clementine stirred the water with the whisk, churning it into large piles of froth. "What's this about?"

A coy smile was all Hildegard offered in return. "I'll send Dmitry in with more hot water. You seem to be cooling off. Enjoy your bath." The madam disappeared through the curtain.

Clementine listened as Hildegard's footfalls moved away, followed by a door opening and closing.

"Was that odd?" she asked aloud in the empty room.

Yes, that was definitely odd.

She sank into the bubbles, submerging her head. She stayed under and scrubbed her scalp. Resurfacing, she began working bubbles into the length of her hair. Maybe she should cut it short. It was unwieldy. She remembered her amma brushing it when she was young. "Your hair is so much like your mother's," her amma would say, her eyes full of sadness. "So thick and shiny."

Clementine used the small pitcher of clean water next to the tub to rinse the soap from her hair. She'd never seen any painting or likeness of her mother, having to form a fuzzy image of the woman who'd birthed her based only on what her amma told her. Her afi had rarely spoken of his daughter. When Clementine would ask him about her, his face would line and he'd turn away.

She wrung the water from her hair, the dark auburn color muted when wet. No, she wouldn't cut it, but a trim wouldn't hurt.

Bang! Clementine stilled. Was that the door to the private bathing room?

"Somebody order hot water in here?" Jack called out.

Jack!? Odin's beard!

"I got hot water here for a Miss Clementine, was it?"

"I do believe that was the name. Let's see if we can find her."

Boone, too? Dammit!

A herd of boots clomped toward the closed curtain.

"*Ah helvete,*" she cursed.

The curtain swished open.

"You order hot water, ma'am?" Jack held up the bucket. "I'll pour for you." He stepped inside the curtain and tipped the bucket into her bath.

The steaming water was almost too hot again. She squirmed for more reasons than the temperature of the water.

Boone peeked over Jack's shoulder, his eyes as big as saucers. "Why, Mr. Fields, I do believe the lady is in the bath."

Jack let the bucket fall to the floor. "Shiver me timbers, Mr. McCreery, I believe you're right. Is this what's considered 'indisposed'?"

"All right, you two flannel mouths." Clementine grinned, sinking up to her chin in bubbles. She had a feeling they were going to stay awhile.

Boone chuckled and tipped his head toward Jack. "You think that means she's sweet on us?" He leaned forward and looked into the tub. "That's a lot of bubbles." He grabbed the towel from the chair and sat, draping it over his knee. "You hiding something in there?"

Jack pulled in another chair from the next bath over, turned it around backward, and straddled it. "Prob'ly got a sword in there."

"Probably. What else do you have in there besides a sword?" Boone waggled his eyebrows.

"I believe I heard three sets of boots." Clementine craned her neck to see past Boone. The curtain twitched. "Am I right?"

Boone and Jack leaned on each other and began snickering hard enough to make Jack snort.

"Uh ... yessum." Hank cleared his throat from where he was

hiding on the other side of the curtain. "I mean, well, yes, Miss Clem. I'd be that third boot. I mean third pair of boots. I'm not a boot. I'm wearin' new boots."

Clementine grinned. "Hank, come in here and join us."

The curtain fluttered and Hank backed in through the opening.

"Close the curtain, Hank. There's a draft."

"Yes, Miss Clem." Hank swished the curtain closed and continued to back toward the tub. He backed into Boone and veered away, continuing until his legs bumped into the tub, making him teeter and almost fall into the water. He stood up straight and still, staring at the curtain.

"Apologies, Miss Clem."

Clementine couldn't help but chuckle. "Will you turn around, Hank?"

"No!" He wiped his brow with the back of his hand. "I mean, uh, I'm comfortable facin' this partic'lar direction presently."

Boone and Jack burst into laughter.

"I'll get you a chair, Hank," Jack said in between chortles.

"No, that ain't necessary, Jack Rabbit."

"That's okay, Hank, I got it." Jack disappeared through the curtain and returned, carrying a third chair. He plunked it down next to his. "There."

Hank shook his head.

"Please sit, Hank." Clementine swished the whisk, making more bubbles. "I assure you I'm completely covered." Although the bubbles were dispersing more quickly than she'd have liked.

"Aw, Miss Clem. I … Okay." He felt behind him for the chair and clunked and banged it around so that it faced away from Clementine. Then he shuffled himself into the chair, all the while keeping his back to her.

"Well executed, Hank." Boone smiled broadly, watching Clementine.

"Okay. You boys have your revenge."

Boone and Jack looked at each other, feigning shock, and shook their heads.

Boone put his hand to his chest. "Whatever does she mean, Mr. Fields?"

"I surely don't know, Mr. McCreery."

"Miss Clem," Hank said to the curtain. "I never would."

No, Hank wouldn't. But the Sidewinders were a wily duo. Clementine stuck her feet out the end of the tub, sinking to her chin. She scooped bubbles into ridges of bubble peaks and carved gulches between. "So, do you boys need my help with something?"

"Looks like the Black Hills made of bubbles," Jack said, watching her sculpt.

"No ma'am." Boone sat back, crossing his arms. "We wanted to make sure you were healthy and happy." He looked the length of the tub, to her pink toes and back. "Seems you have a dose of both."

"I do."

"Well, I'm not here to cause you no distress, Miss Clem." Hank was talking to the ceiling now. "But there was two things I needed to tell ya."

"I'm listening, Hank."

"First thing, word is there's a new undertaker in town. Put his shingle up yesterday."

Clementine stopped playing with the bubbles and stared at the back of Hank's head. "Are you sure?"

"Yes, ma'am."

What did that mean? She'd have an empty table in her exam room a little more often. That would be a relief. Maybe she'd have more time to do the job she came to Deadwood to do. She nodded her head once at the notion.

"So, you just decided that's a good thing." Boone scratched his jaw.

"I think so. My time is mostly wasted there now." She sat up a little, resting her arms on the edge of the tub. "Say, I thought you three were going to find a steak."

"Ever'place is full up or outta decent grub." Hank leaned his elbows on his knees and started batting at the curtain.

"Dmitry and Alexey fed us." Jack pointed his thumb toward the kitchen.

Boone grinned at Jack. "Might be the best beef knuckles and cabbage I've ever had."

"And to think you had to come to Deadwood to get it."

Boone's grin widened. "Remember the rancid pig knuckles in Ruidoso?"

"Ugh. Worst cantina ever. A starvin' dog wouldn't eat in that stable."

Clementine watched the Sidewinders with a small smile, feeling like one of them. The trip to Galena and back had changed something inside of her. Her loneliness was not such an ache anymore. She turned to the oldest of the three *amigos*. "What was the other thing, Hank?"

He stopped batting at the curtain. "Hmm. Let me think. Can't 'member what the second thing was. Take a minute to get my thoughts back to it."

"We have news, too, Miss Clementine." Jack winked at Boone and slapped Boone's leg.

"Please tell me you haven't made the *Trailblazer* again already," she joked, moving bubbles to cover the opening spaces.

"We've offered Keller a price for the livery," Boone said, his voice a little husky. He appeared to be mesmerized by her hands as she moved bubbles.

"Really? So you've decided to put down some roots in this frozen soil?" Clementine knew that Jack had been ready to jump at the chance since their return to Deadwood, but Boone had taken somewhat longer to reach his decision.

"Yep. Keller accepted," Jack told her. "Said he's run his race and he's ready to skedaddle." He slapped Boone's leg again.

"Goin' into the livery business."

"Hank knows a good blacksmith that's arriving' in town soon," Boone added. "So we'll have a look at him. Maybe have him run the place." He looked pointedly at her. "Hank's a good judge of character."

"He's the best you'll get," Hank told them. "Met Rails on the railroad. Don't know if'n that's his real name but he drove spikes like a steam donkey. Has a daughter. She's good with horses. Seems like a fit you couldn't ask for."

"Well, I'm happy for you two. Odin smiles on you." Clementine dipped her cold toes back in the warm water.

"They'll need a place to call home. Pert near ever'place in town is full up." Hank glanced over his shoulder at Boone.

"A daughter, you say?" Jack rubbed his hands together, a playful glint in his eyes as he looked at Hank.

"Nice girl. Cute as a button. She'd be, what, seventeen, eighteen by now, I think. Maybe older. Time's hazy for me."

"Well, we can let them have the loft," Jack offered. "Don't know where we'll be, though. Guess we have that lot next to the livery. Sell off the wagons and such. Build a proper house. Or maybe a shack. Either way."

Boone nodded. "Hank can stay with us."

Clementine raised her brow. She'd not heard Boone talk of settling in Deadwood. Only Jack had mentioned actually taking up residence. Until now.

She gathered her hair and began wringing the water from it.

"Booney! That's a great idea!"

"Well, then. It sounds like it's settled." Clementine twisted her hair and piled it on top of her head, grabbing the pair of wooden hair combs her afi had carved for her to keep it in place.

"I suppose we're still in the middle of our two-day trial?" Jack scowled. "We finished it. Did we finish it? Gotta start again would be my guess. Dammit." He finished the conversation with himself and tapped his heel on the floor.

"Your bubbles are abandoning you, Clementine." Boone's eyes met hers for a moment.

She looked away first, down at the bubbles. Hmm. Her visitors would be able to see something before long. She swished the whisk a few times, smiling back up at Boone as if the dispersing bubbles were no matter.

His gaze narrowed. "I've been meaning to talk to you about that little trick you played in Galena."

"What trick?"

"You used us as bait."

"Yes." There was no denying the truth.

He snorted. "Of course you'd admit it."

"Of course you'd know I was testing you."

"What? You think we're knuckleheads?" Jack pulled a small knife from his belt. He flipped it in the air and caught it.

"No, Jack."

"Well, how'd we do?"

The whisk wasn't doing its job anymore. The few bubbles left weren't covering much. *Hel's teeth!*

"You boys have finished the two-day trial. It's time to move on." She dropped the whisk on the small table near her head. It was also time to call their bluff. "Will you hold that up, please, Boone?" She pointed at the large towel he'd draped over his knee.

With a challenging glint in his eye, he smiled and stood, holding the towel out between them.

Jack looked from her to the towel and back, his forehead lining. "What are you …"

As she began to rise from the water, Jack looked up at the ceiling. Boone turned his head to the side, his eyes closed.

"Goldurn it, Miss Clementine!" Jack sputtered. "You weren't supposed to stand up." He sprung to his feet and turned toward the curtain.

Hank shot up too, knocking his chair into the side of the tub.

He began fumbling for the break in the curtain. "Miss Clem! I declare!" He gave up and covered his eyes.

She took the towel from Boone, wrapping it around her.

"Onto the next step of our training, then," Boone said smoothly, locking eyes with Clementine as she tucked the corner of the towel between her breasts.

"Correct. You did well against the *Höhlendrache*, but I have much to teach you and Jack." She took the hand he offered to help her step out of the tub.

"My vitals!" Jack clapped his hands and then pretended to throw the knife.

The outer door creaked open. Soft footfalls came toward them.

Hildegard poked her head through the curtain. "Your visitors didn't interrupt your bathing time, I trust." Her grin was downright mischievous.

Clementine laughed. "Madam, you are incorrigible."

"Only in the nicest way." She handed Clementine her clean clothes, folded and warmed by the kitchen stove as promised by Dmitry.

"You sent these three troublemakers in here, I presume?"

She shrugged. "I might have hinted that you were receiving guests." She held up a small envelope. "I have a letter for you. It was left with Jurgen." Hildegard handed it over. There was no writing on it.

Clementine frowned at Boone and then Jack, who'd turned away from the curtain upon Hildegard's arrival.

"Might as well read it," Boone said.

Clementine opened the envelope and unfolded the paper it contained. She decided to read it aloud for all of them to hear.

Salutations Undertaker,

She growled. "It's the Rogue's handwriting." She read on …

It is my hope that this letter finds you well and in good spirits. I claim neither myself, however, for I have committed an unforgivable error in judgment. I believe you comprehend, or perhaps you do not, that the responsibility rests not entirely on you, but on me as well. I placed in you unwarranted trust and that is inexcusable.

In my defense, I believed that extending to you the benefit of belief and charity was the professional and proper course, but alas you have proved me misguided, once over.

It pains me to witness your shortcomings and inability to complete the charge you so readily display. I need not remind you of the consequences of your failure. Or perhaps, given my observations thus far, you are in need of repeated prompting.

You refused assistance in Galena, yet Augustine remains free to host his position. It is beyond my fathom how that came to pass. More important, it is my summation that you do not, even yet, realize that he was not and should not have been your objective in that establishment. Your objective left shortly after me and roams free still as well.

It occurs to me that the best course of action is as follows: I will disable, in some way, your quarry. Perhaps shackle him to a standard? Or simply serve him to you on a silver platter.

Pray tell what, short of that and in your estimation, can be done to ensure your success?

Additionally, I still await recompense for my favored dagger. Please attend this oversight directly.

P

Clementine cursed, offering the letter to Hildegard. She wondered if steam was escaping from her ears.

Boone stared at her, his jaw slack.

"Oh my, she is quite confident," Hildegard said, shaking her

head as she scanned the letter. "I will warn Ludek to be doubly careful in her presence."

Jack grinned. "She sounds like a spitfire!"

"She's sure throwin' a lot of dust," Hank said, with his back to Clementine still. "What I wanna know is what skinned those poor fellas in that cabin."

Clementine looked from Jack to Boone, remembering the scene they'd stumbled upon the previous day. Their troubled expressions probably matched hers.

Lowering the letter, Hildegard frowned at her. "A more worrisome question might be who's opening the gates for all of these menaces?"

The End ... for now

Book 3 in the Undertaker Series will be coming your way in 2020!

Read on for the first chapter of Book 3 (Can't Ride Around It).

The Deadwood Undertaker Series

Deadwood (late 1876) ... A rowdy and reckless undertaker's delight. What better place for a killer to blend in?

Enter undertaker Clementine Johanssen, tall and deadly with a hot temper and short fuse, hired to clean up Deadwood's dead ... and the "other" problem. She's hell-bent on poking, sticking, or stabbing anyone that steps out of line.

But when a couple Santa Fe sidewinders ride into town searching for their missing uncle, they land neck deep in lethal gunplay, nasty cutthroats, and endless stinkin' snow. Their search leads them to throw in with Clementine to hunt for a common enemy.

What they find chills them all to the bone and sends them on an adventure they'll never forget.

More Books by Ann

Books in the Deadwood Mystery Series

WINNER of the 2010 Daphne du Maurier Award for Excellence in Mystery/Suspense

WINNER of the 2011 Romance Writers of America® Golden Heart Award for Best Novel with Strong Romantic Elements

Welcome to Deadwood—the Ann Charles version. The world I have created is a blend of present day and past, of fiction and non-fiction. What's real and what isn't is for you to determine as the series develops, the characters evolve, and I write the stories line by line. I will tell you one thing about the series—it's going to run on for quite a while, and Violet Parker will have to hang on and persevere through the crazy adventures I have planned for her. Poor, poor Violet. It's a good thing she has a lot of gumption to keep her going!

Books in the Deadwood Shorts Series

The Deadwood Shorts collection includes short stories featuring the characters of the Deadwood Mystery series. Each tale not only explains more of Violet's history, but also gives a little history of the other characters you know and love from the series. Rather than filling the main novels in the series with these short side stories, I've put them into a growing Deadwood Shorts collection for more reading fun.

About the Authors

Ann Charles is a *USA Today* bestselling author who writes award-winning mysteries that are splashed with humor, adventure, paranormal, romance, and whatever else she feels like throwing into the mix. When she is not dabbling in fiction, arm-wrestling with her children, attempting to seduce her husband, or arguing with her sassy cat, she is daydreaming of lounging poolside at a fancy resort with a blended margarita in one hand and a great book in the other.

Facebook (Personal Page):
http://www.facebook.com/ann.charles.author

Facebook (Author Page):
http://www.facebook.com/pages/Ann-Charles/37302789804?ref=share

Twitter (as Ann W. Charles):
http://twitter.com/AnnWCharles

Ann Charles Website:
http://www.anncharles.com

Sam Lucky likes to build things—from Jeep engines to Old West buildings to fun stories. When he is not writing, feeding his kids, attempting to seduce his wife, or attending the goldurn cats, he is planning food-based booksigning/road trips with his wife and working on one of his many home-improvement projects.

Sam Lucky's Website:
http://www.samlucky.com

Can't Ride Around It

Book 3

Ann Charles
Sam Lucky

COPYRIGHT 2020 ANN CHARLES & SAM LUCKY

Can't Ride Around It

Chapter One – Sneak Peek

Late 1876
Deadwood, Dakota Territory

Jack "Rabbit" Fields was not a complicated man by any means. He knew a good thing when he saw it, whether it be horseflesh, a solid business venture, a sure bet, or a pretty sage hen. When it came to locking horns with any curly wolves he ran into along the trail, he tended to shoot first and ask questions later—a notion that had saved his hide more times than he could count.

Rabbit grabbed a glove full of snow from the top of a wagon wheel and began to shape it into a ball. Nope, not complicated one bit, *unlike* his partner in the livery business, Boone McCreery. Being complicated was part of Boone's nature, along with over-cogitating.

Since they were kids, Boone had been the one who had to think a thing beyond its duration. For instance, take that time they were twelve and Boone was contemplating the purchase of a pig for their uncle at the autumn hog auction in Agua Fria. While prime hog after hog went to the highest bidder, Boone sat by and pondered, too busy considering an undersized ear or turned-in hoof to put in a bid. He'd ended up with the runt of the sale by overindulging his thoughts.

Their Uncle Mort, who'd adopted them when they were wagon-train orphans no bigger than overgrown possums, couldn't decide whether to laugh or bang his head against the barn door most days when it came to Boone's over-thinking habit.

Early on, the tendency to ponder to no end had earned Boone the nickname "Molasses," which Rabbit was fond of using to stoke the fire in Boone when needed.

Boone would have Rabbit believe that thinking things out was the wise man's way. That he had to take the time to contemplate every damned thing since Rabbit never did.

"Somebody's got to watch out for you," he'd say.

But Rabbit's pistol watched out for both of them plenty over the years, and more than ever since they'd arrived in Deadwood, where the streets were filled with some of the best and worst humanity had to offer.

"Jack Rabbit!" Hank Varney called from the street near the front of Keller's Livery. The same livery Boone and Rabbit had bought and registered the papers on just two days prior. They were going to need to change the name soon now that Keller was heading back east to his family for good.

Hank was a fast friend to Rabbit, and he hadn't given Boone time to consider the pros and cons of a friendship. Nope, that wasn't Hank's way. If he had a biscuit, he'd give a friend half in a heartbeat and put an arrow in the ass of anyone who tried to take it from him.

"Hiyo, Hank!" Rabbit waved. "Come back and help us push this buggy outta here."

Rabbit and Boone had gone to work on the livery immediately. They'd sold off the derelict wagons and buggies and tack overcrowding the livery's storage lot even though Boone had resisted the idea at first. Mr. Molasses had struggled to get past the idea that the owners might come back. He'd always had a soft heart for a sad story. Then again, a short time ago Uncle Mort's freight wagon had been one of the many abandoned pieces of equipment in this very storage lot that had been sold before they could recoup it.

Rabbit could understand Boone's hesitation, but the lot needed to be cleared. More equipment and rigs were arriving in town every day, practically every hour, and they had the biggest livery in town. As a compromise, they'd decided to start by selling the older stock first. Unfortunately, that meant moving most of the damned wagons and buggies out of the way to reach those that had been pushed to the back of the lot, wedged up against the crumbly rock forming one side of Deadwood gulch.

"Rabbit, push the neck yoke back and forth," Boone called from the back of the buggy. "This wheel is frozen in the mud. We need to break it loose."

"Wait for Hank. He can help push." Rabbit closed one eye and squinted into the bright cloudless morning sky. The day was colder than a bucket of snowman snot, especially with the dang wind.

Rabbit scooped up another glove full of snow and packed it into the ball he'd started. He gauged the distance and height and then lobbed the snowball, knocking loose a blanket of snow that had accumulated on the roof of the buggy. A small avalanche slid down the backside, landing with a satisfying *swish-ploosh!* Right about where Boone was standing.

"Son of a rat catcher. Rabbit!" Boone popped out from behind the buggy, his hat drooping down over one ear and onto his shoulder, weighed down by a healthy pile of snow.

Rabbit burst into laughter. "Commence to shiverin', icy britches."

Boone leaned forward and gingerly tipped his hat, dumping

the load of snow on the ground. "Went down my neck, you scrawny chicken rancher." He took off his hat, shook it, and flopped it back on his head.

Rabbit held his stomach. "Hoo hoo! Your pretty green eyes were big as wagon wheels. You needed a bath anyway. A shave, too, ya scruffy sheepherder."

Boone glared at Rabbit while he swiped at the slushy snow running down his back. "That's gonna end up on your list of regrets before we're done."

Rabbit kept chuckling. Payback or not, seeing Boone wearing a bonnet of snow and rosy cheeks was worth it.

"Movin' wagons, I see." Hank joined them, slapping Rabbit on the back. Tall and lanky, and tough as nails, Hank reminded Rabbit of an old ironwood tree down in the desert. Not that Hank was that much older than Rabbit, maybe a decade or so was all. This morning, the older man's whiskers had a layer of frost on them.

"Watch that rascal." Boone shook the front of his coat, still trying to get the snow out. "He'll douse ya."

"Ho there, Boonedog! Didn't see you back there."

"Glad you're here, Hank. Now you can help Rabbit give this buggy a push."

Hank eyed the wheel that was buried up to the spokes in frozen earth. "Looks like the wheel there is done for 'til spring."

Boone scowled. "You're probably right."

"What say we cook some coffee?" Rabbit suggested, thinking about the hot, fiery forge inside the livery. "Thaw the innards."

Twenty minutes later they were melted a little around the edges and sitting at the table in the livery loft, warming their hands on steaming tins of coffee.

"You been busy at The Pyre lately, Hank?" Rabbit asked.

The Pyre was one of two undertaker establishments in town. It was a typical house of the dead except for one key thing—it was run by a woman. And not just any woman at that.

Clementine Johanssen had come to town six or so months ago and gone into the business of burying the town's dead, which was a thriving trade in a gold booming town as rough and rowdy as Deadwood. Taller than most *hombres* around town and tough as rawhide, she could knock a man sky-westward and crooked eastward in a flash. Hell, Rabbit had seen her do nearly that more than once.

In addition to burying the dead, Clementine also was an ace at killing troublemakers of the unworldly sort, and made a mighty fine fourth *compadre* in their posse. Trained to fight from a young girl up, she came into their newfound friendship with a healthy dose of gumption. Not to mention her cabinet full of deadly weapons that made Rabbit swoon.

Clementine had been visiting them in the livery every day for over a week, teaching them all she could about the weapons they would use and the creatures they would face if they continued to associate with her and Hank. Rabbit had never chopped and stabbed so many straw men in all his born days. Of course he hadn't. What sane soul would? Boone would probably agree. They were both sore every night from head to toe after exercising muscles they didn't even know they had.

With Clementine coming around so much, Rabbit and Boone hadn't seen the need to visit her at The Pyre. Hell, Rabbit's preference was to avoid that place anyway, if possible. He wasn't exactly squeamish around a dead body, but that place felt like an eerie stage stop on a one-way trip to a long sleep.

"Miss Clem and I ain't busy so much these days," Hank answered Rabbit's question. "New undertaker in town is doin' drop-dead business."

Boone laughed. "That's a good one, Hank. People dying to get into his place, are they?"

"Hoo hoo, Boonedog." Hank shook his finger at Boone.

"Miss Clem appears happy about the situation," Hank told them, taking a moment to sip from his cup. "She's been practicing with her weapons a lot. She works with you boys pert near ever' day, but by herself, too. I think the letter from that rogue character had some affect on her. She even swings that big sword, the *Ulfberht*, around now." Hank's gaze lifted to the ceiling, a smile rounding his whiskered cheeks. "Like watchin' a fancy dancer spin and jump, I tell ya."

Rabbit smiled along with Hank, thinking of the times he'd watched Clementine swing her blades. She moved like greased lightning when she fought. It was a fine sight to see.

Across the table, Boone was scowling at the wall and tugging on his ear, something he'd been doing more often lately, especially when Clementine was around. The last time Rabbit had seen Boone so preoccupied with his damned ear was when he fell for that dark-eyed, sweet-talking *señorita* down in Las Cruces. Unfortunately, it turned out she was married, and to more than one *hombre* at that. Since that fiasco, Boone hadn't paid much attention to the ladies. Hell, not that he was ever a dandy. Mr. Molasses always took his time picking out a woman, the same as he did hogs way back when, often losing out to other stallions in the meantime.

Rabbit cleared his throat.

Boone blinked and looked at Rabbit. "Uh, anyway, I think that rogue is trouble. Wish I'd seen her there in that saloon in Galena. Don't know what I'd have done. Be good to know what she looks like, though."

The Rogue Executioner was another deadly female in town in the same killing profession as Clementine. However, where Clementine followed more in Boone's pondering footsteps when it came to spilling blood, the Rogue was wasting no time slaying. She'd been keeping Clementine's two exam tables busy with bodies bearing their enemies insignia in the form of a tattoo or brand.

"I think that rogue is a real fireball." Rabbit winked at Boone. "I'd like to sit with her a spell. All those kills, nobody knows who she is. She must be wicked to watch in action. Must have a real interestin' story or two in her."

"Sit with her a spell." Boone smirked. "She might just pin your ears back, if you're not careful."

"Oh! Jack Rabbit. Miss Clem gave me this." Hank fished in his pocket and pulled out a linen bag. "Said you musta forgot it when you run off to Santa Fe."

"What? Another blade?"

"Nosiree. Don't feel like one of them blades you been playin' with."

"Playin'? Take a look at this." In one fluid movement he stood, jerked a shiny slender throwing knife from his belt, and flung it across the room. *Thwap!* It stuck into a board he'd hung on a stack of hay at the other end of the loft.

Hank opened his mouth so wide it took up half his face. His round eyes took up the other half. He nodded his head exaggeratedly and slapped his knee. "I'll be a hell-bent horny toad!"

"I know!" Rabbit pulled another knife and held it up. "When she gave me these things, I thought she was pullin' on my rooster tail but, I gotta tell ya, I like 'em. Quick as a sidewinder on hot sand and before you know it, I'll be able to shave those whiskers from your chin from across the loft."

Hank rubbed his whiskered chin. "Better'n a six shooter?"

"Quieter, anyway."

Hank nodded. "Well, here." He handed Rabbit the bag.

"Wonder what Miss Clementine thinks I need." He opened the bag and pulled out a silver and turquoise bear pendant on a leather lanyard.

"Hey now! Uncle Mort's bear."

"Miss Clem says you forgot it when you departed on your Santa Fe gallivant after your uncle's funeral."

"I surely did. Distracted, I guess." Rabbit strung the loop of leather over his head and rubbed the silver bear. He couldn't

help but smile. "Feels like a little piece of Uncle Mort is here now."

Suddenly his head began to spin, but only a little, like what tended to happen when he slammed a whiskey on an empty stomach or sipped a little too much McCuddle's Original Magical Tonic. But he hadn't had either for better than a day.

That was odd. He rubbed his temple, waiting for the feeling to pass. Instead, the back of his neck prickled, same as it did now and then when he was a kid playing in the old horse graveyard in the ravine behind Uncle Mort's woodshed. He felt the air shift behind him. The tingling in his neck spread south, down his spine, making his legs itch to skedaddle.

He looked at Boone and Hank, wondering if they were feeling something far from ordinary, too. The two of them sat at the table, sipping coffee as if they were having tea with the queen of England. Hank broke out a deck of cards and began to overhand shuffle.

Rabbit's stomach weighed heavy. There was something behind him now, he knew it without even turning.

Sheeat! Someone is lookin' at me.

He craned his neck, peeking over his shoulder.

What he saw made him spin back around. "Nope."

"What 'nope,' Jack Rabbit?" Hank looked up, still shuffling the cards.

Rabbit shook his head. "Fuck that."

Yet he couldn't help but glance behind him again. The sight was same as before. He scowled and focused on Boone and Hank.

"You two see that?" He jabbed his thumb over his shoulder.

"The bed? Stairs? What?" Hank asked.

Rabbit frowned. "Boone? What do you see?"

Boone shot Rabbit a wide grin, his eyes sparkling. "I see a real handsome man. Kinda *loco* though."

"Ain't exactly helpful, are ya? Hank, anything else?"

Hank looked up from the cards he was dealing and tilted his head to see around Rabbit. "Don't see nothin', Jack Rabbit. Just the bed over there." He went back to flipping the cards into three piles.

"Jack, turn around." The gravelly voice that spoke sounded far away, yet right in Rabbit's ear. A very familiar voice at that. "Let me look at you."

Rabbit froze, his heart thumping hard in his chest like it was trying to break free and race back to New Mexico.

"Jonathan Virginia Fields." The voice grew louder. "Turn around this minute!"

Rabbit gulped. Only one person had ever used his full name since his mother had died back on that wagon trip west. Rabbit did as ordered, moving slowly, his gaze aimed down at the straw-covered floor. His legs felt like heavy piles of meat with the bones removed.

"Look at me!"

Rabbit let his gaze lift to the bed, in front of which a pair of boots stood with legs attached. His gaze eased up and up, until he locked eyes with his uncle, who'd been dead for way too long to be standing in the loft right now.

"Ain't real," Rabbit said, trying to convince himself.

"What ain't real, Jack Rabbit?" Hank asked.

"What does that mean?" Uncle Mort snorted. "And you know how I feel about you using the word 'ain't,' boy."

"Isn't," Rabbit corrected out of habit.

"What isn't real?" Uncle Mort scanned the room. "Where are we? Looks like a hayloft."

"In the loft of a livery." Rabbit told him.

"I see." Uncle Mort stepped toward Rabbit, his feet drifting a little way with each step as if he were on ice. He was pale, like he'd been whitewashed.

Rabbit took a step back, cringing. *What the fuck!*

"Since when are you afraid of your uncle, boy?"

"Uh, since … you … Well, since you died. I went to your funeral." Rabbit's voice cracked on that last word. Was he dreaming this? He glanced around the loft and ran into Boone's frown.

"Rabbit, what are you doing?" Boone fanned the cards in his hand, not even glancing in Uncle Mort's direction. "Get over here. Hank dealt you in."

Rabbit shook his head. It was a trick. Somehow. Boone was fooling with him. Payback for that snowball earlier. Yeah, that was it.

He looked behind him again. Nope, that wasn't it. What couldn't possibly be his uncle still stood there watching him.

Uncle Mort was dressed in the long, threadbare, light blue nightgown he always wore to bed back home on the ranch. As Rabbit stared, his uncle's body undulated slightly, as if pushed this way and that by the gentle gusts that coursed through the loft. He could even see the bed and wall here and there through his uncle's body.

"Sheeat." Blood rushed and roared in his ears. The room began to tilt, enough to make him reach out with both hands to steady himself. "I must've broke my brain."

"Rabbit." The sound of Boone's voice calmed Rabbit a bit, making the room level out. "Who are you talking to?"

"Uh, Uncle Mort," Rabbit said over his shoulder.

Boone chuckled. "Tell him to join us. We need a fourth hand."

Uncle Mort scowled down at his body and then up at Rabbit. "Do I remember something happening in a … ?" He attempted to put his hand on his chest, but it passed through. "Well, I'll be." He passed his hand through his chest again. Then through his leg. Then he put the tip of his finger on his nose and it sank up to his wrist.

"Jehoshaphat, Uncle Mort!"

"Look at that." His uncle sawed the side of his hand through his silver beard and neck and then flopped his head to the side.

"Uncle Mort! Don't do that!"

Uncle Mort laughed with the same deep belly laugh Rabbit had heard a thousand times growing up. "That would scare the trousers off of Carlos."

Rabbit wondered how Uncle Mort would feel if he found out Rabbit and Boone were contemplating selling the ranch in Santa Fe to Carlos, his uncle's good friend and ranch foreman.

A chair scraped across the floor behind Rabbit. A moment later Boone was at his side. "Right here, is he?"

Rabbit could tell by the sarcasm in Boone's voice he wasn't along for this ride.

"Yep." Rabbit pointed at Uncle Mort. "Right there. You can't see him?" Then he said to Uncle Mort, "Seems I'm more higgledy-piggledy about this than you."

"I'm not higgledy-piggledied," Boone said.

"Not talkin' to you," Rabbit shot back.

"No sense in theatrics." Uncle Mort continued passing his hand through various parts of his body.

"You know," Rabbit said, crossing his arms. "You died a while back."

Uncle Mort paused for a second and then nodded. "Yep. That seems right." He shook his head. "Or maybe not. Hard to tell."

"Torn to ... uh," Rabbit corrected his course out of consideration for the dead. "Killed by a *Bahkauv*."

"That what that thing was? Hmm. Can't remember the particulars too well."

That was probably a good thing. The *Bahkauv* hadn't taken any mercy. Rabbit scratched his head, still having trouble believing his eyes. Sure sounded like Uncle Mort.

"I saw you outside and inside that mine," he told his uncle. "Only you was dead at the time."

"I knew you boys would be upset if you didn't find me, so I gave you a nudge my way."

If that was a nudge, what was this? "And then I saw you again at The Pyre after we paid our respects at the boneyard."

"I tried to explain things that time, but you wouldn't answer."

He hadn't been able to hear Uncle Mort that time for some reason. What was different now besides being in the haylo …

"Ohh!" Rabbit grasped the bear pendant hanging from his neck. "The pendant!" He gaped at Boone. "It's gotta be."

"What is going sideways in that head of yours?" Boone put his hand on Rabbit's shoulder, his forehead lined. He stared into Rabbit's eyes. "You been nipping at that bottle of McCuddle's?"

"Here, hold this." Rabbit slipped the pendant from around his neck and shoved it into Boone's hand. "See anything?" He waved in the direction of Uncle Mort.

"He can't see me," Uncle Mort said, sounding sad about the fact.

"Like what?" Boone asked. "Dancing girls in lacy dresses?" He smiled like a fool, as if he really was watching dancing ladies.

"No, do you see Uncle Mort?"

Boone sobered. "Enough, Rabbit. I miss him too, but this isn't helping anyone."

"Just me then. Hmm." Rabbit's brain ached trying to reconcile the situation. Some McCuddle's might help right about now.

"What are you two goin' on about over there?" Hank held up his hand of cards. "Think I got ya both beat already."

"Uncle Mort is standing right here." Rabbit pointed at his uncle again.

"You don't say." Hank's chair scraped back. He joined the two of them. "Right here?" He pointed in the wrong direction.

"No." Rabbit took Hank's hand and placed it within touching distance of Uncle Mort's shoulder. "Here."

"Well, imagine that. Pleased to meet you, Uncle Mort." Hank stuck his hand out for a shake, right through Uncle Mort's shoulder. "Suppose to me yer just Mort. My name's Hank."

"My pleasure." Uncle Mort stuck his hand through Hank's arm.

"Said he's pleased to meet you, too, Hank." Rabbit found the whole situation becoming, oddly enough, not that odd at all.

Boone crossed his arms. "Okay you two. The jig is up."

"Who is *he* talking to?" Uncle Mort's brow furrowed.

"So, Boone and Hank can't see you or hear you?" Rabbit asked his uncle. "Only me."

"That appears to be the case." His uncle was still trying to catch Hank's outstretched hand.

"Why not? Why just me?" Rabbit grabbed the pendant from Boone's hand and slipped it back around his neck.

"That's ironical, isn't it?" Uncle Mort gave up on Hank's hand. "The one boy who wouldn't listen to me is the only one that can hear me now? Maybe it *does* have something to do with that bear pendant I got from Chief Seiva."

"The old Navajo who lived near the ranch?"

"That's him. He liked Isadora's prickly pear jelly on his biscuits." Uncle Mort made a show of squeezing his head flat between his palms. "She always made the best jelly."

Rabbit's brain got stuck on Isadora's sweet-yet-tart prickly pear jelly for a moment but then came back around. "But how?"

"Remember the ceremony when you turned fourteen? When Chief Seiva gave me that pendant? He gave you one as well."

Rabbit tried to think back, but the time around that ceremony had always been at best a fuzzy memory of dancing, singing, and drinking. That concoction the old Navajo had made them drink had tasted horrible, but boy did it get Rabbit roostered. "I lost mine, I think."

"You did. But I didn't. Do you remember the rite he performed over us?"

Again, that was a fuzzy few days. "Uh, hmm." Rabbit shook his head.

"Well, maybe that was it. Or not."

"Is he talking to you right now?" Hank squinted in the wrong direction, apparently trying to see Mort.

"Yep."

"No, he's not." Boone returned to the table and picked up his cards. "He's hallucinating." He shook his finger at Rabbit. "No more McCuddle's for you."

Hank tipped his head to the side. "Never talked to the departed before. Wearin' clothes, is he?"

Uncle Mort scoffed. "It would be ill considered on numerous counts to wander this earth with my clothes mislocated, although I wouldn't exactly call my old nightwear appropriate for traveling."

"He's wearin' the long, nighttime gown he wore in the winter back home." Rabbit stuck his hand out and gingerly touched his uncle with his fingertips. When his fingers sunk into Uncle Mort's wispy shoulder, he yanked his hand back and stared at his fingers. They felt cold, like he'd stuck them in a snow bank.

Uncle Mort scowled at Rabbit's fingers. "It's disconcerting, this talk about my decease-edness."

"Sorry, Uncle Mort."

Hank rubbed his whiskers. "Miss Clem put him in a nice shirt and trousers before the funeral, didn't she?"

"Yep, but now it looks like he's ready for bed."

Uncle Mort's eyes widened. "A woman clothed me?"

"She's like an Amazon. You'd like her." Rabbit grinned. "Booney, it'd be nice if you'd demonstrate your cordial nature and maybe say 'Hi' to your ol' uncle."

Boone rested his forehead on the table and sighed loud and long.

"Stuck in that outfit is he?" Hank put an index finger to the side of his nose.

Rabbit chuckled a little at the idea.

Uncle Mort looked himself up and down. "Let's hope not. No way for a man to be seen, in his evening attire, drafts blowing about." He felt around close to the top of his head.

"No night cap, Uncle Mort." Rabbit moved over to the table, pulling out a chair for his uncle before sitting next to Boone. "Booney don't believe you're here, Uncle Mort."

Uncle Mort float-walked toward them. "He'll come around. It strains the sensibilities I would think."

"It's strainin' my noggin, that much is sure," Rabbit said. "How about you, Hank?"

Hank returned to his chair and cards. "Workin' around Miss Clem exposes me to some things, but this? I never. What's it like? Ask him for me."

Rabbit picked up the cards Hank had dealt earlier. "He can hear you, I think."

"I can hear him," Uncle Mort confirmed. "Ask him what's *what* like."

"He wants to know what's *what* like."

"Oh, for chrissake!" Boone raised his head, shaking his hands at the roof.

"Well, the afterlife," Hank said. "Bein' a wispy sort."

"I'm a wispy?" Uncle Mort chuckled. "I suppose I am. Hmmm. Tell Hank that sometimes it's dark and sometimes it's light."

Rabbit relayed his uncle's message to Hank, who thought on it for a minute and then asked, "Why are ya back here?"

"That's a good question," Rabbit said, lowering the lousy hand he'd been dealt. "Why are you? Is it because I took your pendant?"

"The pendant is why I'm here. Well, not *why* I'm here. I'm able to be here and talk to you because of that. Possibly. The reason I'm back here is probably because I made a promise to your momma just before she died."

Rabbit frowned. "What promise?" And why hadn't Uncle Mort ever mentioned a promise when he was alive?

The livery door downstairs slammed shut. "Hank?"

Clementine's voice rang out.

Fenrir, her horse, whinnied "Hello" from a stall below.

"Up in the loft," Hank hollered back. "You should probably come see this."

She made fast work of the steep stairs, joining them at the table. Her dark auburn hair was plaited, as usual, her cheeks pink from the cold. She unwound her scarf and let it hang around her neck. She looked from Hank to Rabbit to Boone, holding on the latter a moment longer before returning to Hank. "See what?"

"This is the woman who dressed you," Rabbit told his uncle.

"Jumpin' Jehoshaphat, she's a big girl!"

Rabbit laughed at his uncle's gape-mouthed expression. "You should see her fight, Uncle Mort. She can whip her weight in wildcats. The first time we met her, she lifted a grown man off the floor and then broke both of his arms and his nose."

"She fights?" Uncle Mort asked, still gawking at Clementine.

"And kills. It's what she does."

Clementine's gaze narrowed. "Has he been drinking McCuddle's tonic again?" she asked the others.

"Rabbit thinks he sees Uncle Morton," Boone told her flatly.

"The pendant made him start seein' ghosts," Hank explained.

She focused on Rabbit, her forehead wrinkled. "You can see your uncle Morton? Here? Right now?"

He nodded to all of her questions.

"Can you converse with him?"

He nodded again.

She rubbed her hands together. "Well, isn't this a wonderful surprise."

"I'm not so sure yet," Rabbit muttered.

"You believe him?" Boone asked.

"Of course. In my line of work you soon realize there is always truth behind myths and legends. The *Bahkauv* is a perfect example of a creature thought to be a myth." She patted Rabbit's shoulder. "Turns out we may have a shaman on our hands."

"A what?" Rabbit asked.

"I'm going to need some of that dingdang tonic if this keeps up," Boone said.

Uncle Mort smiled. "So, this is the woman who dressed me, huh?"

"What did ya need me for, Miss Clem?" Hank asked.

"How many bodies were in the shed out back of The Pyre?"

"Plumb full. Stacked like cordwood."

"Full, huh?" She bit her lower lip. "Then we have a problem."

"How's that, Miss Clem?"

"The shed is empty."

**Stay tuned for the next book in the
Deadwood Undertaker Series.**

Made in the USA
Monee, IL
06 July 2020